BIRTHDAY
PRESENCE

BIRTHDAY
PRESENCE

16 Stories with
One Thing in Common

BRIAN L. COX

FOREWORD BY PAUL McCOMAS

iUniverse, Inc.
Bloomington, Ind

Birthday Presence
16 Stories with One Thing in Common

Published by: Two Worlds Productions Inc. in conjunction with iUniverse

www.twoworldsproductions.com

www.birthdaypresence.org

iUniverse books may be ordered through booksellers or by contacting:

iUniverse
1663 Liberty Drive
Bloomington, IN 47403
www.iuniverse.com
1-800-Authors (1-800-288-4677)

ISBN: 978-1-4759-0632-5 (sc)
ISBN: 978-1-4759-0633-2 (ebk)

Printed in the United States of America

iUniverse rev. date: 09/28/2012

For my mother, Connie,
who never tires of saying:
"You can do it, Bri!"

ACKNOWLEDGEMENTS

AN EARLIER VERSION OF "LOST KITTEN, ONE Hundred Percent Chance Of Snow" was published in the Pioneer Press Newspaper in 2002. The story "November Forgets" was published in the 2007 anthology *Further Persons Imperfect*.

Rarely does a book reach publication without the help and support of others. Heartfelt thanks to Christine Cox, Moira Sullivan, Elizabeth Rossman, Drew Downing, Jon Talbot, Heather McComas, James Moeller and Pat Shiplett for their advice, feedback and encouragement, and for reading various early versions of stories in this collection.

Special thanks to Paul (PMac) McComas, a gifted writer, editor and friend. Thanks, PMac, for your keen insights and for being the type of person who knows the dramatic difference between talking about doing something and the hard work and dedication involved with actually doing it!

CONTENTS

FOREWORD

Y OU'RE IN FOR A TREAT.
One might even say, a *birthday* treat.
So please, pay attention, for I know whereof I speak. You see, if there is a Brian L. Cox scholar—someone (other than the big man himself) whose familiarity with Cox's creative compositions is at once intimate and expansive enough that it approaches expertise—well, I guess that would be me.

Allow me to begin with a semi-brief history of our association:

Brian and I met a decade ago, when I was on tour for my novel *Unplugged* (2002, John Daniel & Company), the tale of a suicidal young rock musician, Dayna Clay, her harrowing struggle with childhood trauma and adult depression, and her eventual climb up to the high ground of psycho-spiritual health. Intrigued by my book's link to Nirvana frontman Kurt Cobain (who, incidentally, makes something of a cameo appearance in *this* book, as well)—and by my stated hope that Dayna's story might serve as an inspiration to readers who themselves are wrestling with despair and the aftermath of abuse—freelance-writer Brian sought me out and interviewed me for the *Chicago Tribune*. His subsequent article appeared in the April 16, 2003 issue under the headline "Sending A Hopeful Message About Depression: Recovery Urged in *Unplugged*."

Though we met as reporter and subject, the relationship didn't remain confined to those roles; given our common interests and, especially, common cause, it was perhaps inevitable that Brian and I would find other, varying excuses to work together. We've co-produced, to date, nine short-form narrative films—seven of them award-winners—with number ten currently in post-production. We co-composed and performed a cable-TV-show theme song. More to the point, once I'd read some of his short fiction, I wasted little time in inviting Brian into the private Advanced Fiction Writing (AFW) workshop that I've taught since 2001. He attended for several years and may well be the most prolific writer our "salon" has ever included; rare was the week when he didn't bring in a story, or at least a scene, on which he was seeking feedback. Indeed, many of the pieces that appear in the following pages debuted, in draft form, at AFW and were workshopped there; moreover, this volume's haunting and elegiac anti-war snap-fiction monologue, "November Forgets," began as a response to one of my optional "writing prompts" and first appeared in the second AFW collection I compiled and edited, entitled *Further Persons Imperfect* (2007, iUniverse).

So, yes: I'm well qualified to write about Brian L. Cox and his written work. What's more, I'm here to tell you that, if you pay attention, reading *Birthday Presence* will give you a very good look at both. For while you can learn a great deal *about* Cox from his video work, his journalism, and his still photography, in his fiction there is, if you will, "no 'about' about it." Simply put, he *is* his stories.

If you have a moment, go online to the Chicago Tribune archives, and pay Brian's aforementioned article the attention it deserves. Why? For one thing, it's a well-written and worthwhile piece of journalistic writing; you'll find Cox's reportage to be as well-crafted as his short fiction.

But you'll find something else there, too: a bit of literary foreshadowing. At one point, he describes my coast-to-coast tour for *Unplugged* as being "about more than just selling books . . . it's about getting the word out that there is hope." Well, the same could be said about *this* book, for the best of these stories likewise hold out hope for those in dire need. And happily, they do so, for the most part, not through authorial sermonizing, but though observation and empathy—that is, by bringing full-blooded characters to living, breathing life, plunking them down before us, and coaxing us into their shoes.

Interestingly, it's often in the supporting cast, more so than in the narrators and point-of-view characters, that the crux of Cox's stories lies. Do pay attention to these "also-rans": the aptly named, disaster-fated yet undaunted young Russian immigrant, Katrina, in "The Other"; the mysterious reformed-gangbanger "Mickey the H," in the story that bears his name; the mentally challenged yet insightful neighborhood-bar denizen, Glen, in "The Lion's Eyes" . . . these and other beautifully realized "bench players" might be have-nots in terms of socioeconomic status, but they are rich in wisdom. The hard-won home-truths they personify and purvey more than make up for what they may lack materially and/or in the estimation of others.

Another thing about Cox: "The boy's got range." Again—pay attention, for while his journalism background yields the reportorial approach taken in a handful of these stories (not to mention the utterly credible cop-talk of the authentic and affecting urban drama "What Reggie Didn't Tell Me"), you'll also find between these two covers an impressionistic koan of a narrative (the Zen/Jungian-synchronicity meditation "Lost Kitten—One Hundred Percent Chance of Snow"), a goodly dollop of justified sentimentality ("Four Balloons Andrew Never Received"), and an amusing vignette about unfounded pathological fear wherein silliness meets semiotics . . . with "Unspeakable" results.

In ending the collection with his coming-of-age novelette "Shiner," Cox well may have saved the best piece for last. The young hero, Neil, is characterized—quite aptly, for a story set in (as Pete Townsend called it) Teenage Wasteland—by his *longings*: to escape his warring parents, to make his father face the music, to protect his kid sister, to fit in with his peers, to be cool, to grow out of childhood and into freedom, to learn to play guitar, to "get the girl," and so on. Throughout, Cox's feel for the frustrating liminality, the well-nigh-untenable "in-betweenness," of adolescence is simply spot-on. Thus, while the specific details of Neil's life may be different from yours or mine, "Shiner" takes us back to that period, that place, and that pain as surely as if the story were our own.

All told, these are tales of intensity and indignation, of passion and pathos, of angst and anger, of grappling and grief. They're also tales of both humor and heart—though each of these elements skews, at times, rather dark. Most of all, these are tales of modern males (mostly) wrestling deep into night with their timeless demons—men whose wounded spirits yearn for redemption, reconciliation, release . . . or just a reason to live.

"Okay," you say. "Understood. But what the hell's up with the *birthdays?*" To his credit, Cox doesn't provide a single, clear answer as to why a birthday (or something like it) crops up in every single story in *Birthday Presence*; rather, he has the presence (sorry!) of mind to leave it to each of us, his readers, to figure that out for ourselves. Personally, I come straight back to that *Tribune* article, and to the notion of "getting the word out that there is hope." As we move into and then through middle age, we may not always welcome the addition of yet another year to our running total; still, as they say, "It beats the alternative." Each birthday you celebrate, Cox seems to be reminding us (particularly, though not exclusively, in his paean to perseverance, "Happy Birthday"), is thus a victory—and one that, whether you're one or one hundred, signals the beginning of a brand-new year, rife with possibilities.

Reassuring though that notion may be, let the record show that Cox is not solely an inspirational or "feel-good" writer; rather, he takes chances in his work, often challenging the reader. While some of his protagonists are admirable, relatable, or both, others are anything but. Alongside the everyman heroes are anti-heroes, villains, and even a (figurative) monster or two. Many of his characters, we root for; others repel us. More than a couple of them flirt—or worse—with infidelity, while others commit crimes that, comparatively speaking, make cheating seem like chivalry. Some win us over; others wallow, or—worse—wither. For this author understands, as did his predecessor Arthur Miller with *Death of A Salesman*, that sometimes "Attention must be paid to such a person!" not in spite of his human weaknesses, but because of them. To a man and woman, Cox's narrators and point-of-view characters step right up, grab us by the lapels, yank us toward them and—Willy-Loman-like—demand to be known.

Likewise for Brian L. Cox's singular sensibility and unique narrative voice: they demand to be known. Indeed, "Attention must be paid!" And now, with the publication of *Birthday Presence*, I'm heartened to know that at long last, it will.

Paul McComas
Author of *Unplugged, Planet of the Dates*, and
Unforgettable
Evanston, Illinois

SAY SOMETHING POSITIVE

I'M THE NARRATOR OF THIS STORY, THEREFORE I will tell you something truthful about myself. I am generous. I tend to give people the benefit of the doubt. I assume they have good character, until they show me otherwise.

They often show me otherwise.

My friend believes she can tell a "good person" from a "bad person" within minutes of meeting them. Isn't that a little naive? People are so very talented at hiding their worst side.

Character is defined by the choices people make and the words they speak or, in some cases, don't speak. If you want to know what someone is really like, don't ask their friends, ask their enemies. They will be stingy with their compliments.

Thus is my mindset on a glorious sunny Saturday morning as I walk into my favorite downtown café. It's a charming, modest place, and sunshine is spilling in through the large windows overlooking the street. I pause by the door, and out of the corner of my eye I see, Monika, with her head lowered, reading a book.

Because I am truthful, I admit, I tend to avoid Monika because she has a negative, unconstructive way of thinking. She loves salacious gossip and rarely has a good word to say about anything or anyone. Do you know anyone who always seems to have a doomsday attitude? Then you know what I'm talking about.

I make my way to the counter, order a latté and claim the last open table which is next to Monika. I place my latté on the table and she looks up from the book. "Oh, hi," she says.

"Hi, Monika."

"Kind of hot today for a long sleeved-blouse, don't you think?" She smiles faintly.

"I'm doing laundry today," I reply, "I grabbed this from my closet. Besides, I don't find it too warm. It's just right."

She nods in disagreement. You know the kind of nod I mean. It's the kind someone gives to *imply* they understand and agree with what you're saying when in fact they don't. I'd call it "an insincere nod."

I slide onto the seat. "What are you reading?"

She places the book face up on the table and smirks. "This new book by, Brian L. Cox," she replies, pronouncing the middle initial sarcastically.

"Never heard of him. What's the title?"

"*Birthday Presence—16 Stories with One Thing in Common.*" She smirks again. "A stupid title for a book."

Monika is a world-class smirker. Her first reaction to almost any question, statement, or comment is to smirk, then follow up with a cynical remark. Everyone has to be good at something. I don't think she's ever had any dreams, goals or enthusiasm. It's a protection mechanism. If you assume the worst, the world will never disappoint you. Her glass is definitely half empty, at best.

"*Birthday Presence,*" I say. "Any good?"

A sneer forms on her thin lips. "It's the worst book I've ever read."

I lean forward and glance at the book cover. It's mostly white, probably icing on a cake, with what looks like colorful round sprinkles above the title.

"It can't be that bad. Is it?" I ask.

She shakes her head. "Horrible!"

"What's the 'one thing' the stories have in common?"

She winces, and it looks like she's in pain. "I'm not sure," she replies. "It could be the fact that they're all terrible and badly written. It might have something to do with birthdays."

I point to the cover. "Thus the sprinkles."

She looks down at the cover then back up at me. "Oh yeah, I guess."

"So it's about birthdays?" I ask.

"Maybe. I don't know," she says. "There's always a birthday happening, or in some cases they just mention a birthday." She rolls her eyes. "It's really stupid."

I start wondering why she's reading it if it's so bad—but then she's the kind of person who never has a good word to say about anything. For her to call it "awful" may actually be some kind of backhanded compliment to the writer.

I glance at the book, then up at Monika. "So, you really don't like it?"

She scoffs. "My dog is a better writer."

"Your *dog* is a writer?" I couldn't resist making a bit of a smartass comment.

She exhales sharply, like air escaping from a balloon. "Of course not. I don't even *have* a dog. I was just being sarcastic."

I chuckle. "I know, I was, too."

Suddenly I have an idea, a little challenge to myself. I'm going to keep asking her questions until she says something at least vaguely positive, hopeful or optimistic. "Well," I say, "the stories may be bad, but you've got to admit that's a clever title."

She rolls her eyes again. "He should have titled it *Clichés and Pieces of Shit*."

"It beats reading the newspaper."

She points to the book. "They were out of newspapers; that's why I had to read this."

"That means you saved a buck on a paper."

"I got a parking ticket this morning, so that wipes out the dollar."

"At least your car wasn't towed."

"I wish they *had* towed that piece of junk away. It's always breaking down. It's a money pit."

I motion toward the window. "Beautiful day, especially if you're walking."

She frowns. "It's supposed to turn cool and rain this afternoon."

I will not let her pessimism defeat me! "It's been real dry," I reply, "so we need the rain."

"I don't need it," she says. "My basement floods."

There's another pause as I desperately try to come up with something, anything, to get her to utter one positive word.

"Ahhh . . . The Cubs won last night!"

She shrugs. "I'm a Sox fan, and they lost."

I glance around the café to see if any other tables have opened up. Nope. I turn back toward her ask if I can see the book.

She slides it across the table. "Go ahead."

"So," I ask, picking it up, "nothing at all redeeming about it?"

"Redeeming?"

"Yeah, anything in it you'd give a 'thumbs up' to?"

Her face is a blank.

I open the book at random and look down at the page. "What about the font type?" I ask . . . a bit sarcastically. "Times New Roman? Clean and crisp?"

"It's funny you should say that," she frowns, "it's actually hard on my eyes."

"If that's the case, then it sounds like a perfect book for burning on a cold rainy afternoon . . ."

"I don't have a fireplace."

"Then there's no chance of you having a chimney fire."

"Yeah, but if I had a fireplace, I'd save a ton on heating bills."

I flip to the front of the book. "Foreword by Paul McComas. Did you read that?"

"I started to, but who the hell is Paul McComas?"

I shrug. "What about the Table of Contents? How did that work for you?"

Her face screws up and she snorts. "I didn't read the Table of Contents."

"How do you pick which stories to read?"

"I leaf through it and start reading when I see a story title that interests me."

Got ya! "So, the story titles are good, interesting?"

She leans back in her chair and slowly shakes her head. "No, not really."

"Weren't any of the stories even remotely attention-grabbing?"

"Nope. One talks about unicorns. Unicorns! And there's a real dumb story about some guy who played guitar with Kurt Cobain."

"Kurt Cobain, really?" I reach for my latté. "I like some of his music so maybe? . . ."

She guffaws loudly, then cuts me off. "I never liked that band. Besides, it's not *really* about Cobain. It's just some stupid story about a guy who wants to tear a friend down."

I nod. "I see."

"In another story, some kid drowns. Big deal. Then there's one about a Buddhist cop, and one is about some horny married guy and a hot Russian cocktail waitress."

"Well, *that* sounds interesting."

"Yeah, the waitress is okay," she says, interrupting me again. "But the guy is a jerk."

"Maybe it's an exercise in opposites?"

"I don't know," she sighs, shaking her head. "Then, there's a story about two women talking in a café."

"Two women in a café?" I reply. "Hey, that could be us!"

The corners of her mouth turn down, she takes a drink of coffee and nods at the book. "I doubt I'll finish it."

Her brief description has actually piqued my interest in it. "Since you hate it so much, can I borrow it?" I ask. "I'm always interested in reading new authors."

She looks at me for a moment, then slides the book across the table. "Here, take it."

"You can give it to *me* as a gift," I grin. "Because today's my half-birthday."

She looks confused. "What in hell is a half-birthday?"

I take another sip of my latté, place my cup on the table and lean forward. "Whenever anyone has a birthday on, say, Christmas, or like me, New Year's Day—they get to celebrate their birthday exactly six months after their real birthday. That way, their birthday doesn't get lost in the other holiday."

She snorts. "That's weird."

"So, when was your birthday?" I ask, lifting my cup to my lips.

"Last week."

"What did you do? Go shopping? Go out to dinner?"

"Nah, I stayed home and read this book." She stares down at the cover, then shrugs. "There's nothing better to do."

What I thought about sharing with Monika, is a story from my childhood.

My mother loves birthdays. Absolutely adores them. I always get a card in a crisp pink envelop with a check from her on my birthday, and a long telephone chat. She came to visit on my 25th birthday, and we painted the town.

When I was five or six, she was the one who told me about my "half birthday."

"Your birthday is on a holiday, and you're getting cheated," she had smiled. "You're entitled to a half birthday!" And she told me what it was. This excited me greatly because I did feel a bit "cheated" on my birthday, sharing it with New Year's Day.

"You're lucky," she had said, "because now you actually have two birthdays."

Only a loving mother could give a child two birthdays . . . and the timeless gift of fond memories.

When I was a girl, she'd wrap a few coins in tinfoil and put them in the birthday cake batter. During the birthday party, whoever found a coin in their cake, got to make a wish.

At some point during the party, she'd dim the lights, disappear into the kitchen, and emerge carrying the birthday cake with candles flickering on top. They would all sing Happy Birthday to me, and I got to make a wish. It was my "moment," and she made sure I had it.

But I'm leery my warm memory will elicit a blank stare or a smirk from, Monika. Wishing is abhorrent to certain people, the same way fun or hope is abhorrent. Still, if I don't say something, the shadowy forces of pessimism will win is some perverse way.

I sip my coffee, then place the cup back on the table. "I just had the fondest memory," I say. "When I was a little girl, my mother used to wrap coins in foil and put them in the birthday cake batter. During the party, whoever found a coin got to keep it and make a wish."

She's perplexed. "What if someone bit one of the coins and broke a tooth, or swallowed one?"

I shrug. "That never happened."

"Lucky for your mother."

I rest my arm on the table. "So, you believe in luck?"

"What?"

"Nothing."

There's silence, then I pick up the book and stand to leave.

"Belated Happy Birthday, Monika!" I smile. "Many more. Thanks for the book!"

"Thanks," she frowns. "Another day older, another day closer to death."

For some people, not necessarily the worst thing.

MICKEY THE H

IF YOUR FAMILY BOUGHT A TOMBSTONE OR grave marker of any kind in the Midwest between the years 1877 and 1977, chances are one in four that my family made it for you.

My father died in 1975 and my mother tried to keep the business going, but it was too much work for her. She fell behind and my fathers' business partners took the company over and squeezed her out. My mother died seven years later, but she was happy and relieved to wash her hands of the company.

Despite many business troubles, my mother had an enthusiasm for life. She was an amateur photographer and was the person who got me interested in video and photography. I suffered from allergies and lactate intolerance and she figured hobbies like shooting videos and photography would be good for me.

And she always knew that I never had any interest in the "family business." There was something morbid about it. Even as a kid, I realized that people have the illusion they can leave something behind when they die, a granite marker to say *This is who I was and I was around between these dates.* But even the strongest granite eventually turns to dust . . . and therefore I am vigilant about my health.

The doctor wasn't taking my symptoms seriously so I had started doing research on WebMD. I sat in my living room navigating through the website, the kinetic sounds of traffic filtered up from the street as dusk slowly engulfed the city as if on an incoming tide. The only light came from the soft glow of my computer screen.

I reached for the mouse, clicked on "heart disease," quickly read the page and jotted down a few notes on a yellow legal pad. I continued looking around the site because I wanted to see what other warning symptoms I had for various maladies. I found several things that concerned me.

"Patchy chapped skin." *Hhhmmmm.* It looked like I might have lupus!

I rubbed my eyes, then reached for a bottle of aspirin and washed two down with a gulp of purified water. I was about to check the symptoms for malaria when the telephone rang. I didn't recognize the number on my caller ID, but picked it up because I thought it might be my doctor finally returning a call from earlier in the day. "Hello."

"Hello, can I please speak to Mr. Sloan."

"I'm Ian Sloan."

"Hello, Mr. Sloan. My name is Peter, and I'm with the death negotiators."

"What? Who? The . . . the death negotiators?" I repeated slowly, my breath suddenly shallow as a half dug grave.

"Yes that's right sir. I'm with the death negotiators. I'm calling today because . . ."

I jerked forward in my seat and cut the caller off. "How did you get this number?"

"All phone numbers are dialed randomly by a computer sir," the caller said with a faint smirk in his voice. "So, I guess your number is up."

My heart was pounding. So this is how it happens. "The death negotiators. My God," I said, suddenly unable to take a deep breath. "Why call me? I'm young for God's sake!"

"As you can imagine, we see people of all ages in this business." He paused and I could hear him typing. "Let me see here," he said after a moment. "Our records show that you're a self-employed videographer. Is that correct?"

"Yes," I replied weakly.

"Well, sir, as I said, I'm with the death negotiators and I'm calling today . . ."

"You're calling about my death," I blurted. "The death negotiators? What do you want, to sell me a grave plot, or life insurance, something like that?"

There was a suppressed chuckle on the other end of the phone. "No sir, not the *death* negotiators. I'm with the *debt* negotiators." Then he spelled it out. "The *d-e-b-t* negotiators."

I leaned back in my chair and exhaled loudly. *I must be losing it. Thank God it's only a telemarketing call.*

"Mr. Sloan are you there?"

"Yes, I'm here."

"Sir, this is the time of year when people run up a lot of debts, so we're offering a seasonal consolidation package with low rates that will allow you to combine all your credit card debts . . ."

"No, thanks," I said before hanging up. "I pay off my cards every month." I had to laugh at myself a little due to my mishear on the phone. *"The Death Negotiators."* I guess I was feeling a little paranoid about my health.

I spent another half-hour on the medical website and completed a list of problems I wanted to discuss with my doctor. I knew that he considered me a hypochondriac, but I considered myself a realist.

I turned off my computer, got up from my desk and walked down the short hall to my bedroom. As I lay on my bed staring up at the ceiling, pain started creeping through the back of my head until it settled in a space directly behind my eyes. Probably a brain tumor. But it was the chest pains that concerned me most. My uncle had died of a heart attack when he was only a few years older than I was. Everyone knows that medical problems like heart disease are genetic. I also had reoccurring stomach pain, which could have been cancer. I was in bad shape.

I'm not a hypochondriac, or anything like that, but the Grim Reaper was my constant companion. The truth be told, he's everyone's constant companion. Maybe I'm being overly dramatic, but I could feel his invisible presence with me on the El and on trips to the laundry mat and library. He was always there, draped in black, idly holding a sawed-off shotgun, biding his time, waiting for the right moment to blow me away.

After a good two hours of tossing and turning I finally fell a sleep.

I dreamed I was walking through an airport when I saw my Aunt Melinda, my mother's older sister, who had died a few years earlier. She was always terrified of flying, a deep fear I share with her, and I remember being surprised seeing her in an airport; she didn't travel anywhere unless she could drive or take a train or bus. "There's no such thing as a fender bender at 30,000 feet," she used to say. "I'm not afraid of flying. I'm afraid of crashing."

In the dream, my aunt was sitting in the airport departure lounge calmly reading a book as people trod purposely toward the departure gates and exits pulling suitcases on coasters behind them.

"Aunt Melinda what are you doing here?" I asked as I reached her side. "You hate flying."

She put the book in her lap and looked up at me. "Not any more," she said with a cheerful smile. Then she pointed to her right. "They're not afraid to fly. So why should I be?"

I looked to where she was pointing. Two white-tailed deer were standing in the departure lounge, their large brown eyes seemingly fixed on the ticket counter, their ears perked. One of them was chewing something, its jaw slowly working side-to-side. For some reason, it didn't strike me as odd that deer were standing in the airport waiting to catch a plane.

"They're not afraid of flying," I said, "because they have no concept of death." One of the deer took a half step forward. "They probably think they'll live forever."

My aunt waived her finger though the air. "Deer don't think like that. They're actually wired to live with the idea of their death. They live in the moment. They're brave."

I scoffed. "Bravery is a human trait. A deer's a dumb animal. All it thinks about is eating, making little deer and finding a good hiding place during the hunting season."

My aunt shrugged her shoulders and there was an announcement over the PA. She got out of her seat and dropped her book into her purse. "They're calling my flight," she said, moving with the two deer toward the gate. Then she stopped and looked back at me. "Are you on this flight?"

"No," I answered. "I don't think so."

I was sure that something important happened after that but I couldn't remember what.

The next morning I woke exhausted, and a feeling of dread seemed to hang over me like Damocles sword. I slowly got dressed then called my doctor's office and left a message for him to call me. The doctors and nurses may have thought I was a hypo but they were wrong. When you have time to think of things, your mind will start telling you what illness is stalking you. The medical system today treats people like cattle, in and out, and here's a pill to take once a day. Is it just me, or is it a good idea for everybody to stay on top of potential medical threats?

Walking the two blocks to the café where I usually read *The Tribune* I tried to compile a mental list of my symptoms, but the weather was cool for October in Chicago and I started worrying that I might catch my death.

Inside the café, I chose a window seat looking out on the street. It was mid-morning, but the sidewalks were still filled with office workers and wide-eyed tourists. I was leafing through the newspaper when a story at the bottom of page 18 caught my attention. It had something to do with what experts were saying was exponential growth in the funeral home industry. The part of the story that really stopped me cold was that it said that at least 40,000 people die every day.

I put the paper down on the table and did some rough calculations on the daily worldwide death toll. *My God*, I thought, *that's like eight ships the size of the Queen Mary filled with dead people sailing off into the sunset each day.* This knowledge made me feel a little better about pestering my doctor. I was simply trying to be proactive. There was nothing wrong with catching health problems before they reach a terminal point.

I picked up the paper and continued reading then heard someone call my name from the other side of the café: "Ian is that you? Oh my God, it *is* you. Ian Sloan, how perfect!"

At first I didn't recognize the dwarf-like man rushing toward me in a rumpled blue suit. When he got to my table he grinned then thrust out his hand, which I shook. He let go of my hand then pointed to himself with both index fingers. "Richard Noseworthy, remember?" he asked. "We worked on a sewer documentary together three years ago? I'm the writer."

It all came flooding back to me. It had been a two-week job on the south side. I had been one of three videographers on the project. It was some kind of documentary on the building of the sewer system underneath the city. I never saw the completed film and was pretty sure I had contracted e-coli while shooting it.

I didn't remember much about the project but I did remember Richard because shortly after we had begun shooting someone on the crew told me Richard had been diagnosed with leukemia and was undergoing chemotherapy. Obviously, the treatment must have worked because there he was standing right in front on me.

He motioned to the table. "Can I join you?"

"Sure."

He was five feet tall, with a face as round as the full moon. His ears were slightly pointed and he had full squirrel-like cheeks. He leaned back in his chair. "So you remember me?"

"Yes, of course I remember you, Richard."

He snorted and leaned forward, resting his elbows on the table. "I saw you sitting here and I could not believe my luck."

"Oh?"

"Do you still do freelance camera work?"

"Yes, although my health's been . . . in question lately."

"Anything serious?"

"I'm not sure."

He paused, to look around the café, then back at me. "I have a great short film that's been greenlit by PBS, totally funded, and I'm supposed to start shooting tomorrow."

"Fantastic."

He shook his head and a frown formed on his lips. "It would be except the cameraman I had booked for the next three days was hit by a cab. Instead of helping me, he's being buried."

"Who was it?"

"Ken Silverman. Did you know him?"

I though for a moment, then slowly shook my head. "No. I don't think so. Tragic though."

"It is, but I haven't had a chance to think about it. I'm locked into this shooting schedule and I have to start tomorrow—permits and all that. I've been frantically making calls all morning trying to find a videographer. You know how difficult it is to find a talented shooter on such short notice." He threw up his hands. "Then I turn around and see you sitting here."

I nodded and sipped my latté,

"Well, what do you think?" he asked. "Can you help me out? The money's fantastic."

I was interested in the job because I was barely able to make my rent. But I wasn't willing to risk my life crawling around some sewer. "What's the film about?"

"It's for a series on wildlife living within the city."

"Wildlife in Chicago?"

"That's right. There are coyotes, foxes, possums, skunks and other wild animals living in the city. There was even a wild cougar a few years ago. The cops shot it."

"You're filming possums?"

"No. Someone else is doing a segment on small animals like that. I'm filming a segment on deer."

"Deer?" I was instantly reminded of my dream from the night before. The coincidence was a little unsettling.

He nodded. "There's a family of deer living in a cemetery on the far north side, miles from the nearest woods. They've been there for generations."

"Why does PBS want a short on that?"

He took a deep breath. "Nature shows are hot right now. Deer rarely live longer than 10 years. They get hit by cars, die from disease, starve or freeze to death. They're hunted by packs of wild dogs. Shot by gang bangers. Yet there they are, a whole family, safe inside the confines of a cemetery, in the middle of one of the baddest cities on the planet." He smiled showing small, underdeveloped teeth. "So, what do you think?"

I took another sip. "Can you pay me in cash?"

"How about a check?"

I nodded. "That'll work."

• • •

The following morning I carefully packed my camera then went downstairs to the sidewalk in front of my apartment building to wait for Richard. It was only 7 a.m. and the cool morning air smelled of fall. The sun had created long shadows, which were crawling across the street and sidewalk. It was Thursday, so the street cleaning trucks were out, hissing and puffing, their oval brushes spinning like cartwheels as they kicked up dust, dried leafs and a million germs in the gutters. Standing there, I left another message for my doctor.

Richard pulled up right on time. I stepped between two parked cars, climbed into his van and carefully placed my camera case on the back seat.

"We've got a great day for it," he said, pulling back into traffic.

I fastened the seatbelt. "It's not that great. I prefer not to shoot in direct sunlight. Overcast is better because there's not as much shadow—or too much light. The conditions could be better."

Richard shot me a dismissive look.

"But at least it's not raining," I said, trying to put a positive spins on things. "I can't imagine any place more depressing than a cemetery in the rain."

"I don't know," he said, pulling up behind a taxi. "The last time I was there, checking things out for this shoot, it was raining. I found it kind of peaceful."

"If it's raining, I'd rather sit in a café."

As the traffic began moving, Richard turned on the radio and tuned in a light rock station. After a few more miles we stopped at a Starbucks, then continued toward the north side. We turned off Lake Shore Drive onto Sheridan Road and I sipped my coffee as I gazed out the van's side window, then checked my cell phone to see of my doctor had called. He hadn't.

We pulled up to a red light, and Richard turned toward me. "Thanks again for saving me on this. I'd be lost if I hadn't hooked up with you."

"No problem. At least this shoot doesn't involve crawling around a sewer. I'm surprised I didn't get the plague on that last shoot."

He chuckled. "Yeah, I remember. Pretty nasty stuff. Plus I was fighting cancer at the time."

I hadn't said anything to him about his cancer because I felt like I didn't know him well enough to talk to him about his health. But since he'd brought it up, I decided to ask him about it. "I remember. But it looks like you beat it."

"I'm a lot better than I was that last time you saw me. The whole thing took me to death's door." He took his right hand off the steering wheel and held up his thump and forefinger, about an inch apart. "I was this close."

I shook my head and exhaled. "I hope I never have to deal with something like that."

"Deal with it . . . or you die. And there were some days where I was so sick and tired I almost wished I'd die. The chemo made me so sick I could hardly move. There were times when it felt like it would have been easier to just give up."

"If the cure doesn't kill you . . ."

"The whole thing changed my life."

"Oh?"

"One day in the hospital, I was so incredibly sick that I said to myself; if I survive this, if I make it, I'm going to treasure each day as if it's my last. Well, I gradually got better, and I've managed to pretty much stick to my promise."

"A good attitude helps, I guess."

He turned toward me. "Makes all the difference. I think that's why this film appealed to me. There's a metaphor of some kind there, the way these deer find sanctuary in a cemetery. There's just something about it. Survival of some kind."

I hadn't thought about it until then, but there was something poetic about a family of deer living in a 'big city' cemetery. "How'd you hear about the deer?" I asked.

We pulled up to a red light and a look of excitement formed on his face. "A few months ago I went to the North Side to visit a friend. I parked on the street, near the cemetery, and I was walking toward her apartment when I saw a flash of brown out of the corner of my eye. I turned to look and a deer sprinted past me and took off down the middle of the road. I was like 'Wow' where did *that* come from!"

"You don't see that every day."

Richard grabbed his coffee from the cup holder and without looking away from the road took a long sip.

"It blew right past me, running real fast. It rounded the corner, lost its footing, fell, then scrambled back to its feet and took off. It was scared. It was a minor miracle that it wasn't hit by a car."

"I'll say."

We pulled up to another red light and he turned toward me. "When I got to my friends place and told her about what had happened, she said a family of deer had been living in the cemetery for as long as anyone could remember."

"How did they get there?"

"No one knows."

The light turned green and he stepped on the accelerator then turned onto a side street. We slowed down and Richard pointed to an ancient looking ten-foot-high cement wall. "We're here," he said, pulling up to the curb.

I got out of the van, then pulled my camera bag from the back seat and put it down on the grassy parkway between the sidewalk and street. It was still early, but the fall sun was warm and soothing. Richard came up beside me, unfolded a map and started studying it. I looked over his shoulder. The breeze played with the edges of the map, but it was easy to see the cemetery, which was marked in green and seemed to take up twenty city blocks.

"Where do you want to start?" I asked. "This place is the size of Texas."

He pointed down the street "There's an entrance up this way. Let's start there."

We walked for a few minutes then came to a break in the cement wall guarded by a tall wrought-iron gate. It was open, and once inside, we came upon a narrow asphalt road running down the middle of the cemetery. Smaller dirt paths branched off the main road to the left and right.

"Do you have any idea where they are?" I asked.

"No, let's just start looking. Keep your eyes open because we could walk right past them and not see them. And watch for deer shit."

I knelt down in the grass and pulled my camera out of its case. "Deer shit?" I said, looking up at Richard. "I don't know what deer shit looks like."

He grinned. "A bunch of little brown pellets, the size of marbles."

I shook my head. "What are you an animal tracker?"

"My grandparents had a farm in Wisconsin. Deer used to come up near the house and leave their calling card."

I grabbed my camera off the ground and picked up the case. "I guess you never know when such information is going to be useful," I said, slipping the case's strap over my shoulder. "Camera's ready. Now all we need are your deer."

He pointed off to the right toward a stand of trees about 100 yards away. "Let's try over there."

We started walking on a narrow footpath that wound between grave markers and tombstones and I wondered how many of them my family had made. Some were more than 10 feet high, topped with crosses or angels that cast long shadows. Off to our left, the morning sun, climbing the eastern sky, was sparkling on the surface of Lake Michigan. We passed a large stone mausoleum and came to an open area where a dozen Canada geese were peacefully nibbling grass. I guess they weren't afraid of people, because they barely regarded us, although we were only about 40 feet away. I noticed that there weren't any tombstones in that area, and I figured it was "virgin earth" into which new graves would eventually be dug.

I took off my sunglasses, slipped them into my shirt pocket and pointed at the geese. "I'll shoot some footage of them while we're here."

Richard nodded.

I lifted the camera to my shoulder and shot about five minutes of tape before Richard tapped me on the shoulder and suggested we look for the deer by a stand of birch trees in the distance.

As were walking, he asked, "Smell that?"

"What?"

"The faint whiff of death."

I didn't know what he was talking about and thought his comment weird. "The whiff of death?" I asked after a moment.

"You can't smell it?" he replied, glancing over at me. "It's very faint, a musty smell. It seeps up through the coffins and the soil. All those people, all those stories, underground; a city of the living now a city of the dead."

He was starting to creep me out. But I cut him some slack, because after all, he was a writer and they can be strange. He was looking at me and seemed to be waiting for a reply so I inhaled to see if I could detect the faint "whiff of death" he was talking about. "I don't think I smell anything but the air, maybe some car exhaust from the street."

"I'm not surprised," he said. "My sense of smell became very acute after the chemo."

"That would explain it."

We continued walking and he launched into a kind of running commentary on the dead. I found it unnerving considering our whereabouts and started wondering if "a whiff of death" could be contagious.

"Dusty skeletons underground," he said matter-of-factly, "wearing beautiful dresses and fine silk suits, skulls wearing glasses. Rings on boney fingers. Kids buried in their favorite blue jeans jacket. Shoes filled with nothing but dust and all of them with their boney hands folded on their rib cages."

I hoisted the camera bag high onto my shoulder as we passed between two large granite headstones topped with crosses. I decided to change the subject. "I don't see those deer anywhere. Perhaps we should head back toward the car . . ."

I guess he didn't hear me because he just continued talking as if he were in some kind of a reverie. "They all had stories to tell. Things they believed in. They had dreams. If they were lucky and loved people wept for them."

We arrived at the stand of trees and stopped walking. Richard looked around, then leaned up against a shiny granite tombstone with the name Perdomo and the years 1956-2003 engraved on it.

"People don't grieve for the dead," he said. "They grieve for themselves because there are things left unsaid." He stroked his jaw for a moment and seemed to be pondering his own words. "It just occurred to me," he continued. "What if the dead mourn for the living more than the living mourn the dead? Perhaps there's a silent chorus rising from these graves and they're all saying the same thing 'Live your life to the fullest because you will be one of us soon enough.'"

Jeez, I don't think his sense of smell was the only thing affected by the chemo. I nodded thoughtfully the way you nod to appease someone you think may be crazy.

He looked at me as though expecting a response.

The only thing I could come up with was "The dead mourn the living? I never thought of it in that way. Interesting." I put my camera down and looked around as a slight breeze blew in off the lake. "I don't see the deer anywhere."

He pointed to the left. "Let's try over in that direction."

I picked up my camera and followed. We continued walking past granite tombstones, some tall and majestic, others only a few feet high and engraved with the names of the dead. Some had flowers placed in front of them.

Richard stopped walking and motioned to the right. "Wow. Look at that."

It was a tombstone made to resemble a tree trunk. At about six feet tall, it appeared to be made from cement or limestone and had a rough, bark-like surface with several tiny branches sprouting from it. A name, dates and inscription were carved near the base:

Lillian B. Porter

1924-1943

RIP

Beloved Daughter. Gone Too Soon.

I knew that this type of tombstone had been popular in the 1920s. My great uncles were known for their artistry in this style. Someone had placed a bouquet of freshly cut flowers in a blue ceramic vase at the base of the grave marker. There had to be two dozen flowers: lush red, pink and white roses, brightly colored lilies, sunflowers, and red and white carnations just to name a few.

Richard carefully plucked a small card from amid the flowers and read it aloud. "'These are for you my beloved. Fear not for I am always with you.'"

I moved a little closer and motioned to the flowers. "Looks like they were placed here this morning," I said.

"Considering the dates on the tombstone that's a little surprising," he said. Then he lifted the bouquet to his nose and inhaled deeply. "Ahh, wonderful! You know," he said, turning to me, "an old girlfriend once told me that whenever she saw a bouquet she'd stop and attribute a positive attribute to every flower. She said it was all about living in the moment and that doing it lifted her spirit." He pulled a pink rose from the bouquet, held it by the stem and seemed to be pondering it. "I'll give it the attribute of perfection," he said after a moment. Then he put the rose back in the vase and pulled out a sunflower. "Hmmm? Let's see . . . what about beauty."

I was getting impatient and was about to suggest that we continue on our way when he turned toward me and asked: "You want to try a few?"

I backed away and raised my hands. "No thanks. A flower's just a flower. And anyway, I'm allergic to pollen so the only thing I can attribute to a flower is sneezing." No sooner had a said that when I: "Aaaaaachooooo!" sneezed violently. I pulled a Kleenex from my pocket and blew my nose. "Please put them back. I'm having a reaction."

Richard carefully placed the bouquet at the foot of the tombstone then slowly ran his hand over its rough bark like surface.

"Have you ever seen a tree trunk tombstone like that before," I asked.

"Can't say I have."

"They were a fad in the '20s and '30s," I said. "Trees are, you know, symbols of life."

He knelt beside the tombstone. "When I go, I don't want anything," he said. "Just spread my ashes in a nice place and plant a real tree somewhere in remembrance of me. That's enough." He paused then asked, "What about you?"

I was a little taken aback by his question because it was none of his business. "I haven't really thought about it," I replied curtly.

He stood and strode back to my side. "You might want to think about it because . . . you know, we're all going to die someday."

Was he depressing or what! I looked away and mumbled, "Thanks, very uplifting. I'll keep that in mind."

We started walking again and after a few minutes reached a cluster of bushes covered with tiny crimson colored leaves. As we rounded the bushes we came upon a young African American man crouching in the grass beside a grave maker. We must have surprised him as much as he surprised us because he quickly stood and eyed us warily. He looked to be in his late teens, 20 at the most. His skin was as dark as oil, and he was wearing a T-shirt emblazoned with a picture of a TuPac on it, a baggy black jacket and jeans riding so low they were collecting at his ankles. There were street gangs in that part of the city, and I couldn't help but notice there was a bulge under his coat near his waist. Probably a gun.

We eyed each other for a second without saying anything. Then he pointed at my camera. "What's that for?"

"We're looking for a family of white-tailed deer that live here," Richard answered. "We want to film them. You ever seen them?"

"White tailed deer? Maybe I seen them." His expression suddenly turning hard. "Why you want to film something like that anyway? Why don't you leave the deer be? They're not bothering nobody."

It seemed like he was being protective of them.

"We're not going to hurt them," Richard said emphatically, then pointed toward me. "The only thing we're shooting with is that camera. It's a film for television."

The young man folded his arms across his chest and slowly looked me over. He didn't seem convinced.

"Problem is, people see your program, they come here to hurt the deer. That's just the way some people is." He pointed to his head. "They sick up here. They got the need to kill something beautiful because they think it will take their pain away. But it don't. Understand? You kill something you kill part of yourself. Maybe that's the way God intended it, so there's consequences to the shit you do. You take a life and there's no place to go, you stuck here. Someone take your life and they catch the disease."

He was rambling, and it occurred to me that he was probably on drugs and that we were about to be robbed and killed. I was getting ready to drop my camera and run.

Before I could do that Richard thrust out his hand for the kid to shake. "My name's Richard." He motioned toward me. "And this is Ian."

He looked down at Richard's hand, and for a moment I thought he wasn't going to shake it. But then he took Richard's hand in his. "People call me Mickey the H," he said, flashing a cheesy smile that revealed a golden front tooth. "The H stand for 'Handsome.' Can't you see it?"

No, I couldn't. He looked tough and hard like a boxer who had lost a lot of fights. The word that described him best was "menacing." I imagined he was the product of a tough life and the streets. A jagged three-inch scar above his left eye seemed to confirm my assessment.

"Handsome? Oh, yeah, I can see it," Richard said, obviously trying to humor the guy. "A great face for television."

Mickey snorted, flashed a half grin, and jammed his hands into his pockets. "I wanted to learn how to work a camera and shit. I wanted to make videos because I used to rap. Things didn't work out for me. I never got the chance. I got cheated."

"Why don't you tag along with us," Richard said. "Help us find the deer and see how we do things."

I shot Richard a *what the hell* look, but he ignored me.

Mickey kicked at a twig on the ground then looked up at us. His brown eyes suddenly seemed a little softer. "I suppose I could tag along. I got lots of time and no place to be."

We started walking on a narrow paved road that ran down the middle of the cemetery. "Any idea where we might find the deer?" Richard asked.

"They like moving around," Mickey said. "You got to look for them. Their hearing and seeing is way better than you and me. It's hard to find them because they hear you coming and run away."

"So you've seen them?" I asked.

"Yeah I see em all the time. About six of em. Four big ones and two little ones." He turned toward me. "They trust me because they know I won't hurt em. They real . . ." Suddenly, he stopped walking. "Shit," he said, looking straight ahead, his expression stern. "Here comes bad trouble."

I looked in the direction he was staring. Five guys around Mickey's age were about 50 yards away. Two black pitbulls were sauntering beside them. They were all walking between the tombstones toward us.

"You best come with me, and I mean fast," Mickey said turning. "They be gang bangers, and they ain't nice people. Come on, let's go!"

He started to run. Richard and I exchanged worried glances, and then without saying anything, quickly followed him. Mickey was just a few yards in front of us as we sprinted through the cemetery, trying not to trip over grave markers or run into tombstones. We had run for about a minute when Mickey pointed to a mausoleum. "In here," he blurted as he pushed open the two tiny front doors and ducked inside.

Mausoleums are usually locked, but for some reason this one wasn't. Perhaps the lock was broken and Mickey knew that because he knew the cemetery. Maybe he lived in there. It didn't matter because Richard and I quickly followed him inside. It was the size of a large walk-in closet, and we were barely able to stand due to the low ceiling. It was damp and dark in there and smelled like wet cement. The only light came from the morning sun streaming in through the doorway and tiny slat-like windows. Crouching inside, we tried to catch our breath without making too much noise.

"Would they have done something?" Richard asked in a whisper.

Mickey's eyes widened. His face was shining with sweat. "I'm not worried about me. I can take care of myself," he replied between breaths. "But they might take something off you two. First thing I notice was your camera equipment. It looks nice and expensive. You already in a cemetery and they won't mind one bit messing you up and taking your shit."

"Thanks for helping us," Richard said.

"Yeah," I said. "That could have been a real problem."

Mickey's eyes narrowed and he leaned into the cement wall. "Maybe you still got a problem," he said. "A trust problem. You trusts the wrong people man. You followed me in here because you think I'm better than them, right?"

Richard and I looked at each other and I felt my pulse quicken. Suddenly it was as if the light in there dimmed by half.

"You trust me right?" Mickey asked again. A menacing grin formed on his lips and his eyes narrowed. "You didn't stop to wonder if I was leading you into a trap, if I was luring you in here to take your shit and mess you up."

"We don't want any trouble," Richard said. He pointed to the camera. "Take the camera if you want." Then he reached into his pocket and pulled out his wallet. "Take our money."

There was dead silence for what seemed like an eternity. Then Mickey chuckled softly and crouched beside the wall. "Relax, I'm through with that juvenile delinquent bullshit. I'm just messing with you. I'm just saying you best be thinking about who you can trust in this shit world."

I must have been holding my breath without knowing it because I suddenly exhaled. I looked at Richard and he rolled his eyes. "What about those other guys?" I asked, nervously glancing toward the tiny doorway. What are they doing here?"

Mickey shook his head, and his gaze fell to the stone floor. "Who knows?" he replied softly. "Maybe they looking for me. It's a kind of game we play. They chase me and my boys forever or my boys and I chase them right into eternity." He looked up, and suddenly he appeared much older. "Kind a messed up I guess." He moved silently toward the entrance, paused to listen then turned toward us. "Usually it's safer for me in this cemetery than on the streets." He shrugged. "That's fine, because I like coming in here to check up on my brothers."

"You have friends, family buried here?" Richard asked.

"You know that. Bucks younger than me be buried here wearing all their gold grills and shit." He shook his head again. "They did stupid things. They never knew . . ."

The resignation in his voice seemed to echo in the tiny stone chamber. But it was his expression that said it all. He looked worn out and hard as if he had been alternating between running and fighting his entire life.

What he was saying was pretty compelling stuff so I decided to film him. But when I hit the camera's power button nothing happened. I put the camera down on the ground and mumbled "Damned batteries."

Crouching beside the entrance, Mickey picked up a dried leaf from the smooth stone floor. "No reason for a black man to be shooting another black man in this world that already tilted against the black man," he said, his gaze fixed on the leaf. "It's just ignorance and hormones and playing stupid games." He let the leaf slip between his fingers and it fell silently to the ground. Then he stood and pointed at my camera. "You wanna tell the world something? Tell it this: Black men don't be killing your black brothers. Enough of that shit. We got too many dead brothers in cemeteries . . ." He stopped, then motioned to the outside. "And too many grieving mothers everywhere else."

There was nothing Richard or I could say. Any response would have been trite. We were from a different world, a world where we didn't have to worry about being gunned down by a rival gang member. Mickey must have sensed our discomfort because he motioned to the stone walls. "You know whose crypt we in?"

"No idea," Richard replied.

Mickey smiled and the dim reflected light caught his gold tooth. "This crypt belong to Mr. Dewey Maloney. Born 1857. Died 1934. He was a rich banker."

Richard and I exchanged glances. "How do you know?" I asked.

"I like reading the names on the tombstones and thinking about who they was, what they done with their lives."

Richard took a few steps toward the entrance and peered out the door. "How do you know he was a banker?" he asked softly, without looking back.

Mickey leaned into the wall and a faint grin formed on his lips. "Who else you think get a crypt like this after they dead?"

Richard and I smiled. "Dewey Maloney," I said. "Nicest house on the block . . . and a lake view for eternity. Talk about resting in peace."

Mickey glanced over at me and smirked. "Rest in Peace? You hope. Maybe some of the dead don't rest. Maybe they still got something to say. So they wander, just like them deer you looking for." He crouched against the wall again and clasped his hands together, the reflected morning sun from the doorway lighting his rough face. "Either of you like reading books?"

Richard nodded. "I love reading."

Mickey turned toward me, waiting for a response.

"Books? Yeah," I said after a moment. "I've been reading a lot of medical books lately."

Mickey looked me up and down. "Medical books? You some kind of doctor?"

"No . . . I've had some . . . medical issues."

His eyebrows arched. "You sick?"

"I'm not sure what it is . . . what I have. I'm waiting to see my doctor . . ."

Still crouching beside the tiny doorway, Mickey still seemed to be studying me. "You ain't sick man," he said.

I was surprised by his comment and quipped: "Are you a doctor?"

He turned away from me and muttered: "Yeah, man, I'm a doctor. A doctor of the soul."

"Thanks for the diagnosis . . . *Doctor*. But you can never tell. Just yesterday I read that forty thousand people die every day. That's like eight ships the size of the Queen Mary, filled with dead people sailing off . . ."

He cut me off. "That all? Just forty thousand? It's more than that."

"You mean, just in America?" Richard asked. "Because that seems like a low number for the whole planet."

They were both looking at me waiting for a reply. I suddenly felt like I had been put on the spot. "I thought it was for the entire world," I blurted. "It may not seem like a lot . . . unless you're one of them."

"Unless you one of them?" Mickey snorted. "Ha. Man, you going to be one of them some day. So you better . . ." He stopped then smiled and stood up. "Maybe you thinking you got cancer eating you up or some other disease. Maybe you think you gonna get into a plane crash, or somebody going to drop a piano on you. Splat." He chuckled. "If you worry about tomorrow today, today slips past you like a ghost or you become a kind of ghost. A living ghost. You kind a dead already." He paused and seemed to be thinking. "What I'm saying is everybody holding a ticket for the Queen Mary. They gotta get onboard sometime or another. Nobody live forever and that's a good thing."

He was right, I guess, but it certainly wasn't making me feel any better. I was vigilant about my health because contrary to what people thought, I enjoyed life.

Mickey raised a clenched fist to his chest. "What counts in life is how much heart you have, how much you face down fear."

"Fear?" I asked, genuinely interested. "Fear of what?"

Mickey grinned, showing his golden tooth. "Fear of being hurt or humiliated. At the end of it all what people regret is that they didn't live enough, that they didn't try to find God, that they didn't live boldly, that they didn't invest enough heart, that they didn't love enough." He shrugged. "Nothing else, money, fame, counts at all. You die the same way you're born. Naked with nothing but your body and your soul."

He paused for a moment then turned toward me. "Did you see that angel sitting on top of that tombstone next to where you met me?"

"Angel?" I asked.

"Yeah." His brown eyes were wide as he looked at me and slowly passed his flattened hand through the dank air, like an airplane. "You drop your fear, you got wings like that angel, and suddenly . . . you can fly."

I felt like he was putting me on the spot, that he was somehow calling me out. "I'm not afraid of flying," I lied. "Flying's great! I love flying. I fly all the time . . ."

"You does?" Mickey said with a sly smile. "I bet you got a lot of those frequent flying miles, always flying from here to there . . ."

"I practically live at the airport."

He chuckled. "Good. You tasting life like you should, like tasting fine wine. You gotta savor it, understand what it means. What your obligations is."

Richard stepped back from the entryway. "Obligation?"

"Yeah man," Mickey said, his voice suddenly harsh. "This life ain't no read through. It's the real deal. Make the right choices."

He exhaled loudly. "You know about the Egyptians," he asked.

"The Egyptians?" I replied.

"Yeah, the Egyptians," he repeated slowly. "I read a book that said people in Egypt used to believe that when they die they sail across the Nile to the other side. They meet up with their dead relatives and have a big old party." As he spoke the smile slipped from his face. "That's bullshit. That don't always happen."

I didn't know what to say to that, and obviously Richard didn't either, because he was looking down at his shoes. I thought Mickey was stoned or a little crazy.

There was silence for a moment then Mickey moved toward the tiny entranceway. "Come on," he said stepping out. "Those dumbass gang bangers gone by now."

Richard and I nervously followed him out of the mausoleum into the bright fall morning. Squinting against the sunlight, we quickly looked around. I was ready to start running again but Mickey was right: the gang bangers had disappeared, as if they were nothing more than phantoms.

Richard turned to Mickey. "This is your territory. Where's the best place to look for the deer?"

Mickey motioned for us to follow him. "This way."

We started walking along the narrow path with Mickey in the lead.

"So, you used to rap?" Richard asked as we passed a 15-foot high stone cross.

Mickey hoisted up his pants. "Yeah," he replied without turning around. "We all need to do something to pass the time of day."

"Let's hear one," Richard said.

I could not believe my ears. I glanced at Richard, shook my head and mouthed, "What the . . ."

Mickey stopped and faced us. "You want to hear one of my raps? Really?"

"Yeah," Richard answered, "really."

Mickey pointed at me and smiled. "This rap dedicated to you, Mr. Frequent Flier." Then he cupped his hands over his mouth and started rapping out a beat. "Boom Ba Ba Boom Ba Ba Bomp . . ."

I lifted the camera to my shoulder and tried to film, but again nothing happened. *Damned batteries!* I placed the camera at my feet and Mickey broke into verse:

> I got my Glock.
> I stopped his clock.
> I closed his eyes.
> No time for goodbyes.
> I'm paying here.
> More than years.
> That's forever.
> That ain't clever.
> I'll always remember
> What dead is.
> What life is.
> You feel you heal.
> You dead enough said.
> You living.
> Start living.
> Light's now
> Light's now
> Life's? now . . .

I could not believe I was standing in the middle of a cemetery with a gangster who was actually rapping. What a strange day. I wanted nothing more than to get the footage we needed then get the hell out of there. I glared at Richard who was swaying from side-to-side and clapping in time to Mickey's Rap.

Light's now
Light's now
Life's now
Life's now . . .

Mickey stopped, threw back his head and let out a loud laugh. "Don't think I'll be getting a record contract anytime soon."

"Are you kidding?" Richard said enthusiastically. "It was great." Then they did a fist bump.

Mickey flashed a wide smile. "Thanks, man." He hoisted up his jeans again and pointed down the path. "Go to the west end, and you'll find them deer. At the end, there's a small crypt like the one we just in. It's surrounded by trees. The name on it is 'Moran.' 1902 to1975. I seen the deers round that house in the morning. Be quiet. They hear you coming and they run away."

"You're not coming with us?" Richard asked.

Mickey grinned. "Naw, I got friends to look in on." The clear morning light danced off his golden tooth.

I was relieved he wasn't coming with us because while he had helped, he was also a little threatening. Richard reached out and shook his hand. "Thanks for everything."

I picked my camera up off the ground. "Right. Thanks."

"No problem," Mickey said. "Good luck with your program."

He turned, and we watched him amble away across the grass. When he was about 20 feet from us, he stopped, looked back and gestured to a tombstone. "Death ain't no big deal," he said. "Life, *that's* the big deal."

He continued walking then turned back to us again and yelled: "Don't waste your life building a coffin."

Richard and I nodded in unison. Then Mickey waved and disappeared from sight behind a stand of oak trees.

"Nice kid," Richard said, turning toward me.

"Nice, but a little scary. I think he was stoned—and he had a gun in his waistband."

"Stoned? A gun? You really think so?"

I shrugged. "I thought I saw something when we first walked up on him. And the way he was talking 'live your life or you become a ghost.' Kind of crazy, or high."

Richard looked at me dismissively. "He seemed like a good kid. Rough around the edges maybe but not the type to be carrying a gun." There was disdain in his voice; he obviously didn't like what I'd said about Mickey. I didn't want to argue the point, so I suggested we check the west end of the cemetery where Mickey had said we would find the deer.

With the sun warming our backs, we walked for a while. Then Richard, pointed to a mausoleum some 50 yards ahead. It looked like the burial chamber Mickey had described. "That must be it," Richard whispered.

It was partly surrounded by elm and maple trees with brilliant red and yellow leaves rustling gently in the breeze. I flicked on the camera's power button and to my surprise it actually worked. I don't know why it didn't work earlier. Perhaps in my haste I had flicked the switch in the wrong direction. I had done that in the past.

We slowly approached the mausoleum, which was a dozen feet high with ornate trim around the roof and narrow slits for windows. As we got closer I could see the name "Moran" carved in bold letters above the entranceway just as Mickey had described it.

We were about 30 yards from the mausoleum when I suddenly saw one of the deer. I would have missed it if I had not been looking for it because it was standing very still. Its tan fur blended in perfectly with the fall foliage and the bleak gray stone of the crypt. The deer must have seen us before I saw it because it ears were perked and its brown eyes were wide as it stood beside a tree, staring right at me. I tapped Richard on the arm, motioned toward the deer, then slowly raised the camera to my shoulder and started filming.

Richard knelt beside me. After a half minute the deer took a few steps to its right, lowered its head and started eating the grass at its feet. Within a few seconds three more adult deer and two fawns ambled into view and stood tentatively beside the first deer. They seemed to regard us warily, but then they too slowly lowered their heads to eat. Every minute or so, one of the adults would raise its head and carefully look around.

Richard half stood and moved forward. "Let's try to get closer," he whispered.

I tugged the sleeve of his jacket and quietly scolded him. "Hold on. I don't want to scare them." I pointed at my camera. "I'll use my zoom. We don't have to get closer."

I gripped the camera tightly in my right hand, lifted it to my shoulder and pressed down on the zoom button until the family of deer filled the viewfinder. The two fawns could not have been more than six months old. They looked skinny but healthy, their white bellies spotted with brown. The adults were frightfully thin. Their ribs were plainly visible under their coats, and their fur was matted and patchy in places. One of them had three long scars on it rear flank as if it had been clawed by something large. They looked like fleabags and were probably carrying a slew of diseases. I couldn't believe that they had survived in such a hostile urban environment.

"I can smell them," Richard said quietly.

I was trying to get a tight shot of the two fawns together when the deer I had spotted first stopped eating and once again lifted its head as if listening for something. Its ears were perked and twitching. If there was a noise it must have been inaudible to the human ear.

"Something's spooked him," Richard whispered.

I guess he was right, because suddenly the other five deer stopped eating and all six of them started moving away from us. They walked slowly for several paces then broke into a trot and ran out of sight.

Richard stood and looked in the direction the deer had gone. "Shit," he murmured. He shook his head and turned toward me. "How much did you get?"

I lowered my camera and placed it in the grass next to my knee. "Ten or 15 minutes. Is that enough?"

He crouched down beside me. "Enough for a three minute segment." Then he stood and shoved his hands into his pockets. "Let's pack it up."

That was fine with me because I'd be paid for the entire day, even if we quit early. I turned off the camera, opened my camera bag and reached in for my lens cover. It wasn't there. I turned to Richard. "I can't find my lens cover. Have you seen it?"

He shook his head. "No."

"Shit. I must have dropped it when we met Mickey."

"We'll go back and look for it," Richard shrugged. "It's on the way to the van."

I picked up my camera and we started walking through the cemetery. The sun, climbing the sky in the east, was taking the chill off a lake breeze that had started a few minutes earlier.

"Looking at those deer you kind of forget your problems," Richard said as we passed by a tall tombstone with a statue of the Virgin Mary on top. "It takes your mind off things for a few minutes. If you have any humanity at all you feel for them."

I never thought that I'd have an emotional reaction to seeing the deer, but what Richard had said was right. They were constantly living just out of death's grasp. Perhaps every living thing is. But for the deer, death would likely be found anywhere outside the walls of that cemetery.

"It can't be easy for them in the winter," I said. "I don't know how those fawns could survive in such cold temperatures and without much food."

When we got back to the spot where we had met Mickey we searched the grass and under the bushes for my lens cap. We'd only been looking for a few minutes when Richard blurted; "Oh, my, God, look!"

I turned toward him. He was standing there with his mouth open pointing at a grave marker laid flat on the ground.

"What is it?" I asked.

"Look!" he said, still pointing.

I walked to his side and read the name on the grave marker:

"Mickey Henderson. 'Mickey the H'—You Live On In Our Hearts"

"It can't be," I snorted. "The guy we met must have been putting us on. That wasn't his real name." I pointed at the grave marker. "He knew this guy . . . this Mickey."

"Look at the picture," Richard said, in a voice just above a whisper.

It was one of those tombstones with a photograph of the deceased on it. I moved closer and as I studied the photograph, the hair on the back of my neck stood up. The guy in the photograph did look a lot like the "Mickey" we had just met—but there was something else. He was smiling slightly and it looked like one of his front teeth was off color . . . or possibly gold.

A chill ran down my spine. "This is freaking me out."

"Look at his birth date," Richard blurted.

I stepped forward until I was right above the tombstone. The dates inscribed on it were partly concealed by long blades of grass which I carefully moved with my foot. I had to squint in the bright sunlight. Then I stepped back in absolute shock. "Holy shit. Today would have been that guy's birthday!"

Richard turned toward me. "That's right . . . I think Mickey the H was a ghost!"

I didn't even want to consider the possibility. "That's crazy," I scoffed. "Crazy! It was someone who looked like him—nothing more. Probably his brother who came here to visit him on his birthday."

Richard nodded thoughtfully. "Mickey the H was a ghost . . . a ghost."

"I don't care about the lens cap," I snapped. "I can get another one. Let's get out of here before those gang bangers come back and kill us."

Richard folded his arms across his chest. "I'm not leaving here until you at least admit the possibility he was a ghost."

"What?"

"How can you deny what your eyes are telling you?"

I stared at Richard, then pointed to the grave marker. "All I know is that we met some guy who looks like that guy. Was he a ghost? No. He was putting us on. He didn't want to give us his real name, that's all it was. He was playing us."

Richard's eyes met mine. "Remember what he said about dying and living in fear?" he said. "It all makes sense now. Admit he was a ghost or walk home."

I was getting mad and wanted nothing more than to get the hell out of that cemetery. Then is sheer frustration, I cupped my hands to my mouth and yelled: "Mickey is a ghost! This place is *filled* with ghosts! This is ghost city. Boo . . ."

Then I lowered my hands and turned toward Richard. "You happy?" I asked, unable to conceal the anger in my voice. "I admit it! Okay? Mickey was a freaking ghost, a phantom, and he had some *great wisdom* he needed to impart to us. Can we go now?"

He grinned as he pulled his keys from his pocket. I'm sure he knew I just telling him what he wanted to hear. "At least you can admit the possibility he was a phantom," he said heading toward the cemetery exit. "It'll do you good."

When we got to the van I threw my camera into the back seat and got in front. Richard jumped in, started the engine, dropped the van into DRIVE and turned toward me.

"I'll never forget this day. Amazing. Just amazing. 'Mickey the H' . . . no one's going to believe that."

"I expect to be paid for a full day," I responded without looking at him.

"Of course."

I was still angry at Richard for his little stunt in the cemetery and therefore sat in stony silence as we drove through the city. Besides he was just plain creepy. I was determined that was the last time I'd ever work with the guy.

Traffic was light and after 30 minutes he pulled up to the curb in front of my apartment building, put the van in PARK and turned toward me.

"I was thinking about what Mickey told us," he said. "You know 'Death's no big deal. Life's the big deal.'"

I was still a little angry and felt like telling Richard that he was full of it. But instead, I bit my tongue and slowly nodded. "He's probably seen a lot of both."

"I'll bet he has."

I passed him the tape with the footage from the cemetery "I tried to shoot him but the camera was acting up."

Richard grinned. "Maybe cause someone already shot him."

I rolled my eyes.

He chopped the air with his hand, cutting me off. "Ian, don't you think it's just a little interesting that he not only saved us from those gang bangers but he told us where the deer were? And the way he was talking, and the Mickey the H grave marker, and today's his birthday. All of it. Can't you at least open your mind to the possibility?"

"I believe what my eyes tell me," I replied. "We met some guy in the cemetery. He liked to talk and rap and looked a little like the guy on the grave marker." I shook my head. "Sorry but that's it."

He smiled. "It's too bad you feel that way. You're missing a lot."

"I don't feel like I'm missing anything."

He motioned over his shoulder to my camera on the back seat. "It's like you see the whole world through the viewfinder in your camera. There's no room for anything outside that little box. Nothing on the periphery. Nothing left to your imagination. No room for ghosts. No room for flowers. No room for anything except yourself . . ." He paused, then continued, ". . . and you waiting for a call from your doctor."

He had crossed a line. "My doctor?" I blurted, reaching for the door handle. "You don't . . . oh just forget it." I opened the door, got out, grabbed my camera off the back seat and turned to look at Richard. "Mail me the check." I slammed the door and walked up the stairs into my building as he drove away.

It was early afternoon but I was exhausted. Inside my apartment, I dropped my camera bag by the front door and went to check for messages. There was a voice mail from my doctor's nurse asking me to come in the following morning. She said the doctor had received my test results back from the lab and that he wanted to see me. Hmmm, if he wants me to come in it can't be good news. I quickly called the office but the nurse refused to discuss the test results with me. "I'm not allowed to do that over the phone," she said curtly. "The doctor will share the results with you tomorrow."

Share the results? What did she mean by that? Why didn't she just say he'd "give me the results?" Was she trying to sugarcoat something? "If there's a problem I'd like to know it now," I said firmly.

"The doctor said he'd see you tomorrow."

"Fine," I snapped and hung up.

I put some tea on then sat down in front of my computer. I pulled up Google and typed "Mickey the H" into the search line. I sat there, staring at the screen, then turned off my computer without doing the search. Why? Because it would have been foolish.

I spend the rest of the day reading medical periodicals I had checked out from the library. I had a light dinner, went to bed early and after more than an hour finally fell into dreamless sleep.

The following morning, I got up early, took a shower, got dressed and then sat at my desk browsing Web MD while eating a bowl of corn flakes. I was concerned about what my test results would be, and rather than sit at home and worry, I decided to get to the doctor's office early. I grabbed my jacket from the closet and walked to my car. It was overcast and cool outside, in sharp contrast to the day before.

I walked into the office and checked in at the receptionist's desk. She gave me several forms to fill out. As I was standing there completing them, I noticed a large fresh bouquet of flowers in a blue ceramic vase on her desk. I motioned to it with my pen. "Beautiful flowers."

She looked at the flowers then turned back to me and blushed. "My husband sent them. It's my birthday."

"Really? Most men forget. He must be a great guy."

She smiled and passed me another form. "My Mickey? Oh, yeah, he's the best."

Mickey! The paper slipped between my fingers and landed on her desk. "Did you say 'Mickey?'"

I guess she was a little surprised by my tone because she leaned back in her chair. "Yes, Mickey. That's my husband's name."

"Oh, I see," I said after a moment. "Well then, ahh, happy birthday. Many more."

She smiled. "Thanks. The doctor will see you shortly."

Mickey? I guess all coincidences are rather weird. I took a seat and looked over a couple of old *Time* magazines. But I was worried about what my doctor was going to tell me, and I found it difficult to concentrate. Instead, my attention was drawn back to the bouquet of flowers on the receptionist's desk. There was something about them, and it was more than the fact they were from some guy named Mickey. Then it came to me. My God, they looked exactly like the flowers Richard and I had seen at the foot of the tree trunk tombstone the pervious day! There had to be two dozen flowers crammed into the vase. Red, pink, white and yellow roses, brightly colored lilies, sunflowers, red and white carnations, just to name a few. It was as if someone had taken them from the cemetery and placed them on the desk.

This is too strange!

Their sweet perfume seemed to fill the entire room and to my surprise I wasn't having any kind of allergic reaction. Looking at them I recalled what Richard had said about giving a positive attribute to each flower.

All right Richard; I'll play your silly game.

On the left side of the bouquet was a light pink rose, *Hmm, let me think . . . That's easy. Love.* Next to that was a red rose. *What about . . . prudence.* Next to that was a tiny white rose in full bloom. *Ummm . . . What could that be?* I couldn't come up with anything, and besides Richard's little game was stupid. I picked up the *Time* magazine and started leafing through it. But instead of reading, I found myself trying again to come up with a positive attribute for the white rose.

I turned back toward the bouquet. *Hmmmm . . . what about . . . Joy. Good one!*

I dropped the magazine onto the table and resumed where I left off with the bouquet. There were several yellow and green irises in front. *Let me think . . . Justice?* As I was looking at the flowers a mother and a little girl around nine came into the office, talked to the receptionist then sat down. I watched them for a few moments then turned my attention back to the bouquet. *The sunflowers? Ahhhh . . . Faith! The red and white carnations . . . I'll try . . . kindness. What are those small purple flowers near the top? I don't know what they're called but that doesn't matter. I'm giving them the attribute of . . . courage!*

Richard's game is actually kind of enjoyable.

The little yellow flowers are health, the carnations are benevolence, the small white flowers are . . . wisdom. Wow I can't believe I've come up with so many positive attributes!

An elderly couple came in and sat down but I hardly noticed them because I was totally absorbed in Richard's incredible game. *The daisies are hope, and the green foliage is sharing. The two yellow rose are art? Art can be a positive attribute can't it? Yes of course because it means creativity.*

This is fantastic! *I wish I was in a huge garden with a million blooming flowers and I was assigning a positive attribute to each one!* Sitting there looking at the bouquet something occurred to me—or perhaps it is something that I once had known as the fabric of truth but had forgotten a long time ago.

Just as a snake sheds its skin, people can shed their fear, and life will flow through them. Everything that had happened in the last day confirmed that.

I had seen the living among the dead—and the dead among the living. Who knows what 'Mickey' was? A ghost? Or just some guy? Either way, he had a wisdom beyond his years and he sure knew something about life . . . and death. Some people come to understand way too late.

I turned back to the bouquet. *The purple Irises are charity, the Irises are beauty. The daffodils are serenity, the little blue flowers are tolerance . . .*

The receptionist was saying something but at first I couldn't understand her, because I was so into Richard's flower naming game. She repeated it, and when I turned to look at her, she had what I can only describe as a sympathetic look in her eye.

"The doctor," she said, "can see you now."

FOUR BALLOONS
ANDREW NEVER RECEIVED

YOU'RE IN MICHIGAN ON VACATION, AND YOU'VE just had an argument with your wife because she won't go up in the dunes behind the high grass and have sex with you. Her "cold front" is a dreary counterpoint to the weather.

It's the kind of lazy August afternoon they write about in travel brochures. The pale blue sky is as deep and flawless as a clear mind. A warm breeze out of the south has ushered away the weight and troubles of the world back home.

This would be harmony if your wife had not just spurned you. The beach is practically deserted. Could there be a better day to be a little crazy, to throw caution to the wind and act like a couple of kids in the dunes?

Of course not.

The sun has had the effect of an aphrodisiac on you. It has warmed your blood, arousing within you a mischievous lust. It's not like you suggested that you and you wife have sex right there on the blanket in the open under the beach umbrella. Instead, you pointed to the dune and said: "Let's go up there and get naked," as you softly stroked her bare thigh.

She puts her book face down on the blanket and gives you a scornful look as if she doesn't know what you're talking about.

"Come on, Gwen, it'll be fun."

She frowns. "Are you kidding? Someone could see us. We could get arrested."

"No one's around. It'll be fun. Like the old days."

Of course the old days were only seven years ago.

"Fun? Fun like spending the night in the county jail. That kind of fun? No thanks."

You are losing patience. "No, real fun, *kid* fun. You remember what fun is, don't you?"

"You don't have to be sarcastic," she snaps. "I know what fun is and getting arrested doesn't sound like fun to me."

There is no trace of humor in her voice.

She has successfully destroyed your mood. You bite your tongue so as not to call her a wet blanket, or worse. Suddenly it feels like the temperature on the sun has dropped by a million degrees and instead of August it's December. You were never the type to beg for what you need, so you grab your ball cap and sunglasses off the blanket and stand up. "Forget it. I'm going for a walk."

She is reading a book titled *Water For Elephants*. She picks it up and doesn't answer.

As you stroll down the beach, you ask yourself whatever happened to the woman you married. Then ask yourself how many men have asked themselves that exact same question? When you were dating, she had sex with you in a car wash and in a park. Now she recoils at the idea of a romp in the dunes. Is there a switch that some women flick off when they turn 40 that cuts off the power to their passion?

Maybe they just stop trying.

To your right, the afternoon sun is dancing on the surface of Lake Michigan, turning it into liquid fire. Instead of one large sun there are now 10,000 smaller suns dancing and skipping across the lake. On your left, spruce trees sit on top of massive dunes that seem to be looking west across the lake toward Chicago. You stop walking and stare ahead. The beach runs for miles in a long slow S curve. You decide not to take a walk but to go to your car, listen to the radio and cool down.

You climb the weather beaten wooden steps two at a time to the parking lot. When you reach the top, you are winded. Sweat has formed on your forehead and moistened your underarms.

To your right, about 20 feet from the stairs, a man and woman are standing in the shade of a cluster of tall trees. She is holding a pink balloon, two white balloons, and a purple balloon. The balloons are dancing in the breeze, tugging at the strings of blue ribbon in her hand as if they want to be set free.

The couple look to be in their mid-30s, only a few years younger than you. He has his arm around her waist. Even from this distance it's easy to see that she is sobbing. They do not acknowledge you.

You feel like you are trespassing on something private, so you turn toward the parking lot. As you step onto the asphalt it burns the bottoms of your bare feet so you scamper toward your car. When you get there, you see a woman sitting nearby in front of a sheet of paper placed on an easel. You are reluctant to say anything to her because you feel like you would be interrupting, as if the painting were a person with whom she is having a conversation. But you have to walk right past her to get into your car. And besides, if someone is painting next to your car, they are inviting conversation. Or perhaps, having just been blown off by your wife, you want to have a positive interaction with a woman.

Her easel is set up beside an SUV parked next to your car. Sun sparkles on its windows, chrome and bumpers. The SUV's rear hatch is open, and as you approach, you can see a sleeping bag and camping equipment inside.

You'd guess that the painter is in her mid-40's, which means that she is from your generation. A white visor shields her eyes from the sun. She is looking out over the lake. As you approach, she turns from the painting, puts down her brush and smiles.

You motion toward the canvas. "Great day for it."

"It really is. The light is wonderful. Very clear."

"Are you working in watercolors?"

"That's all I paint in."

"I've always wanted to be able to paint."

She smiles again. "So have I."

You nod toward the canvas. "That looks good to me."

"I try."

"Are you a professional?"

"Professional? God, no! Whenever I get vacation time, I load my painting supplies and an easel into the back of my Rav Four and drive around the countryside, looking for scenes to paint."

You glance at the canvas. It is a tranquil painting of the beach, the tall grass, the trees and the lake. The pastel blues, greens and browns are calming. The painting looks like it is almost completed. There aren't any people in it.

You hear a loud sob and turn toward the couple with the balloons. He seems to be comforting her, whispering something to her.

You look back toward the painter. "That woman seems very upset."

She picks up her paint brush and turns back toward the canvas. "She is . . . they are. It's a very sad day for them."

"It is?"

"Her son, Andrew, drowned at this beach on this day a few years ago. It was his birthday." She stops painting and holds the brush in front of the canvas. "He had just turned four."

You don't ask her how she knows this. You assume she spoke with the couple before you got there, that they have told her what happened. "How sad."

The painter nods, then adds a few strokes to the canvas. She puts the brush down and gazes past you to where the couple is standing.

"Every year, they come here on his birthday and let four balloons go. It's a way of remembering him."

You don't say anything but instead turn back toward the couple. You know that a little boy doesn't drown when his parents are only a few feet away. But suddenly, you can imagine what happened. The scene seems to unfold before you like a vision.

She and her husband, boyfriend or whatever he is, went up into the dunes to have sex. It would only take a couple of minutes. And before they left, they told the boy to stay away from the water. They told him to keep digging a hole in the sand with his little plastic shovel. They were only going over that dune there for a few minutes. They wouldn't be far away.

You can imagine the couple holding hands and laughing as they ran behind the dunes. What they couldn't have known was that as soon as they'd disappeared from sight the lake had called to the boy. It said "Come here and play. Come in the water and have fun." The boy dropped his little blue shovel and went down to the water's edge. He stood there for a moment and looked out across the shimmering lake. He giggled because he knew he was being naughty, disobeying his Mommy, who had told him to stay away from the water. He glanced over his shoulder to see if he was being watched, then went in up to his ankles. The water felt nice on his feet which were hot due to the sand. Then he went in a little farther, to the edge of a drop-off only five feet from the shore. When he reached the drop-off he fell into the deeper water. He tried to get up, but there was a strong undertow. Not 10 feet to the left or right, but right there where he fell.

On the other side of the dune, the boyfriend, or husband, it doesn't really matter, arched his back, and as he came he let out a loud cry while 50 feet away the boy breathed water into his lungs.

When the couple came back, the boy was gone. Gone as if he had dissolved in the breeze, as if he had simply evaporated. Gone as if a giant hand had reached down and plucked him off the beach.

His mother probably noticed first. When she crested the top of the dune, buttoning her sleeveless blouse, she casually looked to where they had been sitting only a few minutes earlier. *Where's Andrew? He can't have gone far! We were only gone for 10 minutes for God's sake.*

But a lot can happen in 10 minutes. The world can end in 10 minutes. You can stop loving someone in 10 minutes.

They started calling his name over and over "Andrew! Andrew!" He didn't answer, and panic swept through their veins. They frantically ran down the beach, still calling his name. "Andrew!" Dear God, Andrew answer me! Please God! If they had stopped to listen, all they would have heard was the breeze, the lapping of the waves on the shore and the drone of a boat engine half a mile away.

It was probably the boyfriend, or whatever he is, that found him. He probably saw something floating near the shoreline. Or giving into his worst fears, he started searching the water for the child.

- 45 -

Now you know the couple's story. Their tragedy. They look different. Smaller.

If you didn't know why they were there, you might think she was drunk and that he was holding her up. You'd think she was crying because they'd had a fight and that he had given her the balloons in apology. That would be a lot easier to accept than the truth. But now you know she cannot stand on her own because she is carrying the immense burden of grief and guilt. For some reason, it strikes you that he seems to be better at carrying that burden.

You don't blame her, because even in her worst nightmare she couldn't have known what would happen. Now she lives with an asterisks next to her name. You don't blame her, instead you blame God. God how could you let that happen? How can you let a little boy drown? Are you there God? God can you hear me?

You're going to have a lot of questions for God when you meet, and you'll want answers.

There is no God.

You're talking to yourself.

Before you left for vacation, you got an email from a guy at work. He said "If you pray—and you remember that you were surprised that he had phrased it that way. "If you pray, could you please say a prayer for my niece, Daphnia." The email said that she was a sixth grader and that she had seven operations to remove cancer from the bones in her face. Or perhaps she was a seventh grader and had six operations. You can't remember which.

But you'd bet your bottom dollar that her parents know the smallest details of her life. They know her favorite color is orange, that she loves her blue jeans jacket and that Friday is her favorite day of the week because that is the day she goes to movies with her friends. They know she likes Cheerios for breakfast and that grape is her favorite soda. They know she loves reading Tiger magazine and that her favorite teacher is Mrs. Kelly. They know her powdery scent. They know she hates math. They know that she wants to be a vet when she grows up.

If she grows up.

The email had resonated with you. It lodged in your memory because you had never heard of something like that before, of anyone, let alone a child, having bone cancer in their face, and having to have their face carved apart to get the cancer out. It strikes you as an unusually cruel cancer, especially for a child.

You look back at the couple just in time to see the woman release the balloons. You and the painter watch silently as the balloons climb into a magnificently blue afternoon sky, a sky without pity or judgment. You both keep watching as the balloons slowly float out of sight over the vastness of the lake.

You glance back at the painter, and suddenly it strikes you that she is an angel. You have never believed in angels but you are sure she is one. In fact, you have never been more sure of anything.

Stop this! You don't believe in angels. You are a slave to the physical world. You are a rational man!

There's no use fighting it. You are absolutely convinced that she is an angel. If you squint you can almost see her wings and halo. You want to ask her why she has been sent to a world where children suffer and die. You refrain because you know such a question would probably freak her out.

You point to the canvas. "I don't see any people in your painting."

She smiles painfully. "I can't seem to get people right."

She pauses then puts her brush down and turns to you. "I do clouds well."

Her chin is trembling.

The sun is too hot, too direct, and there is no shade, no place to hide. You mutter "Goodbye, have a nice day," or something equally as trivial.

The angel is crying now, weeping.

You want to embrace her, to take her pain away, but you know that's impossible because it belongs to her. She owns it as much as she owns her skin. You turn away without saying anything else. Words have become useless.

You decide to walk back to your wife.

You pass the couple, who are now embracing. Is he crying too? You are invisible to them. You pause at the top of the stairs and look out over the lake. You're going to have a lot of questions.

The sun is tumbling down the backside of the sky. You consider swimming the 30-something miles across the lake back to Chicago. Screw that. Why not swim past Chicago, through the Great Lakes, through the St. Lawrence Seaway and across the Atlantic to a new place where no one knows you and they don't speak your language? A place where you are a stranger and no one sends you email.

It wouldn't be that hard to do.

You carefully descend the wide wooden steps one at a time. Strangely, going up the stairs was easier.

As you walk the beach the lake is now on your left, the dunes on your right. The sun has burned its way into your core. You suddenly realize that it wasn't your wife you had sex with in the car wash or in the park. It was someone else. Someone whose name you can't remember. Her face was similar, but she was younger.

As you walk across the sand, you whisper an urgent prayer for that little girl with cancer in her face. You want her to be cured. You want the world to be cured.

When you get back to the blanket, you sit in the elongated circle of shade created by the beach umbrella. Your wife is now beside the umbrella in the sun, lying on her stomach.

Your mood is dark. You consider starting an argument with her, an argument that starts with a single word: *Why?*

She looks up from her book. Her expression is impassive. You notice that her back is getting red. You take a deep breath, then exhale and let go of your anger. You lean forward and reach for the sunscreen.

"You're getting burned," you say. "I'd better put some lotion on you."

WHAT REGGIE DIDN'T TELL ME

R EGGIE MILKS ONCE TOLD ME THAT BAD news spreads in whispers. That's how I heard that Reggie was dead. It was nine in the morning. I had just come off the midnight shift and was leaving the patrol room when I heard someone call out "Buddha." I had picked up that nickname a year earlier after some of the other cops on my shift heard that I'd started practicing Tibetan Buddhism.

I turned to look and saw the shift commander, Brian Murphy, walking toward me. A sergeant, he always wore a tired smile and was quick with a joke or a wisecrack. But as he approached, his cheeks were flushed and his normally soft brown eyes were filled with a cold intensity.

"I heard you worked with Reggie Milks a million years ago?" he asked softly. "Out of the 19th?"

"Yeah, he was my T.O. We were in a radio car together." I leaned against the wall. "Why?"

He shook his head then looked me in the eye. "Bad news, Buddha," he said. "He's dead. Shot himself."

"Murph," I blurted. "What happened? Why?"

He shrugged. "Who knows? Apparently he'd been dead for at least a week. The neighbors complained of a bad smell. A couple of dicks from the 15th went into his apartment to do a well being check. They found him. No note . . . nothing."

I rubbed my eyes. "He'd been dead for a week? Shit."

"Yeah, exactly my reaction." He placed his hand on my shoulder. "I was wondering if you could help us with something?"

"Sure."

"Reggie was divorced, but someone downtown said he had a daughter in her twenties. They've been trying to find her, to contact her. Do you know where she lives?"

Reggie used to talk about his daughter, but I had never met her—or Reggie's ex-wife. "No, I don't," I answered. "I think her name was Brenda—something like that."

"Okay," he said, nodding slowly. "Maybe someone at the 19th can help us find her."

"Yeah," I responded weakly.

"You okay?"

"He . . . he . . ." I mumbled. Guilt forced me to avoid his gaze. Reggie had called me eight days earlier and it now occurred to me that I was probably the last person he talked to before he shot himself. I had not spoken to him in years, and then he called me out of the blue. He was ranting. I thought he was drinking. But if I had listened to what he was saying on the phone that day, if I had taken the time to really listen, perhaps I could have pulled him back from the brink. I didn't listen. I was too busy. Too tired. Too callous. I had let a fellow cop down in his darkest hour.

Reggie had been my training officer when I joined the police force. I was 24, right out of the Academy and green as freshly cut grass. We gradually lost touch after he was transferred to another precinct, but I always thought a lot of Reggie. He had problems; still, he was the guy who took me under his wing and showed me how things on the street really work. I felt that I owed him a debt of gratitude.

I continued staring at the freshly polished floor. I was too ashamed to tell Murphy about the call. "I'm shocked," I finally muttered.

"We all are," he replied. "You sure you're okay?"

"Yeah."

"You knew he was on disability for depression and alcoholism, right?"

"Yeah, I guess I knew that."

"Are you sure you're okay?"

"It's just hard to believe. That's all."

"Well, I'm headed home. I'll see you later." He started down the hall, then stopped and turned back toward me. "Buddha, almost forgot. There's a wake for him at Clancy's tonight. Eight o'clock, if you're interested."

I knew the place. A lot of cops went there.

"Tonight?" I asked. "You going?"

He exhaled loudly. "It's my wife's birthday and we were supposed to go out. But now with all of this . . ." he turned his palms skyward. "She understands cops. She gave me a pass until tomorrow night."

"See you tonight," I said, then walked toward the door.

The beautiful summer morning seemed to mock the bad news I had just received. As I made my way to my car I could not reconcile myself with the fact that Reggie was dead. It rattles you.

I sat in my car and pounded the steering wheel with my fist. Sure, sometimes cops kill themselves but Reggie wasn't just another cop. I had worked with him for three years. After a good 10 minutes, I finally turned the key in the ignition and dropped the car into Drive.

When I got to my apartment I phoned my girlfriend, Vanessa, and left her a message, asking her to call me. I was off for three days and had planned to catch a baseball game and spend time with Vanessa. The last thing I'd expected was to have to go to a wake and a funeral. But if being a cop had taught me anything, it was that death is often an uninvited and unexpected guest.

Standing in my bedroom, I unbuckled my holster, slipped it from around my waist and placed it in the top drawer of my dresser. I got undressed and took a long, steaming shower, then pulled on a clean white t-shirt and a pair of shorts and went into the living room to meditate. Meditation was what originally attracted me to Buddhism. I had read an article that said meditation was a great way to reduce stress. I found a small Buddhist temple near my apartment then began attending workshops and starting incorporating Buddhist practices into in my daily life. Was it my fate to read that article? I don't know. I'm just glad I did, that it resonated with me, and that I took action.

Sometimes, after an especially bad shift, I found myself looking forward to meditating. Like a lot of cops, I had tried drinking as a way of coping. But drinking is just a very harmful way to dull the cutting realities of life. I used to drink two bottles of wine, a 12 pack of beer, or half a bottle of Jamieson whisky a day. It had almost killed me. Meditation was a savior. It was the only real way I could let go of the daily stresses I encountered on the job. Cops tend to put on a good front despite their feelings. That's a mistake because we end up carrying around a lot of repressed emotions. Perhaps that façade is like a suit of armor. But if anyone wears armor too long it becomes very heavy and burdensome. I was determined not to be dead to myself. And considering the bad new I had gotten regarding Reggie, I felt an urgent need to get centered.

Sitting in the lotus position, hands on my knees, palms turned upward, I closed my eyes and slowly inhaled.

Inhale serenity.

Exhale stress.

Inhale peace.

Exhale hate.

Images, faces and smells from my shift started pushing their way into my consciousness like floodwater overflowing a dam.

The angry glare from a 19-year-old kid I had given a speeding ticket to.

The rotting teeth and foul breath of a meth addict.

The crying nine year-old autistic boy who got separated from his parents at a mall.

The Russian woman with her face beaten to a pulp by her alcoholic husband . . .

Let the images come. Let the sensations come. Do not oppose them. Accept them. They will fade on their own . . . Live a deathless life . . . none of this is real . . .

Inhale serenity.

Exhale stress.

Peace . . . serenity . . . peace . . . serendipity.

After 15 minutes I opened my eyes. A yellow light was hovering in the air. Still sitting in the lotus position, I blinked and tried to understand what it was. After a few seconds, I realized that the sun had pushed its way through a small part in the curtains behind me and was shining on the opposite wall. Something about that splash of light was deeply soothing. Sitting there, motionless, I pondered and contemplated it. There was a simplicity and beauty in it that lifted my spirit.

After a few minutes, I got up, went into the kitchenette and poured myself a glass of apple juice. Leaning against the counter, I went over and over in my mind the last time I had talked to Reggie. I gulped down the juice, put the glass in the sink, then went to bed and drifted into a dreamless sleep.

• • •

My alarm clock went off at three that afternoon. Instead of getting up I lay in bed staring up at the ceiling and thinking about Reggie.

He had served in the Navy for a few years before becoming a cop, married young, had a daughter and then divorced. He always went about the job with a grim determination, like a heavyweight fighter slugging it out round after round. He was 12 years my senior, and while I liked and respected him, I always thought he was too tightly wound, and that he let the job get to him. That's an occupational hazard.

He would crack someone over the head or knee with his baton or his flashlight if they were the least bit belligerent. On one of our first calls together, he smashed a drunk so hard that it took 15 stitches to close the gash above the guys' ear. I was astounded at how quickly Reggie had resorted to violence because the drunk didn't seem like a threat. I wasn't saying much and I guess Reggie sensed my astonishment because as we were filling out the arrest report he turned to me and said; "Listen, kid, the number one rule on the street is you've got to protect yourself at all times. We're not social workers. We are one link in the chain that is the criminal justice system. When you run into an asshole, you take them down and let the courts figure it out later. Don't try to reason with drunks or druggies. You'll only get yourself hurt."

But violence begets violence. If you hit someone, they will hit you back. Reggie never understood that. He thought brutality was a good tool for problem solving. Whack: End of problem. It's been my experience that brutal people die a death of a thousand cuts. They create negative energy and often end up physically, emotionally and spiritually sick.

I got up, shaved, then checked my email and voicemail for messages. Vanessa had left me a message. I called her back and told her about Reggie.

"I don't think I ever met him did I?" she asked softly.

"No," I replied, "he was my Training Officer. I haven't seen him in a few years."

"Do you want me to go to the wake with you?"

I hesitated before answering. "It'll just be a bunch of cops. You'd be bored to death."

"I really don't mind."

"I know you don't. Thanks, but it'll be easier by myself."

"I'm really sorry. It's hard to understand why someone would take their own life."

"I guess with some people, it seems as if it couldn't end any other way."

There was silence for a moment. "Come over, or at least call me when you get back okay?"

"I'll come over. I'd like to see you tonight."

"I'll wait up."

I watched some of the Sox's game on TV until it was time to go to the wake.

• • •

It was humid and sunny outside and I pulled my car onto Clark Street just in time to get caught in the crawl of rush hour traffic. By the time I got to the tavern on Damen, a dozen people where already there talking quietly. The place was cool and refreshing compared to outside, and a dozen off duty cops were sitting at a few tables they had obviously pulled together. I recognized a few of the guys and two of the women as dicks from the 24th and I figured the others were people who'd worked with Reggie before he came to the city police force, or were people he had worked with in narcotics.

As I approached Murphy waved and called out. "Hey Buddha, glad you could make it. Grab a seat."

I settled in beside Jehrome Lisle, a sergeant I recognized from the 12$^{th.}$ I had quit drinking 18 months earlier, so instead of having a beer I ordered a ginger ale.

"How did you pick up that Buddha nickname?" Jerome asked as the waitress placed a tall bubbling glass in front of me.

Jerome was a tough, no nonsense guy, so I wasn't sure he'd understand the finer points of Eastern thought like Buddhism. But he had asked, so I took a sip from my glass and turned toward him. "I became interest in Buddhism a few years ago after I heard that meditation is an important part of it, and that meditation is a good way to relieve stress. When I told some of the guys I was into Buddhism, suddenly I was 'Buddha' to everyone."

His eyebrows arched. "Does meditation really help? You feel better afterward?"

"Yeah," I said with a nod. "It really helps."

He raised his glass, took a drink and smiled. "Maybe I should try it. Do I have to shave my head and grow a big belly?"

"Not unless you want to," I said with a chuckle. "But if you're interested in learning more, I can lend you a book. And there's lots of information online."

He shrugged.

I reached for my glass and took another sip of ginger ale. "In reality there's a lot more to it than meditation. It's really a way of life." I stopped there because, as I said, cops tend to be very pragmatic and try to control their emotions. Buddhism had taught me to accept things in the here and now, in the moment. When you do that the pain of the world does not sting so long.

"A way of life?" Jerome asked.

He seemed genuinely interested, so I continued. "At its core is a simple but profound wisdom for living life, for shedding useless desires and needs, for discovering truth and for living a conscious life."

He leaned back in his chair and looked a little confused. "I live a conscious life . . . I'm conscious . . . people live conscious lives."

Obviously he was expecting more of an explanation.

"Buddhists believe that in our pursuit of worldly goods and desires we lose touch with what's really important."

"Goods? What to you mean, TVs and cars, shit like that?"

"Yes, absolutely, that's part of it. Do people really need new big screen TVs, or is there something else, something internal that's more important that they're neglecting?"

"Internal?"

I could tell by his tone that I wasn't doing a very good job of explaining Buddhism to him, so I decided to try a tact I thought he could relate to.

"I've learned to slow down. I was raised Catholic but fell away from the church. I could never understand how God could allow such suffering and grief in the ones He was supposed to love so much. There seems to be an imbalance in the world toward hate, death and violence. Buddhism has helped me understand the causes of all that and how to deal with it."

Jerome took a drink of beer and wiped his mouth with the back of his hand. "It helps to have something, I guess."

"It does, and it's taught me how to simplify my life."

"Less garbage right?"

In a way he had hit the nail on the head. "Right."

He leaned forward in his chair. "So," he asked softly, "what do Buddhists think about a guy like Reggie eating a bullet?"

I winced. "Bad Karma. He'll be reincarnated over and over until he gets it right."

He took another drink of beer then placed his glass on the table. "No afterlife? No heaven? No hell? Nothing like that? Just a lot of bad Karma?"

I decided to take a chance, to try and explain what I understood of it to him. "There's an afterlife, but no dogma involved."

He sat back in his seat. "No dogma? No judgment? No damnation? Shit, I like it already."

Sitting there looking at Jerome, it struck me that there are basically three kinds of cops: Some are sober as a pastor and are Bible pounders, others are drinkers and partiers, and there are some in the middle. I guess what I'm really talking about is three types of people.

"Some Buddhists believe that when a person dies they travel in the afterlife for 49 days before they are judged," I said. "During that period, they are tested many times to see if they achieve enlightenment."

His face screwed up. "Forty-nine days?"

I didn't want the others to hear me, so I leaned forward and rested my elbows on the table. "Yes, but here's the thing. The wandering soul can become terrified of demons, flee, and become lost. The departed spirit must be conscious of what is happening. They must remember that many things are simply constructions of their mind."

"Demons? Constructions of the mind?" He threw up his hands. "You've lost me."

I decided it wasn't a good idea to talk to him about the Wheel of Life or Yama, the Buddhist Lord of Death. Instead, we chatted about work for a few minutes.

Then Murphy stood up thanked everyone for coming. "All of you either worked with Reggie at some point, or at least knew him," he said. "But you may not know each other, so let me do some quick introductions."

He pointed down to the end of the table. "The gentleman in the yellow golf shirt is Gary Hazard, who worked with Reggie as a sheriff's deputy a million years ago. Next to him is Brad Williams; then we have Jennifer White; next to her is Marvin Rosenfeld, and to his right is David Murphy."

He finished the introductions, but before he could take his seat, one of the women asked if anyone had tracked down Reggie's kid.

"Someone from Personnel helped us find her," he said. "She knows about the wake and might show up tonight."

I took a drink of ginger ale, followed by a deep breath and tried to relax. *God*, I thought, *I hope she doesn't come*. I had let Reggie down, and I didn't think I could face his daughter.

"Didn't Reggie start off working as a Sherriff's deputy?" someone asked.

"Reggie started as a Cook County Sherriff's deputy," Gary said, leaning forward in his seat. "He was my TO, seventeen years ago. My first day on the job he told me the golden rule is; never get yourself into something you can't get yourself out of. And he was right. Backup could take an hour to reach you. There weren't any computers in the squads back then, and half the time the radio didn't work."

"Things haven't changed that much," someone said, half-joking.

Hazard smiled, took a swig of beer and continued. "Reggie was a tough guy. I remember one night we saw a bunch of bikers in a forest preserve. Hell's Angels-types. There must have been a hundred of them. I saw a guy walking with a plastic bag and as soon as he sees us, he drops the bag and tries to act nonchalant. We stopped, I picked up the bag and guess what's inside? Twenty lids of grass in plastic baggies. So we're cuffing the guy, and up walks his sister. She doesn't want us to take her big brother so she jumps on my back and tries to scratch my eyes out."

"How touching."

"Without missing a beat, Reggie pulls out his mace and lets her have it square in the face. And this was real mace back then, not the pepper-spray bullshit they use today. So, she's blinded and screaming bloody blue murder. Meanwhile the bikers start to move forward in a huge circle around the squad. Reggie yells at them to stop! They don't. So he grabs the shotgun, cocks it and fires a round over their heads. Not exactly by-the-book, but that stopped them cold. And talk about running the gauntlet! We beat it out of there with them lining both sides of the road leering in at us."

Hazard raised his glass, and we all joined him in a toast. "To Reggie Milks," he said. "He was one tough *hombre*. Taught me a hell of a lot."

A guy across the table from me who looked to be in his early 30s spoke up next: "You know. I heard that Reggie's the third cop from the 24th that's offed himself in the last 12 years."

An older guy next to him scoffed. "Thanks for the feel-good trivia, Simons."

"Sorry, but it's true."

"I don't care if it's true," the older guy said. Then he reached into his pocket, pulled out several $1 bills and handed them to Simons. "Make yourself useful," the older guy said. "Drop these in the jukebox."

Simons grabbed the money, pushed back his chair and stood up. "What should I play?" he asked.

"I don't care. Wedding songs!" The older guy shook his head. "Rookies."

Simons crossed the room to the jukebox and one of the women at the table started telling us about a call she and Reggie had gone on.

"It was a real rough one," she said, shaking her head. "A crack head stabbed his wife and five-year-old daughter, really did a number on them. The mom was gone, but the kid was still alive when we got there. She died in Reggie's arms. That beat him up pretty bad." She paused for a moment, then shook her head. "You know he never seemed to recover from that. He was on disability two months later."

"Damned crack," someone said. "Makes people totally evil and insane."

The woman nodded. "You've got to find a way to exorcise those demons. Those calls will haunt you. If the citizens knew what we do and see . . ." She raised her glass in a toast. "To Reggie. God must have needed a tough cop."

"At least Reggie had a sense of humor," said a black guy who looked to be around Reggie's age. "A few years ago we were serving a warrant on some guy in Lakeview who was wanted by the FBI, some kind of embezzlement thing. Reggie knocked on the guy's front door, and it must have been ajar because it opened. He yells, 'Police.' Before we can go inside, we hear a shot: Bang! We call for SWAT, then go in ready for a war. It was a tactical situation. The guy was upstairs in his bedroom. He had popped himself in the head. He was on satin sheets, and he'd been jerking off watching porn. The tape was still running. Four guys on a platinum blond. The perp's brains were all over the top of the bed. Everybody shows up, the shift commander, the EMTs, two-dozen people are now on scene. We're all there waiting for the ME to arrive, and suddenly, this porno tape keeps stopping and starting, rewinding to all the choice bits and shit. We're like, 'What's going on?' Turns out Reggie was in the next room with the remote control stopping and starting the tape. Real funny guy."

We all chuckled.

"That's not all," he said, smiling. "The coroner finally arrives, and she's not bad. Great stems and in her 30s. Anyway the tape is playing, and the girl is sucking this guy's dick, going right at it, and Reggie says; 'Wow is she ever good at that' as the ME's fishing around in the dead guy's brains. This coroner woman turns to look at the screen and casually says "Yeah we all do that good." Man, we just broke up and fell all over the place. I never saw Reggie laugh so hard."

To most people this kind of talk would seem morbid, even disturbing. But after 15 years as a city cop I had learned how important gallows humor is in maintaining hope and sanity in the face of some pretty horrible stuff.

A guy I knew from the midnight shift lit a cigarette and exhaled a plume of smoke, then leaned into the table and lowered his voice. "I've seen grown men who died with their dick in one hand and a Kleenex in the other. Heart attacks, strokes, whatever, watching porn in front of their computer screen." He snapped his fingers. "Boom. Gone like that. You just . . ."

As he continued talking, my attention was drawn to a splash of sunlight on the wall 30 feet behind him, and for a moment I was reminded of the sunlight on my living room wall earlier in the day. But this light, streaming in through a window at the far end of the bar, had created a shaft of pure illumination that flowed though the air like a shimmering river. Specs of dust were floating in it like tiny suns or moons.

After a few moments I turned back to the table where one of the women from a downtown district was talking about a call she and Reggie had gone on.

"A guy had accidentally hung himself while masturbating," she said. "He had a belt around his neck and had the other end strapped to the coat rack in his closet—you know to heighten his climax. He must have passed out." She straightened in her seat. "His girlfriend found him when she got home from work."

"Hi honey, I'm hanging out in the closet," someone said.

More chuckles all around.

Lust, desire and the blind pursuit of pleasure, I thought, can be killers.

"Reggie and I had a call like that," I said. "This guy in Uptown strangled his girlfriend by mistake while they were screwing. Can you believe that? He said she loved it. When we got there the guy's like, 'It was an accident. I didn't mean to do it!' Reggie was pissed. He freaked out. He grabbed the guy and started shaking him and said, 'You idiot. Didn't you see her turning blue and her tongue sticking out?' I had to pull him off the guy. I mean he was . . . ."

"*Happy Birthday to you. Happy Birthday to you. Happy Birthday dear Trish . . .*"

I stopped talking, and we all turned to see who was singing. It was a dozen people sitting a few tables away. The waitress placed a cupcake with a single candle flickering on top in front of a woman who looked to be 50ish. As the others at the table finished singing, she smiled sheepishly and raised her hands to her cheeks in mock surprise. Some of the people next to the birthday girl cupped their hand to their mouth and said: "Speech. Speech."

A few people in our group continued talking quietly but I watched the birthday girl blow out the candle, then stand to give her speech. It was easy to hear as she was only 15 feet away.

"First of all," she said, smiling widely. "I'd like to know who told you people that it's my birthday because I for one have stopped counting them."

They all chuckled and some of them pointed at another woman sitting at the far end of the table. I guessed she was the person who had organized their get-together.

"Thanks Jen," the birthday girl said, still smiling. "I'll deal with you later." She cleared her throat and continued. "Birthdays are a good time to reflect on things, on life. So let me bore you with some of my reflections since you all organized this grant surprise party. But first . . ."

She reached for her glass of wine, took a sip, then gently placed the glass back down on the table. She looked so happy that she seemed to be glowing.

"When you turn 50, I mean when you turn 45, if you're brave enough, you look back at the totality of your life. It seems like 30 was yesterday and 70 is tomorrow. If you're anything like me, you certainly haven't achieved all you'd hoped. But with grace from God you learn to live with that. You realize life is a series of tradeoffs, successes you never imagined and disappointments you never foresaw. Nothing new there. And if regret and bitterness try to move in, you slam the door in their face." She passed her hand swiftly through the air as if slamming a door shut then continued.

"You know, when I was 20, I was determined to be a vet. Can you imagine me as a vet? I can barely keep my houseplants alive, let alone an animal, but there you go. What I've come to learn in my 50, I mean 45 years, is that things rarely work out as we planned. Still, and I mean this, every day is to be treasured. That's right, treasured, because it is a gift more precious than gold. Count your blessings not your disappointments. All blessings come in the moment. Pain is meant to be part of life and there is no knowledge without sacrifice. Sometimes we find ourselves standing on a high mountain top and endless possibilities seems to be laid out before us. Then there are times where we are in low dark valleys, seemingly devoid of hope. I've learned that these are both states of mind, and neither of them is permanent. We can't live there. I've tried to learn from my mistakes, losses and successes and move on. In the end, friends, family good health and having a relationship with God are what's really important."

She stopped for a moment and, still smiling, picked up her glass and took another drink.

"I guess I've become, dare I say it, an optimist. It's been a great ride, and I just want to thank you all for your kindness in having this party today. You're the best."

Everyone applauded, the birthday girl sat down and they continued their party.

I though it was a nice, positive speech. It struck me that the birthday girl was present and in the moment. She understood what a great blessing it was to be there with her friends who loved and admired her. She looked like she was in bliss.

I was about to say something to that effect to Jerome when he elbowed me and quipped: "I hope she's not driving or else she'll catch a DUI for sure."

Murphy drained his glass then yelled to the waitress to bring over more beer. "I'll tell you what," he said, turning back toward the table. "People fill their lives with money, crazy sex, power, drugs, guns, booze, pills, big houses, celebrity worship, all kinds of shit, but inside they're still missing something."

We all murmured in agreement.

A couple of cops in uniform came in: an older guy and a fresh-faced rookie. Murphy waved them over, then yelled to the waitress. "Honey, get these guys some Cokes will ya?"

They pulled up seats and turned down their radios as Murphy introduced them to the rest of us.

"So, officers," he asked, one corner of his mouth turning up, "what's happening in our wonderful city tonight?"

The senior cop took off his hat, pulled a handkerchief from his pocket and wiped his brow. "We had to pull a decomposing body out of a dumpster. Homeless guy, I guess."

We all knew how sickening those calls could be. I glanced at the rookie. His uniform was pressed, but dirty, and his hair was cut in a military style. He looked queasy and exhausted. I'd seen that expression before. I figured he'd quit in less than a year. Being a cop is a tough job. Overworked and under appreciated.

My attention was drawn back to the shaft of sunlight streaming through the bar. It was glowing so brightly now that it seemed to bathe the entire room in a soft, golden hue. It had created a brilliant rectangle of light that was slowly inching its way across the far wall mimicking the path of the setting sun. Was I the only one who noticed it? How could I be? My God it was the most beautiful thing I had ever seen! I rubbed my eyes then turned toward Murphy who was offering the rookie some advice.

"Listen, kid, if a body is decomposing the smell is terrible," he said. "Use Vaseline. Put it right up in your nose."

Reggie had given me the exact same advice my first week on the job.

The kid nodded weakly as Murphy leaned forward. "Here's another tip kid. I always take the feet when moving a decomposing stiff because bloated bodies explode and the gas and juices get all over whoever takes the top end."

The rookie seemed to turn a light shade of green. He excused himself, got up and rushed to the bathroom.

Murphy repressed a laugh.

A guy from downtown started telling us about a bad traffic accident he and Reggie had worked a few years earlier. "This was on The Drive, before Christmas. A family from the suburbs was wiped out by a city salt truck. Four 10-58s. Mom, Dad and two young kids. It was a bloody mess. They were headed somewhere with a trunk full of wrapped presents which were now scattered all over the road. Reggie was picking up the presents looking at me with tears in his eyes, saying, 'What should I do with these?'"

"They should invent one of those short-term memory-erasing devices like in that movie, *Men in Black*," someone said. "Cops could sure use it after a bad shift. It would be a blessing."

It was quiet for a few moments. Then someone asked; "They found Reggie in his apartment, right?"

"Yep."

"People like to kill themselves in the woods," one of the women said.

"Yeah," someone else snickered. "I guess they feel like they're getting back to nature."

"No it's not that," the female officer continued. "I think it's because they don't want to make a mess at home for someone else to find. Reggie and I were called to a park where a guy was hanging from a tree. He'd used a steel cable."

"Why not a rope?"

"Who knows? Anyway, the ME says a body like that has to come in with the ligature still attached, so we had to get a big pair of cable cutters to get him down. It took us an hour. I'll never forget: we were filling out the report, and Reggie says 'Not a bad place to do it.'"

Murphy's phone rang and he pulled it from his pocket. "Hi Honey," he said in a low voice. "We are . . . An hour or so . . . I will . . . Did you get the birthday card I left you? . . . Good . . . See you in a while . . . . Me too."

The rookie came back from the bathroom, reclaimed his seat and took a drink of Coke.

"You okay kid?" Murphy asked. "Sorry to be so graphic. I got a big mouth."

The rookie shrugged. "Yeah, you do. Buy, hey, no problem."

"The first call Reggie and I ever rolled on together," Murphy said, "was that plane that went down near O'Hare back in the early '80s. Two-hundred-and-something dead. I tagged 24 of them myself. There was a real touching scene; a couple was still holding hands. We had to pull them apart. Of course they didn't have heads." He patted the rookie on the back. "I had to pull a head out of a tree. How do ya like that?"

"Not much."

"The only body not burned was one of the flight attendants," Murphy continued. "They found her in uniform when they lifted the tail, but again, no head."

The rookie's partner sat up in his seat. "It's hard to believe what extreme trauma like that does to a person. The human body is a very delicate thing. Tip a chair over, it bounces off the floor and it's fine. Tip a person over, they break an arm or a hip . . . or their neck."

"We're made fragile on purpose, I guess," Murphy said.

I gazed again into the shaft of sunlight and suddenly it occurred to me that the whole universe was inside it! I wanted to walk over and stand in it, to frolic in it, drink it in, feel the healing warmth of it on my body.

"I wonder why Reggie didn't reach out to someone, a plea-for-help kind of thing?" one of the women asked. "And why wasn't someone from the Department checking in on him? I mean, the guy was depressed, drunk, and all alone with a gun."

Murphy exhaled loudly and shook his head.

I started squirming in my seat and reached for my ginger ale. I just couldn't bring myself to tell them that Reggie had called me and that I had let him down.

"Reggie always said it was the citizens that drove him crazy," a guy at the end of the table said. "He used to say that just because they pay taxes they think they own you and can treat you like crap."

There's not a cop in the world who doesn't know what he was talking about.

The front door opened, and a plump girl of 25 or 30 with short blond hair came in and scanned the room. After a moment, she walked over to our table. "Are you here for the Milks wake?" she asked.

"Yes, we are young lady," Murphy said.

"I'm Brenda," she said quietly, "his daughter."

Everyone jumped to their feet, and Murphy grabbed a chair from a neighboring table. "You can sit right here young lady. What would you like to drink honey?"

"A Coke or juice is fine."

He yelled at the waitress to brink a Coke, then turned back to Reggie's daughter. "Your dad was a great guy and a good cop. Everyone here, and everyone who knew him, liked and respected him. We were just talking about some of the calls your dad and the people at this table responded to. He was a real pro."

We all looked at Reggie's daughter and voiced our agreement.

The waitress came over with a glass of Coke and placed it in front of Brenda. "Thanks," she said.

"What do you do, young lady?" Murphy asked. "Are you still in college?"

"I'm a teacher."

"Your dad was right proud of you," Murphy said. "He used to talk about you all the time."

I don't think Brenda believed Murphy, because I thought I saw her roll her eyes. "I considered becoming a police officer when I finished school," she said. "I told my father and he got mad as hell. He made me promise I'd never do it. He said he hated it. He said he only did it because being a cop was the only thing he knew how to do."

"Your dad was right, you know," Murphy said slowly. "It can be a tough job. I wouldn't want my kids to do it. But it also has it rewards."

Then it was quiet, each of us wrapped up in our thoughts.

After a moment, Murphy took a big drink of beer, wiped his mouth with the back of his hand and turned toward Brenda. "You know something? It seemed like your Dad never had anything to keep him from staying in that black place. That four-o'clock-in-the-morning place."

"He was on disability for depression," someone said. "You'd think they'd have taken his gun away for God's sake."

"I'm sure they tried," his daughter responded. "My dad was a gun nut. He had them hidden all over his apartment. He was paranoid that someone was going to break-in."

Murphy straightened in his seat and I could tell by the seriousness of his expression that he was thinking about something.

"I have a theory," he said. "You got to have something real in life, or you'll end up clinically depressed. And I'm not just talking about cops, either. Everybody's got to have something real to hang onto, to get em through that four-o'clock-in-the-morning place. And it's not drugs or booze or a $20,000 Rolex. You gotta have something. Otherwise, the world will eat you like a cancer."

He pointed at a guy down the table.

"Mike, he's a Jesus freak. He's got that. Me, I got Gail and the kids. You got to have something to hang onto. Call it God. Jesus. Muhammad." He pointed at me. "Buddha. Love. Hope. Family. You gotta have something." He threw up his hands. "Otherwise . . . forget it."

Reggie's daughter turned toward Murphy, her face suddenly a mask of the same deep sadness that I had seen in Reggie. "My dad threw away everything good he had," she said softly. "It seemed like all the bad things he saw got to him, stayed with him and turned his insides black. Like you said 'a cancer.' He turned his back on his family and started drinking . . ." She paused and I could she her chin trembling as she choked back tears. "It didn't take long after that."

I suddenly sensed that it was a lot darker in the bar, and I looked around, trying to understand why. The sun must have slipped behind the buildings across the street because the shaft of light was gone.

Of course.

It was as if someone had flicked a cosmic switch and shut it off. The room was now lit solely by the cheap bar lights and neon beer signs. I turned back to the table and stared into my glass, *through* my glass. The entire room appeared to be elongated, and ridiculous—as if I were in a funhouse hall of mirrors.

Oh my God, here it comes, unstoppable like vomit or a tsunami.

"Brenda, your Dad, he . . . he called me," I said, still staring into the glass. "It must have been the day he killed himself. I hadn't seen him in three years and suddenly he calls me just like that. He was rambling, incoherent, half-crying. I told myself he was drunk. Down on life. He said they were cutting off his medical benefits."

I could feel them all looking at me.

"He wasn't making any sense," I said, half-pleading. "I had just come off a tough 12 hours. I was too exhausted to talk. I told him I'd call him back the next day, then hung up. But I . . . I forgot. How could I know? I was tired. If I had just listened . . . or gone over . . ."

I guess I was expecting Brenda to scream at me or someone at the table to rip into me. Instead they all remained quiet. After what seemed like an eternity, Brenda got up, walked over, bent down, and put her arm around me. As I looked up into her face, the flowery scent of her perfume enveloped me.

"It's not your fault," she said, tears welling in her eyes. "He made bad choices."

Murphy reached over and rested his hand on my shoulder. "Don't blame yourself, Buddha. People need something to get them through when the tough times come, and they always come, sooner or later. Poor Reggie never had anything."

"Thanks, Murph."

I sat there quietly as conversation slowly resumed around me. They were right. I wasn't to blame for Reggie's death. He had been stuck in a painful place for years. My guilt was tied to my compassion for him. I wished I could have saved him, could have shown him the way. But in the end, everyone makes their own decisions, and they are often based on things other than wisdom. Reggie had made many bad decisions, up to and including his last decision in this world.

Sitting there quietly, I was suddenly aware of everyone in the room, my fellow cops, Brenda, the people having the birthday party, nearby strangers, the waitresses and bar staff. I casually looked around the table at all of Reggie's friends. Because of the nature of cops' jobs, we often cross paths with men, women and children at the worst moments in their lives. Everyone at that table could testify to the immense pain and suffering in the world. All the horrific things we had talked about that night were proof of that. There is immense pain and suffering in the world, but I know this: The earth is a witness to it all and dutifully absorbs each drop of blood spilled and every tear ever shed.

Whatever is partly hidden is also partly revealed, and so pain is only part of the truth of life, of existence. There is also an inexhaustible amount of love, hope and charity in the world. All you have to do is to be open to it, and it will come to you. There is a cycle of birth and death and we are all bound to it. We are like that stunning shaft of sunlight, here one moment, and gone the next. It could not be any other way.

I have learned to show compassion for others even at times when my most basic instincts argued against it. I have come to realize what it is that I need to cultivate and what I need to discard. I have eradicated. I have learned. I am my own master.

I am a Buddha.

NOVEMBER FORGETS

I TURN AWAY FROM A SKY LADEN with mercury-tinted clouds and kneel beside the sand fence that runs the length of the beach. Then I button my coat, slip on my headphones and pull up my collar against the stiff November wind.

Early each morning I come here, passing the wand over the sand in slow, even arcs. I search this beach, this universe of sand with its pebbles strewn like dream-filled planets across the Milky Way.

Jeannie was so self-conscious about her crooked teeth that she covered her mouth with her hand whenever she smiled. My beautiful child. I couldn't afford to get her teeth fixed, but I did buy her a telescope when she was 11. She'd read an article about our solar system in the National Geographic, and it had set her imagination ablaze.

Today, November 11, would have been her twentieth birthday.

Jeannie gave me this metal detector four weeks before she left for basic training. She hugged me and said it would be fun, a hobby to help me stay occupied while she was gone. She said treasure hunting would keep me from worrying about her.

She sat cross-legged in the living room and carefully read me the instructions. "Mum," she said, "it's best to pass the search coil wand over the sand in slow, even, arcs." Then she grinned and told me that the Army had a good dental plan, and that she was going to get her teeth fixed when she got back . . .

Now, I watch the gulls watching me with their fierce yellow eyes. Each gull cries out with the creak of a rusty door—but their angel wings are a blessing, like their faint, webbed tracks in the sand.

We all seek warmth and search for the sun, though nothing can thaw my frozen core. All I can do is pass the wand over the sand in slow, even arcs.

I sift through my memories, looking to find driftwood in my mind. Bits of glass, green and brown and clear, shine like jewels underfoot, their edges dulled by tide and time. Everything returns to the place from which it came.

Death was delivered to my doorstep just like a newspaper, at 10:14 on an overcast February morning. I opened the door, and there they were, standing there at attention: a proud man and handsome woman, both in uniform. Their pleading eyes said what their words could not.

I don't remember curling up into a ball on the floor. I only remember a gnawing pain too immense to really feel. It was like trying to swallow this entire Great Lake: it was simply too large. Too black. Too deep.

Too much.

November forgets summer sun-bathers and splash-happy children shrieking in delight. My daughter lives now only in my wounded memory and in an aching mind that my body begs for sleep. I manage slow, even arcs, like the hands of a clock, always swaying between 3 and 9 . . .

Ten years ago, I don't think I could have found Iraq on a map. It was just another hot, sand-filled country somewhere over there. It was not my problem, and my only child was eight, her dreams confined to *The Little Mermaid* and the posters of horses on her bedroom wall.

We came to this beach when Jeannie was just a baby. A beautiful baby. I knew it as a special place, a living thing with a spirit. I wanted to share its power with her—and from the start, she embraced it. By the time Jeannie could walk, the beach—any beach—was her favorite place to be.

I'm sure she lost her virginity here on a hot July night when she was 16. She had gone out with that long-limbed boyfriend of hers. It was past midnight when I heard a car door slam and the sound of the engine fading into the night. She came in with sand in her hair, her blouse inside out and an expression on her face that I'd never seen before.

Maybe that was when the spirit of the beach spoke most deeply to her soul.

The next morning at the kitchen table, I'm sure she wanted to tell me . . . but, like the largest dunes, the walls between even the closest mothers and daughters sometimes seem too high to climb.

I sweep the beach as grains of sand ride the wind and the sun hides shyly behind the clouds. That's OK; it would only sting my tired eyes. They don't believe in anything any more—except, perhaps, the hand at work here.

My daughter's precious blood dried in the desert sun, and for what? For empty footprints in the sand, and for someone else's honor, and . . . and for that "Private Beach—Keep Off" sign standing over there, nailed to a post. War has always been about real estate and greed and this-is-mine!

Whose beach is it? Ask the tall grass at the foot of the dunes. Each blade sways in the breeze, in concert with its neighbors, like a single living thing.

I know the Lord has made a place for my child at His table. Jesus, only You know how terribly I miss her. Oh, Lord, I pray, carry me through this day.

She enlisted against my wishes, and yet I understood. She hated her sales job at Best Buy and often moaned that there must be "something better." Her spirit was withering like a thirsty flower.

Happy birthday my most precious child.

The wind is up, whispering to flags that obey blindly, without thought, snapping to attention, right or wrong. I pass my wand back and forth, listening for answers, but hear only gulls and the empty wind. I bend down to scoop up a handful of sand—of stars—and watch with morbid fascination as they slowly bleed between my fingers.

I must try, try to pass the wand over the sand in slow, even arcs.

One day after work, she came home so dejected about the direction her young life was taking. She sat in the kitchen wearing her blue work shirt and told me that a friend had joined the Army.

"Mum, it sounds way cool. They can teach me a profession. I think I'm going to do it."

"No way, Jeannie! You're only 18."

I feigned anger, but in a way I was secretly proud of her. Perhaps because she was so proud of herself. The pull of the horizon can be strong for a young woman. Like the tide, it beckoned . . . and she answered.

Sometimes, a mother must confine her fear to the shadows. And so I did, even as I whispered urgent prayers for her safety.

Now I search, and all I know for sure is this: I will never be called "Mum" again.

I find scraps of metal, gold bands, tarnished coins just under the surface . . . then a single white feather, shivering in the wind.

This beach is like her bedroom, for both places are alive with her memory. Her room is just as she left it, as if she'd said, "I'll be right back." Her bed is empty; her clothes wait in her closet; two books she'll never finish sit impatiently on her night stand.

Death took us both that February day. But for some reason, I'm still here, searching for answers to the horror that refused to release my tears for a full day afterwards.

Every September, we used to light a bonfire on this beach, Jeannie and I. We'd sit and stare into the fire as it cracked and snapped, the lazy smell of smoke filling our minds with whimsy. We'd watch the sparks and embers fly up into the night sky . . .

Slow, even arcs.

The dunes are having a party; wind and waves supply the drumbeat. Firs and maples dance in place, swaying their broad shoulders as the surf caresses the land, encouraging its sister with a gentle murmur. Jeannie loved parties, and she loved to dance. What wouldn't I give to see her dance here, in the surf, just one more time?

But the wind . . . the wind blows all wishes away. All I'm left with are haunted memories and the glowing curve of the sun.

Before Jeannie left, she smiled her lovely, crooked smile and said, "It's best to pass the wand over the sand in slow, even, arcs."

This beach gives up lost treasure: rings, watches, keys, eyeglasses . . . and something else. So I walk for miles in straight lines, my head down, searching the stars strewn across this beach, flecks of the Moon, Mars, Venus, Saturn, and Jupiter.

Slow, even, arcs.

I know why people come here: to heal. To walk, and to talk to themselves, and to search, like me, asking questions where the water meets the land. There's the hand again, on the liquid surface, stretching to the edge of my imagination.

How easy it would be to wade in . . .

"I'm so sorry," people tell me, "for your loss." Loss . . . as if I had simply misplaced my only child. I didn't lose her; war stole her from me.

My Jeannie. My dear daughter.

"God, why? Why?" I ask each daybreak, as the endless night gives way to something that used to resemble day . . . and the sun speaks with its warm voice, promising that if I'm lucky, sleep will find me tonight.

Slow arcs.

IMAGINE THAT—PERILS
OF A GUILTY CONSCIENCE

OFFICER, SOME PEOPLE, ESPECIALLY MY EX-GIRLFRIEND'S FRIENDS, don't like me. But I'm okay with that. And you know what else officer? I've heard it said that the best place to start telling a story is at the beginning. So that's where I'm going to start at the beginning. Is that okay with you?

Great.

Once upon a time I had a girlfriend named, Cindy. She was the bomb!

Sexy.

Smart.

Gorgeous.

French!

One dreary September afternoon, she called me at work, wanting to know if I was coming straight home from the office when I got off. Her voice sounded different. There was a sharpness, a bifurcation, or maybe a detachment to it. Of course, that's in retrospect because the next day I replayed that phone call over and over in my mind, trying to dismember, I mean dissect every inflection in Cindy's voice.

As a telemarketer, I had become a pro at reading people's voices, just as I'm sure you are, officer. It's been my experience that a slight hesitation on the other end of the phone is an opening to pitch, to ask questions and to sell, to reel them in. In some ways, the voice, just as much as the eyes, is a window to the soul.

"So, you'll be home around 5:30, oui?" she asked, her French accent unusually thick. "You don't stop for drinks with friends from work, no? You come straight 'ome, oui?"

I could understand her asking me that, officer, because on Thursdays my group sometimes went out for beers and nachos at The Galaxy Pub. But don't worry, since I drive home, I only have two beers. I don't want to get a DUI.

Anyway, I placed my coffee mug atop my desk, sat down and leaned back in my chair. "We're not going out," I told her. "I'm coming home. Do you need me to pick up anything?"

"No," she said flatly. "I just want to make sure you're coming 'ome. I see you when you get 'ere."

I hung up and didn't think much of the call. I didn't suspect a thing. My soul content. The corners of my mouth turned up. Maybe she was planning to surprise me with sexy lingerie and whipped cream.

I heard Cindy's voice before I ever met her, when a mutual friend gave her my phone number and she called to invite me over for a glass of wine. She was from some small town in Quebec. Her French accent was delicious and sexy.

On the way home I stopped at the corner store and bought cigarettes, a lottery ticket, gum and a 12-pack of lubricated ribbed condoms. The kid behind the counter's a real jack-off, and as he bagged the rubbers, he pointed at them and said loudly: "Hey Buddy, don't use them all tonight."

"At least I'll have *chance* to use them unlike some losers working in corner stores."

I pulled into my parking space in the lot underneath our apartment building, went into the lobby, grabbed the mail and took the elevator upstairs. I walked into the dining room and dropped the mail on the table. "Cindy I'm home."

She called from the bedroom. "*Je suis ici.* I'm in 'ere."

I pulled off my tie and hurried down the hall. I walked into the bedroom and she was sitting on the edge of the bed, fully clothed, with two of our brand-new suitcases by her knee. She was wearing her blue denim dress, the one she wore when we traveled. Her blonde hair was pulled back into a tight pony tail.

I'd never seen an expression like the one she wore that day: fixed and stern.

"What's going on?" I asked.

"James, I'm not going to beat zee bush, because I still love you." She stood and walked to the other side of the room. "I'm moving out. I wanted to tell you in your face. I owe you that."

I stared at her in disbelief. "What do you mean, you're moving out? Why? How come? What is it? You can't be serious!"

"I serious. Listen, I'm sorry." She shook her head and looked at me, her blue eyes sharp, without a trace of kindness. "*Mon Dieu*, James, surely you felt the distance between us lately. I thought you knew."

"What distance? I don't know what you're talking about. What about the other night?" I was referring to a sexual marathon we had enjoyed a few nights earlier.

She smiled a little. "Yes, we had some fun, but that's not all zare is."

I was about to demand that she explain herself when she stared me right in the eye and calmly said: "I've met another man."

"What!"

"I've met another man," she repeated. "A dentist."

"A dentist? Who is he?"

"No one you know."

"Well, when?"

She cut me off. "Details are unimportant."

My heart plunged at the thought of some dentist drilling her. I rushed to her side and tried to kiss her neck. She pushed me away, and a wave of the CK perfume I'd given her for Christmas wafted in the air.

She gave me a quick, cold hug, the same way you hug someone you don't know that well. "James, I really sorry. I appy I met you. I can't explain it. I didn't mean for ziss to appen. I don't try to looking for someone else or to break your heart." She grabbed a suitcase in each hand and strode to the door. Then she stopped and turned to look at me. "I call you. I owe money for back bills. We can talk."

Well Officer, I vaguely remember the room spinning and my heart pounding as I chased her out the door to a taxi waiting curbside. It was as if I was in a dream, or more precisely a nightmare.

"Cindy," I pleaded, "don't do this. I won't let you leave me."

But inside, I knew it was over. She had probably made up her mind to leave months earlier. The taxi pulled away and I watched the back of her head waiting for her to turn and look at me.

She didn't. She was gone . . . for good.

In that moment, my world, stripped of love, tilted on its axis and I was catapulted headfirst into a nuclear winter of despair. My appetite deserted me. A feeling of emptiness and isolation settled on my life. I lost 20 pounds in a month. I became nervous and easily agitated due to the sudden loss of my lover. To make matters worse, my rent and bills doubled because Cindy had been splitting everything with me.

When Cindy's friends started calling and asking where she was I coldly told them I didn't know the name of the new guy she was screwing and hung up.

A few weeks later, I was sitting on my futon, sipping a beer and looking over the last Visa bill Cindy and I had run up together. She enjoyed eating at nice restaurants and knew a lot about expensive wine. The bill was a whopper and I could barely make the monthly payment. I knew it would be a tight few months financially.

The phone rang. I dropped the bill onto the coffee table and picked up the phone. It was my second cousin, Craig. Someone in the interconnecting circles of our family told him that Cindy had walked out on me and that I was suffering through the emotional carnage that comes in the wake of an abrupt relationship breakup.

"Why don't you come over for dinner on Thursday?" he asked. "It'll be fun. Just you, me and Marla."

Well Officer, as you can imagine I was reluctant because my heart was wounded. I didn't feel like going anywhere and was happy to wallow in my self-imposed solitude feeling deeply sorry for myself. "Thanks Craig," I replied, "but I'll take a pass. I've been working pretty hard, and . . ."

He cut me off. "Come on," he said cheerfully. "It'll be a great chance to catch up on things with me and Marla. Besides, it's Marla's birthday."

It was the third such dinner invitation I'd received in as many weeks. When you've been emotionally gutted, friends and family feel a pressing need to help. It's the best side of human nature, I guess, reaching out to people in pain.

I was too tired to argue. Maybe something about it appealed to a deep need within me. Or maybe I just wanted to eat again. "Sure, Craig," I said wearily. "Marla's birthday? I'll come. What can I bring?"

"Just bring your appetite."

I heard Marla in the background telling him something.

"Marla says to find a parking spot on our block," Craig said. "There's been some robberies in the neighborhood."

Officer, you probably know all about where crimes happen.

"Okay, I will," I said to Craig. "Thanks. See you Thursday."

I hung up, reached for my beer, then slid back onto the futon and glanced at my watch. It was getting late, so I went into the bathroom, washed my face and brushed my teeth. Then I staggered into the bedroom and collapsed on my bed. Nights were hard; that was when I thought about Cindy the most. During the day I kept preoccupied with work, but at night I tended to sleep for a few hours, wake up from a gory nightmare with her in it, then toss and turn until morning.

As I lay there, my eyes were drawn to the chest of drawers across the room. Above it, hanging from the wall, was a sword in a metal sheath that Cindy had given me as a birthday present a few months earlier. At the time I had scoffed.

"Why would you give me something so useless?" I had asked her. But that was Cindy: she had no sense when it came to practical matters.

"Remember when we were in la antique shop?" she had replied with a coy smile. "I saw you looking at it. I can tell you want it. I went back next day and buy it. I 'ave it polished and sharpened. Is tres bien no?"

I pulled the sword from the sheaf and examined the blade closely.

"I have absolutely no use for a sword."

"Every man wants one. Just ask Dr. Freud," she winked. "Now you 'ave one. Take it to office or put it over your bed. It's an art piece. But is very sharp and is well made."

She was right about that. It was a fine weapon. The blade was at least three feet long, double-edged, razor sharp and made from fired steel. I guess it was some kind of ceremonial sword because the sheath was quite ornate.

I had hung the sword over my bureau because I didn't want to hurt Cindy's feelings. I need not have worried: she had charged the thing to my credit card! Four hundred and seventy bucks! As I lay there looking at it resentment, and to some degree guilt, welled up within me. Officer there was just something about it, and I can't really put my finger on it, but there was something about it that made me feel . . . bad? Go figure. I knew I had to get rid of it.

The next morning, I took down the sword and placed it in the trunk of my car. I was planning to give it to a friend who lives in the suburbs. It was razor sharp and I figured he could use it to prune his bushes.

I managed to make it through the week without sobbing in public, and by the time Thursday arrived, I was actually looking forward to dinner with Craig and Marla. But I was tired, so my plan was to eat fast, get home early, then get a good night's sleep.

Driving to their apartment, I thought about Craig and Marla. I hadn't seen them in a few years but remembered that they lived in an old three story brick walk-up just a few blocks from Lake Michigan. It was built in the 1920s, and their apartment had gleaming hardwood floors, glorious high ceilings, fancy moldings and a fireplace with a deep, black hearth. The neighborhood conjured up another age. I could imagine men walking around in fedoras and overcoats which seemed fitting, somehow, for my cousin and his wife.

Craig and Marla are a little strange, though not necessarily in a bad way. Craig's a good guy, a probation officer with a broad white moustache, a beer belly and a truck driver's sensibility. He's an amateur magician and he tends to push his juvenile magic act on people. Kids love it, but I always though it was childish.

Marla is round and short with cat's-eyes glasses. She is unfailingly happy and smiles a lot, as if she's in on the secrets of the universe. She makes jewelry and sells it at craft fairs and on the Internet. There's always been a kind of whispered understanding about Marla in our family, that she's "strange but nice."

I didn't know Marla that well, but I did know she loved unicorns. Absolutely flipped out over them. Everybody who knows Marla knows that. She had dozens of unicorn books, posters, figurines and magazines, and she was all over the Internet, looking up unicorn websites. Childish, don't you agree Officer?

I was like you. I said "Unicorn shmunicorn." I didn't give a rat's ass about unicorns.

And get this. The other really weird thing about Marla is that she firmly believes she can read people's futures and other mystical things by looking at the bubbles in their coffee! She says the little bubbles have a very exact meaning, and, when read properly, reveal things. Can she be arrested for that? I'd seen her do her bubble reading routine at family gatherings, and I always kept my distance.

It was already dark when I got to their neighborhood, and I had to drive around before I found a space a few blocks from their building. It was a drab November evening, perfectly reflecting my mood. Walking along the sidewalk to their door, I pulled up my collar against the damp fall wind that was tugging at my leather jacket and at the bunch of purple Irises I had bought to give Marla for her birthday.

They buzzed me up, and Craig greeted me at the front door with a broad smile and firm handshake. "Good to see you." He nodded. "It's been a long time."

He ushered me into their apartment, where the rich aroma of spaghetti sauce immediately elevated my spirit. Craig hung my jacket in the closet, and we went to the kitchen, where Marla was bent over a large pot filled with what looked like bubbling tomato lava. Her plump face erupted in a broad, loving smile. She dropped a wooden spoon soaked in sauce onto the stove and hugged me. "Oh my God look who it is," she said grinning broadly over her cat's eyes glasses.

I handed her the flowers and wished her a "Happy Birthday."

She filled a crystal vase with water and put the flowers in it. "Dinner's almost ready." She took my hand. "First, let's sit down and have a glass of wine."

Craig poured Merlot, and we went into their living room. It was spacious, with a puffy, cream-colored sofa, a wooden coffee table, two upholstered chairs and a brick fireplace.

"We were so sorry about your girl," Marla said, sitting down on the sofa with her short plump legs crossed. "Sometimes it's hard to see good coming out of things like that. But time heals all wounds."

"Yeah, or time wounds all heels," Craig added smugly, sitting beside Marla on the sofa. "I can't believe she walked out on you like that. Have you heard from her?"

I plucked a potato chip from a bowl on the coffee table and popped it in my mouth. "Nope, and who knows where she is? Her friends keep calling *me* looking for her. Can you believe it? All I know is that she left in our suitcases . . . I mean with our suitcases. Apparently she's living with some dentist." I rubbed my eyes. "I really don't want to talk about it."

I took a big gulp of wine and looked around. I'd only been to their apartment a few times, but as I scanned the room, I was sure something was missing. Then I realized what it was.

"Marla what happened to the unicorns?" I asked. "Last time I was here . . ."

She put her glass of wine on the table and smiled shyly. "Oh, yes," she said, waving her hand through the air. "I think people thought I was getting a little unicorn crazy there."

"You gave them away?" I asked genuinely surprised.

She nodded.

"Any particular reason?"

"No big reason." She leaned back into the sofa. "It was just time."

She explained that, after 50 years of collecting unicorn stuff, she'd sold most of her collection on eBay. Then, she turned toward a small wooden table on the other side of the room, near a window decorated with crystals. "But," she said, pointing, "I still have that one."

It was a six-inch high white ceramic unicorn with a golden mane, nibbling peacefully on a patch of grass under a glass dome.

Marla beamed and ruffled Craig's silver hair. "He gave it to me," she said.

I got up and went over to examine the figurine. "What was the song about a unicorn?" I asked, standing beside the table. "Wasn't it an Irish song or something?"

Marla lurched off the sofa with a wheeze and walked over beside me. "It was recorded by the Irish Rovers back in the late '60s."

Craig got up and went over to his record collection which was housed in a wooden console beside the stereo. "I've got the Irish Rovers right here," he said, pulling out an album.

He passed it to me.

There was a picture on the cover of five smiling guys with guitars and other instruments.

"Yeah, remember how that song went?" Craig said to Marla. Then he started singing an off key verse from the song. Marla laughed and kissed Craig on the cheek. "Yeah, that's it!" she said enthusiastically as she turned to me. "You remember? It's the story of the flood in the Bible. God tells Noah not to forget to take a couple of Unicorns on the Ark. But when the rain starts the Unicorns are playing around and they get left behind."

Craig offered to play the song, but I said I didn't want to hear it, then looked at my watch.

"You know," Marla said, grinning whimsically, "I vividly remember the first time I saw a unicorn. I was three or four. It was in a book with sparkles: this beautiful horse with a lance coming out of it forehead, with magic dust around it."

She took a sip of wine, paused as if visiting the moment in her memory, and continued. "Maybe it was like God for me." She looked down at the figurine. "It was like I recognized it immediately from a past existence or another dimension."

Craig looked at me, then at Marla. "A feeling like that must pack a wallop when you're a little girl."

I sipped my wine and looked down at the insipid little figurine. Marla's story was nonsense. And I certainly didn't believe in

God. Truth be told, I didn't *want* to believe in God, because of you know, the ramifications. "Marla, unicorns are a complete fabrication," I said, barely concealing my skepticism. "How could you think you recognized one from some other place? They don't exist . . . Never did."

I think I hurt her feelings because she turned away from me and went to sit beside Craig on the sofa, leaving me standing alone beside the unicorn figure. "You know something?" she said, reaching over to touch Craig's arm. "I'd hate to live in a world without magic. It would be like living in a world without love or hope."

I thought she was being overly sentimental, but I didn't say anything because I didn't want to hurt her feelings again. There was no room in my life for such cartoonish nonsense. I'd been living in a world without love since I . . . well since Cindy left, and that world had nothing to do with unicorns.

"Know what I like about unicorns?" Craig asked. "They're the most *cuddly* of the mythological creatures—much more friendly that a griffin, a dragon or a sphinx."

Marla nodded wildly in agreement. "Unicorns turn up in old art in Greece and Rome, and even earlier, in the art of Mesopotamia," she said breathlessly. "Some older translations of the Hebrew Bible mentions unicorns."

I scoffed. "There aren't any unicorns in the Bible!"

"Yes, there are," she said as she brushed something off her pant leg. "Some people says it's a bad translation, that they're really talking about an ox. But I choose to believe it's a unicorn." She grabbed a handful of chips and droned on. "People believed a Unicorn could purify a polluted spring by dipping its horn into the water. Medicines made from the horn of a unicorn had all kinds of healing qualities and sold for twenty times its weight in gold in medieval Europe."

I couldn't resist poking some fun at her. "I could use an emotional lift. Can you smoke it?"

"No, Mister Cynical, you can't smoke it!" she balked. "All I've got for you is a spaghetti dinner." With that she tilted back her head, drained her glass of wine and got up off the sofa. "Come on," she said, smiling again. "Let's eat."

I didn't think I was hungry, but I surprised myself by wolfing down two large plates of spaghetti and half a loaf of garlic bread. Over the course of the meal we caught up on family news. As we finished eating Craig, got up and went into the kitchen.

Marla reached over and put her plump warm hand on mine. "You know, of all your brothers and sisters, you were always my favorite. When your mother and father broke up you were a real sad little guy. I took you to a movie. Do you remember?"

I did, and the memory warmed me. But I guess I was starting to feel the effects of the wine because in a very sarcastic tone I blurted out; "I remember the movie. It was *Unicorns from Outer Space!*"

"No!" Marla said defensively. "It was a Jungle Book movie!"

"Right," I said sheepishly. "Sorry."

"When you were little, you used to love looking at the stars, and you used to wonder." Marla was beaming again. "You used to talk about what might be up there. You had such a great imagination."

I wiped my mouth with a napkin. "When you're a kid stuff like that matters. Then, you grow up and do things. Things you can't undo."

Before Marla could reply, Craig came back into the dining room, carrying a birthday cake with candles flickering on top. He started singing "Happy Birthday" to Marla and I must admit that I cringed. He looked down at me, expecting me to join in, which I did, albeit halfheartedly.

Grinning widely, Craig set the cake down in front of Marla. It certainly was a great looking cake. It was covered in chocolate frosting, and the flames from the candles were dancing above a small bouquet of colorful flowers made from icing. "Happy Birthday Marla" was written in yellow frosting below them. "Go ahead, honey," he said. "Make a magical wish and blow out the candles."

She inhaled deeply and, in a single breath blew them all out.

"What did you wish for, Marla?" I asked, trying to conceal the disdain in my voice.

She smiled. "I wished goods things for you."

I leaned back in my chair and folded my arms across my chest. "You shouldn't have wasted your wish on me." Then it occurred to me that there was one thing I would wish for. "I wish I could go back in time and change something I've done."

Marla leaned toward me. "And what would that be?"

"Perhaps I didn't handle the breakup with Cindy very well," I said. "I may have, ummm, overreacted."

"You can't change the past," Craig said. "You have to live with the decisions you make, and, hopefully learn from your mistakes."

"In retrospect," I said sheepishly, "I'd probably handle things differently. She didn't deserve, ummm, to, ahhh, to depart that way."

They both looked at me, no doubt expecting more of an explanation.

"Just forget it and forget her," I said, then looked at my watch.

I was about to tell them I had to get home early when Marla stood and suggested that Craig show me some card tricks.

"Oh, no, that's okay," I stammered. "I have to get going, really."

"Oh, James, you've got to see this," Marla said gleefully. "It's really amazing."

He pulled a deck of cards seemingly out of thin air, fanned them, then told me to take a card and to remember it.

I looked at my card: Queen of Hearts. I leaned over and showed it to Marla.

"Oh, that's a good card," she giggled.

Craig told me to slip my card back into the deck, then he shuffled the deck with great flourish and dropped a three of clubs onto the coffee table.

"This your card?" he asked in a voice like that of a midway showman.

"Nope."

Tell me, Officer, can a person be arrested for being a horrible magician?

Anyway, he looked puzzled. Then he cut the deck and pulled out the nine of diamonds. "Oh, this is it . . . right?"

"No."

He was getting flustered. He cut the deck again and pulled out the Jack of Spades. "Ahhh," he said, grinning. "This is it, right?

"No," I said losing patience. "I had the queen of hearts." And thought . . . *Just like Cindy. But she left me.*

"Oh," he said, clearly embarrassed. "I should have practiced that trick a little more."

"Oh, that's too bad," Marla said comforting him. "It's a great trick when it works."

I could tell Craig felt bad, so I decided to lighten the mood with some self-depreciating humor: "I guess I know a little magic after all," I said, grinning. "I can make a girlfriend disappear."

Marla picked up some dishes and turned to me. "You're lucky to be rid of her."

"You have no idea," I replied.

Craig was slipping the cards back into a box. "Craig," I said. "Have you tried that trick where you cut someone in half? Now *that's* impressive."

He shook his head and dropped the cards on the table, then turned to Marla. "Your turn honey," he said. "How about reading the bubbles in our coffee?"

Marla put down the dishes and curled up beside Craig on the sofa. She took his cup in her palms, looked down, studied the bubbles in his coffee for about 15 seconds, then smiled broadly.

"My dear man," she said, "since when can you walk on water?"

Craig roared. "It happened at work today," he said, slapping his knee. "A pipe broke, and the water was ankle deep."

"I'm on tonight," Marla giggled, turning to me. "Okay, your turn, Mr. I Don't Believe in Anything. Let me see your cup."

She was right about that. I certainly didn't believe the bubbles in my coffee meant anything. My playing along to be nice ended with Craig's cards tricks. My tolerance for those kinds of childish thing was low because they are a waste of time. There's nothing going on. The alignment of the planets doesn't mean anything. The bubbles in my coffee were totally random and meaningless, and there's no such thing as unicorns, never has been. It's all kids stuff, superstitious crap.

But the wine from dinner was warming my blood, so I decided to cooperate. Looking down into my mug, I saw a series of tiny interlocking bubbles floating in my coffee clinging to the side of my cup. If the bubbles were a land formation, then they would have been a little peninsula jutting out into my coffee. I didn't care and was losing interest fast.

Marla smiled and clasped my mug in her chubby hands. She gazed down and after a moment her expression changed. It looked like she had just gotten some genuinely bad news.

Craig must have noticed too. "Okay Marla very funny," he said. "What is it?"

"That's weird," she said, still gazing into my coffee. "It's very rare magic. I see colors. Lots of red, some yellow. Denim? Very unusual." She looked at me over the rim of the cup. "Red. That means big changes are coming your way James."

"Big changes?" I snorted. "I've had enough big changes lately."

Marla smiled, but I could still see the concern in her kind eyes. She handed me back my mug, gathered up the dishes and turned to me with a worried expression. "James, it's late. You're staying right here on the sofa tonight."

I politely refused, saying I had to work in the morning.

Craig offered to walk me to my car, but I declined. "Don't worry," I said, reassuring him, "I'm just around the corner."

At the front door, Marla put her hand on my shoulder. She gave me a big hug and I could feel the warmth from her body. Then she pressed something into my palm. "Take this honey," she said with a kind smile. "It'll give you good luck."

I opened my hand and looked at what she had given me. It was a crystal about two inches long. "Oh, no, Marla, you keep it," I said. "Really, I don't . . . it's your birthday and you're giving me a present."

"Please take it, James," she said, her eyes imploring. "It'll make me feel better."

I mumbled "Thanks" and slipped the crystal into my pocket.

Craig patted me on the back, waved and asked me to call them when I got home. "Otherwise," he said, grinning, "Marla will worry all night."

As I left their apartment, the old wooden stairs creaked and moaned under my weight like a chorus of ghosts doomed to haunt old buildings like that. I was thinking about Marla and Craig and the love they shared. They enjoyed a simple happiness, a peace of mind I'd never really noticed before. I started thinking about Marla reading those stupid bubbles and was a little freaked out by it. Red, yellow and denim. Weird.

Walking to the car, I zipped up my leather jacket and scanned the empty street. The stars were out, and for a moment, I forgot about my problems and paused to appreciate their beauty, their power of wonder. But it was past midnight and the murmur of the cold fall wind through the filigreed branches added to the darkness. I started walking briskly through the cool night air because I was worried about running into trouble.

I know what you're thinking Officer: "This guy had a lot to drink and shouldn't be driving." And maybe you're right, but drinking helped me forget about Cindy.

So, I got to my car, but before I could open the door, two shadowy figures ran in my direction from the mouth of an alley.

"Hey, mister, you got the time?" the first one said, pulling a shiny silver revolver from his pocket. "And I'll take your wallet too, asshole."

Where's a cop when you need one? No offense Officer.

Anyway, living in the city, I knew what to do: just hand over your wallet and don't try to be a hero or you'll get yourself killed. I fumbled for my wallet. "Here take it," I blurted. "It's got everything."

The guy with the gun reeked so badly of Old Spice aftershave I wondered if he had been drinking it. He flashed a greasy smile and pulled $7 from my wallet. He sneered, showing yellow teeth, pointed the gun at my head and waved the few meager bills in front of me. "This all you got dipshit!" he growled as a gust of cold wind blew through the gutter kicking up a bunch of dead leafs.

My heart was pounding, my mouth went dry. I wanted to run but was frozen with fear. "It's got my credit cards," I blurted. "I won't tell anyone. Take them." I plunged my hand into my pocket in a desperate search for more money. Instead of money I pulled out the crystal Marla had given me a few minutes earlier. "This might be worth something," I said, my hand shaking. "Take it."

The guy with the gun grabbed the crystal and examined it. "Worthless piece of glass," he scowled, as he threw the crystal down the alley. Before I could say anything he smashed me on the side of the head with the gun.

I crumpled to the pavement, dazed. I didn't know what had happened.

He pointed the gun at my head while the other guy goaded him on telling him to shoot me. "Put a cap in his cheap head," he said, his unshaven face enflamed with rage. "He don't have the street tax. He gotta die. Go on man. Do it!"

I was still stunned from the blow to my head, but somewhere in the daze, I knew I was going to die. I grabbed the rear bumper of my car with both hands and desperately tried to pull myself up, but instead I slipped back to the pavement. Blood was running down the side of my face, burning my eyes. That, combined with the dark night, gave everything a blurred silhouette quality.

"God, no," I pleaded on my knees, wiping the blood from my eyes. "No, please, don't do it. Please."

It was no use. Squinting through the blood, I glimpsed the evil intent in his twisted face. His eyes were wild like a lunatic, his rotten teeth bared. He wrapped his finger around the trigger. I instinctively raised my bloody hands waiting to be shot. But instead of gunshots I heard a loud noise coming from the alley where the guy had thrown the crystal. It was a sound I knew but couldn't place it. Then, I recognized it as the distinctive sound of a horse galloping like in a western movie. The robbers must have heard it too, because they both turned to look. Before the guy with the gun could turn back toward me, something big, moving real fast, a flash of silver, hit him with a tremendous impact.

I lowered my hands, but with the blood stinging my eyes, I could hardly see. I shook my head and was able to focus a little better but everything was still blurred. I squinted but couldn't believe what my eyes were telling me. The guy with the gun had been hit by a huge animal, a horse, its mass blotting out the street light and stars. And there was something else, in its forehead, a lance of some kind. Oh, my God . . . it was . . . . a unicorn!

It had speared the guy with the gun through the chest. With a thunderous snort and a mighty flick of its head, the Unicorn threw him though the air into a brick wall. He fell lifeless to the pavement in a bleeding heap clearly dead.

The second guy grabbed the gun off the ground. He started yelling, "Ahhhhhh! Ahhhhh!" Holding the gun with both hands he fired at the unicorn. BLAM BLAM BLAM. The Unicorn, this tremendous animal, whined furiously, its eyes filled with rage. It reared up on its powerful back legs, towering above the shooter who kept shooting, and screaming. But the bullets deflected off the unicorn in a rapid series of whizzes, dings and pings. Then, in a single swift motion, the unicorn brought around its powerful back legs and kicked the second guy in the head, instantly decapitating him.

The unicorn landed hard on its flank with a loud grunt. It scrambled uncertainly to its feet and moved toward me, pawing the pavement and snorting furiously from the blood-letting. I wiped my eyes and stared up at it. I was in shock . . . speechless . . . my senses scrambled. My mouth hung open, but I couldn't speak. I rubbed my eyes, but the blurred outline of the unicorn was still standing in front of me breathing heavily, its head slightly lowered like Marla's ceramic figurine. Its ivory fur was shining with sweat. It was a beautiful, muscular animal, six feet at the shoulder, with a blond almost golden mane, huge blue eyes and a white, blood-soaked, three-foot lance coming out of its forehead.

It moved toward me.

I instinctively recoiled, not knowing if I would be killed next.

Then it nudged me gently and licked my injured head.

I realized I had nothing to fear.

Before I could think, before I could move, the unicorn jumped over me, and I was brushed by a gust of wind from its bulk. It smelled sweaty and musty, just like a horse smells. I stayed on the ground, wobbly and dazed, listening to the unicorn galloping away into the night. For a split second, there was utter silence in the alley as if for one brief moment, the world had stopped turning.

Then I was aware of a streetlight buzzing in the damp fall air somewhere nearby, and I heard the piercing cry of an approaching siren. Apparently someone in the neighborhood had heard the gunshots and called the police. I was sitting on the pavement, dazed and bleeding, when they rolled into the dark alley. The blow to my head, the blood in my eyes, the siren, the electric-blue strobe of their emergency lights bouncing off the buildings—it all left me totally disoriented.

Two figures jumped from the police car, probably friends of yours, Officer. One ran over to the guy lying in a bloody heap at the base of the wall. The second cop moved carefully toward me.

"There's another one over there," I blurted, holding my bleeding head with one hand and motioning down the alley with the other.

The second cop walked to where I was pointing.

"Randy take a look at this!" he yelled to his partner, "Holy shit this guy doesn't have a head!"

They found it 20 feet away, as if some kid had left a football in the alley.

They drew down on me with their guns. "Is there anyone else?" the first cop demanded, pointing his gun at me.

"No," I stammered. "No, that's it."

"Okay, you. On your stomach!" he demanded. "Do it now!"

I rolled onto my stomach and threw up my entire spaghetti dinner.

They handcuffed me and the first cop barked into his radio. "This is 53. I need a watch commander, the ME and an ambulance, code three." He paused and took a deep breath. "Two code 10. One in custody."

His radio squawked something and he clipped it back onto his shoulder. Then he bent over and pointed his flashlight directly in my eyes.

Blinded by the light, I winced in pain.

"Okay, you!" he demanded. "What happened here?"

I was still dazed from being pistol-whipped and disoriented from the blood in my eyes, and my head was throbbing. "They were going to kill me," I stammered. "They wanted money and pistol-whipped me with the gun."

"What happened to those two guys?" the first cop repeated angrily.

I told them the whole story, how the unicorn had appeared out of nowhere, how the second guy tried to shoot it, how the unicorn saved my life. "I couldn't see, there was blood in my eyes, and the dark. It happened in a few seconds. But it was a unicorn. I swear."

The first cop turned his flashlight away from my face and I slumped to the ground.

The older cop shook his head and motioned toward the body at the base of the wall. "It looks like someone ran that guy through with a lamppost." He looked down at me suspiciously then slipped his gun back into his holster. "What a mess. He better have a better answer than that. A unicorn!"

They handcuffed me and put me in the back seat of the police car. It felt good to be off the street and away from the two bloody corpses. The older cop turned toward me and rested his elbow on the back of his seat. "What are you on?"

"On?"

"What drugs are you on? Coke? Angel dust?"

"I don't take drugs," I replied wearily. "I had a few drinks with dinner nothing else."

He reached for the police radio, said something into it that I couldn't understand then turned back to me and read me my rights.

"A lot of people are on their way here," he said as he finished. "So you better tell us what happened to those two guys, and none of your unicorn bullshit."

I had already told them what happened, and they didn't believe me. Hell, I wouldn't have believed me either if I hadn't seen it with my own two eyes. I was exhausted, bloodied and in pain. I wanted nothing more than to simply take a long shower, swallow an aspirin as big as my fist and to crawl into bed. I wasn't sure what to tell them. But then, as if by instinct I blurted out: "Someone has to pay, right?"

I don't know why I said that. It was as if someone else were speaking for me.

The first cop examined me with narrowed eyes. "What do you mean someone's has to pay? Pay who? Pay what?"

"Someone's got to pay for the pain in the world, the suffering, the lost hope." I couldn't control myself. It was as if I were sitting there listening to someone else rant.

"What are you trying to tell us, wise guy?"

"What you already know," I responded. "That somebody's got to pay."

"What are you talking about?" one of them asked.

Maybe it was the blow to my head or the trauma of being robbed and almost killed, but I suddenly felt the need to try and explain things to them in a deeper way. "For example," I said. "And this is truly just an example without any bearing in the real world. Understand?"

"Whatever."

"Are either of you married?" I asked. "Got a girlfriend?"

They nodded.

"Good, okay. Let's say you come home from work one day and your woman says she's leaving you for a dentist. A damned dentist! She's like '*au revoir*,' thanks for the laughs. What are you supposed to do with that?"

They looked at each other and shrugged in unison.

"Okay, now you're heartbroken," I continued. "You probably loved her too much and that's what happens when you love someone too much. But let's say this woman of yours knew a lot about expensive wine and nice restaurants and she thinks she can just walk out leaving you holding *la bag* and you're *le sucker*! Understand! The only thing you have left is some stupid impractical birthday present she gave you. What do you do? Jump under a train?"

Their faces were blanks.

"No of course not," I blurted. "You get on your knees and beg her to stay because you love her so much! She doesn't listen. So after it's done . . . it's done . . . you go to that place and you say hey what's going on here? Then the answer comes: She was *le bitch* without feelings. No feelings! Do you understand? Now what, right? Who's going to pay? Not you! Just get rid of the pain. Throw it away in a dumpster. Your life's not over! You're not paying for this!"

I could tell I still wasn't getting though to them so I tried one more time.

"All you have left is what you thought was a useless birthday present and a Visa bill with eight grand charged on it. But you were wrong about the present. It's not useless. You're not getting made into *le sucker*! It's all about who's going to pay. Understand?"

The first cop slowly shook his head. "Buddy, you're on *la meth*, aren't you?"

"No, I'm just trying to make you understand!"

"Listen, I don't know what you're talking about or how you killed those two guys, but I'll find out, and when I do . . ."

"I told you," I snapped. "It was a unicorn!"

. . .

An army of police and ambulances flooded the street and a tired-looking EMT bandaged my head. The police searched far and wide for a "murder weapon" and it seemed like there was only one dumpster in the whole world they didn't peer into.

They took me in handcuffs to the 24th Precinct where detectives sat across a table from me asking over and over what happened. My story never changed, because it was the incredible truth. I was so tired, I even thought about making up a story, telling them that I went into a fit when the guy hit me with the gun and, somehow *I* killed them. But I stuck to the truth. After 12 hours of questioning, they finally let me go and told me not to leave town.

Detectives, probably friends of yours Officer, anyway they found people who knew the two creeps that were going to kill me. Barry Goldner and Stan Cosby. I'll never forget those two names. They were three-time losers from the neighborhood who'd both done jail time. One of their girlfriends said they were out to rob someone that night for drug money.

A few days after everything happened, a television reporter called. She said she's heard my story from the police and wanted to talk to me. I don't know why I agreed to let her interview me.

Perhaps I thought that talking to her would somehow help me get my mind around what had happened.

The next day was drab and rainy, but as promised the reporter and a cameraman rolled up in front of my building in a big white truck with a satellite dish on top. They came into my living room and set up a camera and lights, that seemed to aggravate my head injury.

"So, you're still saying a unicorn saved your life?" the reporter asked, leaning forward. "How can you expect people to believe that? It's impossible. You said it was dark and there was blood in your eyes. Are you sure you were awake? You were hit on the head and dazed, right?"

She was annoying to say the least. Aren't reporters pests, officer? I knew you'd agree.

I paused, unsure what to say to her. "Lady I was awake," I replied after a moment. "I don't think I've ever been more awake in my life."

"But surely," she said, leaning farther forward until she almost fell out of the chair, "you must understand why people, the police are skeptical?"

The cameraman was barely able to control his smirking, which pissed me off.

"Listen, I'm not seeking attention here. You called me. People can be skeptical. I don't care. I'm just telling you what happened, what I saw."

I leaned back in my chair and exhaled.

"Sometimes, people end up paying for their evil deeds . . . sometimes, they don't."

Her ears seemed to perk up like a fox's. "Paying?"

"They paid with their lives right?" I blurted. "When she told me, I didn't care if I lived or died. It was pure reaction like . . . like throwing out brand-new luggage."

"New luggage?" she asked. "What do you mean 'When she told you?" I don't understand."

"Don't you see?" I said. "I had absolutely nothing to lose. Then what happens? The unicorn comes and it's the judge, jury and executioner. It saved my life."

Before I could continue, a rumble of thunder rolled across the gray afternoon sky. I grinned and pointed up. "Sounds like He's backing me up on that one."

She looked at me suspiciously, then nodded as if she understood.

The interview was picked up on cable and broadcast around the country. Soon, other people started saying they'd seen unicorns, too. I saw some of those people on TV, and they looked nuts to me. As far as I could tell, there weren't any other credible unicorn sightings.

A year later, I married a junior producer I'd met at one of the television stations where I was being interviewed. And let me tell you something she would never try to leave me for a damned dentist. We have a daughter and sometimes I listen to her playing and laughing. That laughter is magical.

So officer, after a year, your colleagues left the case "Unsolved." I could tell they were pissed off. I knew they didn't believe my story, but they couldn't come up with any other plausible scenario as to what happened that night. It was as all of civilized society would collapse if they typed the word *unicorn* in their final report.

Maybe it would. And maybe that would be all right.

Officer, I returned to the alley at one point because I was looking for some kind of an answer. My encounter with the unicorn was big news in the city and around the country. You must have heard about it? I hate to admit it, but I guess I became a little bit of a folk hero. A cottage industry of sorts sprang up in the neighborhood where it all happened. There were half a dozen stores selling all kinds of unicorn souvenirs. I rounded the corner onto the street and a stocky man in his early 50s came up to me with a dozen T-shirts slung over his shoulder. It was an overcast summer afternoon, but as you can surely appreciate I was a little leery considering what had happened there.

"Sir," he said showing perfect white teeth. "I've got unicorn T-shirts here for ten bucks! That's five cheaper than the store around the corner. I bet you're a medium."

He held out a T-shirt for me to look at. The front was covered with a cartoonist scene of a unicorn wearing a decorated blanket reared up over a dead woman surrounded by a pool of blood. A set of luggage was sitting next to her. The unicorn didn't look anything like the mythic creature that saved my life and I couldn't understand why there was a woman there instead of those two creeps who had tried to kill me. And what was the luggage all about? It was all very confusing.

I didn't want to tell him who I was, so I just pointed at the shirt.

"Interesting."

"You know," he said, "I saw the whole Unicorn thing. I've been living in the neighborhood my entire life." He pointed down the street to a doorway. "I saw it all from there."

I looked into his wide brown eyes. He was making me a bit nervous. "Oh really," I said with mock surprise. "I thought there weren't any witnesses except for the guy who did it. I mean who was robbed."

He smiled sheepishly. "I didn't want to come forward. I was drinking and stoned that night. I cleaned up my act now though."

I figured he was lying about being there in order to sell t-shirts but I didn't care. Still, I was curious as to what he knew. "So," I asked motioning to the T-shirt. "Why is there a dead woman on the T-Shirt when it was two men that were killed? And what about the suitcases?"

He shook his head and chuckled. "Because she's the dead one."

He passed his hand through the air in a downward motion. "Chop chop. And you know all about the luggage."

Suddenly I felt as if I was in a dream, or more likely a nightmare.

He pointed to the dead woman. "I call her Cindy."

"Cindy? How could . . . ? You're crazy!"

A rumble of thunder rolled across the gray afternoon sky. "Well there it is," he said turning his gaze skyward. "Sounds like he's backing me up on that one."

That's when I realized he was some kind of a demon. Who else could summon thunder? Officer as you can imagine I was gripped with fear. I could almost see the horns coming out of his forehead. How could he know what I did . . . . I mean what happened to Cindy . . . I mean . . .

He put the T-shirt back with the others on his shoulder. "I guess you're not the T-shirt type," he said. "But I got something here I can let you have for a few bucks."

He reached into his pocket and pulled out a crystal. I was shocked. It looked exactly like the crystal Marla gave me that night. I had totally forgotten about it. It was then that I realized I wasn't looking at some kind of demon as I had thought moments earlier. The devil himself was right in front of me!

"Where did you get that?" I demanded. "How could you know?"

He shrugged. "Oh I picked it up somewhere. People throw good stuff away and other people pick it up. People like different things."

"I've thrown away good luggage," I said weakly.

He nodded in understanding. "I know."

He held out the crystal for me to get a better look. Shards of white and blue light seemed to be emanating from it.

"It's yours for twenty bucks," he said smiling wickedly. "Plus I gave you a petty good story, something you can tell you kids right? Consider it an alibi."

I nodded in agreement. What else could I do? I thrust a $20 bill at him, grabbed the crystal and ran away as fast as I could. I never went back there after that.

Officer in the end I look at it all this way: on a fateful dark fall night I took shelter from a broken heart in the home of people who loved me. That night changed my life like a river diverted from its original path.

Officer I'm glad you're getting all this down in your little notebook. And please make a note of this. It's clear to me now that the bubbles in coffee mean something because everything means something no matter how insignificant it may appear to be. You just have to figure out how to read it like Marla read the bubbles in my coffee that night. Red, yellow and denim. Big changes. Absolutely amazing!

I guess what I'm saying is: nothing in this world is random. Everything happens for a reason. The unicorn did more than save my life, it changed my life. When people ask me what I believe in, what my personal philosophy is, I tell them I truly believe there are no mistakes in life.

For example—and this is purely just me pulling something out of thin air to illustrate my point: Let's say someone gives you a nice sharp . . . axe for your birthday. But you don't know anything about axes, never owned one, and you think, what the hell? What am I supposed to do with this? But later something heartbreaking happens, like the person who gave you the axe suddenly dumps you, and the answer comes to you. It dawns on you and you look at the axe and it's like the axe speaks to you. It's a magical axe and it says: Let me help you get rid of that anger, that pain. And you know what? You listen because what the axe is saying is right. That axe has a purpose, it always had a purpose, but you never realized it until that moment. Amazing!

It's the same with the unicorn. I believe in the unicorn because I have no choice but to believe in it. In the end it's better to believe in it than not to because it's easier to sleep at night. And you know what officer? You and your colleagues in the detective division can come to my door as many times as you want and ask me more questions about the unicorn and ask me about Cindy; Wherever she may be. I don't care because the truth is there are no mistakes. Everything happens for a reason and everything in life is connected, like a living tapestry. Cindy, an old sword, a broken heart, great wine, nice restaurants, brand-new suitcases tossed into a dumpster—and, of course, a unicorn. They're all connected! Or in one case "disconnected." Don't you see? It's so beautiful once you understand.

And you know what officer? I have a personal philosophy and while it may be corny, I happen to believe it's true.

I believe stars have the power of wonder.

I believe there are voices in thunder.

I believe in children's laughter . . . and happily ever after!

Now officer, I've told you a million times that I don't know what happened to Cindy or that ridiculous sword she gave me. I have no idea how her head ended up in a landfill. So for the love of God will you please take these handcuffs off of me!

EXTREME OFFICE POLITICS

I WAS SURFING THE NET LOOKING FOR the best way to secretly poison someone when I landed on the Wikipedia website. I poked around there for a few minutes and somehow ended up on the definition for: "Hatred."

> *Hatred (or hate) is a deep and emotional extreme dislike, directed against a certain object or class of objects. The objects of such hatred can vary widely, from inanimate objects to animals, oneself or other people, entire groups of people, people in general, existence, or the whole world. Hatred can become very driven. Actions after a lingering thought are not uncommon upon people or oneself. Hatred can result in extreme behavior such as violence, murder and war.*

> *Philosophers have offered many influential definitions of hatred. René Descartes viewed hate as an awareness that something is bad combined with an urge to withdraw from it. Baruch Spinoza defined hate as a type of pain that is due to an external cause. Aristotle viewed hate as a desire for the annihilation of an object that is incurable by time. Sigmund Freud, defined hate as an ego state that wishes to destroy the source of its unhappiness . . .*

Blah, blah, blah. As usual, those pointy-headed stinking losers are overstating everything, because "hatred," can be boiled down to a single name: Charlie Backman.

And there he is, that happy smiley-faced bitter sick and twisted rat.

My quarry.

He's walking across the parking lot, loosening his god-awful red tie, a laptop in a hideous leather case slung over his pathetic shoulder. It's after work. He doesn't suspect a thing. That idiot.

A grin pushes its way across my face as I put the car into Drive and creep toward him. His hatred for me has driven me to this!

He's walking slowly—ambling—with his misshapen head down, the back of his puke-green suitcoat flapping in the breeze.

I'm only 80 feet away.

He's oblivious, that moron. He doesn't see me. He's parked against a chain link fence at the far end of the lot, which will give me a clear path once he's passed the few cars left.

I've rented a big Buick for this because my Toyota is too small. I planned this carefully, thoroughly, methodically. I realized early on that my own car doesn't have enough bulk or weight to really cream him.

Details are important.

I'm only 40 feet away now, but I've got to have patience. I can see his repulsive face smiling as usual. I'll wipe that smile off his face! I grip the steering wheel so hard that my knuckles turn white as I slam my foot down on the accelerator. The engine roars; the tires squeal.

He hears the car and suddenly, instinctively, looks to his right, eyes wide with shock, his repugnant smile gone and his mouth open so wide, I can see his rotting yellow teeth. It's too late to get out of the way smiley-man.

You're mine!

I'm on him. I hope he sees my face. It will be the last thing he sees.

Smack! There's a delightful thud. Now he's under my tires, screaming. I slam on the brakes but I'm already past him. Looking in the rearview mirror, I see him on the ground, writhing in unspeakable pain. I drop the car into reverse and gun the engine.

He's trying to get up, trying to get out of the way, but he can't because his pathetic legs and arms are broken—no not broken: shattered. He's screaming, shrieking, "No No No No!" as I run him over again. That ass kissing two-faced . . .

Whomp! The rear bumper crushes his head like a tomato. No, not like a tomato—like a hideous, crazy, demented watermelon!

I run him over a dozen times, carefully, gleefully, until he's nothing but a bloody pulp of mashed repulsive bones, a gruesome stain on the asphalt.

I stop the car and pull a handgun—no not a handgun, an assault rifle—from the back seat. I open the door and start getting out. I'm sure that evil loser is dead, but . . .

The phone rings, yanking me out of my fantasy. I angrily grab the receiver and turn from my window overlooking the parking lot. It's Sharon, the ugly-ass secretary. She's blabbering on asking what I want on my pizza.

"Pizza? What?"

"It's Lisa Burton's birthday today. You know, Lisa from Marketing?"

"Yes," I reply impatiently, "I know who she is."

"Anyway, it's her birthday today, so there's a, you know, birthday lunch for her in Conference Room 207."

Now I know what she's talking about, our ridiculous company policy of throwing a lame lunch for employees on their birthday. They spring for a few lousy pizzas, a cheap cake, a card and a lottery ticket. I always considered it nothing more than a free lunch. That is until two weeks ago, when they actually forgot to do it on *my* birthday. Charlie Bachman's in HR, and he probably had something to do with bypassing my company birthday party that SOB.

"It'll be at 1:30 today," Sharon says.

I can see her in my mind's eye, slouched at her desk down the hall, chewing gum. Slouching and chewing are the two things she does best. When she's not chewing gum, she's gnawing the end of a pen like a mongrel dog, her big blonde hair done up like a poodle's.

I'm actually glad she said "no" when I asked her out last year. I don't know what I was thinking! It must have been some kind of temporary insanity. She's such a lowlife stinky slut.

"Julie and Mary don't eat meat, so they're getting mushrooms on their pizzas," she drones. "Kevin and Dexter are getting pepperoni, so you could share with them—or share with Alex; he's getting . . ."

I cut her off in mid-sentence. "Hey, thanks for asking Sharon, just get me a plain cheese pizza."

Dumb bitch. Slut.

I hang up, lean back in my chair and stare at the computer screen. *Hmmmm, on Charlie Boy's birthday, whenever that is, I think I'll sneak a new ingredient onto his pizza. Rat poison.*

• • •

He first came to my attention two years ago. I always get to work early and take the parking space next to the fifth lamppost three rows from the entrance to our building. I park there because the lamppost is easy to see from my office window and it's therefore easy for me to keep an eye on my car during the day.

On July 17 when I got to work, he was parked there. There were other parking spots open nearby, but he had parked in the spot left of the lamp post. My spot. The first time, I wrote if off as an innocent mistake because he was relatively new to the company. But it happened again a few days later, so after work, I waited in my car until he came out of the building, and then I calmly explained that he had parked in my spot.

"I can see my car from my office window," I said, forcing a smile and pointing up at the second floor.

"I didn't know we had assigned parking places," he replied smugly.

"We don't, but everyone knows that's my space," I said. "I've been parking there for five years now."

"I'll try to remember," he said before getting in his car and driving away.

The next day, he snubbed me in the cafeteria and it didn't take me too long to conclude that he was saying nasty things about me to our fellow coworkers. That SOB!

And this brings me to what I hate the most about Charlie. His fake optimism. He's the company cheerleader. *Rah Rah Rah, isn't everything great?* Mr. Happy! Of course we all know that in reality life is shit! But he pretends it's wonderful. In truth everybody hates working here, everybody hates Charlie and everybody talks about him behind his back.

The only personality trait (and I'm using the word "personality" loosely here because he really doesn't have a personality. It's more like a bad attitude) Anyway, the only thing more obnoxious than his insincerity is his hubris. When he had a cancer last year, he was always coming to work. It seemed like he didn't have any energy and he was obviously trying to show everyone up. I could almost hear him saying: "Look at me, everyone. I'm something, coming to work when I have cancer. I'm a model employee." That idiot. At the same time he had absolutely no consideration as to how having a guy with cancer in the workplace might affect other people! Amazingly inconsiderate!

He's also two faced, which is probably why he's in HR. Everyone knows what HR is like. After my divorce he pretended to be nice. I was feeling a little forlorn one day so when Charlie stood behind me in the food line in the cafeteria I mentioned what a psycho bitch my ex was. He nodded—and invited me to his church!

He said, "Keep you chin up this will pass!" I could not believe he took my ex-wife's side! He had never even met that whore! That's when I really came to understand how bitter, sick and twisted he is. That hateful SOB!

It was then that I decided to avoid him at all costs. He was dead to me!

But after a few days, I found myself thinking of him, day and night. After one particularly sleepless night, I resolved to make people see the real Charlie Bachman. Every few days I'd mention something about him to Sharon, who is not only a secretary and the company "pump," but more importantly is the company gossip. I'd come to work in the morning or return from lunch and casually say things like:

"What's that smell? Has Charlie from HR been here? I hate to say this but he smells bad. Terrible! He's got a hygiene problem . . . I think Charlie's got mental issues . . . He's retarded . . . Don't tell anyone but his wife made a pass at me at the company Christmas party . . . He's having an affair with a married woman in Finance . . . Did you see those flower-covered napkins he brought to the company picnic? How gay is that? . . . Didn't I see his name in the newspaper—something about a DUI? . . . you can tell by the way he talks that he's an idiot . . . The guy's a genius and thinks he's better than everyone else . . . Have you ever noticed that his head has a funny shape? I think that indicates some kind of mental handicap . . . I lent him $20 and he never paid me back. It's not the money, it's the principle . . . Has he dropped a lot of weight? Because I think he might have AIDS . . ."

I was trying to create a cyclone of pure hatred around him. I wanted people to despise him as much as I did. To loathe the miserable ground he walked on. If I was successful, perhaps someone would take matters into their own hands so I wouldn't have to. I was hoping that someone else would grow to hate him so much that they would kill him for me and therefore I could avoid jail.

Some people might call me a bare-faced liar and a coward, a bitter sick and twisted man, and they may be right. If that's what I am, it's because that's what Charlie has turned me into.

After the failure with Sharon, I thought I could get Lou in Shipping to kill him by telling Lou, who is black, that Charlie is a member of a white supremacist group and that they all dress like Nazis and walk around doing that Nazi salute while screaming "White Power!"

When I casually mentioned this to Lou one afternoon as he was doing some paperwork he shook his head. "What Charlie B from HR? No way. I really doubt that," he said. "He seems like a nice person to me."

I scoffed. "They all seem nice, until they're dressed like Hitler or the Klan and are burning your house down and lynching your family. I just want you and the brothers to know so you can take action before it's too late."

He stopped writing and looked at me over the rim of his glasses. "Take action?"

"Yeah action. Surely you're not going to let him get away with that!"

He put his pen down on the desk. "Get away with what?"

"Burning your house down. Killing your family. My God stop him now before it's too late!"

He seemed to be pondering what I had said then replied: "I think the Klan disappeared for the most part fifty years ago and besides I've got work to do. But I appreciate you bringing this to my attention. I'll bring it up at the next meeting of the Black Panthers."

I knew I couldn't rely on them taking action.

In the end, what I said about Charlie Boy didn't gain any traction. It was all lost on Sharon, Lou and the others. Anytime I tried to make people see what he's really like, they'd nod slowly then say something like: "I never noticed that. He doesn't seem like that kind of person to me."

I can't even say his name any more because it's like poison in my mouth. Now, I simply refer to him as "it." So one day, I bumped into "it" in the hall following a boring 30-minute presentation he gave our department on the merits of recycling, an idea he stole from me. That stinking, retarted, lying, two-faced bastard! It was idiotic Hawaiian Shirt Day, and he was wearing a pathetic red, blue and yellow shirt, which was the ugliest Hawaiian shirt I'd ever seen. He was walking right toward me, so I figured I had to say something. I know how to play the game.

"C-man, nice job on the presentation," I said with an earnest smile. "I really enjoyed it. You have some great recycling ideas there, you really do. Nice shirt by the way." *I wish I had a knife you miserable lying rat-faced rotten stinking low life. I'd like to rib your lungs out you sleazy back stabbing retard . . .*

He flashed a rehearsed smile. "Thanks Clive, I'm glad you enjoyed it. Every little bit helps. It's nice getting positive feedback." He motioned down the hall. "Are you headed back to your office?"

"Yes."

"I'm going over to Finance, I'll walk with you."

"Fine." *You overbearing egotistical pig.*

"So Clive how are things in your department?"

"My department? Never been better! Wonderful! Just great! Fantastic." *You condescending asshole! I'm sick of your superior attitude you moronic ass kisser. I'm going to cut your head off and put it on a pole you scumbag shit eating . . .*

"Glad to hear it," he said, patting me on the shoulder. "Sharon said you weren't feeling well, that you took some time off? Good to see you're back in the picture."

He was referring to the 14 days I'd spent in the hospital to get treatment for high blood pressure and ulcers. "Glad to be back! It was nothing really—just a little exhaustion. From working too hard I guess. Ha ha. I'm feeling 110 percent now. Better than ever. Absolutely amazingly great." *I'm sick of your pedantic lunatic ranting. I hope your kids die you mendacious suck-up scumbag piece of garbage.*

We reached the point where the hall takes a right turn toward Finance and we stopped walking. Suddenly I had a vision of him in flames. "I'm thinking of having a few people from work over for a cookout," I said as calmly as I could. "Interested in coming?"

"Sure just let me know when," he said with a wave. "See you later."

"See you later." *You bet you'll see me later you miserable sycophant.*

He's real bitter, sick and twisted. He tries to act like a great guy who's eager to help people. I see through his cheap charade. It's all bullshit, calculated brown nosing and sucking up to people so he can get ahead. I hate two-faced people and his behavior has condemned him to death . . . in my imagination. At least for now.

A few days later I was sitting at my desk, looking at Internet porn when a brilliant idea struck me: Develop a Strategic Plan for murdering Charlie Boy! My stinking retard boss, Penny, was gone for the day, so I started typing up bullet points ways of killing Charlie at work.

- Staple him to death.
- Decapitate him with the paper cutter
- Stab him in the eye/ear with a pen/pencil
- Strangle him with the phone/FAX/copier cord
- Jam his head in the file cabinet/drop file cabinet on his head
- Bludgeon him with the company training manual
- Choke him with Post-Its

After a while, I abandoned the Strategic Plan (it was much too confining) and started killing him any way and anywhere I could. I even stopped imagining that I'd make it look like an accident because a hateful two-faced guy like that deserves a painful death. (see car fantasy above.) You probably think I'm exaggerating but they didn't stop Hitler in time, and look what happened there.

I have one little fantasy I use to lull myself to sleep at night. Thinking about it calms me. I lure him into my basement on the pretense of helping me move an air conditioner, then kill him with a hatchet. He's always sucking up, offering to help people out, so I know he'll say "yes" when I tell him my back is bad and I need his help. I'll tell him it's my birthday, which is even better considering how he tricked the company into cancelling my birthday lunch.

In this fantasy, he comes over to my place, and I have plastic sheets down on the basement floor to catch the blood, because there will be lots of blood. When he asks; "What's the plastic sheeting for?" I smile and say, "I'm just doing a little painting."

So, we're down in the basement, and I ask him to move a few chairs so we can get at the air conditioner. When he turns his back, I whack him on the head with the hatchet—but not hard enough to kill him. This will take a while.

Now he's on the floor, and he turns to me with pleading, questioning eyes, blood gushing from his head. I laugh in his face, raise the hatchet and hit him over and over until the walls and floor are splattered with blood and brains. Finally, I chuckle and say: "Told you I was painting."

That fantasy has been immensely satisfying, but it is kind of messy, so I've started thinking about electrocuting him in his shower. That led to the idea of putting a poisonous snake in his bed, and that led to a sweet little fantasy where I invite him over for a BBQ, douse him with lighter fluid, set him ablaze and serve him to my neighbors. (See BBQ invitation above.)

The BBQ killing was great because it opened the flood gates to a slew of other fire fantasies where I light him up and he dies in painful infernos. The best one is an elaborate, ironic scheme in which I use his brown-nosing, *I'll help you* bullshit against him. I pretend to run out of gas on my way home from work, and of course he offers to bring me a gallon or two from the service station. When he comes back, I pour the gas over his head, then casually ignite him with my cigarette. I belong to a Civil War reenactment club, and I used to daydream about shooting him with a cannon.

One day, I came up with the idea of putting meat inside his pockets, then unleashing a dozen starved pit bulls which tear him to shreds. I've injected him with battery acid, beat him to death with a baseball bat and pushed him in front of a train, off a high building and over a cliff. I've stabbed him in the neck with a letter opener, kicked him to death, and planted bombs in his car, in his house and under his desk. It crossed my mind to pay a hit man to torture and kill him but that didn't last long because it wouldn't be nearly as satisfying as doing it myself.

I was at my desk, sketching out a plan for drowning Charlie Boy in the dunk tank at the company picnic, when the phone rang. Once again, it was the scheming, lying, stinking, twofaced, rotten, putrid, devious secretary Sharon.

"I wanted to remind you that there's a lunch meeting in conference room 306," she droned. "It starts in 15 minutes."

"Meeting?" I replied. "I wasn't told about any meeting."

"You didn't get the memo?"

"What memo?"

"It went out last week. It's a must-attend. No exceptions."

"I didn't get any memo, and I was planning on going to a gun shop to do some shopping at lunch."

"It's a must attend meeting," she repeated.

"Oh all right!"

"I almost forgot," she continued. "The boss called and said someone from HR has to be at the meeting. He specifically asked me to tell Charlie Bachman, but the phones are acting up again and I haven't been able to reach him. Can you stick your head in his office and tell him?"

"I really don't have time. Can't you just . . ."

She interrupts me. "Please. I have another meeting right now in the south wing. You have to walk right past his office to get to the conference room 306. I know it's last minute but . . ."

"Oh, for God's sake! Okay I'll tell him."

I hung up, finished sketching my plan for drowning you know who at the company picnic and got ready for the insipid meeting. God, I hate those lunch meetings! It's just another way for the company to steal more of your private time. I glanced out the window at my car (proudly parked in the space next to the fifth lamppost three rows from the entrance to our building) pulled on my suit jacket and left my office. On the way to the conference room, I passed Sharon's desk but she had already left.

When I got to Charlie's office, I paused in front of his door, which was closed. *There must be some way I can use this situation against him? Of course! I won't tell him about the meeting and he'll get fired for not attending "a must attend meeting!"* Sometimes, I'm surprised by my brilliance and ability to think on my feet. Just as I turned to quietly walk away, his ugly-ass door opened.

"Hi Clive," he said. "Did you knock?"

Is this guy creepy or what? "Did I knock? What do you mean?"

"Did you knock on my office door?"

"Yes. No. I was going to knock. Planning to knock but have yet to knock."

"I see. What's up? How can I help you?" He stared at me with deranged bulging eyes waiting for a reply.

You can drop dead! That would be a big help!

"Sharon asked me to tell you about some stupid meeting happening in Conference Room 306," I said. "But it sounds kind of informal, so if you can't make it, I'm sure they'll understand. I'll tell them you have a headache."

He looked perplexed. But of course he'd get perplexed at a traffic light. "Why didn't Sharon call me?" he asked.

Because you're a blithering idiot! "She said there's a problem with the phones."

"Again?"

What am I, the company phone expert? You low life. "That's what she said."

"I was planning on going out for lunch," he groaned, "but I'd better go to the meeting. Let me grab my suit coat."

Brownnoser!

"So, what's new?" he asked as we walked down the hall.

None of your business. That's what's new, you miserable prick. "What do you mean by that?" I asked.

He looked over at me. "I mean how's it going in accounting?"

You are unbelievable. The balls on you, asking me that. What are you going to ask next the balance of my bank account? My blood type? "It's going exactly the same as it was the last time we talked," I replied curtly.

"Oh, I see."

You see! You see! You don't see anything you parking space thief. You mangy dog. You . . .

We rounded the corner and stopped in front of Conference Room 306 where evil Charlie motioned with his arm for me to go first. I pushed open the door, and as soon as we stepped inside, everyone yelled "SURPRISE!"

"What the . . . !"

It seemed like half the company was there.

Skanky Sharon walked up and smiling widely, took Charlie Boy and me each by the hand and led us to a table with two birthday cakes and pizza.

"There was a computer problem," she said, smiling. "It's supposed to let us know about people's birthdays a few days in advance. Anyway, we just found out last week that we didn't have a birthday lunch for you on your birthday, Clive and since today's Charlie's birthday, we decided to have a double celebration."

She stepped back, grinned and threw up her hands. "Surprise!"

"Fantastic," Charlie replied.

Sharon handed us each a blue envelope containing a birthday card. Then everyone started singing a very off-key version of "Happy Birthday."

When they finished Charlie wrapped his arm around my shoulder. "Happy Birthday Clive," he said, raising his glass in a toast. "Birthdays are good for you. The more you have the longer you live."

What did he mean by that? Was it some sort of insult? Was he saying that I was adolescent, childish? *Another day older another day closer to a slow and painful death you wretched fool. Happy 'Deathday' you ignorant characterless HR idiot!*

I felt my blood pressure spike, but to my credit I ignored his hateful toast. I'm not going to stoop to his insidious level. Of course, I was pissed off and humiliated by the fact they had held my birthday party on the same day as Evil Charlie's birthday. Who wouldn't be? But there was nothing I could do about it, at least at the time.

We were still standing by the pizza table when Sharon walked up and held out a pair of lottery tickets. "I forgot to put a lottery ticket in each of your cards," she said. "Go ahead Clive take one."

I grabbed one, shoved it into my pocket and Charlie took the other one.

. . .

A week later I was on my way to the bathroom, after having done research on various techniques for keeping a dead body dumped in a lake from floating to the surface, when I ran into Howard from marketing. He's a moron bean counter type but at least he doesn't try to act all happy and shit.

"Hi H-Man," I said. "What's the good word?"

"Everyone's totally bummed out."

"Why?"

"Didn't you hear?"

"Hear what?"

He leaned against the wall and looked at the floor. "You didn't hear about it?"

"What?"

"Some guy in HR dropped dead yesterday."

My heart started pounding. "Human Resources? Whhhh . . . Whhooooo?"

"Charlie Backwards? Backoff . . . Backsomething . . ."

"Cha . . . Cha . . . Cha . . . . Charlie Bachman!"

"Yeah that's it. Poor guy dropped dead at his desk. Heart attack."

I started gasping for breath as tears welled in my eyes. "He's dea . . . de . . . dead . . . wha . . . wha . . . what?"

"Yep. Did you know him?"

"Deeeee . . . Deadddddd? What will I do now?"

"Are you alright? Were you two close?"

"Oh my God . . . Cha . . . Cha . . . Charlie. I can't breathe."

He placed his hand on my shoulder. "I didn't know he was a friend of yours. Sorry. Keep your chin up. This will pass."

The detachment in his voice sent a chill though me and I knocked his hand away.

"How dare you minimize Charlie's death! How dare . . ."

"I'm just saying his time was up. He went real fast. He didn't suffer."

I slumped against the wall. "You cold-hearted bastard! Charlie . . . Charlie?"

"My God you're hyperventilating. Are you Okay? Your color . . . . sit down."

"Can't live without . . . Cha . . . Cha . . . go on without . . . He's gone?"

"My God man you look terrible! I'm calling the company nurse!"

As I stared into the black abyss of H-Man's evil face a single thought echoed in my mind. "*You cold hearted, stinking, bean-counting egotistical piece of shit . . .*"

LOST KITTEN—ONE HUNDRED PERCENT CHANCE OF SNOW

SOMEWHERE, THERE IS AN AVALANCHE. A SOLID wave of snow and diamond-hard ice roars down the side of a mountain kicking up a 30-foot high plume of white as fir trees snap, and everything in the avalanche's quarter-mile wide pristine path is buried.

This image is pushing its way from the back to the front of your mind as you grope under the weather beaten front stairs of your home. It is almost midnight and you are searching for a lost kitten, the kitten that your ex-wife gave your nine-year-old daughter, Amy, as a birthday present a few weeks ago.

You cannot explain where this mental image of an avalanche is coming from. But in a way it is as unstoppable as a real avalanche. Perhaps this is just the way your mind works because you are a writer and you are trying to write a book. It is not going well.

You stand and brush dirt and bits of dried leaves from the knees of your rumpled blue jeans. Exhaling loudly, you tug up the worn leather collar of your jacket and curse under your breath as if answering the cold November wind taking direct aim at your exposed neck. You inhale deeply, clear your mind, then return to the task at hand. You drop to one knee and using your gloved hands like eyes you reach blindly under the front porch of your house and continue groping in the dark in a halfhearted attempt to find the kitten.

Some people search never expecting to find anything, and this is what you are doing. It is a hopeless pursuit. A hopeless pursuit . . . hmmm the way things are going that may be a good working title for your book.

This will be the last place you'll look before abandoning what you are sure is a futile midnight hunt. You don't expect to find the kitten. You are only searching to pacify Amy, who is inside pretending to sleep.

We all pretend . . .

You are sure the gray and white kitten froze solid within hours of disappearing three days ago. Or perhaps it survived for a few hours, then was dragged away by one of the jagged-toothed possums that lumber through the alley behind the house in the dead of night. Loss, you think, is part of life. But you do not want to lay this sad truth at your only child's feet, not just yet. A storm packing snow and more freezing temperatures is bearing down on the city. It will place a snowy exclamation mark on the whole damned thing, spelling an end to the kitten for sure. A kitten surviving three days outside in this weather would be like trying to survive . . . an avalanche.

Regardless, you will carry on with the charade, go through the motions, do the search, pretend there is a chance of finding the tiny animal. Perhaps, you think, love is all about pretending. You will sit Amy down on Monday, after the storm, and gently tell her that you will take her back to the animal shelter to pick out another pet. The kitten can be replaced. Everything, you think, can be replaced.

Amy named the kitten, "Sky," two weeks ago as she climbed into the back seat of your battered green Volvo. She was giggling and laughing with the tiny animal buried in the puffy arms of her winter jacket. She said she named the kitten "Sky" because its fur looked like the gray and white clouds tumbling silently overhead. You do not think "Sky" is an appropriate name for a cat. Cats should be named "Boots," "Felix" or "Daisy."

Amy immediately showered the kitten with love, cradling it in her arms like a baby and blowing gently on its stomach.

"Oh Dad, look, does he ever like this," she had said to you a day after she got the kitten. "Dad look he's laughing. It's tickling him. He's laughing!"

You could not believe how quickly Amy fell in love with the kitten, because you are a suspicious man and you do not trust or like cats. Why don't you like cats? You cannot explain why, except to say they give you an uneasy feeling.

In fact, you were mad as hell when Johanna gave the kitten to Amy for her ninth birthday. And don't get you started on Johanna! Two years earlier, she sat in the living room of the home you shared, calling you a "perpetual pessimist." "Perpetual pessimist" what the hell was that supposed to mean? She had lost her mind. That's what that meant. What else had she said? Oh right now you remember. She had said that you "don't care about anything!" You thought about how she said it, sitting on the living room sofa, her legs crossed, her black skirt crawling halfway up her thigh. Cigarette dangling from her fingers, she'd told you that you were a weight dragging her down. That's exactly what she said "draaggging meee doowwnn," eyes fixed on you, red lips curled into a hateful sneer. She hit you with verbal broadside after broadside, screaming that you never hoped for anything, that you accepted the good and bad with equal blasé. Finally, she buried her head full of black hair in her hands and told you that she just couldn't cope anymore.

You sat there impassively listening to her rant. Of course, she was wrong. You are a realist. Johanna was a dreamer. It was that simple. You understood life. If there's one thing you know it's this: false hope gives birth to crushed dreams.

Lying flat on your stomach you crawl forward trying to reach past a rose bush and farther under the front stairs. As you slowly crawl forward, a low hanging branch scratches your cheek. You quickly stand. A tear-sized drop of blood trickles down your face and dries on the orange stubble on your chin as a cold damp wind picks up handfuls of golden and brown elm leaves and throws them at your feet. After a moment you resume your search.

"Here kitty. Heeerrrre little kitty. Psssssst. Psssssssst," you whisper, stretching your words out as if they are made of rubber. "Come ooooonnnnn kitty kitty kitty. Heeeeeeeerrrrreee kitty. Pssssst."

The only light that is witness to your search comes from a single, dim bulb above the stairs and the blue glow from a street lamp across the road that hums and snaps in the chilly night air.

Amy had blamed herself for the kitten's disappearance. She was inconsolable. She'd left it alone in the back yard for a few minutes after school on an unusually warm Wednesday while she went inside to telephone her mother. When she came back the kitten was gone, as if some invisible hand had reached down from the clear, blue sky and plucked the animal off the lawn. She tore into the piles of leaves you had raked earlier in the week, but she came up empty handed.

Amy spent a dozen hours over the last two days perched on a rickety high back wooden chair staring out the kitchen window into the leaf covered backyard eagerly watching for any sign of the tiny animal.

You only agreed to this late night search after one of Amy's teachers had told her there would be a better chance of finding the kitten by searching late at night, after the commotion and noise of the day had faded with the evening twilight. Amy also convinced you that you should plaster the neighborhood with "Lost Kitten" notices. You didn't want to give your child false hope. Stupid hope. But you agreed to the posters because the mere idea of doing them lifted her spirits like one of the huge red and blue hot-air balloons pictured on her bedroom wall. You would go through the motions. By the end of the night Amy had convinced herself that someone would see the posters and call up to say they had found Sky.

• • •

The next morning after breakfast, you get up from the oval table in the middle of the kitchen, carry your cereal bowl to the sink, rinse it out and dry your hands on a dish towel.

Time to go through the motions.

You pull out a black marker and a crisp white sheet of paper from a drawer and cross the room to the table where Amy is already kneeling on a chair. Her expression is pensive.

"Dad, did you check under the stairs last night? Did you look everywhere? Did you check by the garbage cans?"

"Honey," you answer softly, "I checked all over the yard and under the stairs." You point to your cheek. "Look I even scratched my face on a bush."

An expression of concern forms on her face. "Does it sting?"

"No. It's only a scratch." You pull the cap off of the thick marker and the sharp smell of ink fills your nostrils. You lay the marker and paper on the table.

Amy grabs the marker and stares at the blank sheet of paper as if she is contemplating some deep truth. After a few seconds she carefully prints: "I've Lost My Kitten Named Sky. Have You Seen Him?" in even, inch high, black letters at the top of the white page. Underneath, in smaller letters, she describes the kitten. She stops briefly, stares at the page, and then carefully adds your address and telephone number. Finished, she lifts the piece of paper to her face, pushes back her long black bangs, and carefully examines the page as if it were a precious document.

"It looks great, Amy," you say. You stand and cross the kitchen to the window where Amy had been holding her vigil and quickly scan the back yard.

No sign of snow . . . yet.

Amy prints up eight "Lost Kitten" notices. She wants to do more but, quietly growing impatient, you tell her she has enough to canvas the neighborhood. You don't want to carry this charade too far. Amy filled with optimism and certain she is only hours from getting her kitten back, rushes to the closet by the back door and grabs her puffy winter jacket off a hanger, then pulls on the black boots with the silver buckles her mother gave her. You put on your coat and gloves, and together, you and Amy step outside into a brisk morning. The fall sun, hanging low in the east, casts off streaks of sunlight that stream through the filigree branches of the maple and elm trees, bathing the backyard in a soft yellow glow.

"Come on, Dad. Let's go. We've got to get these up!" Amy exclaims, without looking at you. "I want to hurry back in case anyone calls."

The wind is shifting uneasily from the west to the north. The maple and elm trees lining both sides on the narrow asphalt street have already surrendered their leaves, which blow around the street in tiny twisters of gold, red, green and yellow. Amy shuffles through the leaves, then stops at a large elm and staples a poster to the tree's rough brown skin.

Tiny flecks of snow begin floating down as she strides up to another tree, holds the poster against the tree trunk with one hand, and uses her other hand to staple the notice into place. She steps back to look at the poster. Seemingly satisfied, she walks toward another tree, then you hear someone calling her name.

"Oh, Amy! Did you find him?" a tiny girl with short yellow hair yells breathlessly as she runs up the sidewalk. "Last night, I dreamed you found him and he was all right. He was all right!"

It is Angela, one of Amy's good friends. She's lived around the corner since Amy was a baby. They are now both in grade four. There is no question that Angela is the unofficial leader of a small group of girls including Amy that seem to hold Angela in some kind of awe.

"Hi, Mr. Collins," Angela says smiling, her cheeks red from the cold. "Did you find Sky? Did you find him?"

"Not yet, but we're putting up notices," Amy answers, waving the remaining sheets of paper through the falling flakes.

"I'm out collecting leaves to press in a book. Look what I found!" Angela proudly holds out a brilliant, liquid-gold elm leaf with luminous green veins. "I want to get as many good ones as I can before they're covered with snow. That ruins them."

The two girls continue walking a little ahead of you stopping every few steps to pick up and compare leaves. They put up the last poster on a tall maple, then return to the sidewalk.

"Dad," Amy says. "I'm going to bring some leaves home to press too okay? This snow is going to cover them."

"You wouldn't like them so much if you had to rake them," you say in a joking way. "I'm just kidding Amy. Go ahead."

Amy twirls a huge, fiery-red maple leaf by the stem as Angela retrieves a similar specimen from the ground. Then Angela turns Amy away from you as you watch a couple get into a car parked at the curb. The two girls start to whisper, but you can still understand most of what they are saying.

"Let's make a wish," Angela says to Amy. "Let's make a wish that you get Sky back. Let's wish on these leaves. Let's wish that if we let them go, you'll get Sky back. Okay?"

"A wish?" Amy replies. "Okay, let's make a wish. Let's let them go. But we can't tell anybody, or it will be ruined."

Their innocence and naïveté make you smile.

The girls drop their leaves, and a gust of snow-filled wind snatches them up as if it had been waiting to return them to nature. Amy watches her red maple leaf tumble along the white ground, take flight and then disappear into a colorful whirlpool of other leaves.

"Don't you want your leaves any more Amy?" you ask.

"It's okay," Amy answers softly, turning toward home. "Can we go back now, in case somebody calls to say they found Sky?"

You say goodbye to Angela, and the two girls hug. Angela raises her mitten-covered hand to her eyes to protect them from the falling snow as she watches you and Amy walk toward home.

When you're almost there Amy stops, turns and points to your footprints in the freshly fallen snow. "Geez Dad," she says, smiling. "Your footprints are way bigger than mine."

You grin and look down at your daughter. "That's the way it should be, because I'm bigger than you."

"No, you're not," she says, beaming. "I'm bigger than you."

"Okay. Whatever you say honey."

Back inside, you grab a banged-up tea kettle off the stove and fill it with water. You turn on the burner, and it erupts with eel-like blue flames that lick at the bottom of the kettle. The flames warm your hands, still red and chilled from the walk. Amy drops her jacket by the back door, takes up her post on the old wooden chair at the kitchen window, and stares into the back yard.

You glance toward the window. The storm is building in intensity. Large snowflakes drift out of the sky, spinning down, dancing like miniature ballerinas, some pausing in the air before covering the grass, bushes and brown garden in a layer of pure white.

"Amy, do you want a cup of hot chocolate?" you ask without looking at your daughter. "And there's still a few Oreos."

Amy rests her chin in her hands with her elbows on the windowsill, her face inches from the glass. "No thanks," she answers without looking away from the yard.

You open a cupboard, then hear a thud on the floor behind you, followed by the familiar sound of your daughter running inside the house. You jerk around just in time to see Amy frantically yanking the back door open. She throws open the screen door and, without a word is gone.

You drop a paper packet of hot chocolate on the counter and run to the door. A cold blast of wind blows into the kitchen as you step outside, where Amy is crouched over in the middle of the yard. She has her back to you, huge snowflakes are settling on her black hair and tiny shoulders. She stands slowly and turns around.

She is holding Sky in her arms.

"I can't believe it. He came back!" Amy exclaims, her blues eyes dancing as she stands in the snow, hugging and kissing the kitten.

You walk silently through the falling snow to your daughter and gaze down at the kitten in her arms. Its fur is clean, and its wide yellow eyes are keen and alert. It is as if the storm has delivered the tiny kitten unharmed from some faraway place.

"Amazing," you mutter, thinking out loud. "Where have you been hiding? I thought . . . for sure . . ." You gently take Amy by the arm. "Come on honey let's go inside."

Back in the kitchen, you stir the hot chocolate as you watch Amy across the room, sitting next to the radiator, with Sky struggling to get out of her arms. But Amy refuses to let the kitten go and instead stands and walks back to the window. She is absolutely giddy with delight. "Dad, it's so pretty when it snows. The first time it snows in the fall, it changes everything." She's still snuggling the kitten. "Mum said little fairies come out when it's snowing, and they do magic."

Of course, that's exactly what Johanna would say. She doesn't have to shovel that god-awful, wet, heavy, heart-attack-causing snow.

Amy gazes down lovingly at Sky, now motionless in her arms. She lowers her head, snuggling the kitten, then cradles it like a baby. She blows gently on the tiny animal's belly, and he seems to tilt his head back and smile.

You stride across the kitchen and gently kiss your daughter on the forehead, then descend the stairs to the basement to look for a snow shovel. You are sure you left the damned thing down there last winter.

Somewhere, there is an avalanche.

THE LION'S EYES

I T'S MID JANUARY AND I'M WATCHING THE TV weather woman decked out in a pink outfit talking about the frigid low pressure front that has parked its icy ass over Chicago. I haven't gone out in two days because I've been off sick with a cold and I'm hoping she'll says it's going to warm up to, I don't know, minus 20 degrees!

No such luck.

"The Siberian Express cold weather front is over in Chicago, making for the coldest day in 17 years." She points to a computerized weather map behind her. "It's so cold outside, the birds are wearing parkas. But there is a silver lining, because this kind of front produces spectacular winter sunsets with some of the most dazzling shades of pink you'll see . . . if you dare to brave the cold, that is."

I reach for the TV remote control, hit the off button, and grab my coat, hat, and leather gloves from the hall closet. It's not that I *dare* to go outside, I think to myself as I lock my front door. I *have* to go outside because I haven't been out in two days and now I'm out of food and cash so I need to hit the ATM then the Lion's Head Pub for dinner.

I step outside the front door of my apartment building, and the frigid air seems to grab and shake me like a dog with an old shoe. The air is so freaking cold it actually stings. I hurry through the wrought iron gates in front my apartment building, then quickly stride down the sidewalk toward the ATM three blocks away.

Steam is rising from manhole covers and dancing ghost-like in the street. It's a few minutes before 5 on a Friday evening. The sidewalks are pretty much deserted, but after half a block I see a familiar figure walking toward me.

Frank.

I instantly recognize his lanky frame and familiar gait. He's wearing a Chicago Blackhawks jacket with a big Indian chief's head on the front. Frank always wears that jacket, regardless of the season, and as he approaches I can imagine the chief saying, "Hurry up, jag-off, I'm freezing."

But Frank's one of those people who seem oblivious to the weather, cold or hot. Some people are like that. They have a natural ability to handle weather extremes with equal blasé.

I'm glad to have run into Frank because I lent him $40 at the Lion's Head a week ago and he has not paid me back. He'd been chatting up some girl and when she gotten up to go to the bathroom, he'd japed me with his elbow and casually asked me to lend him a few bucks so he could buy more drinks and "close the deal." He swore he'd pay me back the following day but instead he'd done a disappearing act.

His head is down as he approaches. A green wool cap is pulled down snugly over his ears. When we are about 20 feet apart he suddenly looks up and grins. "Oh hey man, what's up? Cold enough to freeze the nuts off a bridge." He refuses to meet my gaze and instead motions to the east. "Lake's frozen solid. You could walk across it to Michigan."

I plunge my hands deeper into the pits of my pockets and shrug. "It's January in Chicago. What do you expect?"

"I guess so," he says as the chill in the air turns his words to steam. "Where you headed?"

I study his face for a moment, waiting for him to bring up the forty dollars. The bitter cold had tinged his cheeks with pink. "To the ATM," I answer, "then to the Lion's Head for dinner. Which reminds me. You got the money I lent you last week?"

"Oh that. Right, right." He casts his gaze onto the sidewalk as if it holds some great insight. "Right. I meant to call you."

He is actually shivering, and his teeth are chattering.

"Right," I reply in a monotone. I don't need the money; It's the principle of the thing. He said he'd pay me back, and I'm not going to be played for a sucker.

"Listen," he says, glancing up from the sidewalk. "It's freezing and I gotta do a few errands. I'll bring the money by the Lion's Head later. I'll buy you a few beers as interest. Okay?"

"I'll be there," I reply, transferring my weight from foot to foot in a futile attempt to get warm.

He flashes another grin, then quickly hurries past me.

I stride down the sidewalk toward the ATM as winter's icy fingers grope their way through my clothing causing my shoulder and neck muscles to tighten like steel cables. Lowering my head, I pick up my pace as rush hour traffic whizzes by. To my right, the top curve of the sun has just slipped behind the jagged city skyline as a bank of vibrant pink clouds crawls mutely across the sky.

Approaching the ATM, I pull my wallet from my pocket. My hands are numb so it takes me two tries to enter my password. After a few seconds the ATM whirs, then spits out three crisp $20 bills. To my surprise, they feel warm like they've just come from an oven. I slip the bills into my wallet, hurry across the road and round the corner onto Lunt Avenue. Sprinting down the sidewalk, I pass through tiny cyclones of dead leaves created by the wind in front of The Lion's Head.

I pull open the glass door, and as soon as I step inside, the warm air buffets me like a thick towel just pulled from a clothes dryer. The room, lit by the many grays of a winters' evening, resembles a black and white photograph. Two couples are sitting at a table having dinner and chatting, but the bar is empty. It's a little early for the dinner crowd, which is just how I like it.

I unzip my coat and rub my hands together trying to get some feeling back into them. Then I slide onto a bar stool directly under the old taxidermied lion's head that's mounted high on the wall, above two rows of liquor bottles. The bartender is rinsing glasses in a tiny sink and doesn't see me. I pull a pack of cigarettes from my pocket, tap one loose, and use a tea candle on the bar to light it. At that the young bartender glances up, wipes his hands on a towel and comes over to take my order.

"Evening," he says, placing his hands palm down on the bar. "You're a Heineken with a glass right?"

I nod and flick my cigarette over the ashtray as he turns toward the fridge. He's short and stocky with squinty eyes and a goatee. He looks a little like a hedgehog but he's a likable kid. He started working at the Lion's Head a month ago after Jill, the old bartender, was fired for stealing. His name is Dan, or Dean or Mike or Marty? Or it might have been Lionel. He's told me a dozen times but I always forget. I call him "Buddy," a good catchall name in any situation. He's 20 years younger than me, probably a student at Loyola. He puts my beer on a coaster beside a tall glass then looks at me and asks, "Menu?"

"I'll take a look."

He walks out from behind the bar and into the dining room. After a moment, he returns and places a menu on the bar beside my beer. "Just call me when you want to order."

"Sure, Buddy. I'll let you know."

I glance at the dinner specials, then push the menu away and look up at the TV in the corner above the bar. The news is on, and a reporter is talking about an old man killed in a hit-and-run as they show footage of his wife crying her eyes out asking: "Why, why?" over and over. *Why?* That is a word I have pretty much eliminated from my vocabulary. *Why? Because that's the way things are. That's why.*

The front door opens with a swoosh, and a blast of the Siberian Express Artic air rushes in, followed by a large man wearing an olive-colored parka with a fur trimmed hood covering his head. He stands there for a moment, his face concealed, then stomps his feet for warmth. After a moment, he pushes the hood back, revealing a smiling, unshaven and familiar face. It's Glen, one of the regulars—or in his case, an *irregular*. Glen comes into the Lion's Head all the time. He's from the neighborhood. My guess is that he lives in a nearby home for people *with issues*. Maybe he got dropped on his head as a child. I don't know. All I do know is that he can be a real pest with his moronic questions, and he's always tying to sell this really lame jewelry he makes. I'd guess he's around 40 although it's hard to tell how old someone like that really is. Last week he tried to sell me a ring that had what looked like a piece of chewed gum where the stone should be. He was really pushing it on me and wouldn't stop, so I told him to "bug off."

I don't want him to talk to me, so I lift my left hand to the side of my face and act like I'm totally absorbed in watching the news. There's a crib recall after an infant got stuck in one and suffocated, some CEO is going to prison for stealing his company blind, and a priest is in trouble for sexually abusing a bunch of kids.

I feel a solid tap on my shoulder. I turn to look and Glen is standing there, smiling his idiot smile, his hand outstretched. His hands and cheeks are tinged pink from the cold. His eyes, an intense, sparkling blue, are set deep in his rock-like face. His teeth are yellow and uneven. A bead of saliva is trickling down the left side of his chin, as usual.

"Hi there," he says. "I know you from here? I met you before? Hey, guess what? It's my birthday."

I know it's his birthday because every night for the previous few weeks, he's been dropping hints to anyone who would listen. He continuously told the waiters and waitresses, the bartenders, even the other customers that his birthday was approaching:

"My birthday's in ten days." "I'm an Aquarius." "I'm going to make you guys a cake for my birthday, a marble cake!" "I'm going to give everyone a present on my birthday and buy you guys drinks." "Some people put real money and stuff in birthday cakes. If a kid finds a gold coin in their piece of cake that means they going to be rich. If they find a thimble that means they're never going to get married."

I quickly shake his large hand, which is rough and cold as stone.

"Your birthday?" I say with mock surprise. "No kidding? Isn't that great. Have a happy birthday." *What are you, eight years old?*

I turn back to the television hoping he'll get the hint and go away.

Instead he claims the stool beside me.

Oh great. I keep watching the television, and grimace.

"Boy, he looks great today. Alive!"

I'm not sure if Glen is talking to me, himself, or someone else who has walked into the bar. So I ignore him.

"It looks like he's watching TV, don't it? Just look at him. I'd swear he's watching TV."

He taps my shoulder again and I turn just in time to see him motioning up at the lion's head.

"Look. He's watching TV!"

I exhale and glance up at the lion's head. It's turned slightly in the direction of the television, like it always is. It's been mounted high on the wall for as long as I've been going into the Lion's Head. It's old and wrinkled, with a shaggy mane. Its black lips are slightly parted showing yellowed teeth and a tip of pink tongue. Its brown eyes look moist and tired. It seems to be staring solemnly past the television, through the wall, and into another place—a dream world. I imagine the owners bought it for fifty bucks at a yard sale.

"Nice taxidermy job," I mutter under my breath. "They must have shot it when it was sleeping."

Glen mistakes my snide remark for conversation and immediately responds.

"I couldn't kill an animal, even if it was an animal that could eat me. Even a small animal like a turtle or a bird. Maybe I could kill a worm." He pauses for a moment, then exclaims: "A lion's the King of Kings!"

I'm tempted to correct him; to tell him what he means is that the lion's king of the jungle. But I don't want to engage him, so I sip my beer and look at the TV.

After a minute, Glen turns his attention to the bartender, who is slouched over a newspaper. "Hey Tony. You going to the peace rally on Sunday?"

The bartender responds very unenthusiastically without looking up. "I don't know. I'm trying to do something right now."

Glen slumps on his stool as if suddenly deflated.

"Okay, I'm sorry. I was just wondering." Then, to no one in particular he says: "We're going to get in on next Saturday night!"

I lean away from him, moving to the edge of the bar stool as two waitresses emerge from the dining room and order drinks.

Tony starts making the drinks as the waitresses linger at the bar, chatting.

Glen straightens on his stool, smiles broadly as if recharged, and turns toward the waitresses.

"Hi, Carol. I told my friend about you. He wants to meet you. I'm going to bring him in here next week, okay?"

The waitress he is talking to is in her mid-20s with long black hair, dark eyes, and a slim figure. She whispers something to the other waitress then straightens a pile of menus and looks at Glen with a hard smile. "I told you, Glen! I have a boyfriend. He'd get mad if I started meeting other guys." Then she leans against the bar and in a kind tone adds: "Thanks for thinking of me, though."

Everyone treats him okay. They put up with him, I guess.

Glen nods rapidly. "A boyfriend?" he says. "Oh, I forgot. That's okay. My buddy can find another girl."

There is blissful silence for a few minutes but I can sense Glen beside me, his mouth agape as he looks around the room like a child at a circus. Then:

"He seen it when Jill was stealing money from the register. Yeah, he seen it."

I glance to my left, and Glen is once again staring wistfully up at the lion's head.

"Yep he sees it all," he continues. "He sees the world the same way a tree sees the world. The world moves around it. The King sees it all."

I take a drink of beer and a drag from my cigarette then turn back to the television, but I cannot block the sound of his voice. It is as if there are just the two of us in the room, two of us in the world, and he is talking directly into my ear.

"He watches," he says. "He sees the drunks in here. He seen it when that guy slapped his girlfriend last week and made her cry and her lip bleed . . ."

I scan the room looking for a table as Glen leans against the bar and continues staring up at the lion's head.

"He seen the oil wells burning in the desert. He seen that face, the demon face in those black fires. He sees little kids hunting for dinner in garbage dumps, people dying with AIDS. He sees the liars, the cheats. He seen the buildings fall in New York. He sees it all. He's the King!"

I snatch my beer and cigarettes off the bar and start to stand up. But before I can move to a table, I see a fiery glow in the doorway between the bar and restaurant. Some of the people who work there are carrying something . . . a cake, with pink candles. It's a birthday cake. They're smiling and singing "Happy Birthday." Carol, the waitress, places a wrapped present on the bar and kisses Glen lightly on the cheek.

"Happy birthday Glen," she says sweetly. As they put the cake in front of Glen, the heat from the candles brushes my face.

Out of the corner of my eye, I notice Frank walking in. He comes over, leans on the bar, and motions to Glen and the cake.

"What's up," he whispers, "a party for the 'tard?"

"I guess . . ."

I turn back toward Glen as the glow from the candles dance across his weathered face. His mouth is partly open and his eyes are wide as he stares down at the birthday cake. Someone yells, "Go ahead, Glen. Make a wish and blow out the candles."

Glen inhales deeply, then blows out all of the candles in a single breath, spitting a little on the cake and bar. Everyone applauds. Carol cuts the cake, and Glen, still grinning widely, hands it around on plates.

He puts a piece of cake in front of me but I hardly notice because my attention is suddenly drawn up to the lion's head. I could swear that lion is smiling, and a tear is running down its tired cheek.

SIMON'S GREAT LIE

W E ARE ALL LIARS TO ONE DEGREE or another. We deceive. We tell half-truths. We mislead. Sweet lies roll of our lips like honey. But some lies, like some people, are worse than others.

Simon's lie is especially atrocious.

Simon claims to have jammed, that is he says he played guitar with, Kurt Cobain.

If you don't know who Kurt Cobain was you can stop reading right now because you must be a complete idiot. I take that back. Keep reading, because what I have to say is vitally important. Kurt Cobain was the lead singer, songwriter, guitar player and genius in a power trio out of Seattle called, Nirvana. In 1990, they single-handedly created the worldwide music phenomena known as grunge rock. Their punk rock influenced melodic sound changed the face of music forever and helped them sell a billion records. They were the best, hardest rocking band in the world . . . that is, until Kurt, killed himself in the greenhouse of his Seattle home on April 8, 1994. In memory of Kurt, I take that day off work every year and listen to Nirvana CDs.

In case you haven't figured it out by now, I'm Nirvana's biggest fan.

I'm also a defender of the truth. The most important truth being that Nirvana is the best rock band ever, better than Green Day and Pearl Jam combined. Well at least better than Pearl Jam. I'm sure Kurt Cobain would agree.

Truth is as pure as pain; it cannot, *must* not, be contaminated. Legend counts.

That's why I am determined to rip Simon's "I jammed with Kurt Cobain" lie to shreds.

Most lies, especially elaborate lies, are a house of cards. Remove one card and . . .

I stayed up most of last night, searching the Internet for the wrecking ball I'll need to expose Simon's lie. At 4 a.m., I finally found exactly what I was looking for: a listing of all of Nirvana's tours and the cities and venues they played, from the early years up to the end. This information is my Holy Grail because Simon tells everyone that he meets that he jammed with, Kurt Cobain, and the two other guys in his band Nirvana, after they'd played a show at The Riveria Club in Chicago. My research proved that Nirvana never played there. They played shows at the Metro and the Aragon Ballroom, other Chicago music venues, but they never played "The Riv." Never!

Lies unravel in the details.

Sitting at the breakfast table, gleefully munching cereal, I carefully review the list. I hear a door open; my roommate Greg, stumbles out of his bedroom wearing boxer shorts and a tattered T-shirt. He scratches his chest, mumbles something inaudible, then joins me in our tiny kitchen.

Dipping a spoon into my bowl, I chase the last few floating Cheerios, then eye the printout as Greg forages, animal-like, through the cupboards and the fridge. Then he drops into the seat beside me with a bowl of Captain Crunch in his hand.

"I can't believe we're out of coffee," he moans. "You said you'd bring some home from work."

I'm a barista at a coffee shop called Head Diesel. The pay is shit, but I get one good perk: all the ground coffee I can steal.

"Yeah," I reply. "I meant to grab a fresh-ground pound yesterday but forgot."

Without warning Greg launches into a verbal tirade. "You forgot?" he cries, pounding the table with his fist. "You forgot yesterday and the day before. Don't you understand? I need a cup of coffee in the morning to get going." His eyes are bulging out of his head, his face is a shade of deep crimson and the tendons on his neck are sticking out like rope. "When you moved in here you promised we'd always have fresh coffee from that place you work. That was the reason we took you on as a roommate, the promise of an endless coffee supply. Now you tell me you forgot to bring it home?"

"There's some green tea," I say in a weak attempt to defuse the whole whacky situation.

From his expression of utter dismay I might as well have offered him a cup of piss. "Tea? Are you kidding me? I need coffee. Coffee! Not tea. Who drinks tea?"

"Tea is actually better for you than . . ." He cuts me off.

"I'll tell you who drinks tea," he practically screams. "People in China drink tea. English people love their tea. People in India drink it by the gallon. You know who else drinks tea? Terrorists in Afghanistan drink tea. They sit around, drinking tea, and talk about killing people and blowing things up. Not me! I'm not a murdering tea drinker. Don't you understand? I'm an American! I drink coffee! But in reality, I *don't* drink coffee because we don't have any coffee because once again you forgot to bring coffee home! Now you're offering me tea. Do I look like a tea drinking terrorist to you? Do I?"

"No," I blurt, "you don't look like a tea-drinking terrorist. You look like a crazy American."

"What?"

"Are you losing your mind? Relax before you stroke out. I'll bring home five pounds of Jamaican Blue mountain *coffee* tonight. I promise, all right?"

He exhales loudly, and shakes his head. It appears as if he is regaining his sanity. "You promise to bring some home tonight?" he asks.

"No problema."

Greg nods weakly then rubs his bloodshot eyes. "Oh, man what a night. I should have stopped when those two girls bought me tequila shots."

If Greg were a dog he'd be a Golden Lab. Once he's had a cup of coffee, he's an easygoing, friendly guy, and that, combined with his short dyed-blond hair and athletic build always gets him lots of attention from women. He often regales me with stories about the girls he meets.

"I was so messed up," he rasps, between spoons full of cereal. "All I can remember is that it was one of their birthdays. I think it was the blonde?"

"So there was a party?"

"Yeah, with a birthday cake, presents, the whole enchilada."

"Nice."

"It would have been, but I blew it because I didn't get either of their phone numbers." He pauses, and I can tell he's trying to retrieve a memory through the dense fog of the previous night. "I think I remember one of them kissing me—or slapping my face." He rubs his left cheek then leans back in the chair and nods at the newspaper. "Can I see that?"

I slide the paper across the table, then gather up my dishes and put them in the kitchen sink.

When I go back into the dining room, Greg is engrossed in the sports page. "Hey, what's up tonight?" he asks without looking at me.

"I'm meeting Simon and Robert at Mather's Pub. It's darts night."

"Simon . . . Simon?" he says, looking up at me over the newspaper, obviously trying to put a face to the name. "Simon, that's the guy that jammed with Kurt Cobain right?"

I wince. "You don't actually believe that crap, do you?"

Greg resumes eating his cereal. "I don't know; it probably happened. Somebody else told me they believed it."

I feel like one of those angry cartoon characters with steam blasting out of its ears. It is infuriating to me that anyone can have bought into such an incredible and obvious lie. "They believed it!" I scoff. "How can anyone believe it?"

I've heard Simon tell his lie to people in bars and also to a punk rock girl on the El. It's total bullshit. He said he jammed with Kurt Cobain a few years before Nirvana hit the big time, sold a zillion records and were catapulted to rock and roll superstardom. When I asked Simon why he hadn't told me about this before, he just shrugged his heavy shoulder and said he forgot! *Yeah, right, he forgot!* That's like someone saying they forgot they had tea with the Queen of England. Now, people respectfully refer to Simon as *the guy who jammed with Cobain.*

If anyone jammed with Cobain, it should have been me!

Greg closes the newspaper, leans back in his chair and shoots me a dismissive look. "Simon's all right. That guy's had a hard life."

"Hard life or not," I blurt, "he can't go around saying he jammed with Kurt Cobain. It's not right." I grab the printout off the table and wave the pages through the air like a victory flag. "And I can prove it!"

Greg erupts into a series of dry coughs, eases up from the table and brushes past me. Then he staggers into the living room, flops onto the sofa and grabs the remote control off the coffee table. "I don't know why it matters that much to you," he says. "Simon's an artist, right? A painter? I guess it's a creative thing." He yawns and points the remote at the television.

I stride into the living room and block his view of the TV. "Don't you understand why this bugs me?" I ask. "It's like someone saying they played with The Beatles back in Liverpool before they were on the music radar screen."

Greg passes his hand through the air. "Dude, you're in the way."

I stand my ground and try to come up with a more contemporary comparison. Greg likes rap so I offer an analogy he can relate to: "It's like saying he rapped with Tupac in Oakland, back in the day before he sold any records." I stare at Greg sharply, waiting for him to acknowledge my point.

"Dude," he says shifting his weight on the sofa. "I can't see the television."

There is no way I'm going to move until he accepts the importance of what I am saying. "The truth's significant and Simon's revising history. Cobain's only been gone less than 20 years. It's like denying the Holocaust or the attacks on Pearl Harbor!"

Greg snorts loudly, like a dog, then gets off the sofa and nudges me out of the way. "Let it go man," he mutters, his unshaven face inches from mine. "Lighten up, will you. I want to catch some scores from last night."

It's totally useless trying to make him see the light so I turn away in anger. "I've got to get ready for work." I go into my room, stick the computer printout and a set of darts inside my knapsack and zip it closed. Then grab a sweater and a denim jacket from the closet. On the way out, I pause and glance into the living room. Greg is snoozing on the sofa, his mouth half open and crooked. The remote control is still in his hand.

• • •

Walking to the bus stop, I button my jacket and hoist the knapsack onto my shoulder. The air is cool, the sky a soupy wet cement gray. I am not mentally prepared for winter, the cold, the snow and short days. Just the thought of it makes me shiver, like a lonely dried up leaf on a tree.

Smoking warms me, so when I get to the bus stop I drop my knapsack at my feet, unzip the front pocket and pull out a pack of Camels and my red Bic lighter. Of course, no sooner do I finished lighting my cigarette, when the damned bus rolls up and the doors open with a *swoooooosh*. Muttering under my breath, I glance down at the cigarette. The bus driver, a woman in her 40s with a bad perm, looks me up and down as I flick the cigarette into the gutter and grab my knapsack off the ground. I climb on board and take a seat near the back.

The 20-minute ride is followed by a three-block walk to Head Diesel. I got the job a few months ago after a friend of mine who used to work there quit. His ex-girlfriend, Lilly, worked there too, and before she dated him, she'd dated Simon, who I already knew from another friend, Chris, who I no longer hang around with. We are all into Nirvana, and grunge music in general, but after Cobain died, Chris started listening to Metallica! I couldn't believe it, and I haven't talked to him much since that. Am I a purist? I guess so, or at least I have musical standards.

Lilly and I sometimes talk about Simon when things are slow at work. She doesn't have many details, except to say that he was locked up in a mental ward for a couple of weeks after swallowing about 30 sleeping pills. She once told me that he suffers from depression. Yeah, right! Who doesn't suffer from depression! *Life is depression!*

I push open the heavy glass door and walk into Head Diesel. It's a funky, long, narrow café with exposed brick on one wall where the boss, Geoffrey, hangs shitty paintings by local artists. A counter and a glass display case with muffins-laden baskets and cookies runs half the length of the other wall. I guess the café was considered a "hippy hangout" a million years ago, when people would come in to read poetry or whatever. I consider working there to be a kind of badge or honor. It beats working for a bank, The Gap, or that Seattle-based café retail chain that's taking over the world. You know the one. I won't do them the honor of naming them here. It's hard to believe that that money grubbing company and Nirvana both started in the Seattle area. I'd bet a month's pay that Kurt Cobain never went into that corporate coffee shop.

The aroma of fresh-brewed coffee is a nice counterpoint to the cold air outside. Business is slow so Lilly is leaning into the counter filing her nails. I mutter "Hi," hurry past her, put my knapsack and jacket on a chair in the office and go back out front.

Since I am a truthful person, I must admit that I was attracted to Lilly when I first started working at Head Diesel. "Attracted" may be a little bit of an understatement, because in reality I just wanted to have sex with her. But she never showed any feelings, hot or cold, for me. She's definitely a 'counter-culture girl,' a waif with three piercings in her right ear and a small silver hoop in her left eyebrow. Her shoulder length jet black hair is in sharp contrast to her round face, which is either intentionally pale as a result of makeup or unintentionally sickly due to a lack or iron in her diet. Her purplish lipstick and nail polish are a perfect complement to her dark clothing.

I walk behind the counter and check the coffee pots which are half empty. "I'll start some java," I say, turning toward the sink.

Lilly finishes filing her nails, then holds out her hand like a fan and examines her work. "Already started it," she replies without looking at me. "You can fill the water container."

She's talking about the lousy 10-gallon thermos with a spout we keep on the end of the counter for customers. Everyone knows I have a bad back hate lugging around that heavy-as-hell container. Still, Lilly doesn't have the strength do to it, so I grab the frigging thing, lug it out back, fill it with water and drag it back to the counter.

As I'm struggling to hoist it onto the counter, I glance over at Lilly, who is calmly using tongs to rearrange the muffins in a large wicker basket. Her muffin-shifting routine really bugs me. Whenever business is slow, she moves the blueberry muffins to the front of the basket; then ten minutes later, she moves them to the back, and moves the banana nut muffins to the front. This despite the fact that no has bought a single muffin in the intervening 10 minutes. She moves the chocolate-chip and peanut butter cookies around in the same infuriating way! And she always seems so damned pleased with herself, as if she is accomplishing some great feat.

Still panting from the heavy lift, I lean against the counter and watch her.

"Simon was in earlier," she says, placing the tongs on the counter. "He said he'd see you tonight . . . something about darts?"

"Yeah, it's Darts Night at Mather's," I say, as a sly smile crosses my lips. "And my darts are especially sharp."

Lilly's face seems to form a question mark. "Sharp is good, I guess."

I reach for the coffee pot and pour myself a cup, then dump in cream and sugar, take a sip and lean against the counter. "Did Simon ever tell you his story about playing guitar with Kurt Cobain?"

Lilly sighs dramatically and for the first time since I got to work, makes eye contact with me. "Yeah, I heard about it."

"Do you believe it?"

My question seems to make her uneasy: She turns away, pours the contents of the tip jar onto the counter and start counting it. "Wasn't there, like, someone else there, a witness or something?" she asks as she stacks the coins into tiny pillars. "It was a friend of Simons' but the guy's dead now?" She stops counting and stares up at the ceiling as if trying to remember. "I think I saw a picture of him with Cobain, a few years ago, at some party. It was late, and I can't remember if I actually saw the picture, or if someone told me and I imagined seeing it."

That is so like her: ditzy. It doesn't matter, because I know that the mysterious photograph is just part of Simon's lie.

An old woman in a heavy coat and wool cap comes in and orders a large coffee to go. I pour it into a cardboard cup and take her money as Lilly scoops up the tips and exchanges them for bills from the register.

"You know," Lilly says, turning back to me, "I visited Simon when he was locked up in that mental ward. Very scary place. He cried all the time." Her eyes darken. "It's kind of odd seeing a big bear of a guy like that crying." She picks up the tongs and starts rearranging the cookies. "It shocked me, seeing him like that," she says, holding up a peanut butter cookie with the tongs. "He was embarrassed that people knew he'd tried to kill himself."

I take a sip of coffee. "Oh *that's* it then," I say triumphantly. "He's just crazy, and this whole I jammed with Cobain thing is some kind of weird delusion?"

This bugs her, because she places the tongs on the counter and shoots me an angry look. "Simon's a little whacked. That doesn't mean he's lying or delusional. I don't care either way." She plants her hands on the counter and stares at me. "I like Simon, even though I never got into Nirvana," she says, her voice stern as if scolding a child. "Too intense. I mean, it was sad and everything . . ." She shrugs and backs away from the counter. "I don't think they ever did a positive song. Not one single love song. They were anti-everything, and besides . . ."

I spill my coffee as I interrupt her. "They explored darker themes! There has to be a voice for hopelessness and alienation. The anti-everything, nihilistic attitude is part of the punk ethos."

"Uh-huh, whatever," she says, nodding her head in a mocking way. "I really didn't care for the last act, either. Cobain and his wife, what's her name, had a little girl. I can't imagine leaving a child behind like that."

My reply gets lodged in my throat. "Nothing could have saved him," I blurt after a moment. "Don't you understand? That's the point. Depression . . . it was his destiny, like Jesus. There was no other way for him. The man, his music, his life and death were a . . ." For a moment words fail me. Then I shout: "A manifesto!" I'm not sure if that's exactly what I want to say, but that's what comes out.

Lilly looks absolutely horrified. She raises a boney hand to her mouth and steps back toward the counter. "Like Jesus? A manifesto? Are you serious?" Her thin black eyebrows arch. "He was more like a cautionary tale."

I can feel my blood pressure spiking. "A cautionary tale! He was a great artist . . ."

"It was all about 'him,' and the bleakness he felt," she says waving her hand in a dismissive way. "He was an artist, a very gifted artist. But he was entirely focused on himself and his pain and . . ."

I cut her off. "That was his truth! He rocked!"

She sighs and rolls her eyes. "Life is a struggle, but it's not just darkness. Maybe he didn't have enough love as a child. He was a product of that, and, he channeled that, that loss, that emptiness. There was one song where he sings about his gastric juices. Come on, give me a break!"

"You just don't get it."

She places her hands palms down on the counter and glares at me. "He had the worst case of 'me-ism' I've ever seen. It just so happens he was really blessed . . . or cursed . . . with the ability to put his dark feelings of 'alienation' to a catchy melody, and had great musicians backing him up."

She's right about his talent and his band, but I don't want to agree with anything she says, so I just grunt.

"You ever heard of the painter Vincent Van Gogh?" she asks.

"Of course." I raise my hand to my ear. "He cut his ear off!"

"The guy was one of the greatest painters ever," she quips, "and all anyone remembers is that he cut his ear off."

I shrug and she continues.

"Anyway, he was the poster boy for depression, but at least he celebrated life, living and light in his paintings. Cobain was a product of his time and the media looking for anything that expressed some kind of real emotion, nothing more and certainly nothing eternal. Kids were starved for something real in music, and he supplied it." She leans against the counter and folds her arms across her chest. "Sorry, but that's the way I see it." Then she smiles wryly and asks; "Know what could have saved him?"

"What?"

"The guy should have learned to dance. It would have saved him from himself."

"Learned to dance? What the . . ."

"That's right! He should have learned to dance, and you should too. Life demands it."

My fists and teeth are clenched. "The whole point is, he didn't *want* to dance! I mean to live! He didn't want to *live!*"

I think I frightened her, because she looks real nervous, then mutters something like "Junkies will do that," or "Flunkies have bad backs." Then she turns away, pulls a bag of coffee beans from under the counter and pours them into the grinder.

I stand there absolutely furious, staring at her narrow back and thin white neck. "Dancing is for idiots," I scoff. "Life demands it? Ha. What a bunch of bullshit."

She keeps her back to me, pretending she can't hear above the whir of the grinder. After a few moments I dump my coffee in the sink, then go outside to have a cigarette and calm down.

It's freezing without my jacket, but I'm so angry I don't care. Lilly is way off-base, misguided and misinformed. Poor girl. It's useless trying to have a meaningful conversation with her about one of the true gods of rock. Some people are beyond reach. I slowly grind my cigarette butt into the sidewalk with my foot and go back inside. I leave after my shift is done without saying anything to her.

• • •

On the way to Mather's Pub I tug up my jacket collar against a biting wind. It's getting dark and the streetlights are casting an eerie white glow onto the sidewalk.

My plan is simple. I'll casually ask Simon about some detail of his imaginary jam session. He *loves* talking about it, and once he gets started, I'll methodically take his lie apart piece by frigging piece. I imagine him reduced to tears. Not that I mean to hurt the guy. I simply want to see him pay for telling such a disgusting lie.

I pull open the pub's heavy glass door and a blanket of warm air engulfs me. Pausing, I shove my wool cap and gloves into my knapsack and scan the room, which is filled with people talking and laughing.

Simon's looks like a tank with bad acne, and I immediately spot him wearing a flannel shirt that reminds me of a tablecloth. He's hunched over a table by the dartboard, talking to some guy I don't know. I stride over to the table and set down my knapsack.

"Hey, man," Simon says with a wheeze as he turns toward me. He pats me on the back, then motions toward the bar. "Grab a beer."

The guy Simon is talking to is totally engrossed in whatever Simon has been telling him and doesn't notice me.

I order a bottle of Bud at the bar and take it back to the table, where Simon and the other guy are laughing loudly. I stand there for a few seconds then pull my darts from the front pocket of my knapsack and lay them on the table beside Simon's darts.

He stops laughing and motions to the other guy. "This is . . . what's your name again, dude?"

"Peter," the guy replies with what sound like an English accent. I'd guess he is in his early 20s. And considering his spiked blond hair, black T-shirt and black pants, I figure he's a musician. The guy's so tall and gaunt, I imagine that in profile he'd be invisible.

"Peter plays bass in a band," Simon says.

Peter lifts his glass and nods.

"And it's his birthday today!" Simon adds.

I glance over at Peter. "It's your birthday?"

"That's right mate."

"Well, let me the first to wish you a . . ."

Simon cuts me off. "It's Liverpool, right?" he asks Peter. "You're from Liverpool?"

Peter nods.

"Great place. Never been there," Simon says. "Anyway, we got to talking while I was waiting for you. I was telling him about the time I jammed with Kurt Cobain. Peter's a big Nirvana fan."

I can't believe my timing! Plus, my ambush will yield extra satisfaction if I can spring it on Simon in front of somebody. Considering the graveness of the lie, he deserves it. I look over at Simon who is stroking his chin thoughtfully.

"I just remembered something," he says, turning to Peter, "Oh, my God this is Cobain's birthday too!"

A wide smile spreads across Peter's face. "It is? I never knew that, mate. That's friggin brilliant!"

I figure Simon is telling another lie, but I don't say anything because I'm not sure. I used to know when Cobain's birthday is, but I cannot remember. I make a mental note to look it up when I get home.

I pick up my darts and stand a few feet from the table in front of the dartboard, listening for a chance to spring my trap.

Simon takes a long drink of beer, then belches and puts his glass back on the table. "Now, this was back innnnn . . . 1992—a couple of years before Nirvana hit the big time. They were touring, just like a million other bands trying to make it."

I throw a dart and miss the board by a foot. "Simon," I exclaim, turning toward the table. "Nirvana were huge in '92 biggest rock band on the planet. Their record was on top of the charts. Ninety-two? No way! You can't be right. That's bullshit."

My point was is like water off a lying duck's back. Simon reaches for his cigarette and glances at me. "My mistake," he says, taking a drag. "You're right. It was 1990. Anyway, my friend Carl knew they were a great rocking band so we went down to check them out."

I throw my second dart and miss the board again. "Carl?" I ask sarcastically, clenching the third dart in my fist. "Carl was killed in a car accident three years ago. He's the only guy who was with you? Your only witness?"

"Yep," Simon answers. "That's right."

It's outrageous to me that Simon would use a dead person's good name to validate his lie, but I let it slide and turn toward the dartboard.

"So," Simon continues, "they were playing at The Riv, but there weren't many people there . . ."

BAM! He's walked right into my trap. I scoff loudly, throw the third dart, almost hitting the bull's eye, then march over to the table. "No way, Simon," I say. "Nirvana never played the Riv! I checked. They played the Metro. It's a hard rock venue. I can say for sure Nirvana never played the Riv!"

There is fear in Simon's eyes as I reach for my knapsack.

"As a matter of fact I happen to have a list I got off the Net of all the venues Nirvana ever played." I pull out the list and slap in down on the table beside Simon's darts. "Here. Take a look."

He glances at the list in what I can only describe as a casual manner. I stare at him sharply, waiting for a reply.

"Oh, yeah?" he says after a moment. "I'll have to check that out. It was a long time ago." He stops talking and seems to be pondering my point. "I suppose it could have been the Metro. I was pretty drunk by the time we got there." Then he waves his hand through the smoky air in a dismissive way. "Nope. No," he says adamantly. "I'm sure it was at the Riv." He motions toward the printout with his paw-like hand. "Your list isn't complete."

"What do you mean, 'isn't complete?' It's from the Internet!"

"The Internet's useless," he smirks, "except as a conduit for useless information."

I try to challenge him on this, but he ignores me and goes on for a few minutes, telling this Peter guy all about the Nirvana show and how great it was. It seem like Peter only knows two words; "no shit," because he says them in an excited way every time Simon finishes a sentence.

"So anyway," Simon continues, turning toward me. "We sitting there in the *Riv*, and Cobain announces from the stage that the band is looking for a place to crash that night, something about being tossed out of their hotel."

"No shit," Peter says, his eyes wide.

My ears are ringing, and it feels as if my seat is charged with electricity. I'm tempted to throw my hands up, call Simon a bullshitter and storm out. But I know that the most fantastic part of his lie is coming, and I'm ready.

Simon snubs his cigarette out in an ashtray. "When they finished playing, Carl walked up to Kurt and told him they could stay at his place because his parents were out of town."

"No shit!" Peter exclaims.

Simon pauses for dramatic effect then takes a drink of beer. He looks around as if collecting himself to spew forth the last part of his enormous lie, then lowers his voice to just above a whisper. "We were all drinking back at Carl's place when Cobain pulled his guitar out of the case and told me he was working on a new song based on some *Boston* riff. He played it for me. It was "Smells Like Teen Spirit," what later became their biggest hit. I said, 'Wow, man, that's a great song. Kind of basic, but rockin!'"

Peter's mouth is now agape. "No shit!"

"Yeah man, no shit," says Simon, grinning wildly. "Meeting them was a real high point of my life."

"I imagine," Peter says breathlessly. "Brilliant."

"So, Cobain told me the song needed a bridge. He handed me his guitar, and I showed him a bridge. It ended up in the song. It was a major A cord and a diminished seventh."

Diminished seventh! Diminished seventh! I'm completely incredulous. Anyone who's ever picked up a guitar knows that's not the bridge in that song!

"No way, Simon!" I seethe. "That's not the bridge in 'Smells Like Teen Spirit.' It's more like smells like pure bullshit!" I know I have him on this point so I persist. "Plus Simon, Cobain played left-handed, and you play right-handed, so how could you play his guitar man? Huh?"

He sighs and shrugs his heavy shoulders. "Oh, yeah, you're right," he says, his wheeze getting worse. "I played another guitar that was sitting around. That's what it was. Carl had a guitar, so we all jammed."

Simon continues as a grin spreads across his chubby face. "We talked about everything. Music. Life. Women. Depression. Back then I was so down, I wanted to race into death's outstretched arms. It would be a release of pain. Of addiction . . . just float away . . ." He blew lightly on his fingers then released it with a puff of air ". . . into nothing."

He met my gaze. "I'm glad . . . I didn't do it."

I knew what he meant but I asked anyway. "Do what?"

He grinned. "You know, take a ride on the gypsy highway."

"No shit, man," Peter says softly as he reaches for his beer. "Depression? Sorry to hear that mate. Glad you didn't end it."

"I take my meds, and that get me through the day," Simon replies. Then he smiles broadly as if recalling something pleasant. Staring at his fat face I can see down his throat, deep inside into the bottom of his lying soul. "Know what I really remember most about that night?" Simon says. "Cobain was wearing these real nice Italian shoes. He said he spent any money he had on nice shoes. I said, 'Yeah, good shoes are important, sometimes you gotta come as you are.'"

"No way!" I blurt. "Cobain always wore Converse sneakers: they were his trademark!"

A couple at the next table regard me nervously as Simon calmly lights another cigarette, exhales a large bloom of smoke in my direction and examines me with narrowed eyes.

"Yeah? Those sneakers must have come later. He was definitely wearing these nice pat-leather expensive Italian shoes with his beat-up jeans."

I snatch my jacket and knapsack and get up to leave when Simon turns to Peter and says something that stops me in my tracks:

"You know what? I jokingly asked Cobain for his autograph. I told him it might be worth money some day. He laughed, then wrote me a note on a slip of paper. I keep it in my wallet. Want to see it?"

Unable to speak, Peter just nods.

I'd never heard Simon talk about this slip of paper before and figure he must have lost his mind and that this is a new crazy extension to his story. He swivels in his seat like a circus bear on one of those tiny motorcycles, plunges a hairy hand into his coat pocket, pulls out a bunch of junk and drops it on the table. I stare down at the table and shake my head in disbelief: a fishing lure, a couple of broken crayons, a tattered spiral notebook, a heavy ring with keys, two ballpoint pens, a prescription bottle with a few pills, a crumpled Burger King coupon and two red guitar picks.

Figures.

"Oh crap," he mutters, patting his coat then his pants pockets. "Where's my wallet? Oh, here it is."

He pulls a worn leather wallet from his pocket and drops it onto the table. It's thick and bulky, like a book containing his life story. He opens the wallet, pulls out a slip of paper, unfolds it and slowly passes it to Peter as if it is some kind of precious relic.

Peter, practically trembling, looks down at the slip of paper in his hands. I can see his lips move as he reads whatever is written on it. Then he hands it back to Simon and hugs him warmly. "Awesome, Simon!" he says, smiling broadly. "Absolutely brilliant!" Then he turns from the table and walks into the crowd without even so much as a glance back at me.

Simon must have read the disbelief on my face, because he looks at me with a bemused smile, then starts to put the slip of paper back in his wallet.

"S-S-Simon," I stutter, grabbing for his wallet. "Let me see that!"

He passes me the slip of paper, then rests his elbows on the table.

I look down at the writing on the paper, which is a little faded from time. The handwriting is like chicken scratches but I can still read what it said: "*Simon, you're the biggest bullshitter ever born. Keep up the good work and thanks for the bridge for my song.*" It's signed, in messy but unmistakable handwriting, "*Kurt.*"

I slowly look up at Simon, who is still smiling at me.

"So, that story of yours is a joke?" I say. "A crazy joke!"

His smile drops, he snaps the paper out of my hand and slips it back into his wallet. "It's not a joke dude. It's real. That's what he wrote." He shrugs and shakes his head as if to say *I don't know why he wrote that.* He starts filling his pocket with all the shit that is on the bar, the crayons, the fishing lure, the guitar picks and the Burger King coupon, all of it. Then he stuffs the wallet back into the front pocket of his jeans.

"Cobain was a weird guy," he says shaking his head. "A nice guy, but definitely weird." He shifts in his seat, rubbing his eyes. "It seems like he was marked, like Cain from the old Testament. He didn't follow the crowd, and that can mean living a life of pain."

A smile crosses his face, but it's not the relaxed smile I know. It's more like a grimace, or a pain filled smile like someone wears at a funeral when they're trying to hide the loss they feel. Tears well up in his brown eyes and puts his heavy hand on my shoulder.

"Know what could have saved Cobain?"

I remember what Lilly said. "If he'd learned to dance?"

"Maybe," he wheezes, "that's not what I was thinking."

He takes a long drag from his cigarette, and the orange glow from the tip illuminates his bulky frame.

"Staying in rehab and understanding, and mostly understanding," he rasps. "People simply understanding the pain he was in. Pain like that cuts you wide open. It's like you're buried above ground."

He's staring at me waiting for a response. I try to avert his gaze but can't. He's hypnotized me. He can see into the pit of me, into the darkest part of my soul. I'm at a psychological crossroad. I see something I've never noticed before. Suffering is flowing like tributaries from the corners of his tired brown eyes.

"Understanding," I mutter. "I guess . . . you know . . . that would have helped."

He pushes my shoulder playfully, and grins in a reassuring way. "That's all anyone wants."

Screw it. Who cares? His lie is safe with me. He owns it. It's his fantasy—or the truth. I don't care. What Cobain did to himself was a despicable lie, or a horrible inescapable truth. Sometimes it's difficult to tell them apart. The only real truth is that it was a premature death. Sad and tragic.

Sometimes lies give meaning to the truth . . . and on occasion trump it. People usually lie to deceive others, but Simon isn't trying to deceive anyone; he's just trying to get by. Maybe he jammed with Kurt Cobain, or at least believes he did.

Hope comes in weird forms.

"Simon," I say slowly, shaking my head, "that must have been something, man. Jamming with Cobain. Incredible!"

He leans back in his chair and looks me in the eye. "Yeah, it was incredible." There's silence for a moment then he says: "I guess it's hard to believe, huh?

A grin forms on my lips. "Shit happens."

He burps loudly and raises his glass in a toast. "Happy Birthday Kurt, wherever you are."

I hesitate, then slowly raise my own glass. "Thanks for the music."

I CAN'T EVEN SAY HER NAME

S TRANGERS WILL TELL YOU THE STRANGEST THINGS. Perhaps that's why they're called "strangers." But as usual, I'm getting ahead of myself.

So, a few weeks ago I was in Chicago doing research for a movie script I'm writing. It was half past something on a steamy August evening and I was sitting in a bar asking myself a simple question: Stay for another drink or go back to my hotel room?

I don't know what the bar was called, but it was an "Irish-style pub" named, O'Reilly's or Mulligan's or Mrs. O'Leary's Cow, for all I knew. I'd been in places like that in various cities and I'd guess there are a thousand similar pubs in Chicago. After a while they all start to look alike. Some guy once told me that they're all built from an "Irish Pub kit." Apparently, it comes with a long frosted mirror over a dark wooden bar with brass foot rails and fancy beer taps, or some variation of that. The point is that all those pubs are re-creations, replicas, copies of a hundred other places just like them. But this place had a casual atmosphere, which affirmed my decision to stay for another drink before venturing back to my hotel a few blocks away.

I tipped my head back, drained the last of my gin and tonic with a single gulp, placed the glass onto the bar and scanned the room. Pictures of long-dead writers, soldiers and presidents stared down from the walls. The place was one-third filled with people talking and laughing, obviously in good cheer. Music videos were playing on a flat screen television hanging above the bar. The volume was turned down so everyone in the video appeared to be engaged in some kind of nonsensical mute lip sync. The incessant flashy images, quick edits and in-your-face over loaded photography gave the voiceless performances a kind of strident, oppressive "hyper" quality that offended sight.

I turned from the TV, pulled a crisp $50 bill from my wallet, held it between two fingers and waved at the bartender, who was talking to a waitress at the end of the bar. He was a young man, 20 years my junior, stocky with neat dark hair above a fresh scrubbed face and alert eyes. "The same sir?" he asked politely. "Tanqueray and tonic with a twist?"

I nodded. "Exactly."

The bartender carefully filled my glass with ice, poured the drink, and placed it on a coaster then stepped back, folded his arms across his chest and studied me quizzically. "Haven't seen you in here before have I?" he asked, smiling slightly.

A good bartender will always strike up a conversation with a new patron so I was happy to engage him. "My first time in here," I replied, raising my glass in a lone toast. "I'm only in Chicago for three days. On the way back to my hotel I saw your place and decided to stop in. And besides, I'd bet this is the only bar in the country where they still allow smoking."

He grinned. "Technically we're not supposed, but the boss turns a blind eye. And besides nothing's illegal until you get caught, right?"

I chuckled. "You sound like most of the producers I know."

He leaned in to the bar. "Producers?" he asked. "Do you mean movie producers?"

"Are there any other kinds?" I replied with a laugh.

"So you work in the movie business?"

I paused, then pulled a cigarette from the pack of Marlboros on the bar. "Yes," I replied padding my pockets for a light. "I'm researching a script. I'm a writer and film director."

His eyes lit up like most people's do when I tell them what I do for a living. He pulled a red Bic lighter from his pocket, reached across the bar and lit my cigarette. "You're a movie director?" he asked, his thick dark eyebrows rising. "Done anything I might know?"

Exhaling a large plume of smoke, I placed my cigarette in a square glass ashtray beside my drink. "I work on indies, small independent films," I answered. "I'd be pleasantly surprised if you've seen or heard about any of them."

"Try me," he said keenly.

I was sure he wouldn't know my work because most of my films had been released in Europe and England. But he seemed like a nice guy genuinely interested in hearing more so I threw out the title of my last film.

"*Killer Sex*," I said, eyeing him. "Released in Italy last year . . . and, no, it's not a porno. It's an erotic film."

"What's the difference?"

I leaned back in my seat. "There's a big difference. Erotic films are much more artistic. They're not specifically made to titillate whereas porno is made to arouse the viewer. We use real actors, real scripts."

The bartender nodded as if he understood. "*Killer Sex?* Can't say I know it," he said still holding a bar towel "Who's in it anybody I know?"

"Yeah," I answered. "If you know Carlo Boadicea or Louis Cabrillo, two up-and-coming Italian actors."

He seemed to be thinking about it, then said he didn't know any Italian actors. "I love movies though," he said. "My friend's a film student at Columbia. We were drinking last week and came up with an idea for a blockbuster movie. We thought it would be funny."

I reached for my cigarette. "That's how most scripts originate. With a germ of an idea."

"Great! Like to hear the pitch?"

I offered a reticent "okay," then picked up my drink in anticipation of the long convoluted discourse sure to follow when people tell my they have an idea for a film. But I liked the kid and I'm always willing to talk about movies.

He motioned toward the television above the bar, where a famous female pop singer was mutely grinding away in an overtly sexual dance.

"This movie is about her," he said, pointing at the TV. "It's her birthday today, so they're playing her videos in heavy rotation."

I raised my glass and toasted the TV. "Happy birthday." Then I turned back to the bartender. "So, your movie is about her?"

"Yep, but we can't use her real name because we don't want to get sued. So we decided to refer to her as 'Blank Blank.'"

"Blank Blank?" I replied. "Very creative."

"Well, they're all pretty much the same—at least they're all selling the same thing. Just fill in the Blank Blank."

"You're right about that," I replied, then asked. "Whatever happened to originality?"

He turned his palms skyward. "Who knows? The Rolling Stones were sexy bad boys. Marvin Gay was soul sexy. Hendrix was sexy as Hell. The Beatles had massive sex appeal." He grinned wolfishly. "Every girl in the world wanted to have sex with Sting."

I nodded. "Can't argue with that."

"U2 are sexy and intelligent," he continued. "The Red Hot Chili Peppers are just that, 'hot.' Lady Gaga. Hot as the sun. All those performers have "sex" ingrained in their music. It's absolutely native to their sound. It's not a fabricated backtrack like 'Blank Blank.' It's real. Sex is an indispensable part of their music, in the DNA of their songs. The beat. The melody. The lyrics. The performance."

"You're right. They were all young, once, and original."

His eyes lit up. "There's always Bjork!"

I chuckled. "She's sure one of a kind. A, Yoko Ono, for a younger generation."

"Who's that?"

"A Japanese artist."

He stared at me blankly.

"John Lennon's wife."

"Really? Isn't he dead?"

"He is. She isn't."

He seemed a little confused, but then continued telling me about his movie idea.

"It's all about Blank Blank and others like her, you know, sexual dynamos and how their influence is ravaging our youth and culture."

"Wow, sounds like a crazy script."

"I don't actually have a script yet," he said pointing to his head, "but it's all up here"

"You know what it's about and you haven't even got a script yet? Interesting."

He planted his palms on the bar and leaned forward. "You don't need a script to shoot a movie!"

I figured he was just joking, so I nodded in an inclusive way and he continued. He breathlessly explained that the protagonist in his movie was a man in his early 20's, not much younger then himself who continuously cruised bars looking to pick up girls that resembled *Blank* Blank.

"Then one night," he said, "this guy looks across the dance floor of a crowded club and sees the woman of his dreams. His Grail. Her resemblance to Blank Blank is uncanny. Long blond hair frames her tanned face and tumbles over her shoulders."

"Act Two," I said, smiling. "The plot thickens."

He grinned. "That's not all that thickens."

I raised my glass in toast. "I'm with you."

"She's wearing a midriff t-shirt exposing a tanned trim stomach and a navel ring, tight plastic red pants tied up in the crotch, a suede waist-length jacket with faux fur at the ends of sleeves, and sexy red leather boots."

He leaned over the bar and lowered his voice. "This girl is giving the guy a dead ringer Blank Blank slutty come-hither look from across the room."

I motioned at the TV. "Exactly like her videos. A painted French whore. The girl of his dreams."

"More like the girl of his 'wet' dreams," he said, holding up his fingers as quote marks around the word *wet*.

I laughed and he continued. "The guy is completely blown away by this woman so he rushes over and asks her to dance. They hit it off and spend a blissful evening together, dancing under colored lights, drinking and talking. After midnight the guy casually invites her back to his apartment for a drink. She gladly agrees, so they grab their coats and leave."

I sipped my drink, and the melted ice cubes sang with what I can only describe as a musical tone. "I see a third act coming."

"There sure is," the bartender said taking a breath. "Now here's where it gets Fellini-like."

When anyone describing a movie to me says "Here's where it gets Fellini like," I brace myself. I'm expecting the plot to take one of two turns: enter the clowns and dogs, or cut to the circus.

"They're back at his place," he says breathlessly. "The guy is in full make mode. He's finally going to bed a Blank Blank. He's real motivated because this is a major score."

"I bet."

"They lay down on his bed and this guy runs his hands over her curvy young body. He slowly unbuttons her blouse then slips off her jeans and panties as white light shines in from the street."

"I'm on the edge of my seat."

"Finally, he gets her undressed," he said. "But he can't believe his eyes. He's horrified. It turns out this Blank Blank look alike creature is really a blowup sex doll. She's not a real person." He stepped back looked at me, his eyes wide. "What do you think?"

I figured he wasn't serious, and that he was just having fun. But his "movie idea" was an interesting observation on pop culture and I didn't mind humoring him a little. It had a definite cinematic *Twilight Zone* quality.

I reached for my cigarette and took a drag. "You know who Karl Marx is?" I asked.

He grinned. "Of course. I studied political science in college. How do you think I ended up becoming a bartender?"

I raised my glass. "And a very good one you are."

"Thanks."

Marx said 'Religion is the opiate of the masses,'" I continued. "Today, he'd say sex is the opiate of the masses. Celebrity worship is the opiate of the masses. TV is the opiate of the masses. Crappy movies and music videos are the opiate of the masses. Cheesy pop music is the opiate of the masses." I motioned with my glass toward the TV. "Your girl *Blank* Blank is the opiate of the masses."

He folded his arms across his chest. "Why do they even bother calling sex 'making love?' It's usually people screwing in an elevator, the backseat of a taxi or on top of a desk at work. There's absolutely no love there. It's the opposite of love."

I took a sip from my drink and he wiped the bar.

"All the unwanted pregnancies, abortions, lust, affairs, STDs, pornography," he said. "Casual sex and lust are the real weapons of mass destruction."

I was a little surprised such a young guy would be so down on sex because most guys his age would be looking to get laid as much as possible. I wondered if he might be some kind of religious zealot, a republican right-winger.

But he had engaged me, so I felt like I should give him more honest feedback. I took a sip, then placed my glass on the bar. "Your movie is about the jail bait sexuality sold on television and the overtly sexual themes in the music industry," I said. "Soft core porn in music videos and advertising, all against the backdrop of twenty four seven-television equals we never sleep media, and AIDS ravaging the planet. This soulless music industry fabrication . . ."

He smiled widely, threw up his hands and interrupted me. "Yeah exactly," he exclaimed. "Blank Blank doesn't even know she's a prostitute."

He stopped for a moment and seemed to be thinking as he wiped the bar. "What I'm saying is, she's selling sex. The 12 and 13-year-old girls love it too. They dress like her and end up looking like cheap knock off sluts. They call them 'Prostitots.'"

"Prostitots, really?"

He shrugged and turned his palms toward the ceiling.

I took another sip of my drink, placed the glass down on the coaster and turned toward the TV.

"You know," I said. "*Blank* Blank's sold a billion CDs, so there's got to be something real there, something more than her blatant sexuality and the way she's marketed. Maybe we just don't get it."

"Maybe."

I took another drink. "I hate to think she's someone's daughter."

He glanced up at the TV then turned back toward me and grimaced. "I know what you mean," he replied. "My daughter turned three today."

"It's her birthday?"

"Yep, she has the same birthday as *Blank* Blank." He nodded toward the TV. "My wife and I had a birthday cake for my little girl before I came in today. Candles, presents the whole show."

"Nice."

We both stared up at the voiceless television where *Blank* Blank was straddling a shirtless young man as she whipped his face with her long locks of hair. The bartender had a point and the truth was up there looking down at us.

I took a deep slow drag off my cigarette and met the bartender's gaze. "I like your movie idea. Sell it to Hollywood for millions."

He grinned sheepishly and turned toward the television. We watched *Blank* Blank for a moment then the bartender turned back toward me.

"But man," he said shaking his head. "She has a smokin body."

"Yeah," I said, blindly reaching for my drink. "I'd do her in a heartbeat."

I WONDER IF IT'S SNOWING
IN CHICAGO?

WONDER IF IT'S SUNNY IN TULUM? I wonder if the hot Mexican sun is sparkling on the ocean? I wonder what this vacation will be like? I wonder if Janet and I are going to have kids? I wonder if we're still going to be married this time next year? I wonder if the cab's going to get here through the snow?

All these questions.

For the third time in 10 minutes, I pulled back the living room curtain and glanced outside to see if the taxi had arrived. The ground was covered in a few inches of freshly fallen snow, but no sign of the taxi.

I wanted this vacation to be perfect. But I was concerned we were off to a poor start, that the bad weather will snarl traffic and that we wouldn't get to the airport on time.

The trip was a welcome escape from the icy grip of an especially harsh Chicago winter and a chance for us to work on our marriage. Seven years earlier we had spent our honeymoon in a tiny seaside village called, Tulum. We were hopeful the return trip would let us rekindle the passion we enjoyed in our first few years together, like a gentle breath nurturing a spark into a flame.

Seven years is a lifetime in a relationship. After seven years you know your partner's true self. You see them as they really are, without artifice or a mask. You better be happy with what you see, because if you're not growing together . . . well you know.

Still, the thought of the warm Mexican sun and tropical breezes awaiting us shimmed before me like a warm July afternoon dropped into the stone cold heart of winter.

I heard a car horn blare and went to the window. A yellow taxi was idling in front of our house, its color a sharp contract to the pure white of the street. I turned from the window and called to, Janet, who was in the kitchen.

"Let's go Jan! The taxi's here."

She came into the room carrying half a loaf of bread in a bag swinging like a pendulum.

"I'm putting this out for the birds," she said, holding the bag up for me to see.

I scoffed. "What? There's not time. The taxi's waiting."

She frowned and her blue eyes formed slits. "It'll only take a few seconds."

I knew there was no use arguing. That was her way. She was a patron saint to all little animals. On stormy winter days a look of deep worry would cross her face. I knew what she was thinking because she had said it dozens of times before: *The poor birds and squirrels. It's cold. They'll freeze. They'll go hungry.*"

Her thoughtfulness had ignited a resentment within me. Perhaps I was being selfish, but if she cared half as much about our marriage as she cared about the stupid birds and squirrels we could have saved thousands of dollars on marriage counseling. I can understand giving a few coins to homeless people, but I draw the line at feeding wild animals. Let nature run its course.

Does that make me a bad person? No. It makes me a realist.

I didn't want to upset Janet, so I bit my lip, grabbed the handle of my carry-on suitcase and started toward the door.

"Do what you have to do," I said. "Be quick because I'm betting there's going to be a lot of traffic due to the snow."

"It won't take a second," she replied.

She followed me out the front door, pulling her carry-on behind her with one hand while holding the half bag of bread with the other. It was below freezing outside, and I started shivering as I stood on the walkway hemorrhaging patience while Janet carefully broke up the bread and tossed it onto the snow beside our hydrangeas.

"Janet can you hurry?" I asked impatiently. "I'm freezing and don't want to be late."

Thick snowflakes lighted on her rust colored hair and eyelashes. "Wait in the taxi if you're cold," she replied. "We have plenty of time. The flight doesn't leave for *three* hours."

"Fine."

Exhaust fumes were spewing from taxi's tailpipe as the driver got out, greeted me with a quick "good morning" and put my suitcase in the trunk.

"My wife's coming," I said, brushing snowflakes off my jacket. "She's feeding the birds."

He smiled. "No problem." He was young, in his mid-twenties with dark half circles under his eyes, suggesting he had been driving all night.

I had just buckled my seatbelt when Janet pulled open the door and slid in beside me.

The driver got in and looked at us in the rearview, his tired eyes slits in the mirror.

"Which airline?" he asked.

We both said "United" in unison then exchanged smiles. Janet had a wide cheerful smile and just seeing it helped me relax a little. She pulled a package of gum from he purse, elbowed me gently and quietly offered me some. She had thought of everything. She always did. I shook my head. "No thanks."

• • •

If the adage "opposites attract" is true, then we had that going for us. She had her suitcase completely and neatly packed four days before our flight. On the night before we left, she was casually dropping hints: Don't forget your flip-flops. Remember how angry you were last time when you forgot them? What books are you bringing?

In my defense, I had compiled a "mental list" of things to pack. But on the day before we left I had yet to pull my suitcase from the closet, let alone pack it. I throw everything into a suitcase 20 minutes before leaving. Does that make me a bad person? No I'm a laid back person and I know how to pack for travelling.

But after seven years, Janet tended to cover for me. That morning after I had throw everything into my suitcase, she came into the room, smiled wryly, passed me my passport and said; "Don't forget this."

The taxi pulled up in front of the terminal where a dozen taxis and stretch limos were coming and going as others jockeyed for position next to the curb. Our bleary eyed driver stopped behind a white limousine, jumped out, pulled our suitcases from the trunk and stood there with his hands shoved into his pockets waiting to be paid.

"The snow's letting up," he said looking skyward. "I don't imagine you'll be delayed sir."

"Great," I said, as I handed him two twenties. "Keep the change."

The plane sat on the tarmac for what seemed like an eternity before finally pulling away from the gate. Once we were in the air it climbed steadily, and within ten minutes we were above the storm. It was as if we had entered another world. Sunshine gushed into the cabin through the egg shaped windows. Seeing Janet like that, bathed in sunshine, quietly reading her book, I hoped that a week on the beach, lazing away the hours under palm trees would be the perfect remedy for our problems.

Unfortunately, the problem wasn't *one* thing, it was *many* things. It was the result of being married for seven years, of getting married when we were 23, too young to fully appreciate the commitment we had made. My views on life and relationships had changed in those seven years. Things come and go in relationships, like . . . I don't know . . . people in an airport?

We didn't have kids, although in the past two years we had tried. God, had we tried. Sex had become a chore, like mowing the lawn or taking out the garbage. The joy, passion and pleasure had been pounded out of it. I had once heard that the routine of sex in an attempt to get pregnant is described as "drilling for procreation" And that's what it felt like, work. We had even stopped trying for the time being. We hadn't had sex in weeks. The break was a welcome relief.

Janet really wanted children . . . and I . . . well . . . I thought it was, probably, maybe a good idea? I don't know. The prospect of parenthood scared me. I wasn't sure if I was ready to be that much of a responsible adult, a father. Having a baby would take our marriage in a direction toward heightened commitment.

Does that make me a bad husband? No. I was being honest, to myself at least. Starting a family is an act of courage, because if you are a good parent, the entire focus of your life shifts from yourself to your child. Maybe I was a coward, or self centered. I don't know.

Within a few hours we were over the Gulf of Mexico, an endless blue promise below. As the plane descended, I see could see Mexico's sugared beaches strung like pearl necklaces around the lush tropical jungle.

And I thought: *I'm ready for this* . . .

. . .

As we were walking through the airport terminal I stopped, crouched beside my suitcase, unzipped the side pocket, and pulled out my sunglasses as people scurried past me.

A vacation, or any trip for that matter, is like a board game. In the beginning there are certain perils you have to watch out for. But at the end is the prize. Is this case a week on a sundrenched beach. Sunglasses are vital for the next stage of the trip: Getting out of the airport without being given an intense sales pitch in which you are promised cash or a free day at a resort in exchange for listening to a timeshare sales pitch during your stay. The people selling the timeshares are very good at what they do. They are usually affable young Mexican men and women dressed in white shirts and black pants or skirts. The thing is, time is like gold when you're on vacation. Therefore I called these salespeople "timeshare bandits" because essentially what they're trying to do is to steal time from your vacation. And they don't take "no" for an answer. They wait right outside the baggage claim area and swarm you. In heavily accented English, they promise free this and that just for signing up for a timeshare sales pitch. But I was ready for them. I'd run their gauntlet of deeply tanned skin, dark brown eyes, jet black hair and ivory white smiles on previous vacations. The secret is, don't make eye contact, (thus my sunglasses) and stare straight ahead. At the same time, act as if you only speak Russian. Or better still, makeup a language and watch their blank expression. For them it's a numbers game. There must be ten thousands tourists a day passing though the airport. If they can just get a few dozen to stop. I was in no mood to listen.

Does this make me a bad person? No. I value my vacation time and I have no intention of buying a timeshare. So why even bother doing the awkward timeshare pitch dance?

I slipped on my sunglasses and strode forward. We left the baggage claim area they were on us. "Sir," a clean cut kid who looked like he was 18 said, "I have for you a free day at a luxury spa, all inclusive for you and your lovely wife . . ."

I stared straight ahead, brushed past him and kept on walking. We were only 50 feet from the exit. Sunlight streaming in through the sliding glass doors, like the proverbial light at the end of the tunnel. "Excuse me sir," a girl no more than 20 said as she tried to cut me off. "Would you and your wife like to enjoy dinner at a four star restaurant . . ."

"No gracias," Janet smiled.

Only 30 feet from the exit now . . . In front of us one of the timeshare bandits had corralled an untanned couple, so white, I imagined they were from Iceland, or north of Iceland. He was leading them to the counter, smiling and talking a mile a minute.

"No!" I wanted to yell. "Don't do it. It's not free! At best you'll burn a whole day of your vacation listening to a sales pitch. At worst you'll end up putting down a $10,000 deposit on your credit card just to get out of there."

Perhaps it would be easier for everyone if certain people had "Sucker" printed on their shirt in English and Spanish. I was watching the Icelandic couple being led to their doom when one of the timeshare bandits shoved a flier into my hand. I practically tripped over the guy and therefore had to stop.

He was older than the others. He looked like a Mayan King. Proud, short and dark skinned with broad shoulders, black hair and a cheerful smile revealing nicotine stained teeth.

"Sir, you and your wife look very healthy. You must like to snorkel dive? I have for you free pass for the best diving in Mexico."

I forgot my own rule and mistakenly answered in English. "I don't know how to swim," I lied, happy with my quick response.

"You come to Mexico and don't know how to swim?" he asked smugly. "Do you know how to eat? Because I have gift certificates for the best restaurants."

I didn't like his smartass tone and blurted: "I'm not interested in a timeshare, and I hate Mexican food."

He glared at me. "You will go hungry then amigo," he said gruffly. "Will be alright. We have McDonald's for gringos like you. Or maybe you like to eat dog?"

His eyes filled with hate but he kept on smiling. If looks could kill, he would have laid me out on the airport floor. I was going to tell him to bug off, but before I could, Janet tugged my arm and we kept walking. As we reached the sliding glass doors at the exit she turned toward me.

"Why are you so mean to these people? They're just trying to make a living," she said. "Cut them some slack. Just smile and say 'no gracias.'"

"That doesn't work. And besides that guy was rude. He told me to eat dog."

She frowned. "He meant you could eat a hotdog, not a real dog. You told him you hate Mexican food. You might as well have said you hate Mexicans."

"What! He was an asshole. You're taking his side?"

"Taking his side?" she scoffed. "That's ridiculous. Lighten up will you. You're on vacation."

"I'm light for God's sake," I quipped, before striding through the sliding glass doors into a brilliant sun drenched afternoon. "I'm light."

Outside the terminal it was hot and humid. Small brown men with broad shoulders, wearing short sleeved white dress shirts open at the neck and pressed black pants were loading luggage into the trunks of little while taxis. After a few minutes we reached the front of the line. The taxi driver jumped out and greeted us. "Hola," he said grinning widely. He placed our bags in the truck as Janet and I climbed into the backseat. He got in front and turned to look at us.

"A Donda?" he asked.

Janet and I spoke a little Spanish, but I figured it would be easier for everyone if the driver spoke English.

"No hablo Espanol," I answered. "Habla English por favor?

"Si, a little."

"We're going to Tulum," I said.

He nodded. "Tulum? Muy bien." Then he turned and pulled away from the curb.

"You like the air con?" he asked.

"No," Janet answered as she rolled down her window. "This is perfect."

Once you leave Cancun, the highway to Tulum is a straight shot south for about 60 miles. We drove for a while then stopped for gas. We had just pulled up to the pumps, when a beggar in rags came out of the shadows. He was speaking Spanish and was holding a beat-up Starbucks cup with a few coins in it. As our driver was shooing him away, Janet dug into her purse, pulled out a handful of pesos, motioned for the beggar to come to the window then dropped the money into his cup.

He smiled a toothless smile. "Gracias senorita, Gracias."

"De nada," Janet replied as he staggered away back into the shade.

I shook my head. "You paid for his next bottle."

"How do you know what he's going to spend it on?" she snapped. "Never pass a real beggar, like that beggar, without giving them something."

"Okay. I'm just saying."

As we continued down the highway, sun streamed in through the taxi windows. We drove another half hour, then turned off onto a smaller road with grass pushing up between cracks in the pavement. Lush tropical plants with broad flat leafs like platters and palm trees lined both sides of the narrow road which led to the ocean-side cluster of tiny cottages called, Peace In Tulum, the place where we were staying. After 10 minutes the taxi driver pulled off the thin road into a shaded sandy area where several cars were parked.

"Es aqui, is here," he said as he opened his door, got out and pulled our bags from the truck. It was the middle of the afternoon, and the weather was sunny and warm. Perfect! I paid the taxi driver, and then Janet and I walked up a narrow, winding path to the office. Truth be told, "office" is being generous: it was a modest, unwalled building with a thatched roof, wooden walls, large open spaces for windows and dusty planks for a floor. There were half a dozen tables covered with red-and-white-checkered tablecloths; this area was the restaurant. A handwritten sign hanging over the old wooden desk invited guests to ring a bell hanging from a piece of twine.

Janet dropped her bag beside one of the tables and sat down. "Just how I remember it," she said, resting her elbows on the table. "The basics only."

I sat beside her, took off my sunglasses and placed them on the table. "I think the term in 'rustic,'"

I reached over and rang the bell.

We sat there quietly for a few more minutes, then I rang the bell again. I was starting to wonder if anyone was going to check us in when I heard rustling in the bushes 20 feet away. I turned to look, expecting to see a person, but instead a dog was standing there wagging his tail so hard it looked like his rear end was going to fly off. It paused, looked at us, then ambled toward Janet. It appeared to be a cocker spaniel mix of some kind, mostly white with large brown markings. It was limping, and as it got closer I could see why. It was lame. Its front left leg was partly folded up under the dog, like an L. It limped over to Janet and gazed up at her with adoring brown eyes.

"Oh, is he ever cute," she said reaching down to pat him.

I sat up, getting ready to kick the dog if he growled or tried to bite Janet. "Careful Jan. He could be mean."

"Mean?" she scoffed. "Look at him. He's adorable."

She was right. He didn't seem the least bit distempered. He looked happy enough, and if dogs can smile, he was smiling.

The dog grunted and plopped down at Janet's feet.

After a few minutes the woman who ran the hotel came walking up a sandy path that led to the beach. She looked like she was in her 50s, but it was hard to tell because she was dressed like a hippie, wearing a loose cotton shirt with colored beads around her neck and faded cargo pants. Her feet were bare. Her graying hair and was tied back, framing a deeply tanned face, deeply wrinkled from what I assumed was years in the sun.

"Hola! Welcome," she said as she stepped into the cabana. "You are the Marshalls, si?"

'Yes we are," I said, as Janet and I stood to shake her hand.

"I am the owner, Maria," she smiled. "I have your cabana ready and can check you in."

As I was filling out the registration forms Janet went over to where the dog was lying in a splash of sunlight. "Is this your dog?" she asked gently stroking its belly.

"This dog?" Maria answered. "This is no my dog. He is . . . wild? No he is . . . stray."

Maria planted her hands on her hips and shrugged. "Who knows who owns. They come and go."

"I don't remember him from our last visit," I said looking up.

"You stay here before?" Maria asked.

Janet walked to my side and took my hand in hers. "It was our honeymoon, seven years ago."

"Sorry, I no remember," Maria shrugged. "Have many guests from many countries."

I finished checking in and Maria pointed to a sandy path. "Is this way." We grabbed or bags and followed her. Halfway down the path we met a Mexican man who looked like he was around 40-years-old. Maria said something to him in Spanish and he reached for Janet's bag.

"This is Alex," Maria said. "He is my helper and manager."

He was tall and slim with alert brown eyes. He smiled. "Hola."

"Hola," we replied.

"His English is not too good," Maria said, "but he knows his way around and is a big help."

They showed us to our cabana, which was close-by. Maria pointed to a carved wooden sign above the door that said, *Jaguar.*

"Each cabana named after local animal," she explained. "This is Jaguar cabana, and is very comfortable. Make self at home and enjoy your stay."

I turned toward Janet then Maria and Alex. "Are there jaguars around here?"

"At one time yes," Maria answered. "But not for many years."

"I wouldn't mind seeing one," I said.

Maria smiled knowingly. "Best to see jaguar in a zoo, not in the wild," she said, adding, "Ring the bell if you need me or Alex. Okay?"

"Okay," Janet replied.

They waved goodbye and Janet and I went inside.

"I think this is the same one we stayed in before," she said, looking around.

It was just as I remembered it, as if untouched by the hands of time. The exterior walls, painted a faded sunset orange, were thick stucco. A pair of battered wicker chairs sat on a small porch out front. Inside was a single large room that housed a set of drawers, a wooden table and chairs and a night stand between two beds covered with a white plume of mosquito netting. The floor was smooth cement and there was a small bathroom, a sink and shower in an alcove. There wasn't any air conditioning, and instead a ceiling fan was suspended from the high thatched roof. We dropped our suitcases on the bed, threw on our bathing suits and went down to the beach.

The sand was like a million warm coals under my feet, and I slipped off my sunglasses to get an unfiltered look at our surroundings.

Sunlight sparkled on the ocean, a magical shade of light turquoise. Whitecaps, summoned by a steady breeze out of the southeast, danced across the rough surface of the water. The tropical wind was so steady that it looked like the coconut trees were about to take flight. But it was warm enough to go without a shirt.

The pristine beach was practically deserted. Janet pointed to a pair of high backed wooden beach chairs 30 feet from the waters edge under a palapa topped with palm leafs, which murmured gently in the steady breeze.

"What a view," she said as we settled into the chairs.

We were thirty seconds from our cabana and even closer to the frothy surf crashing on the beach. After a while we went back to our cabana. Janet laid on the bed leafing through a magazine as I stripped off my T-shirt and bathing suit.

"I'm jumping in the shower," I said.

She got off the bed, peeled off her bathing suit and took my hand. "Save water. Shower with a friend." One of the things I always loved about her was that she was an ardent environmentalist.

The water was cool but tremendously refreshing after our long day of travel. I reached for the soap, but Janet took it from me.

"Let me do it," she said softly.

Water flowed in rivulets down my body as she tenderly washed my face and chest then lathered up the rest of me. She always had a sensual touch, and as she continued, I ran my hands over her breasts and hips, then pulled her in tightly and kissed her.

"I don't think I've even been this clean," I smiled.

She grinned mischievously as she knelt in front of me. "Almost done."

It was the first time in a long time that we had done something sexual that didn't carry the weight and expectation of getting pregnant. It was simply sex for sex's sake, and it was liberating.

When we were done, I got out of the shower, pulled on a pair of khaki shorts, a polo shirt and my sandals as Janet finished showering.

We went to the Maria's little restaurant and enjoyed a relaxing dinner of white fish with vegetables and a few glasses of wine. We were back in our cabana by 8:30 and by 9 we were both fast asleep, as night settled on the ocean and lush jungle.

• • •

The next morning we woke late, grabbed a light breakfast and coffee, then took a long beach walk and reclaimed our chairs under the palapa from the previous day. The sun was shining and the southern breeze was still steady and warm.

I turned to look at Janet. "This really is paradise."

She was staring past me and didn't hear what I said. Her tense expression immediately told me that something was wrong.

"What is it?" I asked.

"Look at that," she said pointing to the right.

I turned to where she was pointing. Two dogs, one large and one small, were standing near the shoreline a short distance from us. "What?" I asked. "The dogs?"

"That's the little lame dog from the office," she replied. "That big dog won't let it pass. It's blocking its way. It's threatening him."

"What?" I said looking at the dogs again.

I turned back to Janet who was now standing. "I'm going over there to help that poor little mutt."

"Jan," I blurted, "there's not a problem. I'll bet they know each other. They're probably friends."

She scoffed. "They're not friends. Look how scared the little dog is."

She was right. The lame dog was scared to death. It was cowering, laying in the sand while the other dog loomed over it. Suddenly the big dog nipped the smaller dog on the leg and the mutt yelped.

Janet started walking toward them.

Shit, she'll get bitten. This is not what we want on vacation! Spending a day in a Mexican emergency room waiting for Janet to get a tetanus shot and stitches to close a nasty dog bite.

I jumped to my feet and cursed under my breath, *damned dog!* "Jan wait. I'll come with you. That big dog will kill you."

We had only gone a few feet when I practically tripped over an odd piece of driftwood near the water's edge.

"Jan, hold on for a second."

I knelt in the sand and pick it up. It was a branchless tree limb, five feet long with dozens of knots where there had once been small branches. It was a little water logged but that added to its solidness and weigh, which I would have guessed to be six of seven pounds. I was barely able to wrap my fingers around it. It was straight with a smooth surface as gray as twilight. *Hmmmm, this will be a great equalizer if the big dog attacks.*

"What are you doing with that?" Janet asked.

"Just in case big boy there doesn't listen to reason."

I gripped the staff tightly in my right hand and we walked toward the dogs. When we were 20 feet away Janet cupped her hands to her mouth. "Hey," she yelled in a vain attempt to be heard above wind and roar of the surf. "You leave him alone. Get away from him."

The larger dog, a muscular German Sheppard Pitbull mix, was twice as big as the lame mutt. Its head was large and square, lips curled up in aggression exposing yellowed fangs. It ignored Janet so we moved a little closer.

"Leave him alone," she yelled, angrily waving her arms in the air. "Get away from him."

The large dog took half a step toward us then bared its teeth and emitted a loud growl as the lame mutt stared at us with pleading brown eyes. I gripped the driftwood tightly.

"Jan, let me try."

I stepped past her and held the staff out to my side so the big dog could clearly see it.

I took another step forward and stared the dog in the eye. *I do not want to deal with shit like this on my vacation!* "Listen you big dumb dog," I yelled. "You are not going to ruin my vacation! Get away from that dog now before I bash your head in!"

I raised the staff and took a few steps forward in an attempt to intimidate the dog. We were only 10 feet apart now. My heart was pounding like the surf on the beach. No question, if that dog had lunged at me I would have clobbered it.

There was a loud whistle to my right. The dog heard it too because it immediately looked over to a guy, around my age, sitting in the shade of a coconut tree 60 feet away. He was shirtless and thin, with black facial hair and tattoos on his arms. He was wearing a bright red ball cap, matching shorts and Aviator sunglasses. He had been watching us the whole time. The large dog glanced back at me then sauntered over to his owner. He rubbed the dog's neck then he got up and walked down the beach. I lowered the staff and turned to Janet.

"That guy's an asshole," I said. "He was probably getting off on his dog bullying this little guy."

"What a jerk."

The mutt stood and Janet walked over and dropped to one knee to pat it. "How you doing little man?" she said softly. "Look!" she said, turning to me. "There a cut on his leg where that bastard dog bit him."

I walked over, bent down and scratched the dog's chin. Janet was right. There was a half-inch gash on the front paw of the mutt's bad leg. But it was hardly bleeding and didn't look serious to me.

"It's not that bad. Strays get cut and bruised all the time. They take care of it."

Janet shook her head. "Not that bad? It will get infected."

"Infected? No way. He'll wash it in the ocean. He'll be fine."

"I've got half a sandwich in my purse left over from the flight," Janet said, standing. "I'm going to give it to him. He's thin and looks hungry."

"Jan, don't feed him or we'll never be rid of him."

"I'm not going to watch him starve to death."

"He won't starve. There must be a hundred places around here where he finds food."

She glared at me. "Oh yeah. Where?"

"I don't know. Garbage, and people probably feed him."

"That's right," she said triumphantly. "People feed him and that's exactly what I'm going to do. Feed him."

She turned and hurried back to our cabana leaving me standing there with the mutt. Besides the small cut on his leg, he seemed to have fully recovered from the altercation with the big dog. He was sitting and panting, his pink tongue dangling from the side of his mouth. Janet had such a big heart for little animals, I knew she would practically adopt the thing. I looked over at our cabana and back at the dog.

I gently poked it with the staff. "Shoo. You get out of here. Find someone else to bother. Go on get going."

The dog sat there as if it was deaf. Who knows maybe it was. I glanced toward our cabana again to see if Janet was coming, then pushed the dog gently with my foot. It just sat there looking toward our cabana.

"Go on," I said, raising my voice. "Shoo. Get out of here. Get lost!"

Was I a jerk for trying to get rid of the dog? No. There's a time for compassion and there's a time to put your own needs first. Having the little lame dog around would preoccupy Janet for the whole trip. Before I could get the dog to leave, Janet came trudging through the sand holding the sandwich in one hand and a glass of soapy water and a washcloth in the other.

As she reached my side I motioned to the glass and washcloth. "What are you doing?"

"I'm going to clean that cut."

"You've got to be kidding. He'll bite you."

Ignoring me, she knelt down beside the dog and carefully placed the half sandwich in the sand in front of it. The dog's brown eyes widened and it gulped down the food.

"Okay boy," she said softly, carefully reaching for the dog's paw. "Let me see your leg. Come on now."

The dog recoiled and I got ready to whack it with the staff.

"Janet's he's going to bite you. Leave him alone."

"He's just scared," she said, moving in a little closer.

She carefully took the dog's wounded paw in her hand and gently started cleansing it. The dog looked a little fearful but to my surprise it didn't growl or try to get away. She finished cleaning the cut then rinsed the glass and washcloth out in the surf.

"I hope it prevents him from getting an infection," she said, a look of deep concern on her face. "I wish I had some antibiotic ointment."

I slid my arm around her waist. "You've done enough for this dog for one day. Let's take a walk down the beach."

She smiled.

I was worried the mutt would follow us, but to my relief he stood in place for a few moments then hobbled away in the opposite direction.

It was a blissful beach stroll. We held hands and occasionally waded up to our knees in the surf, the afternoon sun warming our backs.

On the way back, Janet pointed toward the tree line.

"That's interesting."

A large tepee or wigwam of some kind was sitting there. It was made of a heavy brown fabric, perhaps canvas, or maybe animal skins. It was 15 feet high with what looked like a half dozen wooden poles protruding from the top, probably part of its frame. A large flap was pulled over what I assumed was the entrance.

"Do you think someone lives there?" Janet asked, as the wind tossed her hair around.

"I don't know, but they certainly have a great view," I replied.

We stood there silently for a few moments looking at it, then continued a little further down the beach to our chairs. It was late afternoon and the sun was setting behind the coconut and palm trees, which casts long shadows onto the sand.

• • •

That night, after dinner, when we got back to our cabana, Janet flopped onto the bed.

"How about a walk in the moonlight?" I asked.

She yawned. "I'm beat."

It was still early and I didn't feel like going to bed yet. "I'm going for a walk."

Her face screwed up. "Really? Be careful."

"I will."

I locked the door and slipped the key into the front pocket of my shorts. I grabbed the staff and started walking down the beach. The sand was cool, like liquid marble, and the full moon was climbing the night sky as the breeze blew steadily out of the southeast. I had been walking for about five minutes when I heard a loud growling sound in the shadows by the tree line. It was so startling that I froze mid-step. I slowly looked into the darkness where the sound had come from. It took a moment for my eyes to penetrate the shadows, but when they did, I saw the large dog that had been threatening the lame dog earlier that day. It was sitting, and someone, probably the asshole that was with the dog earlier, was also sitting there. Even with the full moon I couldn't see his face because it was dark in the shadows. The dog, still growling, moved menacingly toward me from the shadows into the moonlight. It was only 30 feet away now, snarling and bearings its teeth, which looked like ivory daggers.

I gripped the staff tightly, getting ready to use it as a weapon if the dog attacked. My heart was hammering as sweat beaded on my forehead and the back of my neck.

The guy in the shadows snickered as the dog took another step forward. "Never threaten my dog," the voice said. "My dog does what it wants, and I do believe he wants to see you bleed." He had a distinctive Texas drawl and was slurring, probably drunk.

I raised the staff to my waist and kept watching the dog as I answered: "If your dog comes any closer I'm going to brain it. Call it back . . . now!"

He didn't and the dog continued moving toward me, a thick stream of saliva dripping from its gums.

"He was minding his own business when that mangy lame dog came up yelping," the voice said.

"I don't care. Call your dog off!"

It was only 12 feet away now and was circling to my left. It looked huge in the moonlight, more like a wolf than a dog. There was no use running as it could easily catch me, and at the same time it occurred to me that the dog's owner could have a gun or knife. If I was going to do battle with the dog, it would have to be then and there.

"Why do you and your woman care about some lame mutt?" the voice asked. "My dog could have eaten that mutt for breakfast."

I looked away from the dog for a second in an attempt to see the man's face through the shadows, but he was wearing the same red ball cap pulled down low, which made it impossible to make out his features. "My 'woman' loves animals, what can I say?"

"Soft hearted bitch."

I slowly stepped backward, until my heels touched the water's edge. The dog continued snarling and moving to my left. If it came close enough I was going to smash it on the head with the staff, then run, or go after the owner and let him have the same.

"There's two thing I can tell my dog to do right now," the voice said. "Hit or heel. I'm not sure which one would be better, you Yankee prick."

The dog, only 10 feet away now, growled loudly, its lips curled back in aggression, its eyes black and fierce.

"Call him off!"

"What do you think General, you hungry for some Yankee meat?"

The dog moved a little closer. I was sure it was getting ready to lunge. Before it could do that, its owner stood. "General . . . heel," he said. The dog ignored the command and instead continued snarling at me. "General," the owner repeated in a loud voice, "heel!"

The dog looked back at its owner then sauntered over to his side.

"Your lucky day," the voice snickered. Then they disappeared into the bush through a break in the tree line.

I stood there for a moment and inhaled deeply. I was gripping the staff so tightly my knuckles were white as the moon. *Thank God I had this.*

When I got back to the cabana I brought the staff inside and leaned it against the doorframe. Janet was sitting up in bed reading.

"How was your walk?" she asked, peering up from her book.

I knew better then to tell her what had happened because it would upset her greatly and cast a shadow over the rest of our vacation.

"The moon," I said, "is fantastic."

• • •

The next morning we had finished breakfast and were getting ready to hit the beach, but I could not find my sunglasses.

"Jan have you seen my sunglasses?"

She smiled. "You're wearing them."

"What?" I chuckled and shook my head. "Thanks."

We settled into our beach chairs and I gazed out over the vast expanse the turquoise ocean. The weather was beautiful, a carbon copy of our first two days.

We were sitting in the shade of the palapa reading, when someone called out: "Hola!"

I turned to look. A deeply tanned young woman was approaching. She was smiling warmly and appeared to be in her late teens or early 20's. She looked like a deadhead, wearing a sleeveless cotton blouse and faded denim shorts. Her feet were bare and several necklaces adorned with tiny shells hung around her slender neck. Silver jewelry dripped from her wrists and fingers.

"You are English?" she asked, as she sat cross-legged in the sand beside us.

"Americans," I replied.

"I love America!" she exclaimed gleefully. "From which city do you come?"

Janet leaned forward in her chair. "Chicago."

The girl clapped gleefully. "Chicago! Michael Jordan and Al Capone!"

I smiled. "Neither of them play anymore."

She grinned and pointed to our cabana. "Do you stay at, Peace In Tulum?"

"We arrived two days ago."

"Is good yes?"

"It's basic but we like it," Janet replied.

"Good." She unfolded a white cloth the size of a magazine and carefully laid it in the sand, revealing earrings and other jewelry. "Perhaps you should like to buy something to remember your trip?"

I glanced down at the jewelry. There were earrings, rings, thin bracelets and necklaces, all embedded with colorful stones. It all appeared to be made from sterling silver and turquoise that matched the dreamlike color of the ocean.

Janet took off her sunglasses and leaned across me to get a better look. "It's all very nice," she said.

The girl picked up a bracelet embedded with a turquoise design and handed it to Janet. "Try this, is hand made from excellent Mexican sterling silver."

Janet took the bracelet, slid it onto her wrist and held out her arm. "It's lovely."

The girl smiled and held up a pair of matching earrings, which caught the sun's rays. "These go with bracelet, is a set."

Janet stood, tried on the earrings, then sat in the sand beside the girl and started looking over the other pieces of jewelry.

"How long do you stay?" the girl asked, gazing up at me with wide brown eyes.

"Until the middle of next week," Janet replied.

I pushed my toes into the sand and looked at the girl. She was young but quite pretty, and she seemed friendly enough. My eyes were drawn to a circular tattoo of a ying-yang symbol on her upper arm. I figured she was probably a native Mexican girl from who knows where.

"Do you live in that tent?" I asked, pointing to the tent we had seen the previous day.

She glanced over at it then back at me. "No, I do not live there," she replied. "Native Mexicans are permitted to live on beaches. I think this is what you are seeing."

"Oh really, how nice. Cheap rent."

Janet stood and brushed sand from her knees. "It's very lovely jewelry, but I'm not sure . . . perhaps manana . . . tomorrow? Will you be on the beach?"

The girl smiled. "Si, manana, I come back."

She carefully folded up the cloth holding the jewelry, stood and pushed the long dark hair off of her face.

"I offer table massage, to people, tourists," she said. "Up by yellow boat? Have you seen this boat? Is upside down by trees." She motioned to the right and her many bracelets jangled. "Is 200 meters that way."

"I saw that boat this morning," I replied.

"Have you ever had a massage under full moon?" she asked.

"I can't say that I have."

"Is very relaxing. Perhaps you or your wife like? I give good price."

She was young, in her early twenties, and attractive. My mind conjured up a sexually charged image of her massaging my entire body. But at the same time I knew that this could be a set-up for a robbery or worse.

"I'm not sure," I said. "We're both kind of tired and . . ."

"I am a professional. Do not to worry. You come tonight at 8 o'clock and I will give you massage. The moon will be up." She extended her hand for me to shake. "My name is Aldonza."

"Do you live by the boat?" I asked, letting her hand go.

"Ummmm . . . Yes we live."

She turned to Janet and smiled. "I will come back tomorrow and bring other pieces for you."

"Okay, thank you."

She waved goodbye and Janet and I settled back into our chairs.

"Nice girl," I said. "I don't know about that massage though."

Janet picked up her book and without looking at me said: "You should go. You're always saying you'd like to get a massage. You're on vacation. Just do it."

"Do what exactly?"

"What do you think? Get a massage. Go see her."

"Hmm. Maybe."

. . .

Maria had made seafood tacos and refried beans for dinner, which we washed down with a crisp bottle of chardonnay When Janet left for a few minutes to go to the bathroom, I summoned Maria over to our table and told her about the asshole and his vicious dog from the previous night.

"Could you tell if he was Mexican?" she asked.

"He was American, a Texan, from the sound of his accent."

She looked concerned. "I do not remember seeing a person with a dog like that. Perhaps he left the area today."

I nodded slowly. "I hope so."

"I am going into town tomorrow and I will tell the policia what happened."

"Good idea."

When we got back to the cabana, Janet flopped onto the bed. "I'm tired. I'm going to read. Then crash out."

Sitting at the foot of the bed, I looked at my watch, 7:30. "Maybe I'll go see Aldonza for that massage."

Janet propped herself up on her elbow and smiled. "Good idea. Enjoy it."

I kissed her, then went outside, grabbed the staff and starting down the beach toward the upturned yellow boat. The night wind carried the sweet scent of the jungle mingled with the smoky aroma of burning firewood and the briny smell of the ocean. The moon was so unbelievably bright as it climbed the night sky, that it illuminated everything with a supernatural white glow so brilliant that I cast a shadow. I imagined it was twice as big as the full moons I'd seen in Chicago. I felt like I was truly seeing it for the first time. I could understand why the ancient Mayans and Aztecs were in awe of the sun and the moon and worshiped them as gods. It was as if the moon had a voice and spoke in whispers.

When I reached the overturned yellow boat I didn't see Aldonza, so I walked over and ran my hand over the boat's rough wooden hull, pointing toward the stars. It was about 40 feet long and from what I could tell, had probably been a fishing vessel of some kind. Despite the unyielding brightness of the full moon, the thick woods behind the boat formed a black curtain impenetrable to sight. I looked down at the staff, and was surprised to see that the moonlight brought out a symmetrical design on it that wasn't apparent in the sunlight. Inch long white lines stood out against the dark smooth surface, running the length of the staff. I lifted it to my face to get a better look and ran my fingertips along the white lines, which were like tiny straight scratches.

I laid the staff in the sand and sat facing the ocean. A wide mermaid trail created by the full moon shimmered from the horizon to the waters edge. I was sitting there taking everything in when I heard someone behind me and quickly turned to look. It was Aldonza walking through a break in the thick bush. It was easy to see her smiling in the pure white glow of the moon.

"Buenas noches," she said merrily.

I stood, grabbed the staff with my right hand and used my left hand to brush the sand off the back of my shorts.

"Hola," I replied.

"Where is wife? She does no like massage?"

"Maybe later in the week."

She motioned to the staff. "Why do you bring stick? You no need."

I felt a little embarrassed because she probably knew that I had brought the staff just in case I needed it for protection. "There was a mean dog on the beach last night," I replied. "I brought it just in case he . . ."

She interrupted me. "Is safe, you no need stick.

"It helps me walk in the sand." I lied.

"You can also get here on the road," she said. "There is a sign that says *Zanzibar*, walk in there and you will see our campsite."

"It was nice walking on the beach."

She shrugged. "You keep stick if you want," then motioned for me to follow her. "My table is over this way."

We went through the break in the bushes and down a narrow sandy path lined with lush trees.

"Watch step," Aldonza said, walking a few feet in front of me.

The moon was so bright that I could easy see without tripping over the numerous tree roots which snaked across the trail. After a short walk we entered a clearing. Several dome like nylon tents were erected around a campfire emitting sparks and embers that drifted up into the inky night sky. Two hammocks were strung up between coconut trees. A black Labrador Retriever laying next to the fire raised its head to look at me, and seemingly satisfied that I wasn't a threat, grunted and put its head back on the ground. Half a dozen people around Aldonza's age were sitting on logs near the fire. They were chatting in Spanish and barely regarded us. Aldonza said something in Spanish to a guy who looked to be around 20. He nodded and she turned back to me. I was still a little anxious because I didn't know if these young people were runaways or criminals.

"My massage table is over here," Aldonza said, leading the way.

"Are those people your friends, family?" I asked, following her.

"Si, they are friends," she said without turning around.

We walked 30 feet through the woods before entering a second smaller clearing. To my surprise and relief an actual table covered in a sheet was sitting there.

"How much?" I asked, standing beside the table.

"Is five hundred pesos for one hour," she said, pulling back the sheet covering the table. "You can also give tip if you like."

"Okay . . . es bien."

She smiled. "What do you like Swedish massage? Deep tissue? You have tense, musculo, muscles, si?"

"Swedish es bien," I said.

She pointed to a high back wooden chair near the table. "Take off clothes, place on chair. Lay facedown on top of table under sheet. You get ready and I'll return. Okay?"

"Si, Okay." She headed back to where her friends were as I pulled off my T-shirt, and shorts, placed them on the chair and laid on the table as she had instructed. I was still a little nervous, but as I lay there, the roar of the surf and sound of the wind in the trees helped me relax. After a few minutes Aldonza returned holding a small bottle of massage oil.

"Best for you to concentrate on slow breath," she said, standing at the head of the table.

"Si, I'll try."

Inhaling deeply, she carefully peeled the sheet back until it was down to my waist, poured oil into her hands and started slowly massaging my shoulders.

"You no have burn from the sun," she said quietly. "You are lucky. Many times people have burn from sun and this ruins their vacation."

"I've tried to be careful."

"Good," she said, slowly moving her hands down my back. "When come to Mexico, remember rule number one. Respect the sun."

As I lay there, a small bird or large insect of some kind fluttered into the clearing then just as quickly disappeared back into the starry night sky.

I lifted my head. "What was that a bird?"

She stopped and looked around. "Is probably . . . how is it in English . . . bat?"

"A bat, really?"

"Si, but is okay," she answered resuming the massage. "Tonight the round moon sits on its throne. Bats, birds, insects, animals dance with nature when the moon is full."

"A moon dance?" I asked.

"Si, Yes. It true because Mexico means "Navel of the Moon" in Nahuatl language."

"Nahuatl?"

"Si, is old Aztec language. Mexico comes from word, "mexitli." This word is made up of "metztli" which in English is, moon, and xictli, which translates to "navel.""

"How interesting. I didn't know that."

She lightly touched my temple. "Now you know."

Perhaps it was the intimacy of the situation, but I was struck by her poetic way of speaking. She squeezed more oil from the bottle, moved to my left and ran her hands in slow circular motions over my side and down my arm.

"If you are like me, and you stay still long enough," she said, "you become part of nature. The sun, sea, trees, wind, sand, the moon . . . is as much in you as out of you."

"Really?"

"Si, is like, ahh, orgasm. You not need to try. Just, umm, let it happen."

Like an orgasm. Was she flirting with me? I wasn't sure how to respond, so I simply said: "That's interesting."

She was barely five feet tall and slight in build, but her hands were strong, and she was extremely focused, as if my body were a map she was examining very closely. She moved down to my left leg and turned her attention to my calf.

"Where did you learn massage," I asked.

"My friend showed me," she answered in voice barely above a whisper. "And I learn from feel of the body." She stopped for a moment and took a half step back. "Is too much? Too hard? You please tell me what is good for you."

"Es Good. Muy bien."

She resumed and I closed my eyes, finally able to relax a little. It was quiet for a while and then I asked her how old she was.

"I am no good with English numbers," she answered. "I am veinti and uno, which is . . ."

"Twenty one?" I asked.

"Si."

"Do you live here?"

She paused. "Si, sometimes."

"Are you Mexican?"

"Umm, Si."

"This is a beautiful part of your country. We love it here."

She moved to the bottom of the table and started gently kneading the sole of my left foot with her thumbs. "Is beautiful because is haunted with long memory. Million of years ago, here on the Yucatan, a meteor from space hit the earth."

"Yes, I knew that."

"Did you know it was like sperm to the egg . . . the umm, the day of birth, of the modern world."

"I don't understand."

She kept on massaging. "It was like sperm to the egg. Was a tremendous explosion that shook planet. Was beginning of the modern world. A type of, ahhhh . . . conception, a day of birth? Birthday? A cleansing of the earth. To make room for mankind, our ancestors."

She had obviously been educated somewhere. "Did you study in school?"

"School? No. I love to read books."

"You're smart. Your English is excellent."

"Thank you," she replied, and I could hear a smile in her voice. "I think my English is no so good. I speak to people from many countries. I try English, German, French and Polish. I wish to speak Italian."

"Italian?"

"Si, is because many Italians visit Mexico."

The sound of surf and the subtle fragrance of the massage oil filled my senses as she methodically worked her way up the right side of my body. The warm tropical breeze ushered away any remaining fears I had about Aldonza or her friends. I doubt they were thieves or criminals. Forty years earlier they would have been considered dropouts or hippies. They were living day-to-day off what they could sell to tourists, and in Aldonza's case, what she could make from giving massages.

I was only half awake when she gently placed her hands on my hip and whispered: "Almost done. Please tell me. How should you like to finish?"

I raised my head to look at her. I am not naïve. I knew what she was asking. She was propositioning me. It was subtle, but I could see the suggestion in her brown eyes. Where there had been a gentle softness a few minutes earlier there was now a sharpness and look of expectation. The full moon was overhead, bathing her in a soft light, accenting her smile and the whites of her eyes.

What I wish I had said was: "Muy bien. You don't have to do anything else. But I'm going to pay you something extra anyway so you can buy more books." That's what I wish I had said.

When she finished, I stepped into my shorts, pulled on my t-shirt, grabbed the staff, took five hundred pesos from my pocket and handed it to her. "That was very nice," I said.

She smiled. "Gracias. Now you are good."

"Bien, Si."

I pulled out an additional two hundred pesos and handed her it to her. "This is for you."

She looked down at the money and back at me without saying anything.

"Is that enough?" I asked.

"Did you like?"

"Si, muy bien."

"More appropriate tip for this kind of massage would be additional . . . ahhh, doscientos pesos . . . in English is . . . . two hundred pesos more?"

I didn't feel like squabbling over the price so I gave her the additional two hundred pesos and we walked down the sandy path together back to the upturned yellow boat.

"I will see you manana . . . tomorrow with jewelry for wife," she said before turning and reentering the woods through the break in the bushes.

"Si, es bien."

On the way back to the cabana, I dropped the staff in the sand and waded into the ocean up to my waist. The surf had died down a bit but the water was still warm and moonbeams danced on it dark surface. After a few minutes I waded back to shore, picked the staff and continued walking back to our cabana.

I was almost there when I saw the little lame dog standing by the chairs Janet and I had been sitting in earlier that day. As I approached he looked up at me impassively, his brown eyes wide.

"What are you doing here?" I muttered. He lay down in the sand and grunted. I poked him with the staff. "You go home. You could have gotten me killed." He lifted his head to look at me then put it back down, so, I poked him a little harder. "Get going. Go home." He just grunted again. "Go on get out of here," I said firmly. He didn't even look at me. *Damned dog!* I knew he would be like our shadow for the rest of the trip and that was the last thing we needed, an unwanted intrusion. I gripped the staff tightly, raised it to my shoulder and the dog cowered.

When I got back to the cabana the lights were off. It was so dark I couldn't see anything. I quietly settled into a chair next to the door and when my eyes finally adjusted to the darkness I could see Janet sleeping. I didn't want to disturb her so I decided to go to the restaurant and get a drink. I grabbed the staff and trudged through the sand. When I got to the restaurant it was empty, except for Maria who was sitting at one of the tables counting money. I left the staff leaning against the outside wall by the stairs and went in.

"Is it too late to get beer . . . cerveza?" I asked.

She stopped counting, put the money in a small metal box and motioned to a chair next to hers. "Is no too late. Please sit."

I sat and she went back into the kitchen to get me a beer. She returned and placed the bottle in front of me. I lifted it to my lips and took a long slow drink.

"Is Mexican beer. Is okay?" Maria asked. "Is not Budweiser."

"I don't drink Budweiser," I said placing the bottle on the table. "This is very good."

We chatted for an hour. She chain smoked Camels as I told her about our life in Chicago and she told how she had come to Tulum from Mexico City thirty years earlier. Every time I finished a beer she would go and get me another one. I must have had four or five beers and was getting a little drunk.

"You no have kids?" she asked, taking a drag from her cigarette.

"No, but we'd like to," I answered, slurring my words. "My wife wants. But if we have kids it'll change everything." I motioned to our surroundings. "We can forget about trips like this."

She flicked the ash from her cigarette into the ashtray. "Being a parent is a big job."

"Right, and I'm not sure I'm ready. It if was up to Janet, we'd have three kids, two dogs and a cat by now. I enjoy the simplicity of our lives."

She looked at me with narrowed eyes. "You are not sure about being a father?"

I took a drink of beer before answering. "I enjoy my life the way it is, the freedom we have."

"Freedom is nice," she said leaning forward, "but children can bring you much joy."

I took another drink of beer and placed the bottle on the table. "I guess it's all about tradeoffs."

She smiled and butted her cigarette out in a glass ashtray, then leaned back in her chair. "Life is about tradeoffs."

"Not for Janet. She wants it all, a family, career, a house in the suburbs. In a way I can't blame her for that."

"She is ambitious. Perhaps this is why you were attracted to her in the first place?"

I nodded. "That certainly was part of it."

She smiled widely. "If she wants children perhaps it happens here in Mexico on vacation."

I chuckled. "If we have a girl we'll name her '"Mexico.'"

She tilted her head back and laughed hoarsely. "Mexico is good!"

"She will have her mother's cobalt eyes and her father's mood swings," I said. "She will be tall and beautiful with dark skin and a shy ivory smile. She will love to read and she will respect the sun! Her soul will be filled with blue sky, turquoise, soft warm breezes, white coral, sea turtles and tropical fish."

Maria clapped her hands. "Is lovely! You speak in poetic manor. Do you write the poems?"

"God no."

"No? You should do."

"Really? I never considered myself a poet."

"Everyone is poet if they take time to look, to see. Just let it flow. Let it go."

"To see?"

"Yes to look inside and out. To see. To feel."

"Do you write poetry?"

"Hmm, a little. I like."

I raised my bottle in a toast. "To poetry and my little girl, Mexico."

"To poems and your girl Mexico," she said, raising her glass. She smiled then looked at her watch and back at me. "I must close soon, but first you should like a tequila?"

I was already kind of drunk, so it seemed like a good idea. "Si, gracias."

She went into the kitchen and returned with a juice glass and a bottle of Don Julio Gold.

"Es mucho bien tequila!" I said.

She nodded and filled the glass half way. "Si, is good." Then she stood beside the table. "You have drink. I close restaurant."

She went back into the kitchen as I sat there sipping the tequila. It was so smooth that I quickly finished it. The moon was high and bright, in sharp contrast to the inky blackness of the ocean. A few minutes passed then the restaurant lights went out and Maria returned. I must have looked pretty drunk because she regarded warily.

"You are okay? Perhaps you drink too much?"

"No problemo," I slurred. I pushed my chair back from the table and staggered to my feet. "How much do I owe you for the drinks?"

"Is how you say in English, compliment? No charge."

"Complimentary? Free? Thank you."

She gently took my arm. "I will help you to cabana."

"No necescito," I protested, pulling away from her. "I'm okay. The moon will light my way."

She looked worried. "I am not sure you are okay."

"No problemo. It's close."

She helped me down the wooden stairs and we stood in the sand under the full moon. "Your cabana is that way," she said pointing.

"I know. Don't worry. I'll be alright." I stepped forward, hugged her then waved and turned toward the path. "Goodnight Maria . . . Buenas noches . . . Adios . . . farewell . . ."

"Good night and be careful," she said as she turned toward the dirt parking lot.

There wasn't anyone else around as I stumbled down the moonlit sandy path, past our cabana to the beach. I laid there on the cool sand looking up at a night sky sprinkled with stars like a million children around the mother moon. Soon I was sound asleep, dreaming of a one-armed girl in a bikini . . .

. . . she's walking up the beach looking around for something as the wind whips her long blonde locks over her face. She's in her 20s and is slight. She's wearing a bright red bikini. I am sitting on a towel by myself as she approaches. I suddenly notice that her right arm is missing below the elbow. I don't think she was born that way because there is scar tissue on the nub. What happened? A shark attack, some kind of accident? She looks concerned.

"Have you seen a little white dog?" she asks.

I look at her face because I do not want to make her feel badly by looking at her arm, as most people probably do.

"No, I haven't seen a dog. What does he look like?"

"A white Heinz 57. Cocker spaniel, poodle and who knows what else."

I stand, shield my eyes with my hand and scan the beach. "Is he your dog?"

"Yes, and he's a she," she says, looking around fretfully. "She was chasing birds and got away from me."

"I've been here for a few hours and haven't seen her. Do you need help looking for her?"

The corners of her mouth turn up. "Thanks, but I'll find her. She can't have gone too far."

"What's her name, in case I see her?"

"Sally, or something like that."

God, I want to say, don't you know your dog's name? "I'll keep an eye out and hold onto her if she comes by."

"Thanks," she says, then asks. "This is where the water meets the land right?"

I look out over the white-capped turquoise ocean then turn back toward her. "It is, yes."

She smiles again, starts walking away, then turns back to me and says. "It's hard living on tips only."

I nod as if I understand and she continues down the beach. Watching her walk away, I am struck by what I can only describe as her courage. Most girls in their 20s are completely preoccupied with their appearance. But she is on the beach in a bright red bikini that draws attention to her and her terrible injury. I want to hug her . . .

• • •

"Dan wake up. Come on Dan, wake up. What are you doing here?"

"What? Where am I?" How the . . ."

Someone was shaking me. I opened my eyes. Janet was kneeling beside me. Only half awake, I sat and gazed around. I was on the beach, the first streaks of morning light pushing across the dark eastern sky like long thin fingers.

"What are you doing here?" Janet asked urgently. "I woke up, you weren't there. I was worried and came looking for you."

"Oh," I replied slowly, rubbing my eyes. "I was looking at the stars and must have fallen asleep."

My mouth was dry as sand and it felt as if there was a rock drummer doing a solo inside my head.

"Are you alright?" Janet asked.

"I'm alright," I replied, smacking my lips together. "I just need some water."

She gently grabbed my arm, helped me to my feet and brushed the sand off of me.

"Come on," she said, an expression of concern on her face. "Let's go inside so you can lay down."

Once inside, I undressed and collapsed on the bed, while Janet went into the bathroom to get me something to drink. She returned with a glass of water, handed it to me and sat on the edge of the bed. The room was dark but I could see that she was still anxious.

"I was worried something happened when you went to meet Aldonza."

I gulped down the water and placed the glass on the bedside table. "Nothing happened, it was fine."

"Were you drinking?" she asked, stroking my forehead.

"A little," I answered, then flopped onto the pillow. "I came back. You were sleeping, so I had a few drinks with Maria at the restaurant."

I took her hand in mine. "I left and was star gazing. I fell asleep I guess. I had a weird dream."

She stared at me warily. "Just a few drinks?"

I covered my eyes with my forearm. "And a tequila."

"Thank God nothing happened to you. There are wild animals around here."

I turned to look at her. "I know Jan, but I was close by. Nothing would have happened."

"That's what you think."

She pulled her shirt over her head, striped off her shorts and panties and laid down naked in bed beside me, her body warm and supple.

"I was worried," she said softly. "I'm glad you're okay."

"I'm fine, just tired."

She was asleep in minutes. I rolled onto my side and thought about my dreams. Freud said that we are all the people in our dreams. So I guess that somewhere inside of me is a one armed girl in a bikini. Others have said dreams are a window into the subconscious. I don't know what my subconscious was telling me, but soon I was asleep, the symphony of sound from the ocean, wind and nearby woods filling my mind with peace.

• • •

When I woke sun was spilling in through the wooden blinds and Janet was gone. I looked at my watch. Almost noon. I was feeling a lot better but was still parched. I quickly downed two glasses of water, then threw on my t-shirt, bathing suit and sunglasses and went outside. Janet was on the beach lying in the shade of the palapa reading a magazine. As I approached I could see that the little lame mutt was lying beside her. I thought I was having a hallucination or was still dreaming.

"Hi sweetheart," I said, as I reached her side.

She placed the magazine on her lap and looked up at me over the rims of her sunglasses.

"Feeling better?"

"A lot better."

I motioned to the dog. "I see our friend is back."

She reached over and rubbed his ears. "He came walking up the beach this morning and hasn't left."

I patted him, then stood and stretched. "I guess he doesn't understand English, because I saw him last night and told him to get lost."

"Why?"

"Jan, I don't want you to feel like you have to take care of him. It's our vacation. He's a stray."

"He comes and goes as he wants," she said patting his head. "Don't worry. I'm not going to adopt the poor little guy."

It was as if the dog suddenly understood me because he looked at us both then limped away down the beach.

Janet shrugged. "Like I was saying. He comes are goes as he pleases."

"I guess." I sat next to her and gazed out over the turquoise ocean. The sun was high, over wisps of clouds crawling across a dazzling blue sky. The steady breeze, still out of the south east, was warm and refreshing like the previous days.

Janet sat up and removed her sunglasses. "Another perfect day in paradise."

I was thinking about the massage, and I looked straight ahead. "Absolutely beautiful."

I glanced back at the cabana that housed the restaurant then toward Janet. "Have you eaten?"

"I did. You should go have something."

"Good idea."

I started walking away then stopped and turned back toward her. "Thanks for the help this morning. I was a mess. I overdid it a little last night."

She smiled. "I was worried about you."

I held her gaze for a moment and was suddenly struck by her sincerity and beauty.

"You were?" I asked weakly.

"Of course," she said replied. "What do you think? Why else . . ."

"I'm just hung over. I'm not thinking right."

She motioned toward the restaurant. "Go get something to eat."

"Adios," I said turning away.

When I got to the restaurant Maria was there serving a couple lunch. She was wearing a colorful apron with the ancient Mayan calendar printed on it. She waved, I claimed a seat and after a few minutes she came over to my table.

"How was your sleep?" she asked, her expression filled with expectation.

"It was okay."

"You feel okay today? No headache?"

"A little one."

She grinned. "You would like a breakfast burrito and coffee?"

Nothing ever sounded so good. "That would be perfect."

She left, then returned a few minutes later with a tray holding coffee in a ceramic mug, a small steel container of milk and several packets of sugar.

"Is Mexican coffee," she said placing everything on the red and white-checkered table cloth. "Is strong and will give to you energy."

"Gracias," I said wearily.

Sipping the coffee, I started thinking about the massage Aldonza had given me. I felt like telling Janet what had happened, but I was too ashamed. It would have been like slapping her. We all make mistakes, and occasionally they become our secrets. Confession may be good for the soul, but it's not always good for a relationship. Sometimes it's better to live with mistakes and learn from them rather than hurting those close to us.

A broad expanse of white capped greenish blue ocean was visible from my table. As I was sitting there, a kite surfer in a harness came into view. He was only fifty yards from shore as he skimmed over the rough surface of the water and took flight, flying for 20 or 30 yards at a time before touching down again. I was memorized. He was absolutely free. Nothing ever looked so fun. I was watching him when Maria returned with the burrito and placed it in front of me.

"Customers are gone. Can I join you?"

I picked up my fork and motioned to the chair. "Si, please sit."

It would be impossible to describe how good the burrito smelled, let alone how absolutely delicious it was. It was stuffed with scrabbled eggs, diced ham, fresh peppers, black beans, rice, onions and cheese.

"I sit with your wife this morning," Maria said, sipping from a cup of coffee. "She is beautiful. You are lucky."

"Thank you. She's great."

She leaned back in her chair and looked at me kind of sternly. "Do not let her go."

I shrugged.

"Sometimes people are strange," she continued. "They kill their own happiness. Is a big mistake."

I assumed she was referring to the previous night when I was drunkenly lamenting about starting a family. I placed my fork on the table and wiped my mouth with a napkin. "I guess I was venting a little last night."

Her face screwed up. "Venting is?"

"Is . . . talking too much."

She shrugged. "Was okay. Is how you feel."

"Sometimes, it's how I feel."

"Sometimes is how we all feel," she said raising the cup to her lips. She looked at me for a few seconds without saying anything. It was as if she was taking stock of me, that she thought she knew something about me, that she was seeing into a deep dark corner of me.

"You should to count your, ummm . . . regalo . . . in English is . . . blessings! Yes, count your blessings! Your wife loves you. This is good."

"I suppose." I didn't feel like talking about it so I reached for my coffee mug and gazed out over the beach as Maria stood and gathered up the dishes.

"You like the pizza?" she asked, looking down at me.

"Sí."

"Is good place for pizza 100 meters down the road. Is called *Romane's*. Other visitors enjoy. Perhaps you would like to try?"

"Thank you we might."

I finished my coffee and was getting ready to leave when Maria stuck her head out of the kitchen. "Remember your promise," she said with a wide smile. "You will name your child Mexico."

"Either that or Canada," I joked. I looked over the ocean. The kite surfer was nowhere in sight.

When I got back to Janet, the wind was still up and sun kissed waves were crashing onto the shore. The water looked especially inviting.

"Let's go for a swim," I said, pulling my T-shirt over my head.

Janet put down her magazine and got to her feet. "It's a little rough."

"We'll be fine."

We entered the water and frothy waves broke over our thighs and the roar of the surf filled our ears. I took Janet's hand and we waded in until the water reached midway up my chest. The ocean was so warm and clear that I felt as if it was cleansing me of all my worries.

"I wonder if it's snowing in Chicago?" Janet asked.

"I hope it's snowing and freezing because that would somehow make this feel even better," I replied.

She dove under the surface and came up about 10 feet away. I did the same and for the next little while we swam lazily, or just floated on our backs looking up into the endless blue sky.

When we got back to our beach chairs, I slipped on my sunglasses and let the warm wind and sun dry me. I was looking lazily around the beach when a man came out of the tepee we had seen the previous day. I did a quick double take because to my dismay, he was buck naked. His skin was as dark as mahogany and he didn't have even a hint of a tan line. Dreadlocks tumbled down his back. He was short, muscular and in great shape. He held his head high and chest puffed out, proud like an Aztec sun king. He was a good 60 feet away, but I would have guessed that he was in his late 20s. He glanced around casually, then seemingly oblivious to the few people on the beach, walked down to the water's edge.

I tapped Janet's arm and motioned to him. "You don't see that every day."

She was completely astonished. "I guess we're at the nude beach."

I leaned back in my chair. "He sure wears his pride well, if nothing else."

A few minutes passed, then a young woman holding a baby wrapped in a blanket emerged from the tepee. She was completely naked too, and like the man, she was a fine specimen of a human being. She appeared to be younger than him, probably in her late teens. She was also short, athletic and dark and was very curvy with a prominent v marking her pubic hair. Her long dirty blond hair did little to conceal her nakedness. They both seemed completely comfortable, as if their nudity was as natural as the wind.

Janet was mesmerized. She sat up in her seat and adjusted her sunglasses. "Oh," she cooed. "That must be a newborn."

I tried not to stare, but I was so surprised by what I was seeing, I found it difficult to look away. They were like a mirage, a vision. The man walked to where the girl was standing. They chatted briefly then she went back into the teepee and came out a few moments later without the baby. They swam together for a while then returned to the teepee, pulling the flap over the entrance behind them.

Janet held up her magazine. "I was reading an article on getting pregnant and it said that ovulation can cause a slight increase in basal body temperature."

I thought she had read every article ever written about how to get pregnant but this was something new. I leaned back in my chair. "Basal body temperature?"

"It's your temperature when you're fully at rest."

"Really?"

"Yes," she replied pointing to the page. "It says that to monitor your basal body temperature, you should use a thermometer specifically designed to measure basal body temperature. Then you take your temperature every morning before you get out of bed and plot the readings on graph paper or in a spreadsheet. Eventually, a pattern might emerge. It says I'll be most fertile during the two to three days before my temperature rises. The increase will be subtle, typically less than one degree."

"Use a spreadsheet? That's a lot of planning and work don't you think," I said, then in a slightly sarcastic tone added: "Do you want me to start taking your temperature when you're sleeping?"

She placed the magazine on her lap and a look of slight annoyance formed on her face. "A lot of planning? What do you think we've been doing for the past two years?"

"I'm pretty sure I know what we've been doing Jan."

She sat up and looked at me. "Have your views on us starting a family changed?"

I exhaled and rubbed my eyes. "No. Yes. I don't know."

"You don't know?"

"Sometimes the idea scares me. It's a lot of responsibility and . . ."

She interrupted me. "Since when does having a baby scare you?"

Oh boy, here we go. "The more I think about it, the more it, you know . . ." I paused, then seeing where our conversation was going said: "Scares me' is probably not the best way to state it."

"What is the best way to state it?" she demanded.

"Unsure. Not one hundred percent sure . . . What do you want me to say?"

She stood and glared down at me. "I want you to say you want, no not you want, that you absolutely need for us to start a family."

"I can't say that with totally sincerity."

"Since when?"

"I don't know, Jan."

"You are unbelievable," she snapped. "Why don't you decide what you want to do, and who you want to do it with. We agreed when we got married that we'd start a family, and if you're not onboard with that I need to know."

"I'm just saying the idea scares me a little. I'm not . . . ." Before I could finish she cut me off again. "No wonder I haven't gotten pregnant," she muttered.

"You think you haven't conceived because I have a few doubts?" I scoffed. "That's ridiculous."

"You know what's ridiculous? You are if you think I'm abandoning plans for a family."

"I never said that."

"You might as well have."

There was an icy silence, then she turned away. "I'm going for a walk."

I stood. "I'll go with you."

She started walking away and without turning back blurted: "No. I want to be alone."

The cat was out of the bag. I was actually relieved. I felt as if my doubts were a psychological ball and chain I had been lugging around. Still, I hadn't planned for it all to come to a head like that.

I sat there for a good hour thinking about everything and looking out to sea. I loved and respected Janet. She would be a great mother, but I wasn't sure if I was cutout to be a father. Was I being selfish? No. I was being realistic.

After a while I saw Janet approaching from way down the beach. I continued watching as she grew from a spec in the distance, until she was only a few feet away.

"I'm sorry I got angry," she said quietly, sitting in the sand. "But I thought we were on the same page with having a baby." She took off her sunglasses. "I need to know if you want to start a family?"

"I'm not saying I don't want to have a baby," I replied. "I'm saying I have some concerns."

She reached over and took my hand. "It's natural to have concerns because it's a huge responsibility. And you know what? I have concerns sometimes too. Will the baby be healthy and normal? Will I be a good mother? Can I still have a career? Those are my concerns, but I'm certain I want a family."

"I know."

A single tear ran down her cheek. "I want to have a family and I want to have it with you," she said.

"I know, Jan," I replied softly as I stroked her arm. "I know."

. . .

We slept in the next morning and when we got to the beach after lunch the sun was high. I don't think either of us felt like continuing our conversation from the previous day. Instead, we lazed there for a while then strolled down the pristine beach, holding hands and wading up to our knees in the warm surf. We had a wonderful, carefree afternoon together. I hadn't felt so close to Janet in months.

As we were strolling back to our chairs, I saw Aldonza approaching. When we were about 20 feet apart she smiled widely and greeted us. "Hola."

It was the first time I'd seen her since the massage. I was worried she might say something to Janet, or even try to shake me down somehow. "Hola," Janet and I replied in unison. I wanted to keep walking, but to my chagrin, Janet stopped.

Suddenly the sun felt a lot hotter.

"Is beautiful day," Aldonza said motioning around her. "Is explosion of beauty."

She was dressed the same, in a loose cotton blouse and faded denim cutoffs. Her eyes were shielded by a pair of Aviator sunglasses, each dark lens reflecting the sun.

She smiled at Janet. "You should come for a massage," she said gleefully. "Did your husband no like?"

"It was fine," I said.

"I hurt my hand," Aldonza continued with a slight pout. "I was going too hard."

"Too hard?" Janet asked.

My blood pressure spiked. I felt as if I had been reduced to a mouse, being tortured by a cat.

"Yes, but is okay now," Aldonza replied, limply holding out her right hand for us both to see.

"The sun's real hot today," I said, "I don't want to get burned so we're going to get going."

"I have no jewelry to show you today," she frowned at Janet. "You will be here for how many more days?"

"Three more days," Janet smiled.

Aldonza smiled. "Maybe I was see you on the beach." She waved. "Adios."

As Janet and I continued walking, I wasn't sure if Aldonza was being coy or not. If she was, at least it wasn't blatant. If we saw her before we left, I could always buy a pair of earrings to keep her happy and quiet.

"Maria said there's a good pizza place down the road," I said as we headed back toward our cabana.

Janet smiled. "That sounds like a nice change."

"It's a date."

We got to the pizza place after 7 o'clock. Despite some language problems with our waiter we managed to order margaritas and a delicious cheese and basil pizza. The pizzeria had a half dozen rough wooden tables and chairs and planks for a floor. It was basic, like Maria's tiny restaurant, but a refreshing and spiced night breeze wafted in through the open windows. "This is enough," I thought as I sat there looking at Janet. "This is more than enough. This is perfection."

We had just finished eating when a local couple with two young children claimed a table near ours. I glanced over at Janet who was looking wistfully at the two kids. I knew what she was thinking: When? I took a drink of my margarita and tapped Janet gently on the arm. "Do you have a pen and piece of paper?"

"I think so, why?" she replied, reaching for her purse.

I grinned. "I'm going to write a poem."

Her blue eyes widened. "A poem, really?"

"Yeah, why not."

She took a drink of her margarita and looked at me over the rim of the glass. "Have you ever written a poem before?"

I shook my head. "Nope, but last night when I was talking to Maria, she said all you have to do is to 'see and to feel,' and I feel inspired."

Smiling, she pulled a pen and small notebook from her purse and handed them to me. "Can I read it when you're finished?"

"Maybe."

She stood. "You decide. I'm going to the bathroom."

"I'll be here."

I picked up the pen, thought about Maria had said about letting it flow. I was kind of surprised by the stream of consciousness prose that flowed from the tip of the pen:

> Rule number one respect the sun.
> Like a new moon and old stars dancing across the Zanzibar sky.
> Deep nights when the Mayanians and Aztecs read the heavens.
> They worshipped the sun and got burned.
> I wonder why?

I paused, laid the pen on the table and reached for my margarita. It was tart and strong, the tequila warming my blood, as I wrote:

> I wonder if it's snowing in Chicago?
> I will not destroy my own happiness.
> Then, as if by reflex I scribbled:
> What is happiness?

I stopped and rubbed my eyes. *What is happiness?*

I thought I knew once. It involved living life as fully and honestly as I could. Maybe I was naive, but I believed love held the key to true happiness. Willful naïveté is the romantics blessing, I guess. Still, sitting there, love and happiness felt distant, like a faraway country. They started with Janet, or she was a huge part of it. Even before I met Janet I knew I wanted to have a life partner, a wife. The devil looks for the lone ship. Going through life with someone who loves you is superior to going through it by yourself. Then why was I sitting there asking myself if I was happy? From all outward appearances I should be. Life was good. Jan was a smart and loving woman. She had a sense of humor and compassion for the weak and defenseless. We lived comfortably. I was never cursed with blind ambition. I had a good sales job, and in my own mind at least, I was successful. I thanked God for all my blessings.

Then why . . . ?

"It looks like you've got a lot of your poem done," Janet said, sliding onto her seat. "Can I take a look?"

I tore the sheet of paper from the notebook, folded it up, shoved it deep into my pocket and smiled. "Maybe later, Jan. It's a work in progress."

"No problemo."

We ordered coffee and were sitting there chatting, simply enjoying the tropical night when a man came in wearing shorts and a red ball cap. He sat down near our table and summoned the waiter. He was in his thirties, and was bony with a short beard. A tattoo of some kind was crawling up his right forearm. As soon as he ordered, I recognized his voice, his slow Texas drawl. It was the guy who had threatened me with his dog. I don't think he recognized Janet or I. He seemed drunk and distant, rarely casting his gimlet-eyed gaze in our direction. I sipped my coffee, chatted with Janet and watched him for 20 minutes. When he ordered his third beer, I paid our bill. A few minutes later he got up and went to the bathroom.

"I'm going to the bathroom," I said, as I stood. "I'll be right back."

I am not a violent person, but I will not back down from a fight, especially if I'm cornered. I grew up with two older brothers. I was a middle linebacker in high school. I know the power of violence and I kept in shape. If circumstances warrant it, I take matters into my own hands, and that jerk had really pissed me off.

I slowly pushed open the bathroom door. He was standing at the urinal swaying back and forth, obviously drunk. I casually looked around. There wasn't anyone else in there. I rinsed my hands in the sink, waiting for him to finish. As he was turning from the urinal, pulling up his zipper, I slugged him hard on the left side of his face with my right fist. He flew backwards against the wall, as if shot. His red ball cap landed in the corner and he slumped to the floor. Before he could get up, I grabbed the neck of his shirt with my right hand and raised my left hand in a tight fist.

"Keep your dog on a leash, asshole." I said emphatically.

He was only half conscious and blood was flowing from a deep gash on his left cheek where my punch had landed.

"What . . . the . . . ."

I twisted his shirt tightly around his throat until he started choking. "Be smarter than your dog, asshole. We've told the police about you and you bag of shit mutt."

His eyes were rolling around like marbles in his head, his legs rubber. "Who?" he slurred, "I never saw her . . ." I had obviously knocked the fight out of him, if there ever really is "fight" in meat-headed rednecks like that. I let go and he splayed on the floor, his chin resting on his chest. He was so drunk I doubted he'd even remember how he got hurt.

The knuckles on my right hand were throbbing as I strode back to our table where Janet was looking toward the ocean.

"Are you ready?" I asked, standing beside the table.

She smiled and stood. "Let's go."

Night seemed to envelop us as we walked the narrow road back to our cabana. When we were about halfway there it started raining. We figured it was just a brief shower and it actually felt refreshing, so we didn't hurry. But within a minute it started pouring and then the heavens opened up with warm soft drops the size of nickels. I've been caught in Chicago storms, but I'm convinced there's nothing like a Mexican downpour. It was delightful deluge. It simply felt as if someone had turned on a warm waterfall above us. We were drenched to the skin so quickly we even stopped running.

"Come on," I said to Janet as we reached Peace In Tulum. "Let's walk the beach."

"Are you serious? In the rain?"

"Yeah," I replied, taking her hand. "It'll be fun."

The rain let up a little, but it was still coming straight down in warm balmy drops as we stood on the beach a short distance from our cabana. It was so dark I could barely see as I kissed her and she locked her hands together around my neck.

"Have you ever had sex on a beach in the rain?" I whispered playfully.

Her face was inches from mine. She smiled as balmy rain ran down her cheeks. "I haven't . . . until now."

We stripped naked and laid our clothes flat on the sand like blankets. The soft fat rain on our bodies, combined with the dark night and sweet perfume of the jungle seemed to give everything an erotic flair. I laid on our clothes and Janet carefully straddled me, warm rain dripping from her face and body onto my chest. She put her hands on my shoulders and slowly started riding me as I matched her rhythm with my hips and ran my hands over her thighs up to her breasts. I sat up and she wrapped her legs around my waste, riding me even harder. I kissed her passionately on the neck and mouth and the smoky spices from dinner, mingled with the sharp taste of lime from the margaritas filled my mouth. Sometimes, when you're totally immersed in something immensely pleasurable and real, it transcends time, as if the hands have fallen off a clock. I honestly can't say how long we were there. Ten minutes? Thirty minutes? An hour? If someone had walked past, we wouldn't have noticed, or cared.

When we finished, I laid on my back, facing the night sky, and Janet snuggled in beside me, her body and breath both warm. It had stopped raining and a scattering of stars and the moon were peaking out from behind clouds crawling eastward. We laid there quietly without saying anything, the only sounds our breathing and the breaking surf only 10 feet away.

"I'm not going back," Janet said softly, gazing into the deep night sky. "I'm staying here forever."

I rolled onto my side, ran my hand over her naked torso. She turned to look at me, her eyes as round as the moon overhead. I couldn't believe how beautiful she was. It wasn't physical beauty as much as something deeper, an inward beauty that radiated from her center. I kissed her.

"We can live on the beach, in a tent and sell jewelry to tourists."

She kissed me back and whispered. "If only . . . if only."

She was a pragmatist. I always knew that. I admired that in her. She had priorities. She made lists. She was organized and she knew how to emulate love. She would be a good mother and was a fine wife.

Was that enough for me? I don't know. Maybe it should be. I gazed at the stars. Perhaps I was expecting too much from life? Maybe I had unrealistic expectations? Does that make me a bad person? No. Was I on the precipice of destroying my own happiness? No. I enjoyed simplicity in life, and had worked hard to find it.

After a while we got up and peeled our clothes from the sand. The rain had scrubbed the air clean and the moon and stars sparkled overhead. We didn't even bother getting dressed and instead walked hand-in-hand naked to our cabana, took a warm shower, and feel to sleep in a loose embrace.

• • •

It was mid-morning by the time we got to the beach and we spent a few lazy hours collecting shells, swimming and laying in the sun enjoying our luxuriant tropical surroundings.

Later that day, the young native Mexican couple from the tepee came walking up the beach. They were both deeply tanned, and unlike the first time when we saw them naked, he was wearing tattered denim shorts, a shell necklace and wrap around sunglasses. She was dressed in a loose white T-shirt, a bathing suit bottom and was carrying the baby on her back in a satchel.

They looked like they were in bliss.

It's dangerous to project an idea of happiness on others. Everyone has problems, regardless of who they are or how they live. When it comes to evaluating others happiness, we are all outside looking in. But as the couple got closer, it struck me that despite their bohemian lifestyle, or maybe because of it, they were serine and completely contented. When they were

10 away, he nodded at us and I nodded back. To my surprise, Janet put down her book, and walked over to them. I watched her for a moment and could tell she was asking about the baby. The girl smiled widely and carefully held up the infant for Janet to see. I felt like I had to do something, so I went over to the waters edge where they were standing.

"Hola," I said.

"Hola," they replied.

"They don't speak English," Janet said.

The girl was 20 at the most, still a baby herself. She was robust and strong, her tanned face pretty and worn. The man was a few years older, not much younger than me. His brown chest, biceps and thighs were muscular and sculpted. Thick dreadlocks tumbled down his strong brown back. The baby's soft skin was the color of toffee. It was definitely a newborn, no more than a few months old.

"Es Muy bien, ah es, muy beautiful," I said.

"It's a boy," Janet cooed, as frothy waves crashed on the beach.

The guy smiled widely and said something to me in Spanish, which I didn't quite hear over the surf or understand.

I shrugged. "No hablo."

He smiled and pointed at the baby. "Is my son!"

I nodded. "Es Bien!"

We stood there for a few awkward moments admiring the baby and exchanging smiles, then they continued on their way.

"That is the cutest baby I've ever seen," Janet said as we settled back into our chairs.

I watched them strolling away down the beach. "What a life. How do they manage, living on the beach like that?"

"They get by, just like the rest of us."

They were living like they would have 300 years ago when they would have been chased off land and been forced by nature at defend themselves against nature and wild animals. The character of the threats to their existence had changed since then, replaced by newer stealthier threats. Chances were that they'd never own a computer or a cell phone. But technology, tourists and development were moving in. Of course, everything is relative, and three hundred years from now people will say we lived in a simpler time.

. . .

After dinner I gathered up a few hundred pesos in loose change and small bills as Janet showered.

"Do you have any change, small bills?" I asked as she emerged from the shower and wrapped a thick white towel around her body.

"In my purse. Why?" she asked as water dripped from her hair.

"I thought I'd give it to Aldonza and her friends."

"Really?"

"It can't be easy for them living like that."

She grabbed her purse off the bed, pulled out eighty-three pesos in coins and bills and handed it to me. "It's a nice gesture."

She started drying her hair as I pulled open the front door. "See you in a bit Jan."

She lowered the towel and smiled. "Be careful."

"I will."

Outside, the stars and moon were starting their nightly performance. I grabbed the staff and instead of walking the beach to the upturned yellow boat, I started down the narrow road looking for the *Zanzibar* sign Aldonza had said led to their campsite. Coconut and palm trees in full leaf, lined both sides of the narrow road and therefore it was darker on the road than it would have been on the moonlit beach. It took a few moments for my vision to adjust to the darkness, but once it did, I was struck by how the deep tropical night and lush greenery seemed to blend together. I walked for about five minutes, then saw the *Zanzibar* sign on the left, beside a break in the bushes. I stopped and tried to see down the darkened path. It was well marked and I could see a faint orange glow above the trees, probably a campfire.

I walked down the path and entered a clearing. Three people, two girls and a boy in their twenties, were sitting on logs, their faces lit by the fire's orange glow. As I emerged from the darkness, they all turned to look at me.

"Buenas noches," I said.

"Hola," they replied.

"Hablo English?"

"Yes, I speak English" one of the boys replied.

"Is Aldonza here?"

He eyed me warily. "Aldonza?"

"Yes, Aldonza. She gave me a massage the other night and I have something for her."

He stood. "She is in the tent. I'll get here."

He disappeared into the domed tent and emerged with Aldonza a few moments later. She looked surprised to see me.

"Hola," she said, walking toward me. "You want the massage?"

"Massage?" I replied. "No gracias." I reached into my pocket, pulled out the money and handed it to her. "We go back tomorrow, but I wanted to give this to you, so you can buy more books."

Her brown eyes widened. "Really? Gracias. Thank you." She paused then asked me to wait, as she went back into the tent. She emerged moments later with a pair of earrings. "I made these," she smiled, handing them to me. "Please give to your wife."

They were small and made from turquoise and silver, which seemed to reflect the moonlight. I carefully slipped them into my pocket. "Thank you. She'll love them." In the glow of the fire, she looked like she was about 17-years-old. "Be careful out there," I said.

She smiled. "I will. Adios."

"Adios."

They all started talking in Spanish as I carefully made my way down the path back to the road. I was a hundred yards from the, Peace In Tulum, entrance when I saw it. I don't know how I missed it on the way to give the money to Aldonza.

It was the lame dog.

He was dead on the dirt shoulder of the road. Flies were buzzing all around him. He was on his right side, eyes open and vacant. His tongue was hanging out like a limp pink flag and a pool of blood as dark as oil from his mouth had dried on the pavement. I moved a little closer to make sure it was him. He looked slightly smaller in death, but it was him. He left front leg was much smaller than his right leg and was folded up under him like an L. I moved a few feet closer. There was a tire tread across his neck. He must have been hit by a car, and had been there for a few hours. I prodded him gently with the staff to make sure he was dead. He was. There was nothing I could do, except to make sure Janet didn't see him like that.

I went into the, Peace in Tulum, restaurant. Maria and Alex were cleaning up as a radio blared music in the background. I told Maria about the dog and she raised her hand to her mouth.

"Are you sure it's the same dog?"

I nodded slowly. "Yes, it's him."

She sat and rubbed her eyes. "The cars go too fast for the road."

I sat beside her. "We leave tomorrow. I'd hate Janet to see him like that."

She peered at me over the rims of her glasses. "I will have Alex take him off the road."

"Thank you."

She stood. "Tomorrow is my day off so I will say adios, goodbye, now."

I stood and she hugged me. "Alex will check you out tomorrow. And please say goodbye to your wife."

"I will. We enjoyed our stay here."

She smiled. "Good luck and perhaps next time you will have a baby with you?"

I waved goodbye. "If she's a girl, I'll call her Mexico."

She chuckled. "Mexico is good."

Sometimes people you only know briefly, make a lasting impression on you. Their personality, their soul, their presence. Maria had something scarce in the world, wisdom. She was as utterly comfortable in her life as she was in her loose cotton clothing and shell jewelry.

When I got back to our cabana, Janet was sitting out front reading under a dim porch light. The moon was low in the east, beginning its steady climb up the night sky.

"Did you find Aldonza?" she asked, looking up from her book.

I laid the staff against the wall. "Yes, and she was very grateful."

She smiled. "That was a nice thing to do."

I held out the earrings. "She asked me to give these to you."

She walked to my side and took them. "They're beautiful."

I put my arm around her shoulders. "A nice memento of our trip."

"I can't believe our week's up," she said.

I couldn't either. It had flown by, but at the same time I felt as if I had covered a great deal of emotional territory. It seemed like everything that had happened that week was preordained to somehow prepare me for whatever the future held.

"We'll come back again," I said.

• • •

We woke early the next morning so we could spend time on the beach before heading to the airport. Janet was packed and ready to go the night before. I finished packing after breakfast, then grabbed the staff and went to the beach. Janet was sitting in the sand, looking out over the ocean. She was wearing her new earrings.

The wind had died down. The surface of the water was the calmest I'd seen it since we arrived. Castle-like clouds crawled slowing across the light blue sky as birds scurried after bugs at the waters edge and seagulls bobbed near the shoreline. The salty smell of the ocean filled the air.

There wasn't any past or future in that moment. There's wasn't any fear, expectation or need.

Janet glanced around the beach, the brim of her floppy hat casting a shadow across her face. "I haven't seen our little lame friend since yesterday morning."

Obviously I wasn't going to tell her what happened. "He probably disappears for weeks at a time. He'll be back, some day."

She smiled. "I wanted to say goodbye."

"What about a walk? Maybe we'll see him."

We strolled down the beach collecting more shells and wading into the ocean up to our knees. It would be months before I would be able to walk outside barefooted again, so I tried to appreciate the warm sand, the smell of the ocean; the lofty breeze; the lush vegetation; the cobalt blue sky.

When we got back to the cabana, Janet grabbed her suitcase and started toward the parking lot. I grabbed the staff and stood by the door.

"What are you doing with that?" she asked.

"Putting it back on the beach, where I found it."

"Why?"

I shrugged. "Not sure. It feels like the right thing to do."

"Okay, but don't take. The taxi's waiting."

I smiled. "I know."

I walked to the spot on the beach where I had found the staff. The sun was hot and so near its apex, I didn't cast a shadow. I turned the staff in my hand, carefully examining the many knots and its smooth gray bark. It seemed to symbolize something, or was a relic of some kind. Some people may have dismissed it as a phallic symbol, but to me at least, it was more than that. It was a reminder of a time when the full moon sat on its throne, when the sun and stars had a voice and people listened.

I looked out over the greenish blue ocean. I wanted very much to be present in that moment. Tulum was changing because the world was getting smaller. It would soon be overrun by resorts, developers and tourists. Janet and I were lucky because we visited when it still held a wild innocence and raw beauty. Life and death were in perfect balance in that tropical paradise.

I placed the staff at the water's edge where I had found it. To my surprise, the surf gently surged up and touched it, reclaimed it, embraced it, like an old friend. Then the current slowly carried it away.

I trudged over the sand to the cabana, grabbed my suitcase off the bed and met Janet in the little restaurant where we had registered a week earlier. Alex was sitting at a table checking us out. He only knew a few words of English, but obviously he had experience with this part of the business. When he had finished, he stood.

"Gracias," he said with a smile. "Adios . . ." He paused, and I could tell he was trying to come up with an English word. "Return soon," he said, extending his hand, which I shook.

"I hope so," I replied.

Janet grabbed the handle of her suitcase. "Adios," she smiled.

A little white taxi was waiting in the partial shade of the dirt parking lot. As we approached, the driver jumped out, took our suitcases and put them in the trunk.

"Airporto?" he asked.

"Si," Janet replied.

As we drove down the narrow tree-lined road leading to the highway, Janet offered me a stick of gum.

"Want some?" she smiled.

"Thanks."

I popped the gum into my mouth and handed her back the wrapper, which she dropped in her purse. Her face was bathed in sun streaming in through the window as she turned back toward me.

"Did you ever finish writing your poem?" she asked.

I shrugged. "I'm still working on it. But I've got a working title."

Her eyes widened. "Really? What is it?"

"I wonder if it's snowing in Chicago?"

She grinned. "I hope not."

I placed my hand on hers. Outside, the tropical landscape raced by, teeming with life.

HAPPY BIRTHDAY!

URRY UP AND DO IT. IT'S EASY, just do it now! He had bought the gun a dozen years earlier for protection when traveling on business. At least that's how he had justified the purchase at the time. After all, he often spent long days and nights on the road driving between cities. Better to have the gun and not need it than to need the gun and not have it. But even then, somewhere in the deepest recesses of his mind, he knew there was another reason.

A darker reason.

We all lie to ourselves, either to puff ourselves up or to pull ourselves down. But the worst lies, the most insidious, are the lies we tell ourselves as we gradually lose hope. "You'd be better of dead. The world is shit and if you do this you will make a statement. You are worthless . . ."

"A basic .38 caliber handgun." That's how the woman at the gun shop had described it when he bought it. That was four years earlier. Before his divorce. Before his engineering job, his spirit, and his reason for opening his eyes in the morning were transferred overseas.

It was the gun that he would use to kill himself today.

It was March 11, his 48th birthday.

He didn't want anyone to know it was his birthday because he liked to think of himself as a person not given to sentimentality. He would not apologize for that! That was who he was. Asking him to be soft was like asking him to grow three inches taller. It's not going to happen.

Birthday celebrations, he told himself, were childish and useless. He was an engineer, a man of reason who listened only to his mind. But what he didn't know is that a mind continually preoccupied with itself will give birth to black thoughts, insanity and death.

He had not listened to his heart in years and was now deaf to it, even as it dutifully beat out a steady, ceaseless rhythm. But his heart knew the kind of man he could be. A heart is a simple thing the same way a sunflower is a simple thing. Nothing is better at being a sunflower than a sunflower, and nothing is better at being a heart than a heart. And if he had listened to his heart that day, it would have told him that it wanted to hear two simple words.

"Happy Birthday."

That's ridiculous! He was not a sentimental fool. You might as well thrust a dagger into your heart because sappiness is just as deadly but much slower and probably more painful in the end. Would you rather bleed to death or be blown out like a candle? He'd take the candle every time!

If someone, say a friend, had patted him on the back and said: "Happy Birthday. The world is a better place because of you," he would have smirked his contempt. The world? Ha! This shit world is a better place because of me? Bullshit. This round ludicrous world, this spinning ridiculous world, this foul plastic world? What does it look like from space this world, this planet? It looks like a blue star. A star now that's a laugh! What about the times when it's not facing the sun? What does the dark side of this world, this pathetic planet, look like from light years away? It looks like a cherry pit, something used up, disposable, wretched.

He left his apartment, slipped his keys into his pants pocket, walked to the elevator and pushed the down button. The doors parted. He stepped inside, pushed "L" and descended to the lobby.

He opened the mailbox and a wad of mail tumbled out and fell to the floor at his feet. He slowly gathered it then sifted through it: phone bill, credit card offer, a few fliers.

Back upstairs he dropped the mail onto his dining room table. He walked to the window, pulled back the curtain and looked out over the parkway and the street below. It was a gray, dull day without a hint of spring. The wind was moving the bare branches of the trees. The damned wind: would it ever stop? He turned from the window, walked to his phone and checked for messages.

None.

Now is as good a time as any.

It was as if something, or someone, were coaxing him down the hallway, demanding he take action. A voice was saying, "Hurry up; do it now" like a badly dressed used car salesman trying to close a sale. "Come on. There's no time to waste. Do it."

In his bedroom, he flicked on a light then crossed the room to a nightstand. He pulled the gun out of a drawer and stood looking down at it. He checked to make sure it was loaded, then put the muzzle into his mouth. It would be easy. Just pull the trigger and go to sleep. Come on do it! Make a statement that this world is shit. Hurry up do it now! Don't be a coward. Do it!

He stood beside his unmade bed with the gun barrel in his mouth for 30 seconds, then started to cry. Why am I crying? What is wrong with me?

Every heart has a voice, and what his heart was saying was, "Go ahead and cry. Cry! Feel the pain so you can release it. Angels cry. God cries. The shortest verse in the Bible says: 'Jesus wept.' Cry, and be cleansed of your pain by your tears! Slow down and cry."

He took the gun out of his mouth and used his sleeve to wipe away the tears and a strand of saliva clinging to his chin. He dropped the gun into the drawer, slid it closed, flicked off the light, walked out of the bedroom, grabbed his leather jacket from the hallway closet and left the apartment.

With his newspaper folded under one arm he walked through the cold to a coffee shop one block from home. He ordered a cup of coffee from a skinny, college-aged goth girl with paper-white skin and straight black hair. He studied her bleached face. She was barely 20 but looked sick and tired, like one of the living dead. Dark tattoos crawled up her arms a seeming complement to the piercings in her ears and eyebrows and ball bearing in her tongue. She barely regarded him. He knew her from previous visits. They never spoke except when he ordered coffee.

He dropped the change into her tip jar, poured milk and sugar into his coffee and selected a table near the back of the café. He sipped his coffee, opened the newspaper to the front page and looked at the top right hand corner for the date:

March 11. His birthday.

He leafed through the newspaper scanning stories about the war, a wildcat oil well, and the economy. He stopped on a story about a French scientist who'd committed suicide after spending a year in a cave by herself. The article said the woman was a psychologist conducting an experiment on isolation. She had moved into a cave in the French countryside in order to be separated from all human contact. The article said she'd had plenty of food and water and kept a journal and medical records in order to record her thoughts and health. She emerged from the cave a year later, physically healthy, but people quoted in the story said she had changed. She killed herself with pills one week later. He again looked at the date at the top of the page. March 11. His birthday.

He sipped his coffee and continued to read the newspaper. He stopped on a full-page ad for Sony LCD screen TVs. The price was listed at $199. He had worked in electronics and knew that price was less than half of what they should be listed for, even on sale. He knew this price must be a mistake. He drained the last gulp of coffee, folded up the newspaper and walked home though the cold.

Back at his apartment, he sat in silence at the dining room table and looked down the darkened hall toward the bedroom.

Now?

He turned to the newspaper in front of him and opened it to the page with the ad for the LCD TVs. He glanced at the date at the top of the page:

March 11. His birthday.

He looked at the bottom of the page, where a 1-800 number was listed for ordering the televisions. He picked up the phone and dialed the number.

A woman answered. "This is Sony, how can I help you?"

"I'm calling about the ad in today's newspaper."

"Which ad, sir? We have many promotions right now."

"The ad for the 60-inch LCD televisions."

"Of course, sir. Would you like to place an order?"

He paused. "It's not that. There's a mistake; the price is too low."

"Too low?"

"Yes, I work, worked, in electronics. Those TVs sell for two or three times that amount, even on sale."

"Please hold, sir, I'm transferring you to customer service."

He pressed the phone into his ear listening to the piped-in Caribbean music and thought about what the woman on the other end of the phone might look like. He imagined she was in her 30s, that she had curly blond hair and that she was smiling.

The music stopped, and another woman's voice came on the line. He explained "the mistake" to her. She listened as she had been trained to do. She listened because she was paid to listen. She told him she needed to check it out, and she put him back on hold. He looked around his dining room and his gaze fell upon a calendar pinned to the wall. He silently counted off the days in the month: March 1, 2, 3 . . . until he reached March 11.

The music stopped and the second woman's voice returned.

"Sir, sir?

He sat up in the chair. "Yes, I'm here."

"Sir, you're right! It was a misprint. Those televisions are supposed to be listed for $899."

"That's what I figured. I just wanted to make sure. I'd order 10 of them if $199 is the real price."

"Oh no, sir, but I really thank you for bringing it to our attention."

He glanced at the calendar. "Well, it's my birthday, but it looks like Sony's getting the present."

"Oh, it's your birthday, sir? Well, have a happy birthday."

His heart skipped a beat.

"And thank you."

"No problem," he replied, then asked, "when's your birthday?"

She paused before answering. "My birthday? It's in October, a long way off."

"Yes, a long way off. Let me wish you a happy birthday in advance."

"Why, thank you, sir. And again, thanks for letting us know about the mistake. I hope you have a very wonderful birthday today."

"Thank you. You're very kind."

There was another pause, as if for a moment the woman on the other end heard the isolation and loneliness in his voice. Instead of hanging up, she reached out. She wasn't paid to "reach out" to strangers over the phone. She did it because her heart told her to, and she listened.

"You know sir, it's funny because I read something in the newspaper this morning about birthdays."

"Oh, and what was that?"

"It said that birthdays are very special occasions and that people should acknowledge them. It's like there's some kind of birthday *presence* that happens on your birthday."

He paused, then asked. "Birthday presents happening on your birthday?"

"Yes, but it's spelled p-r-e-s-e-n-c-e, not 'presents'"

"I'm not sure I understand."

"It means you should be very 'present' on your birthday. It's a chance to stop, to slow down, and look at what's good in your life."

"I'm sure Hallmark would agree."

"Sir, did you ever hear of a European writer from a million years ago named, Jean Paul Richter?"

"I can't say that I have."

"I remember when I turned 20, a million years ago, I read something he said. I thought it was so beautiful. I never forgot it."

Silence.

"He said, 'Our birthdays are feathers in the broad wing of time.' Isn't that poetic?"

"Yes, it's nice."

There was a brief silence on the other end of the line, then she continued. "So sir, let me wish you a very happy birthday!"

Then she lowered her voice to a whisper. "I'd sing you 'Happy Birthday' but my supervisor would probably fire me."

Tears welled in his eyes.

The woman chuckled. "The way I look at it, birthdays are nature's way of telling us to eat more cake."

"More cake? That's pretty funny."

He could almost see her kind and smiling face. But it was more than a smile: he imagined she was actually glowing.

"Sir, since it's your birthday today, and since you called us about the mistake, I'm going to mail you a coupon for 20 percent off an LCD TV. What's your address?"

He gave it to her and heard her type it into a computer.

She stopped typing. "There we go, sir. The coupon's in the mail today."

"Thank you. Maybe I'll buy one. I do need a new TV."

"I hope you will. And sir, go have a big piece of cake and have a real happy birthday, okay?"

"Okay," he said, "thank you . . . and . . . happy birthday to you . . . in advance."

She laughed. "I stopped counting at thirty-nine. But thanks."

He hung up.

There wasn't any rush.

THE OTHER

IWAS GETTING QUIETLY DRUNK IN THE Two Keys Pub on Chicago's North Side after watching a Bears game on TV when I met the most beautiful woman I have ever seen. She was not my wife, and she did not even resemble my wife.

The last part of a gray Sunday afternoon was slowly slipping into night as people pulled on their coats and hats and straggled out into the cool October evening. My kid brother Roger was nearby playing pool with a firefighter friend of his while I sat at a table, knocking back the last of my beer. I sensed someone to my right, but before I could look, a heavily accented voice asked: "You need drink?"

I turned and there she stood, holding a round drink tray and wearing a tired smile. Even in blue jeans and a faded pink T-shirt she was strikingly beautiful.

"No, no thank you," I stammered, my senses temporarily scrambled by this goddess standing in front of me. "I've got work, in the . . . the . . . morning."

"No drink?" she replied. "Thank goodness. I very tired. Very busy for game." She quickly looked around the room then pointed at the seat next to mine. Her oval face glowed. "I need time off feet. Is okay to sit for moment?"

I nodded enthusiastically. "Please sit down."

She was between 25 and 30, my height, six feet tall, with a curvy, athletic build. Her light blonde hair, barely touched her shoulders, framing a proud, porcelain-like stunning face that any sculpture would have been honored to use as a model for a statue in Red Square.

She slid onto the seat, put her tray on the table and offered her hand. "I'm new waitress, Katrina." She glanced toward the bar, then back at me. "You are sure I can sit for moment? I am truly exhausted."

"It's fine," I replied as I shook her hand, which was as cool and smooth as marble. "I'm Louis," I said, still in awe of her. "People here call me, Lou."

She smiled shyly, showing perfectly white teeth. "People here call me nickname of 'Russian Wolf.'"

I could see where the nickname came from. Her eyes, large other worldly and emerald green, were sharp, with an animal alertness and a smoldering sexuality. Her shoulders were squared like a dancer. Her skin, a dreamy mixture of silk and milk, was perfect. And that body! Amazing and sensuous. The only thing more striking than her endless curves and long shapely legs was her oval face, which was so symmetrical, beautiful and glowing as to be unreal.

Her only flaw, if I could call it that, was a small scar in the shape of an exclamation mark on her left cheek. It was faded and not real noticeable under her makeup. It wasn't until later that she told me how she got it.

"So you're Russian?" I asked.

"Bello Russian."

We chatted for a few minutes, and my heart rate finally slowed down, although having her next to me seemed to impede my ability to put two sentences together. I didn't want to appear flustered like some schoolboy, so instead of talking, I listened as she told me about her travels across the country that brought her to Chicago.

"You enjoy traveling?" I asked, then tipped back my head and drained the contents of my glass.

"Oh yes," she replied enthusiastically. "Since leave Russia, I travel Europe, America and Canada. San Francisco my favorite city, but very expensive to live."

It was a little difficult to hear her over the sound from the televisions so I leaned forward. "I've never been to San Francisco. But I've been to Los Angeles, for work."

She shook her head dismissively. "I inside L.A. for one day. That was enough. I did no like."

"Just like San Francisco, L.A. is very expensive," I said. "Chicago's a lot more affordable."

"You work in Chicago?"

Before I could reply my phone rang. "Excuse me," I said as I pulled it from my pocket and looked at the incoming number. It was my wife Natalie calling from home. I hit the "Ignore Call," button then slipped it back into my pocket and continued my conversation with Katrina. "I work in the suburbs, for a software engineering company."

"You are technician? Software developer?" she asked, cocking her head to one side.

In that split second instead of telling her the truth, that I was one of a dozen sales reps, I calmly answered: "A technician? No. I'm vice president of sales." Why did I lie? I don't know. It was a reflex. Women find confidence and success attractive, and I really wanted to impress her.

Her emerald eyes widened. "Is good business, yes?"

"We had more than twenty million dollars in sales last year." Another lie. "I don't know what that converts to in rubles, but I'm very happy."

She smiled and brushed her hair back behind her ears with her hands. "Is a lot of rubles."

There was silence for a moment. Then I motioned with my glass to a three-inch high Chinese symbol printed in white on the front of her light pink T-shirt. "Does that symbol mean anything?"

She glanced down at the symbol then back at me. "This shirt is from friend. Symbol means 'dream to dream?'"

"Dream? Dreamy. Of course," I said, smiling, "Looking at you that makes total sense."

She held my gaze for a moment, then looked down at my wedding ring. "You are married?" Her golden eyebrows arched. "Where is wife tonight?"

Shit! I had meant to take off my ring before Roger and I got there. Okay, I admit I do that sometimes. It's slightly sleazy I know, but my marriage of five years was floundering. Natalie and I had hit a wall, we were in a rut, or whatever euphuism is appropriate for a relationship that had lost its vitality.

I leaned back in my seat. "It's boys' night out," I said quickly. "My brother and I always come here to watch the game."

She nodded in understanding. "Wife set you free like dog in yard to run around and sniff."

I wasn't sure if that was an insult, being compared to a dog. Her hands were flat on the table and I noticed a gold band around her ring finger. "What about you?" I asked, motioning to her ring.

She held up her hand and laughed a little as if I had asked a stupid question. "Not wedding ring," she replied. "Sometimes I wear to keep away pests. Men *and* women."

Men and women? I really wasn't sure how to respond to that. "Do you think you'll ever go back to Russia?"

She paused, and a shadow seemed to cross her face. I could tell it wasn't a good idea to pursue that topic. "Who knows? Probably negative," she responded flatly. "I consider move to Florida. I have girlfriend there who can get me employment." She stood up beside the table. "Well Lou, my break is over. I return to work or boss hate me." Then she pointed at my empty glass and asked: "Are you sure you do not want refill?"

I shook my head. "Thanks but I really have to go."

She tilted her head slightly to the side, feigned a little pout as if to say: *"Sorry you have to leave."* "Is nice to meet you," she said.

"Yes," I replied. "I'm sure I'll see you again."

The corners of her mouth turned up as she started to leave. Then she stopped and turned back toward me her smile warm and inviting. "I verk Monday night behind bar, Wednesdays, Fridays and Sundays on floor for game."

"I'll be in again," I replied.

She turned and left, and as I watched her walk away, my mouth may have been hanging open. Roger came over with a pool cue in his hand and leaned against the table. "I see you met Katrina," he grinned. "What a dish!"

"Yeah," I replied, still under her spell. "Absolutely amazing."

. . .

Driving home I could not stop thinking about her. She had awoken something primordial and lustful within me. Our meeting had been fleeting, but I felt as if we had connected on a much higher level. Was there an instant attraction? Yes. I had never met a woman like her and she had taken a genuine interest in me. She'd invited herself to sit at my table, we had a nice conversation and she expressed disappointment when I told her I was leaving.

Hmm, I thought as I pulled into my driveway, I'm going to have to explore that possibility more deeply.

I grabbed my laptop from the backseat and went inside. Natalie was curled up on the sofa watching television. She had let her appearance slip a lot in the last few years, and as I looked at her sitting there she seemed especially unsightly. "There's spaghetti in the fridge," she said.

"I already ate."

She picked up the remote control and hit the Mute button. "Kyle's been running a temperature all night," she said, referring to our three-year-old son.

I slipped the laptop off my shoulder and placed it on a chair. "How high?"

"It's under 100, but I was still worried."

I pulled off my tie. "When did you put him to bed?"

She stirred in her seat. "An hour ago. I tried calling but got your voicemail."

"You called? Really? I didn't get your message."

"I was worried about Kyle and I and couldn't reach you," she said, staring at me accusingly.

"I was talking to somebody about work," I said.

"Who?"

"Just some guy."

"Some guy?"

"Yes, some Russian guy. Vladimir something. He's a software engineer in town on business. We were just chatting."

Over the last few years it seemed like Natalie had become increasingly suspicious of me while steadily losing confidence in herself. She had developed a hair trigger temper, and I sure as hell wasn't about to tell her about Katrina. That would have opened a can of worms I definitely did not feel like dealing with.

She got off the sofa. Passing me on the way to the kitchen she quipped, "I wasn't sure if I should call Roger or that stupid bar you guys like, or send up a damned smoke signal. If Kyle's temperature got any higher I'd have had to call a taxi to take him to the ER."

I figured she was being overly dramatic. "I'm going to check on him."

I walked down the hall, quietly opened Kyle's bedroom door and sat on the edge of his bed. He was sleeping on his back as I carefully placed my hand of his forehead. He felt slightly warm but it didn't seem like his temperature was anything to worry about. I kissed him gently on the cheek, then went back into the living room. Natalie was in front of the TV, eating a big bowl of chocolate ice cream.

"He's asleep," I said, yawning widely, "but I think his temperature is okay."

She put the bowl on the table and glared at me. "Whenever you go out with Roger, it's impossible to reach you and you come home drunk. You shouldn't be drinking and driving. What would happen if you got a DUI? We can't afford that. You could lose you job, and . . ."

"Drunk?" I snapped. "That's ridiculous. I'm not drunk. I had two beer."

"Whatever," she said flatly, reaching for her ice cream.

I didn't feel like arguing, or justifying having spent a few hours with my brother. "I've got an early meeting in the morning," I replied tersely. "I'm going to bed."

Natalie grunted something inaudible as I turned and left the room. I went into the bathroom, washed my face and hands brushed my teeth and then got into bed. Within 20 minutes I was sound asleep.

The next morning when I got up, Natalie was sleeping on the sofa with a blanket pulled up to her chin. I checked on Kyle, who was still asleep. I gently touched his forehead and was relieved that his temperature felt normal. I quickly got dressed, grabbed a banana and a bagel from the fridge and left for work.

I had to work late that night, and as I was driving home, it suddenly seemed as if the car had a mind of its own. Instead of turning right, I continued straight and within 20 minutes was parking outside the Two Keys Pub. Okay, maybe the car didn't have a mind of its' own and I knew exactly what I was doing. I guess I was drawn there by my desire the same way a moth is drawn to . . . well you know.

I pushed open the heavy glass door, walked in and looked around. It was only 7:30 and therefore the pub wasn't crowded. I looked over at the bar and saw Katrina with her head down, counting money. She looked slightly different. Some women are magical like that, like chameleons. It's as if they can change the essence of their appearance without changing their fundamentally beautiful nature. She was absolutely stunning in a silky black blouse and tight black jeans that reminded me of the mystery of a midnight sky. Three small gold hoops sparkled in her left earlobe, while a single hoop dangling from her right ear.

As I claimed a seat at the bar, she looked up at me and smiled.

"Is Lou, correct?" The top few buttons of her blouse were unbuttoned, revealing a small but alluring amount of cleavage. A thin gold necklace with a tiny cross-hung around her delicate white neck. The contrast of her dark clothing against her milky skin made her glow and her green eyes appeared even larger than the previous evening.

"Yes it is," I replied, "and you are . . . Katherine?" I didn't want to appear too eager so I pretended I couldn't t remember her name, although in reality it was tattooed on my libido.

She leaned against her side of the bar. "Is Katrina," she said, correcting me in her thick Russian accent. "Is my mother's name, too."

"Right, Katrina." I met her eyes. "Of course."

"You like drink, Lou?" she asked, her thin golden eyebrows arched.

"A doggie style, I mean an Old Style please."

She shot me a quizzical look, then turned, grabbed a beer from the fridge, opened it and placed it on a coaster in front of me. "Brother not join you tonight?"

"Not tonight," I replied. "I'm on my own. I decided to come by after a long day at the office."

"You need the break, yes?" she asked. "To relax?"

I took a sip of beer, then put the bottle down on the bar. "Exactly."

Two businessmen were sitting to my right, watching TV. From what I could tell, they were also watching Katrina. A blue collar-type guy, wearing a ball cap with the name *Lloyd* stenciled over his shirt pocket was sitting a few seats to my left. Katrina dutifully waited on them and made drinks for the wait staff, but when she wasn't busy, she always made her way back to bar area where I was sitting so we could chat. She seemed genuinely interested as I told her about myself and my software company.

After a little while, I casually asked her if she had a boyfriend.

She shook her head. "I have, then I don't have, then I have again. Now I don't have." She paused. "Is complicated." She shrugged as she rinsed a glass. "Sometimes is simpler to be by self."

I nodded. "I would imagine you could have a boyfriend in a heartbeat if you wanted one."

She looked up at me and smiled warmly. "I'm thanking you, Lou, for this flattery."

I returned her smile. As she started making drinks for one of the waitresses, I glanced at my watch. It was already past ten! It seemed as if I had only been there for half an hour.

I was trying to decide if I should have another beer when Katrina called out to one of the waitresses who was wearing a coat and hat and was headed toward the front door: "Leah," Katrina said, "can you please to drop off books at library branch for me? I forgot to drop and they are much overdone."

"I would," the girl, replied, smiling, "but I'm just going to the ATM. I'm coming back."

"No problem," Katrina sighed. As the waitress left, Katrina turned toward me and pointed to several books sitting behind the bar. "I forget books for one whole week. Now, I bring them and forget to drop off on way to work."

"I can drop those off for you," I said.

Her green eyes lit up. "For me you do this?"

"I'm glad to. I have to drive right past the library and it's time for me to get going anyway."

She picked up the books and placed them on the bar in front of me.

I looked at the titles, which dealt with English grammar, modern art, American history and physics. "You have diverse interests," I said.

She rested her elbows on the bar and leaned forward. "I wish to understand American ways and culture. And I always love physics."

I lifted my jacket from the back of the chair and slipped it on. "I love physics too," I lied. "I studied it as an elective in college."

"Really," she said, obviously impressed. "I have been studying Newton's Laws of Motion. Is accelerating, you agree?"

"Absolutely."

She opened the book on physics, leafed through it, then stopped, pointed at the page and started reading. "'The acceleration of a body is directly proportional to the net unbalanced force and inversely proportional to the body's mass. A relationship is established between force, mass and acceleration.'"

As I watched her reading, the words rolling of her full lips, I think all I really heard was "acceleration, body, force, mass, relationship." The way she pronounced those words gave them an exotic flare.

She looked up at me, expecting some sort of a comment.

Shit, what have I gotten myself into? "It's really remarkable," I said. "What I really love about Newton are his fig cookies. You know? Fig Newtons?"

I was hoping my lame joke would give me some cover. In reality I hardly knew the difference between a molecule and an atom. Katrina seemed to be thinking about what I had said. She closed the book and smiled.

"Formula is of immense usefulness," she beamed. "Knowing any two quantities automatically gives you the third."

"I know," I answered. "Newton was brilliant."

"He is rock star," she replied. I think she actually blushed.

I picked the books up off the bar. "I should be going."

"I am thanking you for this favor," she said. "I owe you for this."

Our eyes met. "My pleasure."

. . .

Desire changes your life, like an earthquake changes the landscape. It awakens within you a deep sense of longing. But desire has a short shelf life, like a flower of fire that has just been picked. It is immediate and consuming. Not just sexual desire. Any desire. The object of your longing gradually moves in until she occupies your wildest thoughts, fantasies and dreams. I'd catch myself thinking about Katrina during boring meetings at work when we were rolling out some new software package. She would come to me in dreams, as an apparition, as I was getting dressed in the morning, or in the shower. My mind would wander. I'd see Katrina's glowing face and perfect body kneeling in front of me.

I loved talking to Katrina almost as much as I enjoyed looking at her. She laughed at my jokes and listened intently to whenever I said. Her lusty intrigue was the same as mine. All of our conversations were laden with some kind of sexual overtone or innuendo. She was flirting with me.

In Russia my grandmother had outdoors shower. I love feeling of shower in outdoors . . . I love swim in nude is so freeing . . . I do SCUBA lessons. We had to strip on beach, but I don't mind, feels good to have nature on body . . . My neck stiff. I need good massage, or long love session . . .

Then Roger told me a fantastically erotic story about Katrina. A firefighter friend of Roger's had dated her for a few months after she arrived in Chicago. He told Roger that she kept a strand of Christmas lights strung over her bed. She liked to strip naked, wrap herself in the lights and climb on top of him. That's how they made love! The thought of it drove me mad with desire, and I have never been able to look at a Christmas tree in quite the same way.

Some married men I know would not hesitate to have an affair with a woman like Katrina. They wouldn't hesitate to jump into bed with a lesser woman. In fact, they would have sex with anything that throws a shadow. I tried, a little, but wasn't able to push Katrina from my mind. She was always nearby in my thoughts, like a lover is. I tried to fight the good fight and remain faithful to Natalie. At the same time, Jesus said that if a man even looks at a woman with lust in his heart, he is committing adultery. I was a serial adulterer. My desire was being continually fueled by lust. My ego was also involved. It continually whispered that I could have a chance with this remarkable woman.

And you know what? I needed to give a woman pleasure as much as I needed to receive it. In nature, fire is sometimes allowed to run its course: make no mistake, a fire was burning within me.

• • •

A few days later I got home from work, and it was if a cloud of discontent had lifted. Natalie greeted me at the door with a broad smile. She had made us a delicious steak dinner, which we enjoyed with a fine bottle of Merlot. When we were finished, she checked on Kyle and I made myself a gin and tonic. She came back into the kitchen wearing the blue silk robe I had given her for Christmas, when she was a lot thinner.

She smiled mischievously. "Let's have dessert in the bedroom."

She took me by the hand and led me to the bed. Candles flickered and bathed the walls in a soft yellow light. She undressed me, then slipped off her robe and let it fall to the floor. Within minutes, we were making love. Natalie moaned and ran her hands over my back. A thin wisp of smoke wafted from a stick of nang champa incense next to our bed. I was doing my best to get into the swing of things, but I was tired and pretty much uninterested. Natalie was probably feeling the same way. The only reason we were doing this was because she felt obligated to perform her "wifely duties." She was doing her "groan-sigh-moan, groan-sigh-moan" routine. She always followed that up with a panting type thing at the end. She wasn't even good at faking it. She probably thought she was doing me a favor.

Wrong!

I turned my head. My gaze fell on the incense. The smoke took on the ghostly form of a beautiful, curvy blonde dancing like a seductress before me . . . My pulse quickened. I fantasized Katrina was beneath me. I thrust into Natalie and I could hear Katrina screaming in ecstasy, heaving off the mattress to meet me. *Katrina, yes, baby*, I thought, *This is how you like it isn't it! Katrina ahhhh.*

I was just about to climax when Natalie punched me hard in the ribs, pushed me off her and jumped out of bed. Her face was red and twisted with anger. "Who's Katrina?" she demanded. "Why were you saying 'Katrina' while you were making love to me!"

Sweat was running down her neck onto her chest as she stood naked beside the bed glaring at me waiting for a reply. Natalie only swore when she was pissed off, and she looked mad as hell.

I sat up. "I don't know anyone named Katrina." I ran my hand over the area where she had hit me. I had to come up with something fast, so I motioned to the window. "You misheard me. I was saying . . . 'curtains, curtains. Close the curtains.'"

Natalie planted her fists firmly on her hips. "Curtains? Bullshit, Lou!"

I exhaled loudly. "I was saying 'curtains!' What if somebody looked in and saw us?"

Natalie balked. "I know what I heard, and it was '*Katrina, Katrina!*' What are you going to say next: that you were calling out the name of a hurricane?" Then she stormed into the bathroom and slammed the door.

I flopped onto my pillow and cursed myself for making such a stupid mistake. After a few minutes, I pushed off the sheet, got out of bed and rapped lightly on the bathroom door. "Open the door, Natalie. Come on, baby. Come back to bed."

"Screw off, asshole," she yelled. "Or better still, screw your Katrina."

I moved closer to the door. "You're going to wake up Kyle," I said sternly. "Come back to bed. I don't know what I said, but I'm sure it wasn't 'Katrina.' There's no 'Katrina.'"

She flung the door open and stood there naked except for the mask of absolute scorn on her face. "There's one thing I'd like to ask you, Lou."

"Go ahead."

"Do you take me for a complete idiot?"

"Of course not."

"Good! Then, let me ask you something."

"Go ahead."

"How many times have you come home after midnight lately with some lame excuse about why you got held up?"

I shook my head. "I don't know. Not that many."

"I do. A dozen times."

Whenever I got home late after going to the Two Keys Pub and Natalie demanded to know where I had been, I offered up lies for her consumption. Lust and desire make anyone a good liar. They are part of the same internal landscape. What you work so hard to hide from your spouse you will gladly show your lover. What did JFK say: Marry the princess and screw the slut. Not that Katrina was a slut!

I do not indulge in self-deception. I am not without morals. A war was being waged within me. One side was enlightened and wanted to be faithful to Natalie. The other side was burning with desire to have Katrina as my lover. There was no way I was going to tell Natalie the truth about Katrina, so instead I had to deflect her questions.

"I told you what happened," I said. "Remember, there was . . ."

She smirked. "Oh, right, let's see now, first there was . . ." Then, in a very sarcastic tone, she started counting off my excuses with her fingers. "'Ben at work needed comforting because his kid got hit by a truck . . . Terry demanded I work late . . . I fell asleep in the car . . . I hit a dog and had to take it to the vet . . . I missed the turnoff and ended up in Indiana."'

She shook her head in disgust. "And my personal favorite: I witnessed a robbery and the police kept me there for hours asking questions." An evil smile crossed her face. "You know what, Lou? You're an idiot. Or, you think I am."

I was pissed off. What if the lies I had been telling her had been the truth? She had absolutely no empathy. "It's been a crazy month, Natalie. I work hard . . ."

She cut me off. "Everybody works hard, Lou! How many of your damned lame excuses do you think I'll believe? And now you call out some other's woman's name when you're in my arms?"

I threw-up my hands and walked back toward the bed. "You can believe whatever you want. Obviously, what I say doesn't matter!"

Natalie wouldn't let it go. She followed me halfway into the bedroom. "Lou," she said, pointing at me accusingly. "I don't know what you're up to. But you're up to something."

The gloves were off. I was sick of her tirade and insensitivity. I turned and glared at her, both of us standing naked in the middle of the room. "Is that right?" I said, my temper reaching a boiling point. "Maybe if you showed the least little bit of interest in me, I wouldn't be out late. I'd have a reason to be home. You think you can jump into bed with me a couple of times a year and that'll take care of everything! Guess what? I need more than that!"

This was a flimsy complaint, a clever salvo fired by my lustful side, little more than pure justification for my desire to bed Katrina. I might as well have told Natalie "you don't understand me." I wasn't a mongrel in heat looking to get laid by anyone anywhere. If I was going to have an affair with Katrina I needed a reason, manufactured or real. My lust didn't care.

I moved a little closer to her. "And what about your weight?" I demanded. "You haven't lost a single pound you gained while you were pregnant, and that was three years ago. Do you ever look at yourself in the mirror?"

Her jaw dropped. "My weight? My weight!" she replied after a moment. "My God, the weight I put on while I was pregnant with your son?" Tears welled up in her eyes, and she turned pale. I felt like I had the upper hand now because what I had said was true. She hadn't lost the weight she gained while pregnant with, Kyle. Without even trying, I had hit on the major reasons married men use as a springboard into an affair:

A: Their wife treats them like a piece of furniture.

B: Their wife lets their appearance slip.

And of course the most prevalent reason, C: No sex, or lousy sex.

"That's right," I said loudly. "You said you were going to exercise and get back in shape. All you do is lie around the house, watching TV and eating! You don't look anything like the woman I married!"

She raised her hands to her face and started sobbing. "I never knew, I never knew you could be so hateful."

I heard a whimper and turned to see Kyle in the doorway, crying and holding his stuffed toy monkey.

Natalie wiped the tears from her cheeks with the back of her hand, then bent down and picked him up. As they were leaving the room, she turned back toward me and in an icy and deliberate tone said: "I hate you." Then she took Kyle back into his room and slammed the door.

"Sure, Natalie," I yelled, standing there, naked. "That really helps!"

I was not going to apologize or feel bad about what had happened. Battle lines were being drawn. I slammed the bedroom door and got back into bed. I was angry, so sleeping was impossible. Lying there, staring at the ceiling, I started wondering what had happened to our marriage. I meant every single word I had said on my wedding day. "Through sickness and health, for better or worse, for richer and poorer," all that crap.

Is love the opposite of water? Does it evaporate when there's not *enough* heat? All I do know is that I didn't feel love for her any more. Something in our marriage was broken. As I lay there, I wasn't sure if I could fix it, or wanted to try.

Katrina occupied my thoughts to the point where I was fantasying about her while having sex with my wife. I'm not an expert on relationships but I'd bet that that's "not a good sign." A man can't deny what he feels in his soul, and fighting it is useless. Katrina made me feel two things I had not felt in a long time: A passion for life and being appreciated as a man.

I stared at the ceiling. After half an hour, I leaned over, blew out the candles and feel asleep.

. . .

I was in the kitchen a few days later when the phone rang. It was my brother, Roger. I had been expecting his call.

"Lou, it's me. I'll pick you up at three."

"See you then."

We were going to the Two Keys Pub to watch another Bears game. I had lied to Natalie, telling her that we were going to Roger's apartment to watch movies and have a few drinks. I told her I'd probably stay overnight at his place. In reality, I was hoping to see Katrina. Considering how good things were going with her, I hoped this might be the night.

Natalie and Roger never got along. She always complained when we went out together. They were like the positive ends of two magnets. They instantly repelled each other. She called Roger an immature playboy. He called Natalie "the Ice Queen."

Contemplating the sumptuous curve of Katrina's hips, breasts and her slender white neck, my mind conjured up the letter S. Following my big fight with Natalie, things settled into a kind of siege. My conversations with her were frosty and short. If I had to attribute a letter to that situation it would have been a "D minus" as in "Disaster." Kyle was the only common ground Natalie and I now shared. I was living with a stranger. She was intentionally remote and detached. I didn't care. I kind of liked it because her emotional "cold front" gave me more freedom.

I brushed my teeth, checked my appearance in the bathroom mirror and dabbed on a little CK cologne. I aim for a clean cut, buttoned down appearance. As I studied my reflection in profile then front on, I was confident I had achieved it. I patted down a few wrinkles on the front of my shirt then flicked off the light and went into the living room.

Natalie was sitting cross-legged on the floor, watching television. She was wearing what had become her unofficial uniform since Kyle was born: a red and black checkered flannel shirt, sweat pants and mismatched socks. Her hair was up in clips and pins. It resembled a bird's nest. She looked like a lumberjack's wife. Kyle, sitting beside her surrounded by his toys, looked up at me and giggled.

"Roger should be here any minute," I said, walking over to where they were sitting. "I'm going outside to have a smoke and wait for him."

"Good," she said, without looking away from the television.

I grabbed my keys off the mantle, then bent down and gently kissed Kyle on the forehead.

"Lou," Natalie said, her gaze still fixed on the television. "Don't drink too much and don't let your brother drive you home if he's drunk."

"We'll be careful." I moved toward the door.

She turned to me, her lips tense, her face now a blend of worry and doubt. "Lou . . . we need to . . . I can't . . ." She shook her head and exhaled. "We need to talk when you get home."

"I told you. I may stay at Roger's overnight, if it's late."

"Tomorrow night, then?" Her eyes welled with tears.

Looking at her sitting there like that, I felt a pang of guilt and I almost reached out to her. I desperately wanted to see or feel something that would remind me of why I married her, a reason for staying together. Anything. Her shy smile, the corny sound of her laugh, her quiet confidence, the playfulness in her eyes, the curve of her breast, her scent.

Natalie for the sake of our marriage get off the damned floor right now. Embrace me tightly and kiss me on the mouth like you mean it. Do it now, Natalie, or I won't be responsible for my actions once I leave this house. I need to see desire burning in your eyes again, as much as I need water to live. Don't you understand?

She didn't move.

Looking at her sitting there, all I saw was a slightly overweight woman, a stranger, the mother of my son, dressed like a slob, looking back at me with what I can only describe as disdain.

At that moment I made my decision, or perhaps she made the decision for me.

"Okay Natalie," I said, turning toward the door. "We can talk. We can not talk. Whatever. I'll see you when I get home."

She turned back toward the television without replying, and I left.

Outside the fall air was filled with the smoky aroma from a dozen of my neighbors' fireplaces in full blaze. Autumn has always unlocked primitive memories from the distant past seemingly locked in my DNA. Echoes of living outdoors in nature thousands of years ago, hunting and gathering, preparing for winter, deep night skies, brightly colored leaves and sitting around, gazing into a fire.

Standing at the end of our double driveway, I fished a green plastic lighter from my jacket pocket, lit a cigarette and watched a plume of smoke slowly drift away. I'd never really adapted to living in the suburbs and often felt the kinetic energy of the city beckoning me. It was Natalie who craved suburbia, with its three-bedroom homes, good schools and square lawns. I simply went along because it seemed like the life plan I had bought into when we married.

But now dragging on my cigarette looking around the neighborhood, I wasn't really sure how I'd ended up there. I guess I'd been swept along by circumstances, fate and time, just like everyone I knew.

I ground my cigarette butt out with my foot, pulled back my coat sleeve and checked my watch. Roger was late. A neighbor drove past in his new Buick and waved. I ignored him. My mood was going from gray to black.

A car turned the corner onto our street. It was Roger. He sped into the driveway, stopped abruptly and playfully tooted the horn. I climbed into his small, fast Japanese coupe, and was struck by what a refreshing change it was from my minivan. I pulled the seatbelt across my chest and buckled it "You're late." I said, settling into the seat. "The game's already started."

He put the car in reverse and looked over his shoulder as he backed up. "Sorry bro. The station called. I got stuck on the phone for half an hour, talking about a shift change."

"Let's go."

We had both inherited our father's curly black hair, tall build and blue eyes. Rodger and I both had the same slight paunch my father developed by the time he was in his 30s. Roger was five years my junior, but everyone instantly recognized us as brothers and called Roger, "Little Lou."

He pulled up to a stop sign, turned on the radio and starting punching buttons trying to find the Bears game. He found it and motioned to a plastic bag on the back seat.

"I got Kyle a toy fire truck. It's in the bag."

"Thanks."

He looked both ways for traffic then glanced at me. "Something on your mind?"

"Same old shit."

He shook his head. "Natalie still busting your balls?"

He knew about my problems at home and the dangerous dance Katrina and I had been doing.

"She hasn't changed."

He pressed on the gas and passed a Camry in the right lane. "What is it this time?"

I gazed out the window at a depressing strip mall. "She's tired. She gives all her energy to Kyle and treats me like a roommate."

We drove down a highway on-ramp, and the engine purred loudly as Roger dropped the car into fifth gear. "She just doesn't give a damn," he said as we eased into traffic. "You have to work at a relationship."

Considering Roger's many short-term relationships, his comment struck me as ironic. But I didn't say anything. I rubbed my eyes, and resumed looking out the window as we passed a semi-tractor trailer. "On the very rare occasion when we do do something it's like she's just lying there doing me a favor," I said. I told him about what had happened when I mistakenly called out Katrina's name while having sex with Natalie.

He burst out laughing and hit the steering wheel with his fist. "No way!"

"She was steamed, still is."

"Bro, listen to me," Roger said, gripping the steering wheel with both hands. "Your mind is telling you what to do. You have to bag the Russian Wolf. Go for it! Europeans are way more open to affairs and sex in general then Americans. Remember that French girl I dated? She wore me out."

Sitting there, thinking about the state of my marriage, I felt like I'd traveled a thousand miles down the wrong road. I was unsure whether I should turn around or continue forward in search of a better destination. That's how life is. You take a wrong turn. Suddenly it's 10 years later and you realize what a colossal mistake you've made.

Roger pulled onto an off ramp, continued onto a side street and pulled up to a red light. He turned toward me. "You know how I feel about Natalie. I've never tried to cover that up. She's ten miles of bad road, bro.'" He smiled his goofy smile. "You need a pit stop called Katrina."

I couldn't help but chuckle. The light turned green. Roger punched the gas pedal and the force of our acceleration pushed me back into my seat.

"You're my only brother. I know what's happening to you," he said, turning a corner. "You're withering on the vine Bro.'"

He looked away from the road for a second and shot me an earnest glance. "You've got a real chance with Katrina. You'll always regret it if you don't do it. So you better do it."

"If it happened, it could ruin my marriage. I'd be lost without Kyle."

"Natalie would never find out! Jeez, what would you do run home and tell her?"

I smiled and slowly nodded in acknowledgement of what he had said. "You have a point there." I looked down at my wedding band. Its shine was gone and it seemed as if it wasn't worth its weight in gold. I pulled it off and slipped in into my pocket.

We found a parking spot right in front of the Two Keys, then got out and walked to the entrance. Roger pulled open the heavy glass door, and I walked in behind him. We scanned the pub, looking for a place to sit. The place was packed so we slowly made our way through the crowd to the bar and ordered two beers.

It was a family business with large screen plasma televisions placed strategically around the L shaped room so everyone could see the game. The owners had a reputation for hiring attractive young Eastern Europeans women as waitresses, which is obviously why they had hired Katrina.

A bar ran the length of one wall and a few dozen tables were scattered throughout the place. Two pool tables and video games were in the section of the room that formed the foot of the L. We stood at the bar drinking and watching the game. I looked for Katrina but didn't see her. After a few minutes Roger saw an open table, which we quickly claimed.

The Bears scored and the room erupted in cheers. Once everyone had settled down I scanned the crowd again, but didn't see Katrina. I guessed she wasn't working that shift. *What shitty luck.* I took a swig of beer and leaned back in disappointment.

Then, out of the corner of my eye, I saw a flash of white at the front door. Katrina had just walked in. She was talking to the doorman, a freezer sized guy with tattooed biceps. Some other guy was standing beside her and she was introducing him to people who worked there.

Katrina's co-workers liked and respected her. She was the poster girl for an Alpha female. If women are like cats, she was the top cat, but she didn't abuse her position. She must have felt the weight of my stare because she looked across the pub, waved and started moving toward us, holding the guys' hand, leading him through the crowd.

My pulse quickened.

"Hi, guys," she said, walking up to our table. She motioned to the guy at her side. "This my friend Alex. He come from Moscow. He is poet, playwright and software engineer." She looked directly at me. "He seeks software job."

Alex bowed slightly then shook my hand. He slurred a quick "Pleased to greet you," then swayed a little, like a tree in the wind. He was around Katrina's age, maybe a few years older.

He reeked of alcohol and had clearly been drinking before they arrived.

As they reached our table, I noticed that there was something different about Katrina. Then I realized she had cut a few inches off the length of her hair.

"You cut your hair." I said.

She smiled widely. "I always do before big move."

"It looks fantastic."

"Really? I am thanking you for this compliment."

I invited them to sit down. Alex plopped onto a seat next to Roger and Katrina sat beside me. Her hair was back in a short pony tail, and even in a simple denim skirt and a plain white blouse, she was as gorgeous and desirable as ever. She put ice and sexuality together in a perfect treatise.

Was Alex her lover? If so, that could ruin everything for me.

He was tall and wispy, a furious combination of points and angles. The dominant feature on his thin, pockmarked face was a long carrot-like nose that seemed to loom over his thin purple lips. His chin, covered with a reddish goatee, looked like a wedge. His rust-colored hair was short and unkempt. His cheek bones were sharp, below beady, bloodshot eyes. He kept his arms and legs crossed the whole time which formed more angles. He was thin and wiry, the opposite of Katrina, not a smooth curve on him.

His Russian accent was thick, but his English fair. He said he had come to Chicago from Moscow a few weeks earlier. With the football game as a backdrop, we all chatted. I determined that he and Katrina were only "friends," and that she was letting him stay with her while he looked for work. That made sense, as he was clearly out of Katrina's league.

Looking at her sitting there, laughing and having a good time, I couldn't help but think that she personified beauty and elegance. It was almost as if she wasn't real, or at least not mortal. A lot of Russian women had immigrated to Chicago since the government there drew back the iron curtain. So many arrived so quickly, it was as if there was some kind of pipeline moving Soviet women to Chicago. I saw them in the malls and restaurants speaking with thick accents. They looked slutty, wearing their cheap furs, designer clothing, pancake makeup, and reeking of perfume. Perhaps I was being overly critical. Next to Katrina, everything in the world seemed tired and flawed.

Alex was wearing an ill-fitting, rumpled navy blue suit coat, a white dress shirt and jeans. He suit was covered in cigarette ashes and burn holes. His shoes were scuffed, just like his personality. As we all chatted, he banged back whiskeys that Katrina bought him and chain smoked Camels.

The Bears scored again and the room erupted in more cheers. Alex looked around then snorted. "Football is for idiots," he smirked. "Run, kick and catch. Is game for monkeys." He spoke rapidly and between breaths flicked his cigarette ashes on the floor.

My brother slid an ashtray in front of him. "Here, buddy use this," he said, smiling. "We wouldn't want to start a fire."

"Oh guys, let me tell you," Katrina said, her emerald eyes wide. "Alex fall in sleep with cigarette reading magazine. Thanks God he does not burn down apartment."

Alex looked at her and grinned, showing nicotine-stained teeth. "That is because American cigarettes are shit," he said dismissively. "Camels are shit. In Russia we have real cigarette."

He was getting drunk. Katrina looked at him sharply for a moment, then changed the subject. "Alex not only software engineer, he also study literature at Moscow University. Tolstoy, Dostoevsky, others."

I mentioned Anton Chekhov, the only other Russian writer I could remember.

Katrina seemed impressed. She reached over and touched my arm. "I love Chekhov!"

"Russian writers are real good?" Roger asked.

Alex's eyes widened. He slammed his fist on the table, and the ashtray trembled. "Russian writers are best," he slurred loudly.

I took a drink of beer and glanced at Katrina, then at Alex. "I think we've got some pretty good American writers too."

This seemed to interest Alex. He smiled coyly, shook his head, took a drag of his cigarette and studied me with narrowed eyes. "I bet you a drink no one in this place can name one great

American writer," he said, the cigarette now dangling between his bony fingers.

The corners of Katrina's mouth turned down. She stirred uncomfortably in her seat and placed a hand on her friends arm. "Alex, please stop."

He pulled away from her and smirked. "I mean it. Americans don't even know their own culture. Watch this."

A girl in her 20s was passing our table; Alex tugged the sleeve of her sweater. She was African American and heavy set with glasses and braids. She stopped and looked at Alex.

"Excuse me Miss," he said. "I have wager with these gentlemen. Can you tell us please name of one great American writer?"

We all looked at the girl, waiting for a response.

She seemed a little confused, but after a moment she gave us a puzzled look and said; "How about F. Scott Fitzgerald, Henry Miller, and my favorite is . . . Ernest J. Gaines."

Alex slumped disappointedly in his seat as if defeated. After a moment he smiled sheepishly at the girl who was still standing there. "Okay, I'm thanking you so much." After she'd left, he frowned and took a drink of whiskey. "Who is Gaines?" he said flatly. "I'm surprised she did not say Stephen King."

Roger lifted his glass. "The bet was a drink, right? I'll have a good Russian vodka."

Alex scowled at Roger, then said something is Russian that I suspected was a curse word.

The smile dropped from Katrina's face and she seemed to be studying her friend. "Poor Alex," she said with mock pity. "He drink more whiskey than write poems. I do not understand why he so mad?"

Alex took another gulp of whiskey and glared at Katrina. "Why? Why ask why?" he slurred. "Why are we the only of God's creatures that have disappointment? I drink because life is toilet of disappointments."

I glanced across the table at Roger who rolled his eyes.

"The young are stupid," Alex continued, waving his hands through the air. "Naiveté is curse around tender neck of young. Listen up child, learn right first time. Life is shit!"

I didn't know what to make of the guy. He was like a bad windup poet with a key in his back.

"Oh shut up, Alex, you're so depressing me," Katrina said, turning to look at Roger and me. "He sad man," she pouted playfully. "He need good woman to give him, how you say, light? No, to give him hope."

Alex raised his glass in a drunken toast "To hope," he slurred. "If I get too much more hope, I'll kill self!"

Katrina sat stiffly in her chair, clearly uncomfortable with her friend's drunken rant. Her lips were terse as if to say something, but before she could speak her phone rang, and she pulled it from her purse.

She stood. "Excuse to me, I must take call outside where I can hear." Then she turned to Alex and said something in Russian.

He replied in Russian and dismissed her with a wave of his hand.

Four college-aged guys at the next table turned from the television in unison and watched Katrina walk away.

I tried to get the waitress' attention to order a few more drinks, but she was on the other side of the room and didn't see me.

After a moment, Alex tapped me on the arm. "Let me tell you something." He leaned forward, his breath reeking of booze. "Real Russians don't come to America. The good Russians stay at home."

I don't think he realized he was talking about himself. I thought he was an asshole, and I was tempted to tell him that I agreed with him.

Before I could do that, Roger leaned into the table and thoughtfully cocked his head to the right. "I don't know about that," he said. "Katrina's one of the good ones. People here really like her."

Alex tilted back his head and drained the last of the whiskey in his glass. "She is exception," he said, sitting back in his chair. "Katrina, she is . . . *The Other*. She has IQ of 153. She belongs to Mensa. She is sage." He turned his palms up to the ceiling. "She is genius." He muttered something in Russian, then returned to English. "She is . . . impossible love? True food?" He looked at me, his mouth and his eyes forming a jealous smile. "She likes you," he grinned. "God knows why, but she likes you. I can tell."

He seemed happy just to be near her, like a tiny insignificant moon orbiting the sun. Roger looked at me and mouthed, "Go for it bro.'"

Katrina came back to the table carrying three bottles of Budweiser, clinking together. "Here guys," she said placing a beer each in front of Roger and me. She sat down and took a sip from the third beer.

Alex frowned and said something to her in Russian.

"No more for you," she said sternly. "You've had enough. You drink too much, you get ugly."

Alex shook his head and snorted, his face crimson as he slammed his empty glass onto the table. He wiped his mouth with the back of his hand then smirked at Katrina. "Ugly?" he smiled fiendishly. "The truth is ugly. I arrive here in ugly city and see fat Americans. Americans! Lazy, stupid, *ugly* Americans . . ."

I was about to tell him to shut up or go back to Russia. Before I could say anything Katrina abruptly cut him off in mid-sentence. There was real anger in her voice. She spoke Russian, so I didn't know what she said, but it was a sharp rebuke, her words ripping into him like bullets of ice.

He sat erect and his bloodshot eyes widened. He spat out something in Russian, but Katrina didn't back off an inch. Instead, she moved forward and blasted him with a few more choice words, like a machine gun. Then she sliced the air with her hand and gave him an intensely arctic glare. It was a display of real anger I'd never seen her unleash before.

Alex looked like a dog that had been kicked. He got up without saying anything and staggered away. Katrina watched him coldly, like a predator stalking its prey, as he disappeared into the crowd.

"I apologize about him," Katrina, said turning to us. "He is very upset about our country's fate."

I imagined her breath were forming puffs of steam, as if she was outside on a cold January day in St. Petersburg. Any emotional attachment I had to Natalie disappeared. At that moment, I would have given up everything for just for one night of passion with Katrina.

This would be that night.

"Alex is bitter." Roger's words snapped me out of my daydream.

The glow in Katrina's face dimmed. "He has too much pride in our country. Pride is what kills Russia, hanging onto past. He dies with Russia. He is angry at America for its success . . . and weaknesses."

I leaned into her personal space. Her face was only six inches from mine. "If he hates it here so much, why doesn't he go back to Moscow?"

Her expression turned from exasperation to sadness. She shifted in her seat and looked me in the eye. "The future in Moscow is uncertain. Everyone's future is uncertain."

Then she sat up straight in her seat and smiled broadly, erasing the gloom the same way the sun erases the fog. "Guys," she said excitedly. "Call earlier was from friend in Florida. I will move there next week."

I felt like a punctured tire. Still, I determined to lay my cards on the table with her, to tell her how much I desired her.

"Much to do before move," Katrina said, waving her arms through the air. She leaned forward and gently placed her hand on mine. "Perhaps you like to have books? I have Chekhov! You can come to apartment on Saturday night and select books you love." She paused, and our eyes met. "Is my birthday Saturday, and because for you I will give present of books."

I didn't care about the books. I would have said anything to be alone with her in her apartment. It would be even better than trying to pick her up at the pub that night. I glanced over at Roger.

His smile was as wide as a keyboard.

"Absolutely, Katrina," I said. "I'd love to look at whatever you've got."

. . .

And so the stage was set for my infidelity. I was actually surprised by the lack of guilt I felt. But everyone knows that a dog that isn't fed at home will beg at a neighbor's door. Roger was right: I sure as hell wasn't going to pass up on the opportunity of a lifetime. And you know what? Having an affair would do my marriage good by allowing me to let off a little steam.

Reason takes a backseat to desire. But, I'm not a sociopath. I understand that messing around on one's wife is wrong. The truth is, my mind had lost the battle to be faithful to Natalie. My body had won. The prize was Katrina. My skin was demanding to have a woman's hot flesh pressed against it. It was as if Katrina was a choice between life over death. What man with a pulse wouldn't choose life?

• • •

Driving to Katrina's apartment a few days later, I imagined slowly running my hands over her naked body. I could see her in my mind's eye, the only light in her bedroom coming from the string of Christmas lights Roger's friend had told him about. I imagined her back arching and her moaning as I passionately kissed her neck, then slowly moved down her torso. Gripping the steering wheel with sweaty palms, I could feel the heat between her thighs. Thinking of her naked, adorned in the lights, I was getting aroused and pushed down the gas pedal to make good time.

I found a curbside parking spot and briskly walked the half block to her apartment. It was a dreary, foggy night, wet leaves carpeting the sidewalk and street. It was her birthday, so I'd brought a bottle of expensive champagne, and put a big pink bow on it to help set the mood. I slipped it under my arm and approached the door of her two-flat.

I pushed the intercom buzzer, and Katrina's voice crackled over the speaker. "Who is it?"

"Katrina, it's me. It's Lou."

"I push button and you tug door hard," she replied.

The front door opened with a click. I sprinted up the stairs two at a time to the second floor. She opened the door, and I almost dropped the champagne. She was wearing a dazzling blue silk robe, and her hair was wet. Her clean scrubbed appearance did not detract from her beauty and in fact somehow enhanced it. "Come in please Lou," she said with a wave of her arm. I stepped in, and she closed the door. "I just jump from shower. I work late. Everything crazy getting ready for move." She raised a mint colored towel to her hair. "Please sit while I get undressed."

Undressed!

As she passed me, the smell of apples from the shampoo or soap she'd used trailed behind her.

"I brought some champagne," I said, holding out the bottle for her to see.

Her eyebrows arched. "Oh thanks Lou, but not necessary."

"It's a birthday present."

She came to my side, took the champagne bottle from me and examined it. "We do no practice this birthday giving so much in Russia," she said after a moment.

"I think it was started by the greeting card companies," I replied with a half smile.

"Greeting card companies? I think not," she said. "This tradition started with the early Greeks who thought every person was born with a protective spirit that watched over them throughout their life."

"The Greeks? Really?"

"Yes," she replied, her wide green eyes meeting mine. "They think the spirit had a mystic relation with the god on whose birthday the person was born." She turned her attention back to the champagne bottle and seemed to be reading the label. "The Romans also have this same idea," she said without looking up. "Is carried down in human thinking and later manifested as guardian angel, patron saint and Tooth Elf."

"You mean the Tooth Fairy," I said.

She turned toward me with a puzzled expression. "Tooth Fairy? Tooth Elf?' What is difference?"

I chuckled. "I don't think there is a difference."

She handed the bottle back to me and smiled coyly. "Is sweet for you to gift me this."

"I didn't have time to bake a cake with candles and all that."

"Ahh, yes of course, candles," she said, lifting the towel to her hair. "Tradition of burning cake candles on birth date also originates with Greeks. Honey cakes round like full moon and lit with candles were placed on the temple altar of god Artemis. In folk belief these candles are given special magic for granting wishes. Birth date candles are tribute to newborn child and bring good luck."

"Really," I said, genuinely impressed. "I did not know that."

Some smiled shyly and shrugged. "I like to read many things."

I held out the bottle of champagne. "Consider this your first-ever birthday present."

She pointed to the kitchen. "Thank you, but consider it a trade for the books. Glasses by sink in cupboard above."

I crossed the floor into the kitchenette and pulled two wine glasses from the cupboard. "Where's Alex tonight?"

"He have job interview in Wisconsin. Gone overnight," she said, hurrying down a short hallway into her bedroom.

Perfect.

I poured the champagne and watched the bubbles race to the rim, then I went back into her living room. A half-dozen cardboard boxes, which I assumed contained her belongings for the move, stood in a corner beside a tall bookcase. A large potted fern and several other plants were scattered around the room. There was a small television and stereo on a stand in the corner, and framed travel posters hung on the walls. A glass-topped wicker coffee table sat in front of the futon.

"Lou," Katrina called from the bedroom. "Look to see what books you like in shelf. More in here you can see in moment."

More in here! Her bedroom!

I picked up my glass and crossed to the bookshelf. It was packed with books on science, philosophy, engineering, art and the humanities. Most were in English, but a few were in Russian.

"Take what you want. I bought most in secondhand stores."

I turned to look. Katrina was standing in the middle of the room, smiling, wearing a rumpled plaid shirt, sweat pants and mismatched socks. Her hair was still wet. She was absolutely gorgeous. She obviously had many faces of beauty. I handed her the glass and offered a toast: "Youth is happy because it has the ability to see beauty. Anyone who keeps the ability to see beauty never grows old." I lifted my glass. "Katrina, may you never grow old."

Her eyes widened as she lightly touched her glass to mine. "You know Kafka!"

"Love him," I replied, unable to bring myself to tell her that I had found the toast online.

She took a sip, then looked at me over the rim of her glass, mischief playing in her eyes. "I have more books in bedroom. Come look."

As I followed her down the hall, her beautiful figure was somehow accentuated by her loose fitting clothing. I could barely control my breathing.

Her bedroom was small and sparely furnished. There was a trace of fresh perfume in the air. An unmade double bed, night table and lamp were set against the far wall. I scanned the room: no Christmas lights. I figured she had already packed them for the move. A chest of drawers and a full-length mirror stood against the other wall. A few dozen books were stacked in piles under a window, and empty cardboard boxes sat beside her bed. Framed black and white photographs of cities adorned the walls. An original painting hung over the bed: a lone white wolf, howling at a full moon, in a snow-covered clearing of evergreens.

I motioned to the painting with my glass. "Do you paint?"

She pushed back her golden bangs and giggled. "I took art class once." She pointed at the painting. "This is how I got 'Russian Wolf' name."

I went over to get a closer look. It was done in oils. It wasn't technically very good and it seemed to have been painted with a great deal of emotion. "Wolves are solitary animals," I said.

She walked to my side and thoughtfully lifted her index finger to her chin. "I think not. Lone wolf is myth. Every animal needs others like it."

Our eyes met. "Yes we do."

Do it now.

I leaned forward to kiss her. Before I could, she stepped away, took a sip of champagne, and turned to the stacks of books. "What do you prefer Lou? Art? History?"

"I'm really open to everything."

She gave me a sideways glance and yanked a book from the middle of one of the stacks. She sat on the edge of the bed and opened the book. "You may like this one."

I sat down beside her and our knees touched. She didn't move away. It was a boring book of Russian history with grainy photographs of onion-domed buildings, bleak-looking old people bundled up for winter and the Russian countryside.

"Take what you want," she said, offering the book to me. "Is good introduction to Russia. Will help you to understand my people, and their . . . how you say in English, desires?"

Her face was inches from mine, her lips slightly parted, her eyes wide and glowing like emeralds.

Now.

I placed the book on the bed, then leaned over and kissed her on the mouth.

She jerked away jumped up beside the bed. I fell on my side, spilling champagne on her blankets. "What are you trying!" she exclaimed, standing in the middle of the room. "What do you think?"

I sat up and put my glass on the night side table. "I thought we got along so well that, you know, and we're both adults and . . ."

"You are married!" she blurted. "I would never . . ."

"You invited me here. It seems like you like me, and . . ."

She placed her glass on a dresser. Then she planted her hands on her hips and shook her head in bewilderment. "Lou, sorry if I gave to you wrong information. I do like you, but like brother, friend. Not lover."

She liked me like a brother? No! It was like a bullet of ice through my libido. Shame, embarrassment, and to some degree disappointment welled up from my feet, filling my entire body. I flopped back onto her bed, covered my face with my hands and muttered: "How could I be so wrong! I'm such an idiot."

I dropped my hands and looked up. Katrina was still standing in the middle of the room, looking down at me, her green eyes sharp, her expression a combination of anger and confusion.

I slowly got off her bed, and the box spring creaked as if to mock me. "I don't know what I was thinking," I said. "Things are really bad at home: my wife and I are on the verge of divorcing."

She stood there speechless.

"Katrina," I continued sheepishly. "I don't want to bother you. I'll just leave."

She slowly backed away as I moved toward the bedroom door. "Yes," she said flatly, "you should go."

I went into the living room, grabbed my jacket off the futon and started toward the front door as Katrina stood at the mouth of the hallway watching me. I stopped and turned back toward her. "I'm sorry," I said. "My marriage is a wreck. I thought you were as interested in me as I am in you." I turned toward the door.

Katrina moved forward. "Lou, wait."

I pulled my hand away from the door knob and turned to see her stepping forward.

"I told you, I am friend," she said calmly. "If there are problems with wife, you can talk to me. Perhaps I can help."

I stood on the threshold for a few seconds, unsure which way to turn. My ego was bruised. But there was something in her voice, a gentleness, a sincerity, that drew me back.

"My wife doesn't care," I said. "Everything changed after our son was born."

Katrina moved toward me, a tender smile on her face. "Come in and sit down." She paused and added: "Just friends, right? No kisses."

I nodded.

She led me to the futon. "Okay, if you like, tell me what is happening. I have female point-of-view."

I didn't hold anything back. Talking to her had the power of confession: It lifted a heavy burden from my shoulders. Katrina sat with her back erect against the futon, hands in her lap, her ears seemingly perked. She listened closely and nodded in understanding as a torrent of frustration flowed from me. I must have vented for 20 minutes or more until I finally ran out of laments. In a way it was like an orgasm, because when I finished I felt unburdened, even relaxed.

Katrina studied me for a moment then moved to the edge of the futon. "Let me ask you something, and you think before answer," she said, her words carrying the weight of expectation. "Do you love wife?"

I sat back. "She's a good wife, but I really don't know if I love her. I wonder why we stay together?"

She shifted on the futon, then reached for her champagne and took a sip. "Marriage is difficult. I know from experience."

I looked at her in disbelief. "You were married?"

She nodded, her pristine face suddenly blank as a sheet of paper. "Yes, for three years in Moscow. I was very young bride, only 19."

I was surprised that she had been married, but absolutely blown away that any man would have let a woman like Katrina get away. "You're divorced? Widowed?"

"Divorced." She replied, waving her fist through the air. "It ended badly. He was older man, and beat." She leaned back into the futon. "He call me, 'beautiful Kat' buy me furs and diamonds. I don't care for such things. I just want to be good wife so I try and stay with him." She got up and went to the front window overlooking the street. "Was no good. He almost kill me," she said staring into the night. She turned and started pointing at various parts of her body. "He break my ribs, black my eyes, break my arm . . ." She paused, then pointed at her cheek. "And this scar, from his ring. I take one month in hospital. Police in Moscow blame *me*! Can you believe?"

I didn't know what to say. Suddenly my marriage problems seemed insignificant. I felt like a self-centered little boy. "Thank God you left him," I finally said.

She smiled weakly and sat back down on the futon beside me. "Yes I leaved him, but I find out two years after divorce . . ."

She stopped talking, lowered her head and started to weep. Then she looked up at me, tears running down her porcelain cheeks.

"He give to me the HIV."

I was totally shocked. She seemed so vibrant and healthy, like the kind of person who never got so much as a common cold, let alone . . . I was at a complete loss. I didn't know what to do or say. After a few seconds I managed to mumble: "Katrina, I'm so sorry. I had no idea."

She looked away. "He was monster. I love wrong man and I pay for this." She toward me, her jade eyes imploring. "Lou, maybe you will leave wife but first try everything. You said she is good woman, so talk to her. Tell her your deepest feelings. Make her to hear you. Play all cards."

I muttered something about Natalie never wanting to have sex and how lust and frustration overshadowed everything good in our marriage.

"Sex is important for couples. But not everything. Lust is like dinosaur in movie *Jurassic Park*. It gets loose and tears everything up."

I couldn't help but grin at her analogy.

She gave me a curious look. "Perhaps you should try and see past desires," she said softly. "Passions of the night are like firework, like candle flame. They flee and cold spot settles in." She squeezed my knee and stood up. "Now go home to wife and child. You are blessed to have them."

I didn't know if I was blessed or not; the future of my marriage was still uncertain. But all the things Katrina had said resonated with me. I slipped on my jacket and started toward the door.

"I walk you to car," Katrina said, pulling a puffy winter coat from the closet. "I need night air."

Outside, the fog seemed to have thickened, like a dense smoke in the cool night.

"Street lights are grim tonight," Katrina said, walking by my side, her hands stuffed into her coat pockets. "Will be better in Florida."

"When do you leave?"

She smiled. "Saturday I go to place of sunshine of light."

We got to my car, and I turned toward her. Her face was glowing like the moon. "I'm sorry for what happened in the bedroom," I said shamefacedly. "I'm a jerk."

"You are a man," she said. "This I know."

"I'm glad we're friends," I said, reaching for the door handle. "And Happy Birthday."

A mischievous smile crossed her face. "Yes, of course, and since we are friends, could you and brother help me load truck for move. Alex will also assist."

"I'll help, and I'll ask Roger." I stood there for a moment unsure if I should hug her, shake her hand or just get in and drive away.

Before I could decide she leaned forward and lightly kissed my cheek. Then she looked up into the night sky and inhaled deeply. "I will miss you guys, people at pub," she said, smiling broadly. "And thank you from my heart for the birthday gift."

A flood of emotions swirled in my mind. I felt an urgent need to tell her what I thought of her. "It's you that deserves the thanks. You helped me see things. Get a new perspective." I got into the car, put the window down and looked up at her.

"Maybe you are good man after all," she said, waving goodbye.

"I am a man," I replied. "This I know."

She laughed. "Okay. See you Saturday, moving man."

I nodded, started the car and drove home through the fog.

• • •

Despite Katrina's heartfelt advice I wasn't able to muster the energy or will power to talk to Natalie about our marriage. The ball was in her court and she wasn't interested enough to work on our problems.

I called Roger from my office the next morning, and he agreed to meet me at Katrina's to help load her rental truck. I gave him her address, and he wrote it down.

"What happened last night, bro?" he asked. "You did it. You bagged that Russian Wolf."

If he had been there, I would have hit him. "Oh shut up," I replied. "She's not like that. Nothing happened."

There was a pause. "I can't believe you messed up. Bro, that was the opportunity of a lifetime."

"Grow up, Roger," I said, then slammed down the receiver.

On Saturday morning, on the way to Katrina's, I picked up a thermos of coffee and a box of donuts. It was cool, but the sun was out and the morning sky was pale blue, in a sharp contrast to the weather a few days earlier when I'd last seen Katrina.

I parked the car around the corner from her apartment, grabbed the coffee and donuts from the passenger seat, and walked briskly toward her street. The chilled air was spiced with the smoky scent of something smoldering nearby, probably from someone's fireplace.

Rounding the corner onto her street, I was confronted with a scene of chaos. Fire trucks were parked at odd angles in the middle of the road as firefighters in heavy rubber coats and boots trod over long hoses that criss-crossed the street like snakes. Black water ran in the gutters as groups of people stood around, talking in hushed voices.

I was surveying, the scene trying to make sense of it, when I heard someone call my name. It was Roger. He was crossing the street walking toward me, his breath proceeding him in puffs of steam.

"What up?" I asked.

"There was a fire . . ."

"How are we going to load their truck with all this shit in the street?"

A shattered look filled his blue eyes. He pointed at one of the firefighters. "Lou, I talked to the captain over there. The fire was in Katrina's building, early this morning. She's gone, bro, and so is what's-his-name, that drunk, Alex."

"What do you mean gone? Gone where?" I though he meant they had loaded the truck and left.

Roger stepped in front of me, put his gloved hand on my shoulder and looked me square in the face. "Lou, they were killed in the fire. Bro, they didn't make it out."

It was the steam carrying his words that I noticed most at that moment. They fell out of the air like birds that died in flight. My knees buckled and I slumped into my brother as the coffee and donuts tumbled into the street. I could only gasp a single word response:

"What!"

My stomach lurched followed by a wave of nausea. Dazed, I half sat and half collapsed onto the curb. "My God, there's got to be a mistake. Are you sure?"

Roger sat down beside me. "Yeah, I'm sure. They think 'someone' fell asleep with a cigarette." He shook his head in disgust. "Probably that Alex guy. Asshole."

I stood and staggered to the front of Katrina's brick building. The windows were smashed out; shattered glass and charred debris were scattered on the lawn and sidewalk. Soot-covered icicles hung from the eves and sills. It was a strange, still image of horror. The heavy and sick smell of smoke wafted over everything.

Roger came up and took my arm. "Lou, there's nothing we can do here. Let's go, I'll buy breakfast."

"Breakfast? I can't eat anything," I said, tears welling in my eyes. "I need to stay here for a minute."

"Take your time." Then after a moment he said: "Lou, she was a great lady."

Some of the firefighters were throwing half-burned debris through the gaping hole that had been Katrina's front window. One of them dropped a load of stuff which crashed to the ground. On top of it all was a scorched poster or painting. It was burned up, and the frame was broken, but as I stood there shivering in the cold, it occurred to me that it could have been Katrina's painting of the wolf howling at the moon. I stared down at it for a minute then turned my back on the tragedy and walked away.

Roger was standing on the curb across the street, the sun shining on his face. "You okay, bro?"

I slowly buttoned my coat and shook my head. "I just can't . . . I can't believe it."

"Neither can I."

I pulled on my wool cap. There was nothing left to do there. "I'm going home."

"Call me later."

"Yeah, sure."

Driving home in a daze, I ran over and over in my mind what Katrina had said to me about being honest and open with Natalie.

"Play all cards."

I pulled into the driveway and sat there for 20 minutes, completely numb.

When I went inside, Natalie was sitting at the kitchen table, drinking coffee, leafing through a catalog. I sat down, and she turned toward me, a quizzical look on her face. "You smell like smoke," she said.

"I know."

She must have read my expression, because she suddenly looked concerned. "What's the matter Lou?"

"Natalie . . ." I reached across the table, took her hand in mine and met her gaze. "We need to talk."

UNSPEAKABLE

ETECTIVE, WHAT CAN I SAY TO HELP explain this unfortunate bloody mess? I guess you could say it all started with a single word.

It was the second week of my marriage and the radiant glow from our recent nuptials was still very evident in the linked-hearts of my husband and I. People might as well have stopped getting married, because we had perfected it. I can honestly say that we were the ideal couple . . . then my handsome new groom had to go and say that unspeakable word!

I was sitting at the dinner table reading the newspaper and drinking a glass of Chardonnay from one of the crystal glasses we'd been given as a wedding present, when he called to me from the kitchen: "I talked to your mom today," he said cheerfully.

"Great," I replied. "How is she?"

"She sounded good. She said her birthday is next week."

"I know. We should do something with her."

"I invited her to dinner on Friday."

God, isn't he great! Inviting my mother over for a birthday dinner. How many sons-in-law would do that in the first few weeks of their marriage?

"A birthday party would be wonderful," I replied. "We'll have a cake with candles, presents and all that."

He came into the dining room carrying a large wooden bowl filled with a fresh tossed salad. "I'll buy the cake."

I leaned over and kissed him on the cheek as he placed the salad on the table. I just loved the way he put the salad down, with such class. My heart swelled.

"I love you," he said.

"Me too. Did she have any news?" I asked.

"Not really," he replied with a giggle.

What an adorable giggle! It is one of the many small things I love about him! "What's so funny, sweetheart?" I asked.

"Your mother told me about your 'unspeakable word,'" he replied, pouring himself another glass of wine. "You should have said something to me about it."

My heart rate quickened. "I was planning to . . . at some point . . . it's uh . . . I don't know . . . it's weird, I guess, huh?"

He smiled, showing that amazingly cute gap between his front teeth, then placed his warm loving hand on mine. "I've just never heard of someone who can't stand to hear a certain word."

"I know it's unusual," I replied. I gazed into his beautiful amber eyes. "I'm not sure what it's all about. But it's better for everyone if I don't hear that word. The last time . . . the police got involved . . . ambulances . . ."

He took a bite of salad and motioned toward me with his fork. The way he moves his fork through the air to illustrate a point is so charming! "I think the best thing to help you deal with this is for me to say the word," he said. "That way it'll be out there and we can get past it. What would happen if I said it by mistake?"

I cleared my throat. "I was going to write you a letter explaining it and ask you to be sure not to say it."

"A letter? Don't be foolish. I'm just going to say it right now. Otherwise it'll always be like the 800 pound gorilla in the room."

I've got to admit, I don't like being called "foolish." But he had said it in a very respectful, thoughtful way, and it certainly wasn't the unspeakable word. Still, in order to make a point, I brought my hand down firmly on the dinner table and the plates trembled. "Please don't say it," I said.

He looked at me and grinned mischievously. His grin is so attractive! "I'm going to say it. You need to hear it. It will do you good to hear it."

I nervously eyed the steak knife next to my plate.

"Just don't say it, okay?"

He poured himself more wine and took a sip. I could tell that he was getting drunk. He over does it with the wine sometimes and truth be told it does bother me . . . just a little.

"I'm just going to say it right now," he slurred. "I'm getting ready to say it. I can taste it in my mouth right now . . ."

I stood up beside the table in an attempt to intimidate him, to assert myself. "Listen," I said, "if you say it, I can't be held responsible for my reaction."

He scoffed. "That's ridiculous."

I really detest scoffers, but considering all his good qualities I was willing to overlook his scoffiness.

"I'm not kidding," I said. "Something bad could happen. The last time . . ." I rubbed my eyes. "It's better for everyone if I don't hear that frigging word."

He seemed to be thinking about what I had said. A row of wrinkles formed on his forehead. But they were the most handsome wrinkles you'll ever see! "The only way to address something like that is by bringing it out into the open," he said. "By saying it over and over. Face your fears."

I could feel my blood pressure rising, and my palms were drenched with sweat. And I've got to say that if there's a second unspeakable word, or should I say an unspeakable phrase, I can't stand to hear, it's "Face your fears."

"I know it sounds crazy but I can't help it," I said, fighting to control my breathing. I tried to force a smile, but it's hard to smile when your teeth are clenched together. "It's just one of those unexplainable things, I guess," I seethed.

"This is childish," he said after a moment. "I'm just going to say it and be done with it."

"Please don't do that," I replied, surprised by the pleading tone in my voice.

He looked at his fork and seemed to be studying his reflection in it. After a few seconds he carefully placed it back on the table and turned toward me. "You should see a shrink. It's only a word. I've never in my life heard of some who's afraid of hearing a single word, especially an innocuous word like . . ."

Is it just me, or does everyone get very agitated when someone suggests they see a shrink? I sliced my hand through the air and cut him off.

"I'm not afraid of it!" I blurted. "Think of it as a deadly allergy, if that helps. When I hear that word, I have a bad reaction. Would you give a peanut butter cookie to someone who is allergic to peanuts? Huh? Would you?"

He threw up his hands and exhaled loudly. I really don't like people who exhale loudly because there's something very impolite about it. Very impolite!

"What would happen if you were in a public place, say a grocery store and you overhead someone say it?" he asked.

I started to hyperventilate. "I don't think I'd hear it in a grocery store," I replied firmly. "Besides, I intentionally avoid places where people may say it."

"That's nuts!" he scoffed. "It's all in your mind. That's why you need to hear it. To get it out there. To get past hearing it."

Did he just call me nuts? Why that little . . . I shook my head. "You don't understand, and that's okay. Maybe I am nuts when it come to that word. It's just one of those things. Please drop it."

He took a big, ugly gulp of wine and leaned back in his chair. "Okay," he said matter-of-factly showing that unattractive gap between his front teeth, "what if I start by saying a word that rhymes with it?"

I exhaled in exasperation. My back teeth were grinding together, and I think I may have been growling. "There aren't any words that rhyme with it," I snapped. *Don't you just hate people who have to rhyme things?*

"I can think of one. Mus . . ."

He started to say a word that rhymed with it, but once again I cut him off in mid-sentence. "Rhyming is for idiots and this whole conversation is making me very uneasy," I said, barely able to control my anger. "Do you understand? Very uneasy." My heart was pounding like a drum in the African night and my eyes were drawn to the poker beside the fireplace. "Let's just drop it okay?"

He drained his glass of wine and burped loudly. He was obviously drunk. Very unattractive! "Enough of this bullshit," he said smiling wickedly. "Are you ready? I'm going to say it . . ."

"No, please don't!" I yelled. "For God's sake, have some sensitivity!"

But the unspeakable word was already on his lips. I could see his mouth forming the first letter. When he said it, it was as if he were talking in slow motion in a deep demonic voice. The word hit me like a blast from a double-barrel shotgun. I vaguely remember staggering to the table and blindly reaching for the steak knife as the word . . . rang in my ears.

It was the last word he ever spoke—if you don't count "No!" and "God!" and something that sounded like "Arrrrrghhhhh!"

So, officer, I'll write that unspeakable word down for you. But whatever you do, please don't say it, because the last time . . .

SHINER

I WOKE FROM A DEEP SUMMER DREAM to the sound of my father berating my mother, his cruel and cutting words seemingly flying up the stairs into my room with razor-like edges.

"There's one thing I want in this house," he screamed. "Before I go to my clinic to earn money to support this family, I want a glass of orange juice!"

I turned over, reached for my glasses and looked at my watch: 7:37. It was mid-August, less than a month before I was to start the ninth grade. I wanted to simply roll over and go back to sleep. That was impossible, so I flopped back onto the sheets and listened to my father's vindictive tirade.

"Why is it so hard for you to get anything right?" he yelled.

"But Gregory last night . . . . you," my mother replied in a pleading voice.

He cut her off. "Is that too much to ask? A simple glass of orange juice?"

"Gregory you *drank* the orange juice . . ."

"Why are you arguing with me?" he screamed. "Why must you disagree with everything I say?"

My mother was desperately trying to explain to him that *he* drank all the orange juice the previous night when he had come home late and drunk. Rage had made him deaf to the truth. I could see him in my mind's eye in the kitchen, glaring at my mother, black eyes filled with anger, face red and twisted, teeth bared. It was a face I knew only too well, as did my mother and my little sister, Claire. Even Alice, our moody dachshund, was often the object of his wrath.

I was about to turn on my Walkman when my bedroom door creaked open and Claire padded in wearing pajamas with little blue bunnies on then. She jumped into the bed beside me as rows of worry creased her forehead. Claire loved baby powder the way some children love candy, and its soft smell now filled the air.

"When Dad yells," she said in a voice barely above a whisper, "it really hurts my ears."

She was on the verge of tears.

I put my arm around her tiny shoulders. "I know. Don't worry; he'll be gone to work soon."

At least that's what I hoped.

The morning sun had pushed through a small space between my bedroom curtains, forming a long yellow rectangle on the wall above us.

"And what about my damned shirts and lab coat?" my father screamed. "They're not pressed. I told you a hundred times to take them to the cleaners . . ."

Then he slammed his fist into something, probably a cupboard.

My mother shrieked.

I was thankful that he hadn't struck her this time. He was short and stocky, with powerful shoulders and arms. He had been a fullback at Western Ontario University, and I later learned that even then he had a reputation as a man with a mean streak who would cleat opposing players when they were down.

"I don't need this kind of bullshit before a day at my clinic. Don't you get it?" he yelled. "You think I like being angry?"

Yeah, I though, *I think you do.* Later in life, when I came to know the full spectrum of human emotions, the one emotion I associated with him more than any other was rage, followed closely by brooding. They were like his shadow, always nearby.

I was sure that in some corner of my father's mind he knew *he* drank the orange juice when he was drunk. I guess the truth really didn't matter to him. He needed to blame someone for his unhappiness and my mother was the closest person to him.

I learned early in life about the petty and cruel things that are played out within the walls of a seemingly normal suburban family.

I sat up in bed and faced the window. As my father erupted into another verbal barrage, Claire snuggled closer to me and buried her face in the blankets. Everything about Claire was little. She had tiny fingers, feet and toes, a little head and tiny teeth. She was like a doll. She also had a little voice, unless she was angry and then it became loud and mad.

"Claire," I said, nudging her. "I've got a good trick you can try so his yelling doesn't hurt your ears so much. Watch this."

She pushed back the blankets and gazed up at me, blue eyes wide, expression much too serious for an eight-year-old wearing bunny pajamas.

I stuck my index fingers in my ears. "Go ahead," I said, nodding toward her. "You do it."

"I tried that," she replied gruffly. "It doesn't work."

I pulled my fingers from my ears. "Did you try the singing part?"

"No."

"Come on. Do like I do."

She knelt, then plugged her ears.

"Okay, Can you hear me a little?"

She nodded.

"The secret is to hum a song you like because that blocks out the noise."

"What song?"

"Any song you like. Go ahead try it."

She looked puzzled, as if she couldn't think of a song. Then, she pulled her fingers out of her ears. "What about the Rainbow Song?"

I didn't know that song, but nodded my approval as she started humming.

"Fingers in your ears," I said. "That's really important."

"Oh yeah," she said, raising her hands to comply. "I forgot."

She looked at me and resumed humming.

I mimed as if I was talking loudly.

A smile crossed her lips and her pale blue eyes widened. "Wow," she giggled. "It really works!"

I reached over and carefully pulled her tiny hands away from her ears. "Don't forget," I said, pushing the blonde curls from her forehead. "You can do it whenever you don't want to hear something."

The smile slipped from her face and she looked at the floor. "Sometimes, I wish I was deaf."

My stomach turned. I was only 15, but mature enough to be disturbed by her comment and the resignation in her voice. "Nobody wants to be deaf," I said. "If you were deaf, you'd never hear anyone say, 'I love you . . . Barf-face.'"

She smiled a little as I took her tiny hand in mine.

"Okay, Snot-head, who loves you more than your big brother?" I asked.

"Nobody, except for maybe Lois?" she said. "Lois loves me too. That's what she said. She loves me."

Sometimes, I heard Claire playing alone in her bedroom, talking to her imaginary friend, pretending to serve tea in the tiny cups imprinted with fairies. *"Lois, would you like cream and sugar? More tea, Lois? Have another cookie."* At the time it seemed like a charming childhood fantasy. Years later, I understood it as an early symptom of Claire's mental illness, a precursor to her inability to deal with the pain of the real world.

I tugged Claire's pajama sleeve and looked into her eyes. "Maybe Lois loves you. But not as much as your big brother." I leaned toward her. "Give me a hug Snot-head."

She backed away and shot me a look of indignation.

"I'm not a Snot-head," she blurted. *"You* are!"

I sat up on the bed. "Oh yeah," I said, suppressing a grin. "If you're not a Snot-head, then you're a Fart-face."

Her lips were pursed tightly. "You're a Fart-face and a, and a . . . Balloon-brain!"

I playfully pushed her shoulder, but before I could reply, my father yelled another obscenity at my mother. Claire immediately turned away from me and toward the bedroom door.

He screamed something inaudible, then stormed out the front door, slamming it behind him. A few moments later we heard the sound of his car engine as he roared out of the driveway.

At last.

A calmness like the serene stillness after a storm immediately settled over the house.

Claire turned back toward me, her face once again filled with concern.

"Don't worry so much, Claire," I said. "He won't be back until late tonight. You'll be asleep by then."

"You promise?"

What could I say? I wasn't sure, but that had been his pattern. Stay out late, or not come home at all.

"I promise."

She exhaled loudly and looked down at the blankets. After a few seconds, she looked up at me again. "Neil, what's 'adopted?'"

Her question surprised me. I wasn't exactly sure how to answer. I knew that Claire and I had been adopted as babies seven years apart. No one had told me, but I had figured it out by the time I was nine. Whenever Claire or I did something to annoy my father, he immediately scolded my mother, saying things like If they were my real children or It was your idea to get them. But I didn't think Claire had any idea.

"Who told you that word, 'adopted?" I asked.

"I heard Mum talking about it to somebody on the phone."

I slid off the bed, crossed the room and pulled back the curtains. Bright July sunlight flooded the bedroom and I squinted against its glow. Standing by the window, I turned back to Claire who was now curled up lying on her side, sucking her thumb.

"What do you think 'adopted' means?"

"I don't know," she replied.

What it meant to me was that our parents needed children to fill in the portrait of the happy, successful family they wanted to present to the outside world. Claire and I were simply the cutouts of children they ended up with. We could have been anyone. I was sure it was my mother's idea to adopt us, and my father went along because he liked the idea of being the head of a "happy" suburban family.

I walked over and sat on the end of the bed, next to Claire's feet. "Adopted means . . . you're really lucky," I said, grabbing her ankle. "You're lucky because someone chose you from all the other babies in the whole world."

She jerked away from me and sat up, pulling her knees to her chin until the legs of her pajamas climbed half way up her calves. She sat like that for a moment, pondering what I had said. "You mean like the time I picked out Angel at the store?"

This was one of her favorite dolls. I flopped onto the bed and stared up at the ceiling. "Yeah," I said, turning toward her. "Kind of like that. But it's not something you should think about until you're . . . twelve."

That seemed to be enough of an explanation for her. She nodded slowly. Then she jumped off the bed and looked at me, eyes wide with excitement. "Neil," she said. "Are we making ice cream today? You promised, remember? Pleeeaaase? You promised."

Our mother had been given an electric ice cream maker by one of her friends a few weeks earlier, and ever since Claire had been bugging me to show her how to make ice cream. I had told her I would, but always blew it off in favor of hanging out with my friends.

I rolled over onto my stomach and rested my head on my arms. "We don't have the ingredients. Mum was supposed to . . ."

Claire cut me off. "Mum bought the ingredients yesterday. Milk, salt and the other stuff too. You promised."

I got off the bed, pulled a T-shirt from my drawer, slipped it on and turned toward Claire. "Promises to pea-headed little girls aren't like real promises, you know."

She glared at me, hands clenched into tight fists. "Yes they are! Promises are promises!"

I didn't have anything better to do that day than hang out with my friends. And it was a far more interesting way of spending my day than making ice cream with Claire. Still, I felt guilty because I had been putting her off for more than a week. I walked to the window and glanced outside. It was a beautiful summer morning drenched in golden sunlight. The sky was deep blue and flawless.

"Okay," I said, turning back toward her. "I'll meet you here at three o'clock and we'll make ice cream . . . like I promised."

Claire's face erupted into a broad smile and her eyes sparkled like blue stars. "Yay," she said triumphantly. "Let's make chocolate ice cream, okay?"

"I hate chocolate," I said, just wanting to give her a little bit of a hard time.

"No, you don't!" she said, standing in the doorway. "You love chocolate."

"Just kidding. We'll make chocolate. Chocolate's okay."

She started shuffling out of the room, then turned back toward me. "Thanks," she said softly, "for showing me how not to listen . . . Pea-head."

"No problem Bird-breath."

I heard her singing softly to herself as she returned to her room.

Claire was often a pest but I felt protective of her. I wasn't sure where that paternal instinct came from. Perhaps it was because even as a teenager I sensed how incredibly fragile and sensitive she was and how at the age of seven she seemed to carry the weight of the world on her tiny shoulders. There were times I'd look at her and thought one of my fathers' screams would break her in two.

Leaning against the window frame, I looked out into the back yard. The lawn rolled 50 feet from the rear of our house to a line of tall spruce and maple trees in full leaf. It was the heart of summer and the morning sun washed over the entire yard, bathing the stone patio and picnic table in a vibrant yellow glow. A landscaping crew looked after our yard, and the lawn was always as trimmed and neat as the grass on a golf course fairway.

I heard the screen door slam, then saw my mother walk out onto the patio, her pink bathrobe shimmering in the bright morning light. She loved the color pink and had incorporated it into her wardrobe and throughout our house. The upholstery on our sofa and chairs were tinged with pink, the lamp shades were light pink, there were hints of pink in many of the paintings in our house, and there were always pink and white towels in the bathroom. My father scolded her about it all the time, saying things like: *"Why do we have to have all this pink shit in our home? It looks like we live in a whorehouse."*

Perhaps pink, for her, was the color of hope. More likely it somehow numbed her against my father's anger and represented an escape of some kind.

A plastic grocery bag dangled from my mother's right hand. I knew what the bag held.

Every night, before my father came home, she drank a half dozen miniature bottles of liquor, then carefully hid the empties in a plastic bag under the kitchen sink. In the morning, after my father had left for work, she threw the bottles into the trash. I don't know why she drank miniatures. Maybe she thought small bottles meant her drinking was not a big deal.

A week earlier I'd taken a half-dozen of the bottles out of the garbage and put them on my windowsill because I liked the way the light reflected through the blue, brown and clear glass. Later that day, I was lying on my bed reading a music magazine, when my mother came in to collect laundry. She lifted a pair of my jeans off the floor and was about to put them into her plastic laundry basket when she suddenly stopped and pointed at the bottles.

"Neil," she asked sternly. "Where did you get those?"

"Get what?"

"The liquor bottles," she said angrily. "Where did they come from?"

I put the magazine on my lap and turned toward the window. "From the trash."

Without saying anything, she gathered up the bottles and dropped them into the laundry basket. "Neil, they're not toys," she scolded. "What are you doing digging around in the garbage, anyway? Keep out of the garbage. It's filthy."

"I just thought they looked cool . . ."

"Well, they're not cool," she snapped. "And if your father saw them, he'd get very angry. Do you understand?"

"Yeah, I guess," I said sheepishly. "I don't know what the big deal is. They're empty and everything."

She dropped the basket onto the floor, strode to the edge of the bed and grabbed my arm. "That's not the point." Her face was red with anger. "For God's sake, Neil, for once just do what I tell you."

I pulled away from her. "Yes, okay," I said, rubbing my arm. "I'm sorry, Jeez."

Now, looking down at her from my bedroom window, I could hear the tiny bottles clinking together as she slowly lifted the cover off the garbage can and dropped them in. She put the lid back on, then rubbed her eyes and stood there as if thinking.

I desperately wanted to rush down and comfort her: to hug her, to tell her that I loved her, to tell her I would protect her, that I would buy orange juice out of my allowance so my father wouldn't have anything to get angry about.

But I didn't. After a moment, she nodded as if she were agreeing with someone, then turned and went inside.

Maybe she stayed with my father for appearances, and to some degree, for and Claire and me. But even then, I knew that "appearances" are often false and treacherous. It takes a lot of energy to cover the truth. It's like trying to put a blanket over something that's large and moving. Marrying a successful dentist fit into her L.L. Bean catalog version of what a suburban family should be, so she did what a lot of abused wives do: She blamed herself for his tirades. I could almost hear her thinking: *If only I had bought another carton of orange juice, everything would be all right.*

I turned away from the window, flopped onto my bed and pulled the sheet up to my chest. The house was calm except for some songbirds in the yard and the murmur of a light breeze through the trees beside our house. Dogs were barking somewhere nearby. Children were laughing as the drone of a lawnmower hovered in the August morning. I stared up at the ceiling and considered going downstairs for breakfast. But I was still tired and within 10 minutes fell into the kind of dreamy slumber that only comes on a summer day.

• • •

The doorbell ringing over and over awakened me. I figured my mother would answer it. When that didn't happen I tried ignoring it. But whoever it was kept ringing, so I flung off the blankets, reached for my glasses and descended the stairs. Still only half awake, I staggered to the front door and pulled it open. The brightness of the day forced me to squint.

The newspaper delivery boy was standing there with sweat running down his forehead in tiny rivulets. He was a kid from the neighborhood, a few years younger than me, probably twelve or thirteen. He was heavy-set with what looked like a crew cut. A bulky blue canvas bag filled with newspapers was slung over his right shoulder. The armpits of his droopy red T-shirt were stained with sweat.

"The doorbell's not broken!" I said. "If you ring and no one comes, you go away and come back later."

He cast his gaze downward. "Sorry," he said in a high-pitched squeaky voice, "but I need to get paid today." He passed me the newspaper.

I took it and rubbed my eyes with my other hand. "How much is it?" I asked, trying to suppress a yawn.

"You owe for five weeks. It's $17.50."

"What?" I said, jolted awake by the amount. "Five weeks?"

The paperboy nodded. "Every week for the past five weeks, your mother told me to come back and collect next week."

I turned and yelled into the empty house. "Mum, the paperboy's here. He needs to get paid."

Silence.

"Mum, are you there? They paperboy needs to get paid . . . Hello? Is anyone home?"

More silence. I figured my mother and Claire had gone out. I leaned against the door frame and looked down at the paperboy. "My parents aren't here. Come back Monday and someone will pay you."

He grimaced and shuffled in place. "I'm going on vacation with my family, so I need to collect from everyone on my route before that."

I dropped the newspaper on the floor, plunged my hands into my jeans pockets and pulled out some change and a few crumpled dollar bills. "How much did you say it is?" I asked, sorting through the coins and bills in my palm.

"Five weeks. That's $17.50."

My money totaled five dollars and sixteen cents. I slipped it back into my pocket. "Just a minute. I'll see if I can scrape it together." I motioned for him to come in. "It's hot today; wait in here."

He stepped inside, dropped the bag of newspapers at his feet with a thud, then wiped the sweat from his forehead with the sleeve of his shirt.

I turned and went to the kitchen to forage for more money. My mother kept spare change and small bills in a ceramic coffee mug in a kitchen cupboard above the range. I dumped it onto the counter and quickly counted it. Four dollars and eighty-four cents in singles, quarters, dimes, nickels and pennies. I scooped up the money, slipped it into my pocket and stood there, wracking my brain, trying to think of some other place where I could find a few more dollars.

My father's desk!

The only problem was that the desk was in my father's den, which was off limits to everyone, even my mother. When he got home from his dental clinic he would disappear into the den for hours at a time, emerging only for dinner or to go out somewhere. He would be mad as hell if he knew I had been in there. But I only needed a few more dollars and the paperboy was waiting, so . . .

It was almost noon but the curtains in the den were closed, and the room was half dark. My father's mahogany desk stood against the far wall. I flicked on the light and glanced over the desktop, looking for money. Nothing.

I moved stealthfully and deliberately, trying not to leave anything out of place which might have tipped my father to the fact I'd been rooting around in there. I sat down in front of the desk, pulled open the top drawer and sifted through the contents. All I saw were pens with logos from various dental companies my father dealt with, paper clips, business cards and a checkbook.

I was about to close the drawer when something caught my attention. It was a light blue greeting card envelope. "To Peter, the love of my life" was written on the front. Peter was my father's name. I looked down at the card and suddenly it was as if someone had whispered "Read that" in my ear. I pulled the card out of the envelope and studied the romantic cover drawing of a couple in a garden, kissing.

I looked toward the door then opened the card and quickly read it:

> "Greg, I love you. Last night was the best night ever. I can't stop thinking of you, especially when we're at work. All the times we spend together are magic. Why do you stay with your miserable wife and those two little brats? Don't you see? We can have a wonderful life together. My Love, leave them now before it's too late."

It was signed "Bridgette." She had drawn a heart beside her name.

I stared down at the card. It was as if someone had slapped me. "Bridgette" worked as a hygienist in my father's clinic. Obviously the card was from her, and obviously she was having an affair with my father. *Holy Shit!* Half-stunned, I dropped the card on top of the desk, and in a daze, went back to the front door where the paperboy was waiting.

"I can't find any money," I said, guiding him out the door. "Come back tomorrow when my mother's home and she'll pay you."

He winced. "Tomorrow? It's been five weeks and . . ."

"I know it's been five weeks," I blurted angrily. "You already told me that. Come back tomorrow and talk to my mother. She'll be here."

He looked around sheepishly. "Okay, alright," he mumbled. "I'm come back tomorrow."

I slammed the door and went back into my father's den to reread the card. Sitting there staring down at it, I couldn't fully absorb the emotional impact of what I had just discovered. I was only 15, but I wasn't naive and had no illusions about my parents' crappy relationship. Their marriage was a train wreck. But seeing the card from his lover hit me as hard as my father would have if he'd known that I'd read it. He was a volatile combination of a violent temper and a short fuse.

. . .

Two months before, right after school had let out for summer, my father had sat me down in his den for a father-to-son chat. He didn't "chat" with me very often, and I was thankful, because the few excruciating chats we'd had usually served as a chance for him to tell me how much I disappointed him. And besides, "chat" implies a two-way conversation when in reality I simply sat and listened to him, offered terse two-word replies to his questions and nodded in agreement with whatever he said. I had learned to tell him what he wanted to hear.

"I need to discuss your grades with you," he had said sternly. "I don't understand why they're so damned low."

My grades were low because I was had been blowing off homework and skipping class whenever possible. I liked hanging out with friends at school but had pretty much lost interest in the academic side of things by the seventh grade. "Some of my teachers are lame," I replied. "I tried . . . I'll try harder next year."

He exhaled loudly. "You'll try?"

"Yes."

"Trying is for idiots," he said angrily. "People who have success don't try. They do."

"That's what I mean," I offered weakly. "I'll do it. I'll try to do it."

He rubbed his forehead, obviously frustrated with the direction our chat was going.

"All your teachers say you're very capable. You're not a moron like some of the kids at your school. You're smart, and it's time you showed it. You have to focus."

"I will."

"When?"

"In the fall. In grade nine."

He looked at me sharply. "Do you know why I became a dentist?"

Oh God, please, not again! He had told me this story half a dozen times in the past but it was boring and I had pretty much forgotten it. I just remember he always framed it in heroic terms as if he had overcome some great hardship and that graduating from dental school was his crowning achievement.

"I wasn't a spoiled kid like you," he said. "At your age, I was working my ass off in my father's plumbing business after school. When I got to university, I looked around to see who was successful and well off. Who do you think it was?" He regarded me fiercely waiting for a reply. I knew the answer but shrugged. I guess I wanted to push his buttons a little. It worked, because he rolled his eyes and exhaled in exasperation. "It was the dentists, the orthodontists!" he blurted. "I studied very hard to get into dental school and graduate. We have this house in this nice neighborhood, my new Mercedes, the expensive clothes you and your sister wear. All of it is the result of me applying myself, working hard to get somewhere. Do you understand?"

I nodded. "Yes."

He leaned back in his chair. "Do you think I like looking down peoples' throats all day and listening to their endless complaints?" he asked, then answered the question himself. "No, of course not! I do it for the money."

I remember thinking what an awful fate it must be to have to go to a job your hate, just so you can earn a lot of money. I figured there had to be a better way to go through life.

He clasped his hands together, rested his elbows on his knees and leaned forward. "If you want to be accepted into dental school," he said firmly, "the hard works starts now."

Then he sat back, and a look of genuine concern crossed his face. He had mentioned his long-range plans for me attending dental school a few times before, and the very thought of it made me ill. If there was a list of occupations I could choose from "dentist" was at the bottom below road-kill collector and crime-scene cleaner. I knew better than to tell him that though, because it was the one hope he held out for me. He assumed I would be his protégé. Was I ungrateful? Maybe. Perhaps I was lucky enough to understand what I didn't want to do for a living more than what I wanted to do. I really hadn't given much thought to a career (unless there was a job where you could play video games and watch TV all day) Still, I knew I would never be a dentist. I hated going to the dentist, in this case my father's clinic, and the idea of becoming one repulsed me.

When I was 10 my father thought it was cute to let me to wear one of his white lab coats. It was so big that it swallowed my arms and reached my ankles. It had a foul chemical smell and I grew to hate that lab coat so much that I finally hid it in the bottom of a closet so I wouldn't have to go through the charade of wearing it. I remember him saying to my mother, "I'm missing my favorite lab coat. Surely you didn't forget to pick it up from the cleaners?"

I knew what my father needed to hear from me that day, and figured he probably wanted our chat about my grades to end as much as I did. "I'll really apply myself in the fall," I said as earnestly as I could. "I want to get into dental school and make a ton of money. I'll bring my grades up."

"Good," he said, "because I don't want to have this conversation again."

God, neither do I! This, or any other conversation with you!

He smiled a little, ruffled my hair and told me to take out the garbage.

. . .

I carefully placed the love letter back in my father's desk, exactly where I had found it, pulled the chain hanging from his desk lamp to turn off the light and left the den. I felt like someone had told me a secret, a dangerous secret, and I was unsure what to do with the information.

Back in my room, I slipped on a pair or cutoffs and headed for the garage to get the lawnmower. That summer, my father had gleefully told a half-dozen of our neighbors that I would mow their huge front, back and in some cases side lawns. He had told me that a little hard work and breaking a sweat would do me good. He was right about breaking a sweat, but it didn't do me any good. It was hot, monotonous work. Instead of instilling some kind of work ethic, what it really did was make me grow to hate lawns and appreciate the value of goofing off. I didn't cut the grass every week as I was supposed to. I let it slide for 10 days or longer. But this time I had pushed it too far, and the previous day one of our neighbors had called our house asking when his lawn was going to be cut. Of course, as soon as my father hung up the phone, he flew into a rage.

I screwed off the gas cap, checked to make sure the lawnmower tank was full then left the coolness of the garage and headed to our neighbor's home under a blistering August sun. As I cut the grass that sweltering afternoon, my thoughts were centered less on how to mow in a straight line than on how to deal with the explosive information I had just discovered.

After I finished that first lawn, I peeled off my T-shirt, pulled a red bandanna from my shorts pocket, wiped my brow and surveyed my work. I had missed several large patches of grass. Obviously my head was elsewhere. I went on to the next neighbor's lawn, and it was late afternoon by the time I finished all of my mowing. I was pushing the lawnmower home when my friends Craig and Phil came riding up on their bikes. Craig was 16, a year older than me, which at that age means a lot. Older boys tend to outrank younger boys. More than that, Craig was outgoing, where I was painfully shy. He was also extroverted and tough. I didn't play sports, but Craig was a talented hockey player with an awesome slap shot. His father owned an import/export business, and sometimes Craig offered me exotic foods like chocolate covered ants, seal flippers and pickled pigs feet. He was the first person I ever knew who had a *Penthouse* magazine. In grade seven he had pulled the magazine from his backpack at school, flipped to the centerfold and held it up for me and several other wide-eyed boys to see. As we were gawking at the naked beauty, he laughed and said: "Her favorite interests are wind surfing and bubble baths."

His older brother, David, had died of a drug overdose a year earlier while living in Toronto. He was seven years older than Craig. Craig had idolized him and he was still struggling to come to term with his brother's sudden death. Sometimes I'd catch him referring to David as if he were still alive. I had gone to the funeral with my family and I remember I was taken aback at how grief stricken Craig had been. I had never seen him so vulnerable and weak. He eyes were crimson and swollen from crying and he was almost unable to speak. David's death was made even more tragic by the fact that he was Craig's only sibling and therefore Craig was now an only child.

Craig was a true friend, whereas Phil was more of a "friend by association." You know the kind of "friend" I mean. He was an ape-like jerk, showoff and bully who enjoyed making snide remarks, usually aimed at me. He was a hockey-player friend of Craig's, and while he was 15, like me, he wouldn't have acknowledged my existence if I hadn't been Craig's friend.

"Dude, you're drenched," Craig said as they coasted to a stop a few feet in front of me.

My face, chest and back were drenched from hours of mowing in the heat, and my hair was plastered with sweat to my head. It must have looked like I'd gotten caught in a downpour. I had even quit mopping my forehead with the bandana because it was completely soaked after the first hour.

Phil mockingly pinched his nose with his fingers. "Dude, try some Ban, man."

"I just finished mowing four lawns, front and back, and I have two more to do tomorrow," I snapped. "Why do people have lawns, anyway? They're a major pain."

Phil gripped his handlebars and laughed. "Not as long as you're the one mowing 'em."

"You're getting paid, right?" Craig asked.

"Barely." I sat on the curb and rested my elbows on my knees. "My father thought mowing grass would be good for me." I kicked a few pebbles. "I'm beat."

"That's because you're not in shape," Phil said. He pointed at my chest. "You need some muscle, Dude," he smirked. "You should lift weights. You're built like a girl."

I was self-conscious about my slight build, and Phil's comment hit a nerve. "Muscle? Like the muscle between your ears?"

Phil's eyes widened. "What did you say?"

"You heard me."

He got off his bike, laid it on the ground and started toward me.

I jumped to my feet, sure that I was about to get pummeled.

Craig got off his bike and stepped between us. "Relax, ladies."

Phil threw his hands up and backed away. "I'm not going to do anything. I'm just saying he should work out once in a while."

I reclaimed my seat on the curb and wiped my brow with my sweat-soaked bandana. "Whatever."

I guess Craig figured it was a good idea to change the subject. "Guess who I'm going out with tomorrow night?" he asked.

Phil and I both turned toward him. Craig was good-looking and very popular so it could have been any of a number of girls.

"Who?" I asked.

"Julie Ginsburg."

I'm not sure if it was sweat in my ears or the shock of hearing Julie's name. Whatever it was, I only managed to mutter a single-word response. "Who?"

"Julie Ginsburg," he repeated.

I felt as thought I had been kicked in the gut. Julie's family had moved into the area at the beginning of the school year. The first time I saw her was in the school gym. Actually I didn't see Julie until after I'd heard her laughing. She had a high-pitched loud laugh that made you want to smile. She was tall and pretty with curly brown hair that tumbled down her back. She played on the volleyball team and was wearing sneakers, shorts and a tight blue T-shirt. She was also developing a shapely figure that the boys at school had not failed to notice. I'm sure most of us boys secretly desired Julie, and many of the girls were jealous of her.

I was shooting hoops that day in the far-flung hope that endless hours of practice might actually help me make the basketball team that fall, and as Julie was leaving the gym with two of her friends, she smiled and said, "Hi." I was so shocked I could only mumble a feeble "Uh . . . hello" in response.

I had admired her from a distance for months. If unrequited love is an illness, then I was in critical condition.

Craig didn't know I had a huge crush on her, or if he did somehow know, he hadn't mentioned anything about it to me. I had seen him talking to Julie at her locker at the end of the school year, but a lot of girls liked Craig.

Sometimes I daydreamed of taking Julie to a movie or a school dance, although I could never work up enough nerve to ask her out. And I never did make the basketball team. Can life get any worse?

"Julie Ginsburg? Man oh man," Phil said, grinning widely. "The body on her. I'm going to want to hear all about it."

Craig smirked. "Hopefully I'll have a few juicy details to share with you."

I felt like I was going to puke, and suddenly the sun felt a lot hotter. "Where are you taking her?" I asked tersely.

"A movie, then out for a burger, then . . . who knows?" He shot us a wolfish grin.

Okay, here are the crazy thoughts that flashed through my mind in that moment. In order to stop my good friend Craig from taking out the girl of my dreams, I could: a.) Kill Craig. b.) Find out the movie theater they're going to and call in a bomb threat. c.) Pour sugar into the gas tank of his mother's car so the engine seizes and he can't pick Julie up. d.) Kill myself. This may not prevent him from taking out Julie but at least I won't be around to suffer thinking about it. e.) All of the above.

I'm just kidding, but there's no question I was insanely jealous.

"The movie you select is very important," Phil said thoughtfully. "You'll want to see something with lots of sex so she'll you know, get in the mood."

"We're going to see *Aladdin*," Craig said.

Phil looked puzzled. "Is there any sex in that?"

I was actually relieved that they weren't going to a racy movie. I shook my head and looked up at Phil. "It's an animated Disney movie so I really doubt there's sex in it. Unless they show the camels making out."

"She chose the movie," Craig said.

"That could work," Phil said. "I mean, if there's a touching scene or something you can put your arm around her to show you're sensitive. Girls like that."

I glared at Phil. At that moment, all I wanted to do was to get the hell away from them. I stood up and grabbed the handle of the lawnmower.

"This piece of shit is almost out of gas," I said. "I'm going home to fill it up and finish my mowing."

"What are you doing tonight?" Craig asked.

I stopped and looked at him, then raised my hand to shelter my eyes from the sun behind him. "I don't know. Nothing."

"I'll call you."

I didn't reply and instead started pushing the lawnmower down the street as Craig and Phil got on their bikes and rode off in the opposite direction.

Within a few minutes, I was back in the garage, which was cool and dark in contrast to the sunny August heat. I left the mower in a corner of the garage and glanced at my watch. It was almost six o'clock.

I crossed the lawn, and as soon as I walked in the house Claire confronted me in the front hall. "Where were you?" she demanded angrily.

"Where was I?" I answered. "Why do you care where I was?"

"Because we were supposed to make ice cream this afternoon. Remember?"

"I forgot," I replied wearily.

"But you promised," she said, "you promised."

"Claire," I said, the level of my voice rising with my temper, "I had to mow a bunch of lawns. Just leave me alone. Bug off. All right?"

"But you promised," she repeated.

Maybe it was the heat, or more likely I was in a black mood after hearing about Craig's date with Julie. Whatever it was, I stared down at Claire and said, "I blow you off on making stupid ice cream and you act like your heart is broken. Grow up for God's sake, will you? And while you're at it, shut up and leave me alone. You're a pest! What I want is a little brother, not a little sister who nags me and won't shut up."

She looked as if I had hit her. "I don't nag you Neil, I, I . . . ." she stammered.

"You know what?" I continued. "I'm never making ice cream with you. Never! You'll be lucky if I ever talk to you again. You're a pain in the ass. Do you understand me? A pain in the ass! Get out of my sight. I hate you!"

I couldn't stop myself. Isn't that how it is sometimes? You unleash some hateful little part of yourself, and suddenly it's like a full-blown eruption.

Her mouth was hanging open. Her wide blue eyes filled with tears.

"You know what Claire? You're not even my real sister. You're just some adopted kid like me that someone threw away, that our real parents didn't want."

She started crying, then sobbing. My harsh words had obviously cut her deeply. I didn't care because I was wrapped up in my own thoughts, feeling like a complete loser.

Claire bolted from the front hall, sobbing loudly.

As I was untying my sneakers my mother confronted me at the base of the stairs. "What did you say to Claire?" she demanded. "She's crying so hard I can't tell what's she saying."

"She was bothering me," I moaned. "I'm exhausted. I've got heat stroke. She won't leave me alone."

Red-faced, my mother shook her finger at me. "You listen to me Mister. You don't have heat stroke. You're acting like a jerk. Your sister is hysterical from crying! You wait until your father gets home and hears about this."

I scoffed. "Do you really think he cares about this family, about us? Ha! He doesn't. All he cares about is his stupid clinic, his stupid hygienists, making money and having a nice car. That's what he cares about. You don't know the truth about him, what he does."

She looked at me sternly. "Neil, you listen to me. Your father works very hard to put a roof over our heads. It's not easy . . ."

I cut her off. "Do you really believe he works so hard? You don't know the truth, what's really happening."

"Oh, really," she replied, planting her hands on her hips. "Then why don't you tell me the truth? What's happening, Neil?"

She glared at me, waiting for a reply.

It was on the tip of my tongue . . . but I reeled in back in.

"Just forget it," I yelled. "I don't want to talk about it, or talk to you."

I turned and started walking up the stairs to my room.

"You get back here mister!"

"Just leave me alone!" I yelled, "or, better still, go and have a drink. It's that time of day, isn't it?"

"What did you say to me?"

I stopped on the stairs and without turning yelled. "Nothing!"

Then I stormed into the bathroom and slammed the door shut. I peeled off my sweat-drenched cutoffs, underwear, T-shirt and socks, left everything in a heap on the floor, turned on the shower and got in. The water was cool but not cold, which revived me. It also seemed to wash away some of the anger I was feeling. As I lathered up, I thought about my biological parents and what life might have been like if they had kept me. But in reality I had absolutely no interest in finding a second set 2of parents somewhere out there. Could there be anything worse? Claire and I were little more than well-cared-for orphans. Despite my father's success and our nice house in a nice neighborhood, I realized that love is what makes the difference between a house and a home.

After my shower, I gathered my clothes, went to my room, locked the door, put on a fresh pair of underwear, shorts and T-shirt, crashed on my bed and listened to Depeche Mode.

As I lay there with my earphones on, the day's events swept over me like a tsunami. I was sickened by the thought of Craig's date with Julie. Of course, the biggest thing on my mind that day was what to do about the love letter to my father. It was an A-Bomb of information. I was torn between showing it to my mother and the real fear of my father's rage. I wanted to do the right thing. But loyalty can be dangerous. It means sticking your neck out for someone. Taking their side. Having their back. And who was I being loyal to? My mother? Perhaps, but more likely I was being loyal to my romantic notion of what a real family could be: happy, contented and pulling together. Why did the love letter bother me so much? I don't know. Perhaps it was an affront to something I believed in, but I'm not sure I could name what that something was.

Outside my window the maple and oak trees were in full August bloom, their fat leaves gently murmuring against the window. Lying there I wondered what bands Julie listened to. What her date with Craig would be like? What I would do with my life? How could I survive grade nine?

I pulled out my earphones and stared at the ceiling as the sounds and smells of a suburban summer evening filtered into my room: the smoky aroma of our neighbor's BBQ; the drone of a lawnmower; the scent of freshly cut grass and gasoline. A neighbor's dog barking; birds singing; the faint cry of a distant police or ambulance siren; the neighbor's kids laughing and playing; the smell of whatever my mother was cooking for dinner. As I lay there, half asleep, everything came together like a symphony, and for just a moment, the world seemed to make sense.

After a while, my mother called me from the bottom of the stairs to come down for dinner.

"I'm not hungry," I yelled back, although in reality I was starving from mowing lawns all day. I didn't feel like facing her. I wanted to get out of the house, so after a few minutes I got up, shoved my Walkman into the front pocket of my shorts, pulled on my sneakers, snuck down the stairs, quietly left the house and headed toward a small park a few blocks away.

My friends and I often spent summer evenings hanging out in the park, but as I entered, it was completely empty. It was a beautiful August evening with a light breeze that carried a calming, pine-scented perfume from the woods nearby. The temperature had cooled a little, but the air was still warm, and as I sat at a picnic table and put in my earplugs, I looked up into the star-filled night sky. Sitting there in the dark, I could imagine Craig's date with Julie. I could practically see them: smiling at each other, kissing . . . and probably more. My mood was about as dark as the starlit night.

I had been listening to music for about half an hour when I saw someone approaching from the park entrance. Not until he was about 10 feet away did I recognize it was Craig. He sat down across from me, and I pulled out my earphones.

"I called, and your mum said you went out," he said. "I thought you might be here."

"I needed to get out of the house."

He nodded, then pulled a cigarette from his shirt pocket. I had never seen him smoke and was surprised he had a cigarette.

"Since when do you smoke?"

He smiled slyly. "Now and then."

"I thought you'd be home, getting a good night's sleep for your big date tomorrow night."

"Big date? Are you kidding me? I'll probably be home by 10 o'clock."

I looked toward the woods. "Whatever."

He lit the cigarette, and as he inhaled, the orange glow from the tip illuminated his face. He exhaled, and a plume of smoke slowly drifted past me.

"Is that a joint?" I asked.

He nodded slowly. "Yep."

"Where did you get that?"

He shrugged. "It's my brother's dope. I found a baggie of it in his closet the other day. My parents still haven't cleaned everything out of his room." He held it out and offered it to me.

I had not smoked pot before and didn't know what to do. At the same time, I had heard a lot about it and was interested in trying it. Still, I hesitated. "What if somebody sees us?"

He smirked. "It's dark."

I glanced around the park. No one was in sight.

"Come on," Craig said, "try it."

"Ummm, okay." I carefully took the joint between my thumb and index finger. I raised it to my lips and inhaled. "It tastes sweet," I said.

"If you say so."

I passed the joint back to him. He flicked the ash from the tip into the grass and leaned into the table. "What was up with you this afternoon today?" he asked. "You seemed out of it, distracted or something."

"I've got things on my mind."

There was no way that I was going to tell him that I was insanely jealous about his date with Julie.

"What things?" he asked, taking another puff off the joint.

"You know, just things."

"Things?"

"Yeah," I snapped. "Things, okay?"

"Okay. Jeez you don't have to tell me if you don't want to."

"Good."

We sat there quietly in the dark for a few minutes, smoking the joint. Then Craig cocked his head sideways, like a dog listening for something. "Do you hear that?"

"What?"

"Music. Can't you hear it?"

He was right. The faint sound of music was coming from somewhere nearby.

He flicked the joint into the grass, ground it out with his foot, then stood up. "That sounds like a band," he said. "Let's go."

"Where?"

"Where do you think? It sounds like a party."

I shook my head. I was happy sitting in the dark, sulking and feeling sorry for myself. I certainly didn't feel like crashing a party. "You go ahead," I said grimly.

He grabbed me by the arm. "Don't be a wuss. Let's see what's happening. They might have booze. Let's go."

I slowly got to my feet, and we started walking in the direction the music was coming from.

"Did you get a buzz off that joint?" he asked as we left the park.

I thought about it for a second before answering. "I'm not sure," I replied. "I'm a bit dizzy, I guess."

He laughed heartily. "You should be more than dizzy. But, don't worry. Not everyone gets high the first time."

I shrugged as we continued walking, side by side. The closer we got, the louder the music, mingled with the sounds of people laughing and having a good time. We walked until we came to one of my neighbors homes. From the street, it was impossible to see what was happening, but the music was clearly coming from their back yard, which was lit up. The people who lived there had moved in a few months earlier and I didn't know them very well.

As we were standing there, two couples who looked to be in their late teens or early twenties passed us, carrying cases of beer. They rounded the corner of the house and went into the back yard.

Craig motioned toward the house. "Come on."

I was hesitant, but I followed. Any fear I had was temporarily trumped by my curiosity. We ambled toward the back yard, careful to step over a bunch of kids' toys and a baseball bat that someone had left in the middle of the driveway. We turned the corner and stood at the edge of the back lawn, staring in awe at the fantastic scene in front of us.

There had to be 100 people there, standing in groups laughing, talking, eating and drinking. Brightly colored Chinese lanterns were strung throughout the trees. A dozen helium-filled balloons with "Happy Birthday" printed on them in crazy lettering were tethered to a picnic table. Two guys holding bottles of beer were tending to two smoky barbeques jammed with hot dogs, hamburgers and chicken. I had tasted lots of barbeque before but this particular barbeque somehow smelled better. The band we had heard was set up on a stone patio playing covers of country rock songs I had heard on the radio.

Wow! I'd been to sock hops at school and parties with my friends, but nothing like this.

Craig elbowed me in the side. "It's someone's birthday. Cool. Let's get something to eat."

I balked. "Are you kidding? We can't stay."

"Just act like you belong here, okay? Follow me."

I think that was my first real attempt at trying to act nonchalant. Crossing the lawn, I felt as if we were walking across a huge stage. I was so nervous and self-conscious that my arms and legs felt as if they were filled with water. We made our way to a picnic table at the far edge of the lawn and sat down. The table was covered with plates of cold cuts, bread, salads and other great-looking eats. No one seemed to notice us; if they did, they probably thought we somebody's little brothers.

Craig promptly made us each a sandwich, then said he was going to steal us some booze.

"Booze!" I whispered urgently. "No way. We'll get busted. Just get some Cokes."

"Don't worry. I'll put it in a plastic cup. No one will know." Obviously, he had some experience with this type of thing.

He got up, and I was left sitting there by myself. After a few minutes, the band took a break. Watching the people, I noticed that a lot of the girls were talking to the guys in the band. One of the things that struck me the most was that the women were gorgeous, but the guys with the band weren't even good looking.

Someone had left a guitar leaning against a chair a few feet from where I was sitting. One of the guys in the band must have seen me looking at it because he came over with his girlfriend and picked it up.

"Hey, kid," he said with a toothy grin. "Your father's a dentist, right?"

"Yep."

He looked familiar, and I figured he lived in the house. But it was his stunning girlfriend who really caught my eye. I'd noticed her as soon as I sat down. She had been across the yard, talking to people, but she'd stood out from the rest of the crowd. A broad smile; an hourglass figure; long black hair falling over her shoulders. She was a knockout. A deeply tanned knockout, wearing a yellow halter-top and tight jeans.

"So, your old man's a mean prick, eh?" the guy asked.

His girlfriend slapped him on the arm. "What are you asking him that for?"

He shrugged.

Apparently everyone on the street knew my father's reputation.

"Do you play guitar?" he asked.

"No," I replied. "I was just looking at it."

"You like music?"

"Yeah, I guess. I like listening to it. I thought it would be cool to know how to play."

He sat down beside me and his gorgeous girlfriend snuggled in beside him. "Guitar's easy," he said. "You want to learn a few chords?"

His question surprised me a little because I didn't know him, but he seemed like a nice enough guy, and his girlfriend was dazzling, so . . . "Yeah, I guess."

"First, let me make sure it's in tune." His breath reeked of beer and he was slurring. "That's your first lesson, kid. Make sure the guitar's tuned before you play it." He strummed the guitar a few times and passed it to me. "Okay, it's in tune," he said. "You take it."

The guitar had the soft aroma of wood polish and cedar. I didn't know how to hold it and mistakenly held it upside down. His girlfriend raised her hand to her mouth to suppress a giggle as her boyfriend smiled, then reached over and turned the guitar right side-up.

"Try it this way," he said. Then he leaned forward and grabbed my left hand. "Okay," he said, tugging on my index finger. "Take this finger here and put in on this string, right here. That's called a fret. Put your finger right there."

He pressed my finger down on the string, but my fingers were stiff and didn't want to cooperate.

"Arch you fingers and press down hard with your fingertips."

I did what he said.

"Okay, put this finger here on this string and *this* fret. Press down hard, now."

It hurt the fleshy tip of my finger, but I kept on trying.

"Okay, now your fingers are in the right place," he said. "It's called an A chord. Here's the pick."

He held up the pick. It looked like a big brown fingernail. He passed it to me then said: "Hold it between your thumb and forefinger, like this and strum down, slowly."

He passed his hand through the air in a slow downward motion.

I hit the top string, and the pick popped out of my hand and fell into the grass.

He chuckled, then bent over and picked it up. "That's okay," he said, passing me the pick. "Hold it more firmly. Now, try again. Strum down, nice and easy."

I strummed down across all six strings, and it was like the guitar spoke to me! I couldn't believe it. I had made music! My eyes shot open, and my glasses almost fell off.

He grinned and pushed my shoulder. "Hey, kid, you're a natural."

"Nice job," his girlfriend added with a playful smile.

He showed me two more chords, then leaned back and looked at me impressively. "Now you know an E, an A, and a B seventh," he said. "Shit, son, you're ready to start a rock and roll band!" He put his arm around his girlfriend and pulled her close. "Playing music will take you places like nothing else can," he said sagely. "You'll have girls like Rachel here begging to be with you. Guitar player. Gunslinger. The ladies love guitar players. They know we're good with our hands."

His girlfriend laughed and slapped him on the arm. "Stop it. He's just a kid."

He planted a wet kiss on her mouth, then turned back to me and grinned again. "Go ahead, practice as long as you like. Just don't drop the guitar okay."

I nodded.

Then, as they were leaving, he stopped and looked around the yard.

"And, you guys, where's your buddy? Stay away from the beer."

"We will."

They started walking toward a group of people, but his girlfriend said something to the guy, then came back and picked up a plastic cup off the table.

"I forgot my drink," she giggled.

"I wasn't going to drink it."

She smiled, revealing perfect teeth. "I didn't say you were."

I looked at the ground.

"You were pretty good on that guitar," she said. "You know, for a beginner."

I looked up at her, but I was instantly tongue-tied and didn't know what to say. "Really?" I finally muttered. "Thanks."

She pointed at her boyfriend, who was pulling a beer from a cooler. "He shouldn't have said anything about your father," she said. "I love my man, but sometimes he has a big mouth."

"It's okay," I replied weakly.

She brushed her midnight black hair back behind her right ear. "He's right about playing guitar, though. It's fun and helps you meet people. It's how I met him. He was playing with his band at a club in the city. I couldn't stop looking at him."

"I'm not old enough to get into a club," I replied.

She chuckled. "I know, but if you start practicing now, in a few years, who knows? You may be the next Eddie Van Halen."

Her voice was as sexy and sultry as she was. The light August breeze was playing with her hair.

"The hard work starts now," I replied in a slightly sarcastic tone.

She took a sip of her drink, then tilted her head to the side as if sizing me up. "It's not work if you enjoy it," she replied, "if it gives you pleasure and satisfies you."

"I'm not going to be a musician," I said tersely. "I'm going to be a damned dentist."

She paused for a moment as if thinking. "'A damned dentist?'" she said in a slightly disappointed tone. "Hmmmm. Really? That doesn't sound like much fun to me."

"It may not be fun, but you make a ton of money," I said, meeting her gaze for the first time.

There was a soft kindness in her dark eyes and as I looked up at her I suddenly felt a little better, as if her mere presence next to me had the power to heal.

She took another sip of her drink, looking at me over the rim of the cup. Then she smiled widely.

"The world needs dentists," she said. "Besides, even dentists can learn how to play an instrument."

I managed a feeble smile. "Yeah I guess so." I think I may have blushed. "Thanks."

She gave me a little wave goodbye, then turned and sauntered over to her boyfriend's side. I've got to say that she looked just as gorgeous walking away as she had looked walking toward me. After a moment, I turned my attention back to the guitar, trying to remember how to play the chords I had just learned. I was concentrating so intensely, I didn't notice that Craig had returned with a blue plastic cup in each hand.

"What you doing?" he asked.

I pointed across the yard. "That guy over there in the blue shirt with that hot girl, he showed me how to play a little."

I strummed the guitar.

Craig nodded in approval and sat down at the table. "Cool," he said. Then he whispered, "I got us some rum and Coke."

"Rum and Coke?" I replied. "Really? I don't know about that. If we get caught . . ."

Our usual roles. He was fearless. I was a coward.

He slid one of the cups in front of me. "Relax. No one's going to know."

I reluctantly took the cup and sipped from it as Craig chugged his in gulps. Meanwhile, the party continued on around us. After a few minutes, I noticed a fat short guy standing near the BBQ, eyeing us. I recognized him from the neighborhood. He worked as a mechanic in a garage near the city. He had greasy hair, and tattoos of skulls and winged demons crawling up his arms. He always had a mean glint in his eye and was constantly hoisting up his pants, which is probably why his friends teasingly called him "Lugnuts."

He strode over to where we were sitting and glared at us. "What are you two punks doing at Bryan's birthday party?" he demanded. "You don't know Bryan."

He was right about that. I had no idea who "Bryan" was. My heart leapt into my throat as I glanced over at Craig.

"We're not bothering anybody," Craig replied.

Lugnuts grabbed the cup from my hand, took a drink, then threw the contents into the grass and scowled at us. "This is rum! How did you little pricks get this?"

"Someone gave it to us," Craig answered in a smartass tone.

Lugnuts smiled menacingly. "No one gave nothing to you little punks! I saw you walk in here all by yourself and steal those drinks."

"Bullshit," Craig muttered.

Lugnuts snorted. "You two get out of here before I kick your ass and call your parents."

Call your parents! I jumped up to leave but Craig started giving him lip: "You're not going to kick my ass," he said emphatically. "My brother's going to kick your ass, you . . ."

Lugnuts grinned fiendishly. "Your brother?" he smirked. "Your dead druggie brother. Even before he turned into a dope addict and died, he was a pussy."

I looked over at Craig. His eyes were wide and filled with an intense hatred. "What did you call my brother?" Craig growled.

Lugnuts kept on sneering as I tugged Craig's shirt sleeve. "Come on, Craig," I urged "Let's go."

But he pulled away from me. "Leave us alone," he told Lugnuts. "It's not your party, you creep."

I could not believe Craig was talking back to Lugnuts, and with pure defiance in his voice!

Lugnuts scowled again and swatted Craig on the head. "You little punks get out of here before I pimp-slap you all the way home."

Craig's eyes narrowed in anger and I thought he was going to hit the guy.

I carefully put the guitar back where I had found it and turned to my friend. "Come, on Craig," I pleaded. "Let's go. Now."

Craig gulped down his drink, carefully placed his plastic cup on the picnic table and stood up.

"We're leaving," he said "but not because *you* told us to."

Then he flashed "the finger" and hoisted up his pants, clearly mocking Lugnuts. Before Lugnuts could react, Craig muttered "Dumb ass butt cleavage" under his breath.

Lugnuts' eyes widened and his face turned as red as a tomato.

I turned to look at Craig, but he was already running for the street. I took off after him, with Lugnuts right behind us, cursing and yelling. We rounded the corner of the house, but before I could catch up to Craig, Lugnuts grabbed me by the collar and started slapping me on the head and face.

"You little pricks, pricks . . ."

"Stop," I pleaded. "Stop, please stop."

But Lugnuts was furious and wouldn't stop hitting me. My knees buckled. My glasses went flying.

"Where do you live?" he yelled as he continued slapping me around. "I'm telling your parents you're drunk! Where do you live?"

"No don't, please, please. Stop . . ."

I don't know where rage comes from, but suddenly an intense anger erupted within me. I started yelling and swinging my fists in rapid, windmill-like motions. I was totally fearless. I landed a blind punch on the side of Lugnuts' head, causing him to lose his grip on my collar. He stepped back and glared at me, the demented pig. In that moment, I didn't care if he tried to kill me. I was hyperventilating, my hands in tight fists, my teeth clenched.

He lunged forward. "I'll teach you to fight back against me!"

He smashed me in the left eye with the back of his hand, and I fell dazed to the ground. Before he could grab me again, I sprang to my feet and ran headlong into him. We collided with a tremendous *thud*. But he outweighed me by 60 pounds, and within seconds, he had me in headlock. I couldn't breathe. I was trying to yell but that too was impossible because Lugnut's forearm was jammed into my throat . . .

WHOMP!

Lugnuts let me go with a squeal of pain and dropped to the ground, gripping his knee. Craig was standing over him holding the baseball bat we had stepped over in the driveway earlier. He lifted the bat to his shoulder and snarled. "What did you call my brother you stupid, ugly oaf?"

Lugnuts tried to get up, but Craig brought the bat down hard on his back.

WHOMP!

"And why are you hitting my friend, Lugnuts?" Craig yelled. "Pick on someone your own size."

Lugnuts was writhing in pain, cursing. He tried to get up again but Craig brought the bat down hard on his leg, and Lugnuts slumped to the asphalt. "Ahhhh . . ."

I was sitting on the ground, still dazed from the beating while Craig stood over Lugnuts, who was yelling, "Stop it! Stop it!" I looked up a Craig. His face was so twisted with rage, I almost didn't recognize him. He slowly raised the bat and was getting ready to bring it down on Lugnuts' head when someone grabbed Craig from behind.

"What's going on here?" It was the guy who had showed me the guitar chords.

Craig dropped the bat and pointed at me. "Lugnuts was beating him up."

"Lugnuts, what are you doing beating on kids?"

Lugnuts staggered to his feet, hoisted up his pants and sneered at us. "Bryan, they were stealing drinks and were giving me lip when I told them to go home." He pointed at Craig. "That little son-of-a-bitch hit me with a bat. I know you two. I'm going to . . ."

The other guy pushed him.

"Shut up Lugnuts. You're not doing anything. They're only kids. Get back to my party."

Lugnuts continued pointing at Craig, his arm shaking. It looked like he was going to cry. "Bryan, that kid hit me with a bat . . . my leg . . ."

"You're all right," he said, pushing Lugnuts toward the back yard. "You can have one of my beers. Get back to my party. Go on!"

Lugnuts said something about kicking ass, then turned and limped around the corner.

Bryan walked over and muttered: "That idiot."

My nose was bleeding a little, and my left eye was starting to swell shut. I was gasping as I fought back tears.

"Let me see your face," Bryan said. He turned me in the direction of the porch light and examined my eye. "You'll be all right," he said as Craig passed me my glasses. "You'll have a big old shiner tomorrow, though."

"Oh, just great," I muttered.

He placed his hand on my shoulder and looked me in the eye. "If anybody asks what happened, how you got hurt, tell them you fell off your bike. Do you understand me? You fell off your bike."

I nodded slowly.

He shook his head and exhaled loudly. "I teach you how to play guitar and this is how you repay me, on my birthday? Stealing drinks?"

"Sorry," I replied. "We didn't . . ."

"I took the drinks," Craig interrupted.

A stern expression formed on Bryan's face as he turned to Craig. "I don't care about you guys drinking, but not at my birthday party. I could catch a lot of grief from your parents. I don't need that kind of aggravation. Next time, I'll *let* Lugnuts beat the shit out of you two."

Craig smirked. "Not if I have a bat, he won't."

Bryan looked Craig up and down, apparently trying to size him up. "Your brother's the guy who died, right?" he asked after a moment.

Craig took a step toward Bryan. "Yeah. What about it?"

Bryan stepped back and raised his hands in mock surrender. "Relax, kid. I heard he was a great guy. That's all."

"He is a great guy, a *real* great guy," Craig said angrily. "He could kick Lugnuts' ass. If I tell him what happened . . ."

"Okay, kid, okay," Bryan said calmly. "No worries. Don't tell anyone anything, all right? Nobody likes a troublemaker."

"Lugnuts started it," Craig snapped.

"I know," Bryan said softly. "He's a complete asshole."

"You got that right."

He walked over and put his hand on Craig's shoulder. "You had a tough year, kid."

Craig looked at the ground without responding. He may have been crying, but it was hard to tell in the darkness. I wasn't sure what to do. Before I could do anything, Bryan motioned toward the street. "You guys get going," he said, "and do not, I repeat, do not, tell your parents or anyone else that you were here drinking. Do you understand me?"

"Yeah, yeah," Craig replied weakly. "We're not going to say anything."

"Good. Now get outta here."

We started to walk away, then Craig stopped and turned around. "Hey, just one more thing."

Bryan's eyebrows arched. "What's that?"

"Happy Birthday, man."

Bryan let out a belly laugh and motioned to the street. "Thanks. Now you two go the fuck home."

He stood in the driveway with his arms folded across his chest as Craig and I slowly walked away. We had gone about a block when everyone at the party burst into a rousing rendition of "Happy Birthday." The joy in their voices made me feel even worse. What a miserable day. I felt like a coward for crying and letting Lugnuts smack me around. Worst of all, Craig, the guy who was about to date the girl of my dreams, had saved me.

"I could have taken that Lugnuts guy," I said, breaking the silence. "I didn't need your help."

"Right," Craig replied mockingly, "you were really kicking his ass."

"He got me in a headlock, and . . ."

"I did see you smack him on the head," Craig said, grinning widely. "Impressive. He was pissed."

"I could have taken him! You stood up to him."

He stopped walking and stared at me. "Yeah only because I had a bat and he wasn't looking. You saw me running from that creep. He's an idiot and only picks on kids. Nobody likes him."

Standing in a pool of light from the street lamp he pointed at my eye. "Wow, nice! It should be good and purple by tomorrow. A real shiner."

"Great," I moaned, "that's all I need."

He nodded thoughtfully. "You earned it, Neil. A badge of courage for fighting Lugnuts."

"Whatever. I shouldn't have run from the guy in the first place."

We resumed walking side by side down the middle of the street, then he stopped and turned toward me. "Don't be so hard on yourself."

His comment made me angry because I felt like he was calling me weak. In reality, I was probably just jealous and still upset after being knocked around by Lugnuts.

"You don't know jack shit," I blurted. "What are you, some kind of psychologist? I'm not being hard on myself. I'm just saying I shouldn't have let him hit me."

Even in the dark I could see that what I had said made Craig mad. "Neil. Sometimes, man, sometimes I could just . . ."

Before he could finish, a car turned onto the street and started driving toward us, its headlights cutting a yellow swath through the dark summer night. I thought it might be my father, and I knew that if it was him he'd stop and ask what we were doing. It wouldn't take him long to figure out we'd been drinking.

"Shit," I muttered. "That's probably my father."

I darted to the side of the road and crouched behind a parked car, leaving Craig standing alone. The car passed, and from my vantage point, I could see that it wasn't my father. When I stood up and stepped back into the street, Craig smirked.

"Tell your old man to bug off. He's a bully, just like Lugnuts."

I shook my head in disbelief. "He'd kill me."

Craig laughed and raised an imaginary rifle to his cheek. "You can borrow my .22," he said, then pointed at his forehead. "Let him have it right between the eyes."

I knew he was just kidding but for an instant the idea resonated with me. "My mother's the one who's going to kill him," I said. "I found out today he's having an affair with a woman where he works."

Craig stopped in his tracks. "What? Really?"

"Yeah, really."

"So, your mother knows about it?"

"I don't think so. But if she finds out . . ."

As we continued walking, I told Craig about the love letter I had found earlier that day. He didn't say anything. He just listened intently and nodded once in a while. I finished and I turned toward him. "I think I should tell my Mum about the letter."

He stopped walking. "Tell her? I don't know about that." He paused and seemed to be thinking. "Just forget about it Neil," he said after a moment. "Don't say anything. Lots of people have affairs. The way your old man is if you say anything he might take your head off."

He was right about that. "I don't know what to do."

"Then don't do anything."

It was after 10 o'clock. The neighborhood was still and shrouded in the sweet darkness of a deep summer night when you're 15, and your whole life lies before you like an endless road.

We continued walking without saying much. After a couple of minutes, we reached the point where our routes home took us in opposite directions. Standing in the pale white glow of a streetlight I shoved my hands into my pockets. "That party was something," I said, "except for Lugnuts that jerk. I liked the rum and Coke, but I'm not sure about that joint we smoked."

Craig grinned. "It's not for everybody. David always gets the good stuff, though."

I sensed an opening. "I guess you still miss your brother a lot, eh?"

He looked at me for what seemed like an eternity. "Yeah, I miss him," he replied softly. "I still can't believe he's gone, that's all. Every time I walk into a room there's something there that reminds me of him."

The only response I could come up with was: "I can't believe he's gone, either."

It didn't matter because Craig seemed to be a mile away in his thoughts: "I remember last summer, he told me something on my birthday," he said softly. "He was home from school and he took me aside and said, 'You're young, but always trust in who you are. Don't ever let anyone look down on you. Nothing else is important.'"

It seemed like good advice to me. "Do you think he was right?" I asked.

Craig shrugged. "I don't know. He was probably stoned and forgot all about it the next day." Then he smiled widely and playfully pushed my shoulder. "You were pretty good on that guitar. Like it was something you could learn. You should take lessons, ask your mother to buy you a guitar."

"I don't know. Maybe."

"Yeah, you should do it." He looked up into the night sky, then turned back toward me. "I'm not sure if I'll take Julie out tomorrow," he said. "She's great, but if someone else wanted to take her out, I'd be cool with that."

I was surprised at him saying that right out of the blue. "What are you telling *me* for?" I blurted.

"I don't know. I guess I thought *you* might like her." He stared at me, waiting for a reply.

I don't know how he had figured it out, but God, I hated him at that moment. Despised him! I hated him for saving me from Lugnuts. I hated him for being a good hockey player and popular at school. I hated him for having a father who cared about him. I hated him for being brave and tough. But most of all, *most of all*, I hated him for taking pity on me, for offering to blow off his date with Julie.

I mumbled "That's crazy" and looked down at the pavement. It would have been too humiliating to admit.

"My mistake," Craig said. "It just seems like everyone's crazy about her."

"I guess."

We stood there for what seemed like an eternity without saying anything. Yet another first for me. A very awkward silence.

"I'm going sailing tomorrow," Craig finally said. "You want to come?"

"I don't think so," I replied curtly before looking up. "I've got things to do with Claire."

His eyebrows arched. "With your little sister? Are you serious?"

I nodded. "Yep."

"Okay," he said. "It's going to rain anyway. I can feel it." He took a few steps, then turned and waved. "See ya later, Jimmy Paige."

"See ya." I stood there in the middle of the street watching him walking away. He had gone about a block, when he stopped and yelled something, but I couldn't make out what it was. Then he waved again and disappeared into the night.

I walked home past my neighbors' houses. Some were dark, while light spilled from the windows of others.

As I quietly opened the front door to our house, Alice started barking, then she growled at me and wagged her tail at the same time. Her normal psychotic greeting. I was still in a bad mood, so I pushed her out of the way with my foot. She bared her teeth, then turned and went back to her bed.

The house was still. My father's car wasn't in the driveway, so I figured he was still out, probably with his hygienist. I slowly climbed the stairs, and when I got to the top I noticed light seeping out from under Claire's door. I carefully pushed the it open and found her sitting up in bed.

"What are you doing awake?" I asked.

"Alice was barking."

"She was barking at me. Go back to sleep."

She pushed the golden locks from her forehead and stared at me. "What happened to your eye, Neil?"

I didn't want her to wake our mother, so I closed the door, crossed the room, sat on the edge of her bed and raised my index finger to my lips. "Shhhh. You'll wake Mum."

Claire looked worried. "You got in a fight, didn't you?"

"No," I replied firmly, practicing my lie. "I fell off my bike."

"Does your eye hurt?"

"A little, but I'm okay."

A row of wrinkles formed on her forehead. "You better show Mum. It's purple like a grape, and it looks like it hurts."

"It's okay. I'll show her in the morning. Go to sleep."

"You hate me, don't you?" she asked as I was getting up to leave. "This afternoon you hated me a lot."

I sat down and slowly shook my head. "Claire, I don't hate you. Sometimes, people get angry and say stupid things, ugly things they don't really mean."

She seemed to be thinking about what I had said, so I reached out and gently grabbed her ankle. "I was a jerk, Claire. A real jerk."

Her lips were pursed.

"I was mad at other things, and I took it out on you," I continued. "I didn't mean one word I said today. I'm really sorry."

"What things were you mad at? Because you were really mean."

"I was mad at stupid things, people things. It had nothing to do with you. I was a bully."

She looked perplexed for a moment, then blurted: "You're a bully! You beat me up. You said I'm not your real sister and I'm a nag and . . . you sounded like Dad when he's mad at people."

You sound like Dad when he's mad. She was right. I was turning into my father. I was blaming everyone else for my unhappiness. The realization made me want to scream.

"I'm sorry Claire. Will you forgive me?" I asked after a moment.

"Can I hit you?"

Her question made me smile a little. "If hitting me makes you feel better, go ahead. I deserve it."

She looked up at me, her expression suddenly filled with concern. "You already have a sore eye. I'm too sleepy to hit you. I'll tell you tomorrow if I forgive you."

"That's smart, Claire. Don't be too quick to forgive people who have hurt you or they may hurt you again. But I hope you'll forgive me some day."

"Maybe" she said softly. She looked at me for a moment without saying anything, her blue eyes half closed. Then she laid her head on the pillow and sighed. "I'm sleepy."

"Go back to sleep, then. Sorry about the ice cream. We'll make it soon, I promise. Okay Pea-head?"

She was already asleep, her mouth partly open. I reached over and quietly turned off her bedside light, then went back into the hall. My mother's bedroom door was closed, and the lights were off.

I quietly made my way down the hall, went into the bathroom and examined my reflection in the mirror. My left eye was swollen half shut. *That idiot Lugnuts.* I washed my face, being careful not to touch the tender bruised area around my eye. I slowly patted my face dry with a thick towel then flicked off the light and went into the darkened hallway.

I started toward my bedroom, but halfway down the hall I stopped and stood in the dark for several minutes. That's when I knew what to do. It just came to me as if someone had whispered in my ear.

I went back downstairs, crept into my father's study, pulled open his desk drawer and took out the love note from his hygienist. I must have stood there in the dark for 10 minutes just looking down at it, running my fingertips over its smooth, perfume-scented surface.

Do it.

I left the den and walked into the kitchen with the card at my side, the only light coming from the back patio. I carefully placed the card face-up on the kitchen table where my mother always had her toast and coffee first thing in the morning. A slight smile formed on my lips as I turned, left the room and climbed the stairs to my bedroom.

It felt good to be back in my own room. I was safe. I quietly undressed, left my clothes on the floor and crawled into bed. The sheets were cool and fresh. My curtains were parted, and shadows from the trees limbs in the back yard danced over the walls. There was a flash of lightning, quickly followed by the low rumble of thunder. Then it started raining.

Lying there half asleep, staring at the ceiling, I imagined I was a guitar player in a rock band at a school dance. There were dozens of girls in front of the stage, gazing up at us in pure adulation. Soon, all but one of the girls faded from sight.

It was Julie Ginsburg. She was looking up at me and smiling.

CPSIA information can be obtained at www.ICGtesting.com
Printed in the USA
LVOW040854081112

306271LV00003BA/1/P